LOST TO THE
DESERT WARRIOR

BY
SARAH MORGAN

MILLS &
BOON

First published in Great Britain 2013
by Mills & Boon, an imprint of Harlequin (UK) Limited.
Harlequin (UK) Limited, Eton House, 18-24 Paradise Road,
Richmond, Surrey TW9 1SR

© Sarah Morgan 2013

ISBN: 978 0 263 90701 8

Printed and bound in Spain
by Blackprint CPI, Barcelona

'You are reluctant to take off your robe,' Raz said softly, **'but once we're married you are going to be naked when you share my bed.'**

Layla felt her stomach curl. Everything inside her twisted and heated. She felt dizzy and strange.

Nerves, she thought. 'Does this mean you're agreeing to my suggestion?'

Without warning he lifted a powerful hand and pushed back the swathe of fabric covering her head. His handsome face was taut and unsmiling, as if he were weighing up a decision of enormous importance.

Layla tried not to flinch, even though the gentle brush of those strong fingers against her cheeks made everything inside her clench. She told herself he had every right to look at the woman he might marry.

Her heart started to pound. His forefinger traced the line of her jaw.

His eyes dropped to her mouth.

'You have strength and honesty and I respect those traits.' He rose to his feet, sure and confident and very much the one in control. 'There is no time to lose. We will be married within the hour. Oh, and Princess…' He paused by the entrance to the tent, his eyes a wicked shade of black. 'You have no need of the *Kama Sutra*. When the time comes I will teach you what you need to know.'

USA TODAY bestselling author **Sarah Morgan** writes lively, sexy contemporary stories for Mills & Boon® Modern™.

RT Book Reviews has described her as 'a magician with words' and nominated her books for their Reviewers' Choice Awards and their 'Top Pick' slot. In 2012 Sarah received the prestigious RITA® Award from the Romance Writers of America. She lives near London with her family. Find out more at www.sararahmorgan.com

Recent titles by the same author:

AN INVITATION TO SIN
  (Sicily's Corretti Dynasty)
SOLD TO THE ENEMY
WOMAN IN A SHEIKH'S WORLD
A NIGHT OF NO RETURN
  (The Private Lives of Public Playboys)

Did you know these are also available as eBooks?
Visit www.millsandboon.co.uk

LOST TO THE
DESERT WARRIOR

CHAPTER ONE

'The Persians teach their sons, between the ages of five and twenty, only three things: to ride a horse, use a bow and speak the truth.'

—from *The Histories by Herodotus*, Greek historian, about 484-425 BC

'Shh, don't make a sound.' Layla slammed her hand over her sister's mouth. 'I can hear them coming. They mustn't find us.'

She wished she'd had time to find a better hiding place. Behind the long velvet curtains in her father's private rooms hardly seemed like an obvious place for concealment, and yet she knew in some ways this was the safest place. No one would think to look for the princesses here. They were never allowed in his bedroom. Not even today, on the day of his death.

But Layla had wanted to see for herself that the man who'd called himself her father lay cold and still in his bed and wasn't about to leap up and commit some other sin against her or her sister. She'd stood there, hidden by the curtain, and heard him seal her fate with his dying breath. His last words hadn't expressed regret for a life misspent. There had been no demand to see his daughters, nor even a request to pass on a loving message to make up for years of cold neglect. No apology for all the grievous wrongs. Just one last wrong—one that would seal her fate forever.

'Hassan must marry Layla. It is the only way the people will accept him as ruler of Tazkhan.'

Hearing footsteps, Layla kept her hand pressed over her younger sister's mouth. Her forehead brushed the curtains and she could smell the dust. The dark was disorientating and she held herself rigid, waiting for the curtains to be flung back, afraid that the slightest movement would give them away.

From behind the protection of rich, heavy velvet she heard several people enter the room.

'We have searched the palace. They are nowhere to be found.'

'They cannot just have vanished.' The voice was harsh and instantly recognisable. It was Hassan, her father's cousin, and if his last wishes were carried out, soon to be her bridegroom. Sixty years old and more power-hungry even than her father.

In a moment of horrifying clarity Layla saw her future and it was blacker than the inside of the curtain. She stared into darkness, feeling her sister's breath warm her hand, afraid to breathe herself in case she gave them both away.

'We will find them, Hassan.'

'In a few hours you'll be addressing me as Your Excellency,' Hassan snapped. 'And you'd better find them. Try the library. The older one is always there. As for the younger one—she has far too much to say for herself. We're flying her to America, where she will be out of sight and out of mind. The people will soon forget her. My marriage to the eldest will take place before dawn. Fortunately she is the quiet one. She has nothing to say for herself and is unlikely to object.'

He didn't even know her name, Layla thought numbly, let alone her view on the world. She was 'the eldest'. 'The quiet one'. She doubted he knew or cared what she looked like. He certainly didn't care what she wanted. But then neither had her father. The only person who cared about her was currently shivering in her grasp.

Her young sister. Her friend. Her *family*.

The news that they were planning to send Yasmin to America intensified the horror of the situation. Of everything that was happening, losing her sister would be the worst.

'Why rush into the marriage?'

Hassan's companion echoed Layla's thoughts.

'Because we both know that as soon as *he* finds out about the old Sheikh's death he will come.'

He will come.

Layla knew immediately who 'he' was. And she also knew Hassan was afraid. So afraid he couldn't bring himself to speak the name of his enemy. The formidable reputation of the desert warrior and rightful ruler of the wild desert country of Tazkhan frightened Hassan so badly it was now forbidden to speak his name within the walled city. The irony was that by banning all mention of the true heir to the sheikdom he had increased his status to that of hero in the minds of the people.

In a small moment of personal rebellion, Layla *thought* the name.

Raz Al Zahki.

A prince who lived like a Bedouin among the people who loved him. A man of the desert with steely determination, strength and patience, who played a waiting game. Right now he was out there somewhere, his exact whereabouts a secret known only to those closest to him. The secrecy surrounding him increased tensions in the Citadel of Tazkhan.

Footsteps echoed on the stone floor of the bedroom.

As the door closed behind them Yasmin pulled away, gasping for air. 'I thought you were going to suffocate me.'

'I thought you were going to scream.'

'I've never screamed in my life. I'm not that pathetic.' But her sister looked shaken and Layla took her hand and held it firmly as she peeped around the heavy velvet curtain.

'They've gone. We're safe.'

'Safe? Layla, that wrinkled, overweight monster is going to marry you before dawn and he's going to send me away to America, miles from home and miles from *you*.'

Layla heard the break in her sister's voice and tightened her grip on her hand. 'No, he won't. I'm not going to allow him to take you away.'

'How can you stop it? I don't care what happens, but I want us to stay together. It's been the two of us for so long I can't imagine any other life. I need you to stop me opening my mouth when I should close it and you need me to stop you living your life in a book.'

Her sister's voice was soaked with despair and Layla felt crushed by the weight of responsibility.

She felt small and powerless as she stood alone against the brutal force of Hassan's limitless ambition.

'I promise we won't be separated.'

'How can you promise that?'

'I don't know yet. But I'm thinking…'

'Well, think fast, because in a few hours I'll be on a plane to America and you'll be in Hassan's bed.'

'Yasmin!' Shocked, Layla gaped at her sister, who shrugged defiantly.

'It's true.'

'What do you know about being in a man's bed?'

'Nowhere near as much as I'd like. I suppose that might be one of the advantages of being banished to America.'

Despite their circumstances, a dimple flickered at the corner of Yasmin's mouth and Layla felt a lump in her throat. No matter how dire the circumstances, her sister always managed to find a reason to smile. She'd brought laughter to places without humour and light into the dark.

'I can't lose you.' She couldn't even bear to think of that option. 'I *won't* lose you.'

Yasmin peered cautiously across the room. 'Is our father really dead?'

'Yes.' Layla tried to find some emotion inside herself but all she felt was numb. 'Are you sad?'

'Why would I be sad? This is only the fifth time I've ever seen him in person and I don't think this one counts so that's only four times. He made our lives hell and he's still making it hell even though he's dead.' Yasmin's unusual blue eyes darkened with fury. 'Do you know what I wish? I wish Raz Al Zahki would ride into the city on that terrifying black stallion of his and finish off Hassan. I'd cheer. In fact I'd be so grateful I'd marry him myself and give him a hundred babies just to make sure his line is safe.'

Layla tried not to look at the figure on the bed. Even dead, she didn't want to see him. 'He wouldn't want to marry you. You are the daughter of the man responsible for the death of his father and his beautiful wife. He hates us, and I cannot blame him for that.' She hated herself too, for sharing the blood of a man with so little humanity. For sharing in his shame.

'He should marry *you*. Then no one would be able to challenge him and Hassan would be finished.'

The idea was so outrageous, so typical of Yasmin, Layla's instinct was to dismiss it instantly and preach caution as she always did. But how was caution going to help them when her marriage was only hours away?

Her mind picked at the idea gingerly. 'Yasmin—'

'It is said he loved his wife so deeply that when she died he made a vow never to love again.' Yasmin spoke in an awed whisper. 'Have you ever heard anything so romantic?'

Layla's courage evaporated along with the idea. *She*

couldn't do it. 'It's not romantic. It's tragic. It was a terrible thing.'

'But to be loved that much by a man as strong and honourable as him—I want that one day.'

Yasmin stared into the distance and Layla gave her a shake.

'Stop dreaming.' The whole thing was alien to her. The only love she knew was her love for her sister. She'd never felt anything remotely romantic when she'd looked at a man. And nothing she'd read on the subject had led her to believe that would change in the future. She was far too practical a person, and it was the practical side that drove her now. 'If they take you to America I'll never see you again. I'm not going to let that happen.'

'How can you stop it? Hassan is at his most dangerous when he's afraid and he's terrified of Raz Al Zahki. He won't even allow his name to be spoken in the city. But everyone *does* speak it, of course. Especially the women. I've been listening.'

'You've been to the *souk* again? Do you have no sense of danger?'

Yasmin ignored her and her voice was an awed whisper. 'They say his heart is frozen into ice and only the right woman can melt it. It's a bit like the legend of the Sword in the Stone you read me when I was little.'

'Oh, Yasmin, grow up! A man's heart cannot be frozen into ice unless he finds himself lost in Antarctica with insufficient equipment. A heart is responsible for pumping blood around the body. It cannot be "frozen" or "broken".' Exasperated, Layla wondered how two sisters could be so different. Their experience was the same, except that Layla had protected Yasmin from the worst of her father's actions. 'This isn't legend, this is *real*. Stop romanticising everything.'

'They think he will come.' This time there was an undertone of excitement in her sister's voice. 'He has been playing a waiting game while our father and Hassan plotted. With our father dead, he has to have a plan for taking up his rightful place as Sheikh. Hassan is terrified. The council is terrified. They have extra guards on the doors at night. They've sent patrols into the desert, although goodness knows why because everyone knows Raz Al Zahki knows the desert better than anyone. No one is sleeping because they're afraid he might enter the Citadel at night and murder them in their beds. Frankly, I wish he'd just get on with it. If I bumped into him in the dark I'd show him the way.'

Layla covered her sister's lips with her fingers. 'You need to be careful what you say.'

'Why? What else can they do to me? They're splitting us up! I'm going to America and you're going to marry Hassan. How much worse can it get?'

'I'm not marrying Hassan.' Layla made her decision. 'I'm not going to let that happen.'

'How can you stop it? Hassan can only be the next ruler if he marries you. That's a pretty powerful motivation.'

'Then he mustn't marry me.'

Yasmin looked at her with pity. 'He is going to make you.'

'If he can't find me, he can't make me.' Not daring to give too much thought to what she was about to do, Layla sprinted to her father's dressing room and removed a couple of robes. She thrust one at her sister. 'Put this on. Cover your hair and as much of your face as you can. Wait here for me behind the curtain until I come and fetch you. I need to get something from the library before we leave.'

'The library? How can you think of books right now?'

'Because a book can be many things—a friend, an escape, a teacher—' Layla broke off and hoped her sister didn't notice her high colour. 'Never mind. The important thing is that we're going away from here. It will be like the game of Hide we played as children.' She caught her sister's horri-

fied glance and wished she hadn't used that reference. Both
of them knew what that game had really meant. She changed
the subject quickly. 'Those horses you love so much—can
you actually ride one if you have to?'

'Of course!'

Her sister's hesitation was so brief Layla told herself she'd
imagined it.

'And I've read extensively on the theory of riding and the
history of the Arabian horse, so between us I'm sure we'll
be fine.' She hoped she sounded more convincing than she
felt. 'We'll take the back route to the stables and ride into the
desert from there.'

'The desert? Why are we riding into the desert?'

Layla felt her mouth move even though her brain was telling her this was a terrible idea. 'We're going to find Raz Al
Zahki.'

The wind blew across the desert, bringing with it whispers
of the Sheikh's death.

Raz Al Zahki stood at the edge of the camp and stared into
the darkness of the night. 'Is it truth or rumour?'

'Truth.' Salem stood next to him, shoulder to shoulder.
'It's been confirmed by more than one source.'

'Then it is time.' Raz had learned long before to keep his
feelings buried, and he kept them buried now, but he felt the
familiar ache of tension across his shoulders. 'We leave for
the city tonight.'

Abdul, his advisor and long-time friend stepped forward.
'There is something else, Your Highness. As you predicted,
Hassan plans to marry the eldest princess in a matter of hours.
Preparations for the wedding are already underway.'

'Before her father's body is even cold?' Raz gave a cynical laugh. 'Her grief clearly overwhelms her.'

'Hassan must be at least forty years older than her,' Salem murmured. 'One wonders what she gains from the match.'

'There is no mystery there. She continues to live in a palace and enjoy benefits that should never have been hers to begin with.' Raz stared at the horizon. 'She is the daughter of the most ruthless man who ever ruled Tazkhan. Don't waste your sympathy.'

'If Hassan marries the girl it will be harder for you to challenge the succession legally.'

'Which is why I intend to make sure the wedding does not take place.'

Abdul shot him a startled look. 'So you intend to go ahead with your plan? Even though what you're suggesting is—'

'The only option available.' Raz cut him off, hearing the hardness in his own tone. It was the same hardness that ran right through him. Once, he'd been capable of warmth, but that part of him had died along with the woman he'd loved. 'We have considered every other option, and—' He broke off as he heard a commotion in the darkness and then lifted a hand as his bodyguards emerged silently to flank him.

They were men who had followed him for fifteen years, since the brutal slaying of his father. Men who would die for him.

Abdul thrust himself in front of Raz and that gesture touched him more than any other, because his trusted advisor was neither physically fit nor skilled with weapons.

Gently, but firmly, he moved him to one side, but Abdul protested.

'Go. *Go*! It could be the attempt on your life we have been expecting.'

Aware that Salem had his hand on his weapon, Raz fixed his gaze on the slim figure of a boy whose arms were gripped by two of his men. 'If my death were the objective then surely they would give the responsibility to someone I could not so easily crush.'

'We found him wandering in the desert along the border with Zubran. He appears to be alone. He says he has a message for Raz Al Zahki.'

Knowing that his men were protecting his identity, Raz signalled for them to bring their captive forward.

His hands were tied and as they released him the boy stumbled and fell to his knees. Raz stared down at him, noticing absently that his robes swamped his thin body.

It was Salem who spoke. Salem, his brother, who rarely left his side. 'What message do you have for Raz Al Zahki, boy?'

'I have to speak to him in person.' The words were mumbled and barely audible. 'And I have to be alone when I do it. What I have to say is just for him and no other.'

The guard closest to him gave a grunt of disgust. 'Someone like you wouldn't get close enough to Raz Al Zahki to wave from a distance, let alone be alone with him, and you should be grateful for that. He'd eat you alive.'

'I don't care what he does to me as long as he hears what I have to say. Take me to him. *Please.*'

The boy kept his head bowed and something in the set of those narrow shoulders drew Raz's attention.

Ignoring Salem's attempts to hold him back, he stepped forward. 'So you're not afraid?'

There was a brief pause. The wind blew across the desert, whipping up sand and catching the edges of the boy's robe. He clutched it desperately.

'Yes, I am afraid. But not of Raz Al Zahki.'

'Then you need to be educated.' The guard dragged his captive to his feet and the boy gasped in pain. 'We'll keep him here tonight and question him again in the morning.'

'No!' The boy struggled frantically in the man's grip. 'By

morning it will be too late. I have to speak to him now. Please. The future of Tazkhan depends on it.'

Raz stared at the boy, half shrouded by robes that were too big for him. 'Take him to my tent.'

Salem, Abdul and the guards looked at him in disbelief.

'Do it,' Raz said softly, but still the guards hesitated.

'We'll strip-search him first—'

'Take him to my tent and then leave us.'

Abdul touched his arm, his voice low. 'I have never before questioned your decisions, Your Highness, but this time I beg you, at least keep the guards with you.'

'You think I can't defend myself from someone half my height and weight?'

'I think Hassan will try anything at this late stage in the game. He is frightened and desperate and a desperate man should never be underestimated. I think it could be a trap.'

'I agree.' Salem's voice was hard. 'I'll come with you.'

Raz put his hand on his brother's shoulder. 'Your love and loyalty means more to me than you can possibly know, but you must trust me.'

'If anything happened to you—'

Raz felt the weight of it settle onto his shoulders. He, better than anyone, knew that there were some promises that shouldn't be made. 'Make sure I'm not disturbed.' He dismissed his bodyguards with a single movement of his hand and strode into his tent.

He closed the flap, muffling the sound of the wind and protecting them from prying eyes.

The boy was on his knees in the furthest corner of the tent, his hands still tied.

Raz studied him for a moment and then strolled over to him and cut the rope with a swift movement of his knife. 'Stand up.'

The boy hesitated and then stood in a graceful movement, only to fall again a moment later.

'I don't think I can stand—' The words were uttered through clenched teeth. 'My legs are stiff from riding and I injured my ankle when I fell.'

Raz looked down at the slender body bowed at his feet. 'Tell me why you're here.'

'I'll talk to Raz Al Zahki himself, and no one else.'

'Then speak,' Raz commanded softly, and the boy lifted his head in shock.

Under the concealing robes, dark eyes widened. 'You're him?'

'I'm the one asking the questions.' Raz sheathed his knife. 'And the first thing I want to know is what a woman is doing creeping around my camp in the middle of the night. What are you doing walking into the lion's den unprotected, Princess?'

Layla was in agony. Physical agony from her fall from the horse, and emotional agony from the knowledge that her sister was missing and alone in the vast emptiness of the baking desert and it was all her fault.

She was the one who had suggested this stupid, crazy plan. She, who never did anything stupid or crazy. She, who studied all available evidence before she made a decision, had acted on impulse. Which just proved that a cautious nature wasn't to be mocked.

It would have been better had Hassan sent Yasmin to America. At least then Layla would have known she was alive.

As it was, Yasmin was lost, and she was now a captive in the desert camp of Raz Al Zahki, a man who had more reason to hate her than any other.

A man who knew who she was.

Staring into those cold black eyes, she suddenly knew the meaning of the phrase 'between a rock and a hard place.' If her cousin was the hard place then this man was the rock. He stood legs spread, handsome face unsmiling as he stared at her. His body had the muscular structure of a warrior's, his shoulders broad and hard. She knew he had suffered terribly and yet there was no sign of suffering in face. This man wasn't broken, he was whole and strong—at least on the outside. There was nothing soft about him. Nothing vulnerable. Even before he'd revealed his identity she'd sensed his place at the head of the pack. He had the confidence and authority of a man born to lead others, and even though Layla had expected nothing less still he intimidated her.

'You knew who I was the whole time?'

'Within five seconds. You have a memorable face, Princess. And very distinctive eyes.'

It was the first personal comment anyone had ever made to her and it took her by surprise.

She'd studied him on paper and committed all the facts to memory, from his year and place of birth to his impressive military career and his degree in engineering. She knew he was a skilled rider and an authority on the Arabian horse. She knew all that, but was only just realising that facts could only tell you so much about a man.

They couldn't tell you that his eyes were darker than the desert at night or that the power he commanded on paper was surpassed a thousand times by the power he commanded in person. They couldn't tell you that those eyes were capable of seeing right through a person to the very centre of their being. They couldn't tell you that meeting those eyes would make your heart thunder like the hooves of a hundred wild horses pounding across the desert plain.

She was fast realising that a list of dates and qualifications didn't convey strength or charisma.

Unsettled that the facts had given her such an incomplete picture, Layla remembered what her sister had said about the rumours. That Raz Al Zahki was a man who knew women. Before he'd fallen in love he'd been wild, and afterwards he'd locked it all away. Every emotion. Every feeling.

'How do you know me?'

'I make a point of knowing my enemy.'

'I am not your enemy.' And yet she could hardly blame him for thinking that, could she? His family had suffered terribly at the hands of hers. They stood on opposite sides of an enormous rift that had divided their families for generations.

'Which brings me to my second question—where is Hassan? Or is he so lacking in courage he sends a woman with his messages?'

Layla shivered, but whether it was his tone or his words that affected her she didn't know.

'I'm not here because of Hassan. I was with my sister, Yasmin, but I fell from the horse.' She saw his beautiful mouth tighten. 'I'm sorry—I—you have to help me find her. *Please.* She's alone in the desert and she won't have a clue how to survive.' The thought filled her with despair but still he showed no emotion. No sympathy. Nothing.

'So where is Hassan?'

'He could be back at the palace, or he could be out there looking for us. I don't know.'

'You don't know? And yet this is the man you're supposed to be marrying in a matter of hours.'

And if Hassan found Yasmin first—

His words slowly seeped into her numb brain. 'You know about the wedding?'

'I know everything.'

'If you think I want to marry Hassan then clearly you *don't* know everything.' The tent was dimly lit, but there was enough light for her to see the flash of surprise in his eyes.

'How did you leave, if not with his consent?'

'We escaped. My sister loves horses. She took the fastest horse in the stables. Unfortunately she omitted to tell me she couldn't control him.' Layla rubbed her palm across her bruised back. 'He proved too much for both of us.'

'*Both* of you?' A dark eyebrow lifted. 'You rode one horse?'

'Yes. We're not that heavy and we didn't want to be separated.' Layla didn't tell him that she'd never ridden before. This man was renowned for his horsemanship. She had a feeling he wouldn't be impressed by the fact she knew everything about the breeding history of the Arabian horse, but nothing about the reality of riding one. 'Something scared him and he reared up. I fell and he bolted with Yasmin on his back. She won't be strong enough to stop him. She's probably fallen, too.' Panicking, she tried to stand up again, but her body protested so violently she sank back onto her knees just as two large dogs bounded into the tent.

Terror sucked the strength from her limbs. She was at eye level with the two beasts as they came to a standstill, teeth bared.

Raz said something to them and they whimpered and sank down to their bellies, huge eyes fixed on him in adoration.

'Saluki?' The fear was so sharp Layla could hardly breathe. 'You own Saluki?'

'You recognise the breed?'

'Of course.' Her mouth felt as if she'd swallowed all the sand in the desert. If dogs could smell fear, she was doomed. 'The Saluki is one of the oldest breeds in existence. They have been found in the Pyramids of Egypt, mummified alongside the bodies of pharaohs.' She didn't reveal that her familiarity with the breed came from a darker, more personal experience. An experience she'd tried to block from her mind.

'You said you were escaping. What was your destination?'

'You. You were my destination.' Reminding herself that the dogs were unlikely to attack without provocation or command, Layla kept utterly still, watching the animals. 'We were trying to find you.'

'On the night your father died? From the lack of tears it would seem you have inherited his lack of sentimentality.'

Was that what he thought?

Shocked, Layla almost corrected him, but she knew this wasn't the right time. Misunderstandings could be corrected later. Or maybe they didn't even matter. 'It was my father's dying wish that I marry Hassan.'

The darkening of his eyes was barely perceptible. 'So why come looking for me?'

She'd practised a hundred alternative ways to say what she wanted to say but every word vanished under that icy scrutiny. 'You are the rightful ruler, but if he marries me that weakens your claim and strengthens his.'

There was a sudden stillness about him that suggested she had his full attention. 'That still doesn't tell me why you're here.'

Only now did Layla realise just how much she'd been hoping he'd be the one to say it. He was praised for his intelligence, wasn't he? Couldn't he see for himself why she was here? Couldn't he see the one solution that would solve this once and for all?

But perhaps he could see and chose not to look.

'I don't blame you for hating us.' The words tumbling out of her mouth weren't the ones she'd rehearsed but when she looked at him all she could think of was the loss he'd suffered. 'If I could change who I am then I would, but I'm asking you to put that aside and do what needs to be done.'

'And what,' he prompted softly, 'do you believe needs to be done, Princess?'

No man had ever asked her opinion. Not once since the day she took her first step to the day she and her sister had slid out of the window of their father's bedroom. Not once had anyone treated her as anything but a weapon in the considerable armory of the house of Al Habib.

But this man had asked her.

This man was listening to her.

He was regal, she thought, proud and sure of himself. In that moment she caught a glimpse of why so many trusted him and protected him. He was as different from Hassan as the ocean from the desert.

'You *know* what needs to be done. You have to take your rightful place. You have to end this before Hassan finishes what my father started. Before he ruins our country in the selfish pursuit of power...' She paused, wondering whether to mention Yasmin again but deciding this man would be motivated more by his duty to his people than sympathy for her sister. 'And to do that you have to marry me. Now. Quickly. Before Hassan finds me and takes me back.'

CHAPTER TWO

He'd been planning to do whatever was necessary to prevent her wedding to Hassan taking place. Yet he had not considered the option of marrying her himself, nor had any of those surrounding him dared to suggest it despite the fact it was the obvious solution.

The tactician in him could see the benefit. The man in him recoiled.

He'd thought there was no price he wouldn't pay to fulfil his duty.

He'd been wrong.

Tension rippled down his spine. He felt as if he were being strangled.

'No.' He'd trained himself to shut down emotion but that skill suddenly failed him and his refusal came from somewhere deep inside him. Some dark part of himself he no longer accessed. 'I had a wife. I don't need or want another.' His voice sounded strange. Thickened by a hundred layers of personal agony. One of the dogs growled, a threatening sound that came from low in the animal's throat. He saw her gaze flicker to the dog and sensed her fear although he didn't understand it.

'I know about your wife.' Her brief hesitation suggested she was about to say something else on that topic, but then she gave a little shake of her head. 'Obviously I'm not suggesting myself as a replacement. This would be purely a political arrangement, advantageous to both sides.'

Raz tried to detach his mind from the pain he carried around inside himself. 'Political?'

'Hassan's position is precarious. Marriage to me is his way of securing his place as my father's successor. He has no support in Tazkhan and has never taken the trouble to earn it. For him, ruling is about what he can gain rather than what he can give and that approach makes him neither popular nor secure.'

Raz hid his surprise. He'd listened to men talk for hours on the problems facing Tazkhan and yet this girl had summarised the situation in four blunt sentences, devoid of emotion, exaggeration or drama.

'Perhaps he didn't expect your father to die so soon.'

Again there was hesitation, and it was obvious she was being selective about what she told him. 'Hassan knows that the only way he will be accepted is to marry me, and he is willing to do anything to make that happen. Do not underestimate him.'

Her words were like the scrape of a knife over an open wound because he'd done exactly that. In his righteous arrogance he'd thought himself untouchable and as a result he'd lost someone he'd loved deeply.

'You seem very familiar with the workings of his mind.'

'I've studied him. I think there is a strong chance he is clinically disturbed. He demonstrates some of the elements of a sociopath, shows no remorse or guilt for any of his actions.'

Her words were serious, those beautiful, almond-shaped eyes steady on his.

'He has no care for the feelings or opinions of others and an overinflated idea of his own importance. He is a dangerous man. But you already know that.'

'Yes.' He did know. What surprised him was that *she* knew. Raz realised he'd made assumptions about her based purely on her bloodline. He also knew she was right that the marriage had to be prevented. He didn't reveal that he'd had his own plans for making sure it didn't happen.

There was no doubt her plan was better. Permanent.

And safer for all concerned.

Except for him.

For him, it meant breaking a vow.

His tension levels soaring into the stratosphere, Raz paced the length of the tent.

Whichever way he looked at it, it felt like a betrayal. It pulled him down and tore at him. 'I cannot do it.'

'Because I am the daughter of your enemy?' She spoke in the same calm voice. 'Aristotle said "a common danger unites the bitterest of enemies". We have a common danger. I am proposing we unite. It is the right thing to do and you know it.'

Raz turned with a snarl that drew the dogs to their feet. 'Never assume to guess what I am thinking, Princess.'

Her head was slightly bowed but he could see her eyes were fixed in terror on the two animals now crouched low on the floor of the tent.

'I beg your pardon.' She held herself absolutely still, her voice barely more than a whisper. 'It seems a logical solution to me. I assumed it would seem so to you.'

It did. The fact that his emotions defied logic frustrated him. 'Do you apply logic to everything?'

'I didn't apply logic when I chose to steal a horse and point him towards the desert, so the answer has to be no, not to everything. But to most things. I find generally the outcome is better if the action is given the appropriate consideration.'

He'd never met anyone as serious as her.

He wanted to ask if she'd ever laughed, danced or had fun, and then wondered why he was even interested.

'You are suggesting something I cannot contemplate.'

'And yet you know it is the right thing for Tazkhan. So

your reluctance must be because you once had a wife you loved so very much.'

Raz felt the blood drain from his face. The tips of his fingers were suddenly cold. Anger sharpened his brain and tongue. 'Logic, if not an instinct for self-preservation, should be warning you that you are now treading on ground that is likely to give way beneath your feet.'

'I did not bring up that topic to cause you pain, but to try and understand why you would say no to something that is so obviously right.' Her fingers shook as she smoothed the robe she was wearing. 'You loved her and exchanged promises, and now you never want to marry again. I understand that.'

'You understand nothing.' He heard the growl in his own voice. 'You have condensed a thousand indescribable emotions into one short sentence.' The force of his anger shook him, and it clearly shook her too because her eyes flickered to the entrance of the tent, gauging the distance. Raz felt a rush of shame because whatever his sins, and God knew there had been many, frightening women wasn't one of them.

She spoke before he did. 'I'm sorry.' Her tone was a soothing balm against the raw edges of his pain. 'And you're right, of course. I don't understand what you're feeling because I've never loved anyone that way. But I understand that what you lost is somehow linked with your decision never to marry again. And I just want to make clear that what I'm suggesting has nothing to do with what you had before. Ours would be a marriage of political necessity, not of love. Not a betrayal of her memory, but a business arrangement. If you marry me, you take your rightful place as ruler of Tazkhan. You would be unchallenged.'

Not a betrayal of her memory.

So maybe she did understand him better than he'd first thought.

'You think I'm afraid of a challenge?'

'No. But I know you love your people and want to give Tazkhan a peaceful and prosperous future.' Suddenly she sounded very tired, very alone and very young.

Raz frowned as he tried to remember her age. Twenty-three? Younger?

'And what do you gain from this arrangement, Princess? How do you benefit from entering into a marriage where feelings play no part?' In the flickering candlelight he could see a hint of smooth cheek beneath the voluminous robes, but very little else except those eyes. And her eyes were mesmerising—as dark as sloes and framed by long, thick lashes that shadowed that smooth skin like the setting sun. Suddenly he wanted to see more of her. He wanted to reach out and rip off the robes that concealed her and see what lay beneath the folds of fabric. He'd heard whispers about the beauty of the elder princess and ignored them all because her physical attributes had been of no interest to him.

Disturbed by the sudden flare of his own curiosity, he stepped back. 'How do you benefit from this "business arrangement"?'

'If I am married to you, then I cannot be married to Hassan.'

'So I am the lesser of two evils?' Could that truly be the reason? Raz struggled to decipher her intentions. She seemed innocent and yet she came from evil. She appeared to speak the truth but those who surrounded her spoke only lies. Feeling the weight of responsibility, he suppressed his instinct to trust her. 'You are expecting me to believe that you crept out of the Citadel tonight, stole a horse and rode aimlessly into the desert in the hope of tripping over me so that you could propose marriage?'

'I had more to lose by staying than leaving. And it is well known that there are plenty of people who know your whereabouts, Your Highness. I trusted that someone would bring me to you.'

She'd called him 'Your Highness'. It was an acknowledgement he wouldn't have expected from her, given that they were on opposite sides.

Raz narrowed his eyes. 'Your loyalties are easily shifted.'

'My loyalties are to Tazkhan, but I understand that you are afraid to trust me. I do have other reasons—more personal ones.'

'What other reasons?'

'If he finds her, Hassan intends to send my sister to America.' Desperation shook that steady voice. 'He wants her out of the way.'

'Why would he want her out of the way?'

'Because we are stronger together than we are apart and he wants to weaken us. Because my sister has an uncomfortable habit of speaking her mind and she becomes harder to control with each passing day. She is dreamy, passionate, and challenges everything. And Hassan hates to be challenged.'

'And you don't challenge him?'

'I see no point in poking an angry dragon with a stick.'

'And where is your sister now?'

'I don't know.' There was fear and anxiety under the veneer of calm. 'The horse galloped off. I'm scared she might have fallen and been injured. I'm scared Hassan's men will find her before you do.'

Raz lifted an eyebrow. 'That is almost inevitable since I'm not looking for her.'

'But *will* you look for her? Once I'm your bride, will you also offer your protection to my sister?'

So that was why she was here, he thought.

She'd risked everything for love. Not romantic love, perhaps, but love all the same.

'So to keep your sister with you, and protect Tazkhan, you

would marry a stranger. That is the least romantic proposition I have ever heard.'

'Possibly. But we've already established this is not about romance. You wouldn't want that and neither would I.'

'Why wouldn't you?'

'I am not a romantic person, Your Highness.'

That matter-of-fact statement might have been unremarkable had it come from someone several decades older than she was. Her eyes were dark, luminous pools of pain and he wondered how those eyes would look if she smiled.

'You don't believe there can be love between a man and a woman?'

'Yes, I do believe there can be. Just not for me. I'm not like that. I don't have those feelings. I'm a very practical person,' she said with disarming honesty. 'As you don't want love either, I assume that won't be an obstacle for you.' She brushed it aside as easily as the desert winds shifted sand.

She had no idea, he thought. No idea that love was the most powerful force known to man. No idea how much havoc could be wrought by that emotion.

But *he* knew.

He'd been caught in the wake of devastation and still ached from his injuries.

'You say that this is a political arrangement to secure the future of Tazkhan, but for a marriage to be legal and binding in our country it requires more than simply the exchange of vows and rings.'

Her spine was rigid and her eyes were fixed on the ground in front of him. 'I am aware of that. It's important that Hassan isn't able to challenge our union so I've already familiarised myself with Tazkhan marriage laws.'

Raz found himself intrigued and exasperated in equal measures. 'So you understand what marriage entails?'

'You're referring to the physical side and, yes, I understand that. I know it has to be a full and proper marriage. I accept that. It won't be a problem.' She'd dipped her head so that the folds of her robe almost obscured her features. 'From what I've read, it shouldn't be a problem for you, either. A man doesn't need love in order to be able to perform the sexual act.'

'Perform?' Raz was torn between amusement and disbelief as he stared down at her. Under the protective folds of the robe she was shy, fragile and clueless. 'What exactly have you been reading? Whatever it is, it sounds an unusual choice for a girl like you.'

'I'm not a girl. I'm a woman.'

Not yet. The thought flew into his head and he stared at her for a long moment.

'You are contemplating a lifetime with a man who cannot love you.'

'But you will respect me.' Lifting her head, she looked him directly in the eyes. 'You will respect me for making the decision to do the right thing for Tazkhan. And that is all I need.'

Raz stared at her for a long moment.

Respect.

Was that really all she needed?

It sounded like very little, and yet right now he wasn't sure he could deliver even that.

Feeling the weight of responsibility pressing down on him like a thousand tons of sand, he turned and strode to the doorway of the tent. 'I need air.'

I need air.

Layla sagged. She needed air, too. She couldn't breathe. She was suffocating under the heavy fabric of the robes and the stifling heat in the tent and she was terrified she'd blown everything by mentioning his wife. And as for the rest of it— she'd never thought talking about sex could feel so uncomfortable. It was a natural act, performed by animals—of which man was one—since the dawn of time. Why a discussion on the topic should leave her hot and shaky she had no idea.

It was *him*.

There was something about him—a raw physicality that made her understand for the first time why women talked about him in dreamy tones.

Confused, exhausted and desperately worried about Yasmin, all Layla wanted was to strip off the robes she'd taken from her father's rooms and lie down.

She looked longingly at the low bed covered in richly coloured silks that dominated the far side of the tent.

His bed?

Just for a moment she had an image of him lying there, strong limbs entwined with the beauty who had been his wife, sharing their love. The image shocked her. Apart from images of the sculptures of Michelangelo she'd never seen a man naked, so she had no reason to be imagining one now.

Her body ached from head to foot and she wanted to stretch her limbs and examine her bruises, but she was too afraid to move with the dogs guarding her.

She watched them as she carefully tried to ease herself into a different position.

The bag she'd tied under the robes pressed uncomfortably against her hip and she pulled out the two books she'd taken from the library. One was her favourite—a book she'd read so many times she almost knew it by heart. The other—

'What is that?' His voice came from the doorway of the tent and Layla jumped and dropped both books onto the thick rug that carpeted the floor of the tent.

'Books. Just books. I brought them from home.'

Before she could snatch them back he stooped and picked one up. And of course it was *that* one.

There was a tense silence while he scanned the title of

the volume. Dark eyebrows rose in incredulity. 'The *Kama Sutra*?'

'If I'm proposing marriage then it's important I have some knowledge of what is required. There is no skill that cannot be mastered with sufficient studying. I'm ignorant, and in my experience ignorance is never bliss.'

She could hear the blood throbbing in her ears. She felt her mouth dry as if she had swallowed all the sand in the desert and her heart pounded like the hooves of the Arabian stallion who had thrown her onto the sand with such disdain.

His prolonged silence was more humiliating than a refusal and she was grateful for the semi-darkness of the tent that gave her at least some protection from his scrutiny.

Her expectations of this encounter had been modest. She hadn't exactly expected him to embrace the idea of marriage with enthusiasm, but she'd thought he'd say *something*. She certainly hadn't expected him to walk out of the tent.

But perhaps the thought of marrying her sickened him. Perhaps people were wrong and Raz Al Zahki *wouldn't* do anything that needed to be done for his country. Perhaps even he wouldn't stoop so low as to marry the daughter of the man who had destroyed his family.

Perhaps he didn't want a woman whose knowledge of the world had been gained from the contents of her father's library.

'You're not going to need this.' He handed the book back to her and her face burned like the desert in the midday heat

Tears formed a hot burning ball in the back of her throat and she almost choked on it.

He was refusing to marry her.

'I understand. In that case I need to try and find my sister myself, before Hassan does. He is at his most dangerous when he is angry and he will be very angry.' She struggled to her feet, but her legs cramped from kneeling for so long in one position and she lost her balance.

He caught her and scooped her into his arms.

Afraid of being dropped to the ground for the second time in one day, Layla gripped his shoulders and her fingers dug into an unyielding layer of solid muscle.

In her day-to-day life at the palace she didn't encounter men like him. Her father had surrounded himself with men like Hassan: men whose flesh was softened from inactivity, sycophants whose purpose in life was to indulge to the fullest.

She doubted Raz Al Zahki had ever overindulged in his life. He was lean, athletic, super-fit—and dangerous in every way.

As she turned her head, her eyes met the fierce black of his. Curiosity turned to fascination. Her eyes dropped to his mouth, now terrifyingly close to hers. Hassan's mouth was full and fleshy, but this man's lips were firm and perfectly shaped. His face was beauty blended with hardness. Hardness in the savage slash of his cheekbones and the lean line of his darkened jaw. Hardness in the grim set of his mouth and the glint in his eyes. And that hardness gave him an edge of danger. Even she, with no expertise or interest in men, could see why women might describe him as spectacularly handsome.

Something tightened deep in her stomach. Heat washed across her skin and poured through her veins.

They stared at each other and then his mouth compressed. He strode across the tent and lowered her onto the silken cover draped over the large bed, standing over her, powerful and imposing in every way.

'Where does it hurt? Explain your injuries.'

That curt command jolted her out of her dreamy state of contemplation.

Layla told herself there was no reason to feel intimidated. He couldn't help his height. He couldn't help his powerful build. And she could hardly blame him for not smiling in the circumstances.

He'd asked about her injuries.

All the talk of romance and emotions had stressed her beyond belief, so the practical nature of his question soothed her. She preferred the definable to the indefinable and her injuries were definitely definable.

'I ache all over, but particularly my legs, my back and my arms. I suspect it's a mixture of stiffness from unaccustomed muscle use and bruising from the fall. Based on the symptoms, I don't believe anything is broken.'

His eyes gleamed with irony. 'Presumably you have studied medical texts along with Aristotle and the *Kama Sutra*? Your reading matter is diverse, Princess.'

She didn't tell him she hadn't even started the *Kama Sutra*. 'I read a lot.'

'You read. Your sister talks.' He studied her for several long and deeply unsettling minutes. 'Take the robe off.'

'What?' Feeling like a tiny mouse in the sights of a predatory eagle, Layla stared at him. 'Why?'

'Because I want to assess the state of your injuries for myself.'

'I don't have any injuries,' she said quickly. 'Truly, it's just muscular. Superficial. Nothing for you to worry about but I appreciate your concern.' She'd been desperate to be out of the robes, but now she was equally desperate to keep them on. The thought of removing them in front of this man unsettled her.

With a sigh he sat down on the bed, his thigh brushing briefly against hers. 'You say you want marriage and yet you're afraid even to remove your robe in my presence? Are you proposing that once we're married we go to bed fully clothed?'

'No, of course not. That's different.'

'*How* is it different?'

He was testing her. He thought she couldn't do it.

Desperation blew away modesty. If he refused to marry her she would never see Yasmin again.

'I will be fine. I will take the responsibilities that come with the role very seriously.'

'Responsibilities?'

'Physical intimacy is one of the responsibilities of a wife. I understand that. I understand exactly what is involved.'

'Are you sure?' Those dark eyes swept her face with disturbing intensity. 'How much of the *Kama Sutra* have you read, Princess?'

If she said she'd read the whole thing cover to cover would he marry her?

Layla opened her mouth and then closed it again, because she knew her skills at lying were on a par with her horse-riding abilities. 'Not much.' She hoped honesty wasn't going to kill her future. 'In fact just the title so far. But I'm a fast reader,' she added quickly, afraid that her lack of knowledge might put him off. 'And *you* have experience.'

For some reason just saying that made her body warm.

Because looking at his face made her feel hot and uncomfortable she stared instead at his hands, but for some reason that didn't make her feel any better. She felt as if she'd had a shot of adrenaline straight into the heart.

'You are reluctant to take off your robe,' he said softly, 'but once we're married you are going to be naked when you share my bed.'

Layla felt her stomach curl. Everything inside her twisted and heated. She felt dizzy and strange.

Nerves, she thought. 'Does this mean you're agreeing to my suggestion?'

Without warning he lifted a powerful hand and pushed back the swath of fabric covering her head. His handsome face was taut and unsmiling, as if he were weighing up a decision of enormous importance.

Layla tried not to flinch even though the gentle brush of those strong fingers against her cheeks made everything inside her clench. She told herself he had every right to look at the woman he might marry.

Was he looking to see if she were as beautiful as his wife? Or was he deciding if he could look upon her every day and not see the face of her father and Hassan and think of the destruction they'd caused in his life.

He continued to look, his gaze disturbingly intense as his fingers trailed slowly over her cheek.

She knew her face was flushed. She could feel the heat and knew he would be able to feel it, too, with those fingers that seemed in no hurry to cease their exploration of her skin.

Her heart started to pound.

The seconds passed and a minute became two minutes and longer.

His forefinger traced the line of her jaw.

His eyes dropped to her mouth.

Layla was rigid with discomfort. She had no idea of the correct etiquette in this situation. Was she supposed to do something? Say something? Was it some sort of test?

She remembered Yasmin telling her that his wife had been stunningly beautiful.

Was this all about comparison?

When he spoke, there was something in his tone she couldn't identify. 'You are brave.'

Torn between relief that there was at least one thing about her he liked and disappointment that such close examination hadn't uncovered anything else to commend her, Layla felt obliged to tell the truth. 'I'm not very brave. I ran away from the palace.'

'And you ran to me and offered me everything, even though deep down the thought of it frightens you.'

'I'm not frightened.'

'So far I believe you have been honest with me. I advise you not to change that.'

She hesitated. 'I don't think you'll hurt me.'

His eyes darkened. 'I will inevitably hurt you—as you would know if you'd read the book.'

Was he talking physically? Out of her depth in a conversation that felt like a swim in boiling oil, Layla had never felt more mortified in her life. 'If there is pain then I'll bear it.'

'You seem determined to pursue this course, but what you are proposing will tie us together for a lifetime, so I urge you to think carefully and be sure this is what you want.'

'That's why I came to you and suggested it.' Surely the facts spoke for themselves? Why did he keep asking her? 'The alternative is being tied to Hassan for a lifetime and you must see that lacks appeal for so many reasons.'

There was a glimmer of something in his eyes. It might have been admiration or it might have been pity or even humour.

'You have strength and honesty and I respect those traits. If respect is truly all you need from a relationship then I can promise you that. It will be done.' He rose to his feet, sure and confident and very much the one in control. 'I will send Salem to find your sister and instruct him to bring her here. I agree that there is no time to lose, so you and I will be married within the hour. I will send someone to help you prepare. Oh, and princess…' He paused by the entrance to the tent, his eyes a wicked shade of black. 'You have no need of that book. When the time comes I will teach you what you need to know.'

CHAPTER THREE

'I AM TO search for a princess who talks too much? What sort of a description is that? Every woman I know talks too much.' Salem sat relaxed on his horse, a look of incredulity on his handsome face as he looked at his brother. 'If the stallion she stole is the one we think it is, he was bred for speed and endurance. He could have carried her for miles. She could be anywhere. Or lying dead somewhere in the desert.'

'The fact that she talks too much should make her all the easier to find and we both know that with your abilities you can track anyone.' Raz rode alongside him, controlling a horse who snorted and pawed at the sand, yearning for speed. 'Be careful. Hassan will be looking for her and the horse. And also for you.'

'And for *you*. You should not be asking me to leave you at this time.'

'I'm not asking you. I'm giving you an order.'

'Is it true that you are going to marry the Princess tonight?'

Salem's voice was soft and Raz kept his hand steady as he soothed the horse.

'It is the right thing to do. The only thing.'

'It may be the right thing for Tazkhan, but is it right for *you*?'

Raz ignored the question. 'You will do everything in your power to find the younger sister.'

'You vowed never to marry again.'

No one but his brother would have dared make such a personal remark and the words were like the sharp flick of a whip.

'There is more than one type of marriage. This will be a marriage of the head, not of the heart.'

'And the Princess?' There was a creak of leather as Salem shifted his position in the saddle. 'She's young. Is that the life she wants?'

'She claims that it is.'

'Does she know about—?'

'No.' Raz interrupted him before he could finish the sentence. 'But she understands exactly what I am able to offer her.'

'And you trust her? You can live with her, knowing who she is?'

'I will learn to live with her.' He blocked thoughts of her heritage and instead thought of her sitting huddled on his bed, gripping the oversized robe in clenched hands. He thought of the book she'd chosen to bring from the library to equip her for her new role. *Thought of the courage it must have taken to come to him.* 'She has very little life experience.'

'Whereas you have decades too much. You're not an easy man to know, Raz—are you being fair to her?'

'I will endeavour to be as fair as possible.' Frowning, Raz released his hold on the reins and urged the stallion forward. 'You're wasting time. The key to my bride's happiness will be finding her sister safe and well. Make that happen.'

Salem rode away from him. 'Just watch your back, brother.'

'His Highness instructed us to bring you clothes.' The girl dropped a dress on the bed. Resentment and animosity throbbed from her and it was obvious she wished she had not been the one chosen for the task.

'Thank you.' Having washed away the dust from her fall in the water that had been hastily provided, Layla stared at the exquisite fall of silk, caught at the waist with a silver belt. 'I didn't expect a dress.' Especially not a dress like this one. *A romantic dress.* Where had he found it?

She remembered his comment about romance and felt a flash of panic that Raz Al Zahki would think she was secretly nurturing dreams about their relationship, and then remembered that he was the last person to encourage such a delusion.

He didn't want this any more than she did.

'You cannot marry His Highness in dusty robes that swamp you. You have to look your best on your wedding day.' There was censorship in her tone and something else. *Jealousy?*

Feeling desperately alone, Layla missed her sister more than ever. She suppressed the urge to point out there was no reason for anyone to feel jealous. That this marriage was driven by loyalty to his country and no other emotion.

Surely it was obvious?

'The Sheikh and I met for the first time a few hours ago.'

'But you have been chosen as the one to warm his bed and his heart.' The girl removed the bowl of water that she'd placed by Layla's feet. 'You carry a big responsibility.'

The words did nothing to ease the churning in her stomach. Layla knew she'd warm the bed simply by lying in it, but she also knew that wasn't what the girl meant. She did not feel it appropriate to point out the absurdity of being chosen to warm his heart when his heart was in his thoracic cavity and more than capable of maintaining its own temperature. No, what the girl was *really* pointing out was that she was filling the gap left by his wife. Suddenly Layla realised that it was all very well to speak blithely of a different sort of marriage but in the end this union was about a man and a woman spending their lives together, and she had no idea if he would even be able to treat her with civility, given everything that had happened.

But what difference did it make? Her alternative was marriage to Hassan and nothing could be worse.

Rationalising that, Layla only half listened as the girl braided her hair and continued to praise Raz in terms close to hero-worship. She was aware of the worsening throb in her head and the steady gnawing of anxiety about her sister. And beneath all that there was anxiety about herself. About what lay ahead. About *him*.

It was all very well to state bravely that this was what she wanted. Quite another thing to contemplate the reality.

I will inevitably hurt you—as you would know if you'd read the book.

'The book' was safely tucked away in her bag, along with the other book she'd smuggled out of the Citadel. Raz had told her she didn't need to read it but she couldn't think of anything worse than relying entirely on someone else for information.

She wished she could have time alone to study it before the wedding, but there seemed to be no chance of that and she couldn't argue with his decision to proceed as quickly as possible.

Hassan would be out looking for her. *And for Yasmin.*

She winced as the girl's fingers encountered a fresh bruise.

'His Highness told me you fell from your horse. It's a shame that you can't ride because he is a magnificent horseman.'

The implication being that he couldn't have picked a worse match in her.

Her confidence plummeting as each of Raz's qualities was revealed, Layla sank into gloom. She was starting to wonder if this might not have been the worst idea of her life.

And then she heard noise from outside the tent and sat up,

clutching the towel, terrified that Hassan might have found them. 'Who is that?'

'The wedding guests. A Bedouin wedding gives everyone a chance to dress up and celebrate. Word has spread that His Royal Highness Raz Al Zahki is to marry Her Royal Highness Princess Layla of Tazkhan.' There was a brittle note to her tone. 'Even though it is short notice, he wants as many of the local people here as possible. It's important that it is witnessed.'

He wanted rumour spread. He wanted Hassan to hear and be afraid.

'Even when I'm married to Raz Al Zahki, Hassan is unlikely to step aside.'

'His Highness will know what to do.'

Layla was surprised by how much faith people seemed to have in him. She was used to living in an atmosphere of negativity and resentment, not of trust.

Nothing about this new life seemed familiar, and certainly not the dress.

She had never worn anything so beautiful. Her hair, now shiny and clean, was concealed by a veil and her eyes had been accentuated by kohl. The shiny gloss the girl applied to her mouth felt sticky and strange and Layla felt utterly unlike herself.

Any hopes she'd had of being able to sneak a look at the *Kama Sutra* died as she was immediately led outside. It seemed that she and Raz Al Zahki agreed on at least one thing, and that was that the marriage should take place as fast as possible.

And clearly he had also decided that there should be as many witnesses as possible, because a surprising number of people had poured into the desert camp in the time it had taken her to wash and change.

The wedding itself was a blur, conducted with an urgency

driven not by feelings of sentimentality but by the knowledge that any delay could give Hassan an advantage.

Layla kept her gaze focused ahead of her, aware of what felt like a thousand pairs of eyes fixed on her—some curious, others with unconcealed hostility.

And all the time she was aware of Raz next to her, tall and powerful, doing his duty for the good of his people, his own personal wishes set aside.

The event held no emotional meaning for either of them, but they stood side by side, spoke the words required of them, and Layla felt a rush of relief that came from the knowledge that no matter what happened now Hassan couldn't make her his wife.

As Raz turned towards her relief was washed away by reality.

She was now living in the enemy camp with a man who had no reason to feel anything but animosity and contempt for her.

The fact that this was a marriage of expediency didn't seem to bother the guests, who danced and celebrated until Layla was almost dropping with exhaustion.

And he noticed, of course, because it seemed he noticed everything—from the slightest change in the wind's direction to a child who had wandered off unattended.

'Come.'

Just a single word, but delivered with such authority that it didn't occur to her to contradict him. Or maybe it was that she was too preoccupied with what lay ahead.

She hoped the physical side of their relationship didn't require too much input from her because she was fairly sure she was going to fall asleep the moment she lay flat.

They were halfway towards the tent when there was a sound in the distance. She heard horses and shouts and Raz tightened his hand over hers and hauled her close to his side.

Moments later two men she recognised from her arrival at the camp galloped up with the Sheikh's stallion—that same huge black beast that had become as much of a legend as its master.

Layla strained her ears to catch what they were saying and then gasped as firm hands grasped her and swung her onto the back of the animal. Less than thrilled at being back on a horse so soon after her last experience, she clutched at the stallion's mane feeling unbalanced and horribly unsafe.

Moments later Raz vaulted on behind her and locked his arm around her waist.

'I'm sorry to do this to you when you're still bruised after your last encounter with a horse, but Hassan has discovered your absence.' His mouth was right by her ear. 'Right now he is doing everything in his power to find you. It isn't safe to stay. We must move on.'

'But now that we're married—'

'That does not make it safe. No matter what circumstances led to our marriage, you are mine now and I will protect you. You have my word on that.'

Layla heard the steel in his voice and wondered if he were thinking of his wife.

Did he blame himself for not preventing the accident that had killed her?

Had she given him yet more responsibility to add to the load he already carried?

'Could we use a different mode of transport? I'll slow you down. I can't ride.'

'I am the one doing the riding. You are merely the passenger.'

'I'll fall off.' She glanced down and then wished she hadn't. It was a long way to the ground. The stallion was enormous and she felt the power of him beneath her, felt the quivering suppressed energy, and remembered how the horse Yasmin had taken from her father's stables had shot forward like an arrow from a bow, leaving her in an aching heap on the sand.

His arm tightened around her. 'I will *not* let you fall.'

'Can't we use a helicopter or a Jeep or something?'

'One of my men is flying the helicopter and another is taking a Jeep to provide a decoy. They will not expect us to be on horseback. It is the safest way.'

Thinking that he had a very different idea of the definition of 'safe', Layla gripped tightly with her legs and felt the warm flanks of the quivering horse pressing against her bare thighs. 'I'm not dressed for this.'

Even as she said the words a cloak was wrapped around her and he said something to someone close by.

'There is no time to change. You will be fine. Trust me.'

Layla was about to point out that she didn't trust him any more than he trusted her, but the horse sprang forward and she squeezed her eyes shut.

'Is it wise to ride at night?'

'No. Which is why Hassan will not look for us on horseback.'

'Is that supposed to be comforting?' She thought she heard him laugh but decided it must have been the wind, because who could find such a dangerous situation amusing?

'I know this area as well as you know the palace. We are following the stars and the riverbed. Now, relax and go with the rhythm of the horse. You are very tense and that will make the whole thing more uncomfortable.'

Go with the rhythm of the horse...

She told herself that last time she hadn't had a skilled rider in control or a strong male arm wrapped around her.

'Pull the scarf across your mouth.'

She released her rigid grip on the horse's mane to do as he instructed.

She wanted to ask where they were going, but knew the

question was not only superfluous but also potentially hazardous because the hooves of the horses sent sand flying into the air and she only had a thin layer of scarf protecting her. So she kept her mouth closed and tried to remember what she'd read about riding, and then realised it didn't matter because *he* knew and was driving the horse forward, controlling the animal with one hand on the reins while the other remained firmly locked around her waist.

She was aware of the dull thud of hooves on sand, of the feel of Raz's thighs pressed hard against hers and the brush of the cool night air on her face. A sensation tore through her that she didn't recognise and it took her a few moments to realise it was exhilaration. With the responsibility for controlling the horse in someone else's hands, the ride on the back of this powerful animal was the most exciting, breathtaking experience of her life. In her restricted, regimented life this was the closest she'd ever come to freedom, and it felt so good she smiled behind the protective covering of the scarf. She couldn't remember when she'd last smiled, but she was smiling now as each pounding stride of the horse took her further away from Hassan. It felt like the end of something—and then she remembered that Hassan was unlikely to give up that easily.

And Yasmin was out in the desert alone and lost.

Her smile faded.

She hoped Salem's knowledge of the desert was as good as it was reputed to be and that he'd find her sister quickly.

They rode for several hours, until time blurred and sleep overcame her. Several times she was jarred awake as her head hit his shoulder, and eventually he shifted position to give her somewhere to rest her head.

'Sleep, Princess.'

And she did, because her body gave her no choice, exhausted by the exertions of the past twenty-four hours. Her last coherent thought before her brain shut down was that sleeping against his chest like this was the safest she'd felt in her life.

CHAPTER FOUR

SHE WAS SNUGGLED against him, lulled to sleep by the movement of the horse.

The closeness of her disturbed him as much as the realisation that she was nothing like he'd imagined her to be when people had spoken her name. He'd visualised someone pampered and privileged. Someone spoiled and entitled. When he'd first seen her in his tent he'd assumed she was an opportunist, switching sides to protect herself before the inevitable shift in power.

At some point from her arrival in the camp to her falling asleep against him his view on her had become clouded, and now he was forced to admit he didn't know what he was dealing with.

Dawn rose over the desert, and in the distance he saw the familiar shape of trees and tents clustered around the small, lush oasis that marked one of his favourite places on earth.

His heart clenched as it always did when he arrived here.

Perhaps he shouldn't have brought her, but what choice did he have?

Alerted to their presence, people emerged from tents. The rising sun glinted off the dunes and Raz brought his horse to a halt.

'Princess?' He spoke the word softly and she stirred against him, her hand locked on the sleeve of his robe.

Raz looked down at that hand. Her fingers were slender and he realised this was the first time he'd seen any part of her other than her face. 'Layla!' He used her name for the first time and she came awake with a start, her eyes blurred with sleep as she tried to focus and orientate herself.

'I fell asleep?'

'For several hours.' He held the stallion steady and then dismounted in a smooth movement. 'Swing your leg over the saddle and I'll help you down.'

She did it without fuss, but the moment her feet touched the ground she winced and gripped the horse for balance. They'd ridden for hours and she was already aching and bruised from her ride from the Citadel. He knew virtually nothing about her but suspected only dire need would drive her to steady herself against his horse.

The stallion gave a snort of disapproval and threw up its head in disgust.

Raz put his hand on his horse's neck and spoke calmly. 'Your muscles will soon become accustomed to riding.'

'I'm fine, really.'

'You are hoping never to see another horse in your life,' he said dryly, 'but horses are an essential part of my life. I own several stud farms. Two in the US, one in England and one here in Tazkhan.'

'I know. Your aim is to promote the highest standards in breeding. You specialise in endurance and racing. People send mares from all over the world to be covered by your stallions. You rode in the endurance team on your favourite horse, Raja.'

He hid his surprise. 'You know a great deal about my horses.'

'I know nothing about your horses.' This time she was the one to speak in a dry tone. 'But I will try very hard to learn.'

'Is that what you want?'

She hesitated. 'Of course. Although I can't promise I'll show any aptitude. I'm not very coordinated and I'm not sure animals like me much.' Hesitant, she reached out and patted the stallion's neck. 'Is this Raja? I'm incredibly grateful to him for not throwing me off.'

'I bred him. He was sired by my father's stallion.'

'He's beautiful. But big.'

Presumably her legs had steadied because she stepped back and looked around her for the first time.

'Where are we? We can stay with these people? In their homes? Will we be welcome?'

There wasn't a place in the desert where he wasn't welcome, but he didn't say that to her.

'The Bedouin pride themselves on their hospitality. A visitor may stay three days and three nights, after which he is considered sufficiently refreshed to be able to continue his journey.'

'Is that what we're going to do?'

Raz didn't reply. He wasn't used to sharing his plans with anyone, least of all the daughter of the man who had ripped his life into shreds. 'The oasis here is famed for its beauty. You can relax here, knowing you are safe.'

'And my sister?'

'When I have news from Salem I will tell you. And now I have things I must do.'

She didn't ask what things. She simply stared at the red-gold of the dunes as they rose against the sunrise as if she were seeing the desert for the first time, while Raz found himself looking at her profile. She had to be exhausted and in pain after the long ride, but she hadn't once complained.

He wondered what she was thinking.

Was she still relieved not to have married Hassan?

Was she nervous? Regretting her decision to marry a man she didn't know?

On impulse he reached out to touch her shoulder, and then changed his mind and withdrew his hand. 'The waters of the oasis are good for muscle ache.'

'I'll remember that, thank you.'

A young woman emerged from one of the tents and Raz felt a sudden rush of tension. In an ideal world he would have prepared for this encounter with more care, but the world was rarely ideal.

'This is Nadia. If there is anything you need she will help you.'

Nadia looked from him to Layla, unable to hide her dismay. 'So it's true? You married her?'

Her voice shook and Raz shot her a warning look.

'Yes. And you will make her welcome.'

For a moment he thought she was going to refuse.

Their eyes met and suddenly he wondered whether her feelings about this development were more complicated than he'd imagined.

Nadia's breathing was shallow, but she gave a brief nod. 'Of course. Come this way, Your Highness.' The correct mode of address was spoken through clenched teeth, but Raz decided to overlook that for now.

His sudden marriage would have come as a massive shock to Nadia. It was fair that she be given time to adjust.

Raz saw Layla glance towards him and wondered if the other girl's open hostility had upset her.

Or perhaps she was suddenly realising that this marriage was real.

Out of the frying pan into the fire?

'Bathe, eat, rest,' he told her quietly, 'and I will see you later.'

Bathe, eat, rest.

All of it seemed to be leading to one thing. The night.

I will see you later.

Layla tried not to think about it. It was something to be done, that was all. She would endure it as she had endured the long gallop on the horse and a thousand other discomforts in her life. Really, how bad could it be?

'His Highness gave instructions that you are to swim. He says it will ease the pain in your muscles.' Nadia was barely civil as she led her towards the tents, but Layla was starting to get used to that attitude from everyone close to the Sheikh.

She felt as welcome as a scorpion in the heel of someone's boot.

All the same, she wondered what the other girl's relationship was with him. She'd seen the look they'd exchanged and it had been obvious to her that they knew each other well.

She wondered if the woman had been his lover, but told herself she had no reason to mind even if she had.

Baking hot under the desert sun, Layla removed her cloak. Nadia turned pale.

'Where did you get that dress?'

Layla glanced down at herself and noticed that the silk was discoloured by sand and dust from the ride. 'I was given it. Why?'

'No reason.' Nadia's lips were bloodless. 'I will leave towels on the rocks, Your Highness, and lay out clean clothes in the tent for you to change into when you have finished.'

'I can't swim,' Layla admitted. 'Is the oasis deep?'

Nadia led her along a narrow path. 'Not if you enter the pool by the rocks on the far side.'

The rocks on the far side.

Layla committed that to memory because she didn't want to get it wrong.

Nothing about her first glimpse of the camp had prepared her for the beauty of the oasis. Shaded by date palms, the still pool of water looked temptingly cool after the long, dusty ride.

This part of the pool was secluded, the view from the

other tents obscured by palms and citrus trees. Just one tent stood close by and Nadia gestured with her head. 'That is His Highness's tent. I will leave clothes there and put food in the tent. If you need anything, just call, but the pool is safe in the daytime. I'll go and fetch towels.'

Layla didn't ask what happened at night. She was too busy wondering who had given up their tent for the Sheikh.

It was obvious it had prime position, set apart from the others and opening onto what effectively became a private pool.

But not *that* private.

Layla glanced around her, aware that anyone could walk past at any time.

Having only ever undressed behind a locked door, she decided to keep her dress on. It was ruined anyway, so she might as well get one last use out of it.

Removing the belt, she walked to the rocks at the far side of the pool, as Nadia had instructed, and slid into the water.

Stretching out her legs, she felt for the bottom with her feet—but there was no bottom.

Too late, she realised how deep it was and clung tightly to the slippery rock with her fingers, trying to pull herself out again. Just as the thought flashed into her head that Nadia had deliberately sent her to deep water she sank under the surface, dragged down by the weight of the saturated dress.

Trying not to panic, Layla attempted to haul herself up, but her fingers slipped and she sank under the surface, choking.

Water flooded through her mouth and her ears and she kicked hard, but the dress wrapped itself around her ankles, pulling her down.

Just when she'd thought there was no way she was ever going to get out of this alive she felt a disturbance in the water next to her and strong hands hauled her upwards, towards the light. Layla broke the surface of the water, gasping and coughing.

'Are you trying to drown yourself?' His black hair plastered to his head, Raz lifted her onto the rocks and then launched himself out of the water next to her, water streaming from the gleaming, pumped muscles of his bare chest. 'What were you thinking, swimming in a dress?'

Layla couldn't answer. She was too busy coughing and trying not to be sick.

Cursing softly under his breath, he smoothed her soaked hair away from her face. 'You are all right now. You are safe. It was lucky I decided to come back and check on you.'

'I went under—'

'Because you chose to swim in your dress,' he breathed, and she shook her head.

'I never intended to swim. I can't swim. I was just going to dip myself in the water.'

'Fully clothed?'

It sounded ridiculous, spelled out like that, and her face turned fiery hot. 'I thought someone might walk along and see me. The dress was ruined anyway so I thought I'd just keep it on and paddle.'

'In the deepest end of the pool?'

'I thought it was the shallow end.' Layla glanced up at him, puzzled, and saw his eyes darken dangerously.

'Why would you think that? Who told you it was the shallow end?'

She wasn't going to tell him that when there was already friction. 'It was my fault,' Layla muttered 'I should have checked for myself.'

Without speaking, he unfastened the back of her dress. 'Take this off. Go to the other end of the pool where the water is only waist deep. You will be safe and undisturbed, I promise.'

'Where are you going?'

'There is a conversation I need to have and it would seem

that it can't wait.' His voice vibrating with anger, he vaulted to his feet and strode back towards the tent.

Moments later Layla heard his voice and winced, because it was obvious to her that however much Nadia had loathed her before this, she was going to loathe her a thousand times more by the time Raz had finished ripping strips from her in that icy voice of his. She thought she heard muffled sobs and closed her eyes, because the whole situation was turning into a complex mess and without the facts she had no idea how she was supposed to handle it.

Taking refuge in the practical, she peeled off the soaked dress and forced herself back into the water again—more because she didn't want to let fear beat her than because she wanted to wash. This time she was relieved to feel the bottom under her feet. As he had promised, the water only reached her waist and she washed herself quickly, still shocked by how close she'd come to drowning in this beautiful place.

The sun sent sparkles of light dancing over the still surface of the pool. Somewhere nearby she heard children playing, their laughter cutting through the stillness of the baking hot air, and the sound surprised her because she hadn't expected to hear children.

She couldn't think of the time she'd last heard children laugh like that. It reminded her of when Yasmin had been very young and Layla had been constantly putting her hand over her mouth to stifle her giggles in case the sound drew unwanted attention. But here no one was trying to muffle the sound and the children played happily, unrestricted.

Thinking of her sister brought a lump to her throat.

Where was she now?

If only she were at least alive, Layla would never complain about anything ever again.

Listening to the children, she was tempted to go and watch them, but then decided she'd encountered enough hostility for one day. Instead she wrapped herself in the towels that had been left for her and walked the short distance to the tent, hoping that Nadia wouldn't be there.

Stepping inside, she stopped in surprise.

She'd expected something basic, but this tent was not only fully furnished but luxurious, decorated in rich reds and deep purples. There was a seating area piled with soft cushions and a low bed covered in silk sheets, with a thick cover for cold desert nights.

It was idyllic.

It was—Layla swallowed hard—*it was romantic*.

Someone had laid food on a low table near to the door, but Layla wasn't hungry. She couldn't even think about food after everything that had happened. Did Nadia really hate her so much she would want her dead? And what had Raz said to her that had caused her such distress?

Feeling sick from nerves and oasis water, she pulled on the clothes and sank onto the cushions.

Despite worry about Nadia, and anxiety for her sister, her mind was dominated by thoughts of the night ahead.

She would have spent the day reading, but her books had been left behind at the first camp so she had nothing but her imagination to occupy her time, and by the time Raz finally appeared she was so worked up she jumped out of her skin.

'You startled me.'

His gaze rested on the untouched food and a faint frown touched his forehead. 'You haven't touched the food. Are you unwell after the incident earlier?'

'No. I just wasn't hungry.'

'If you do not eat you will make yourself ill.'

She didn't tell him that she already felt ill. That nerves had created an uncomfortable lump in her stomach, leaving no room for food. 'I won't be ill. I'm very fit.'

'But you can't swim?'

'There is nowhere to swim in the palace so I've never had opportunity.'

'Then that's something we must fix.' A ghost of a smile touched his mouth. 'Swimming in the oasis is one of life's pleasures.'

Her heart was pumping so fast she worried she was going to pass out, and when he took her hand and drew her towards him she stopped breathing.

'I am sorry for what happened to you.'

'Is Nadia—?'

'I don't want to talk about Nadia. She has no relevance to what is happening between us and I've dealt with her. Now you need to relax.' His voice soft, he smoothed her hair back from her face. 'You are very tense and there is no need to be.'

Behind him, through the crack in the tent, she could see the sun turning dark red as it set and it shocked her because she hadn't realised it was so late.

'I'm not tense.'

'Yes, you are, and that is hardly surprising.' His fingers lingered in her hair. 'This is not how you dreamed your wedding night would be, I'm sure.'

'I never dreamed about it. I'm not a dreamy person, Your Highness.'

'Raz.' He let a strand of her hair twist itself around his fingers, frowning as she flinched away from him. 'You don't have to be afraid of me.'

It wasn't fear that made her stomach cramp, but she wasn't sure what it was because it was a feeling she didn't recognise.

All she knew was that she'd never felt more uncomfortable in her life. He clearly thought she'd spent her formative years dreaming of weddings and happy endings whereas nothing could have been further from the truth.

'I am not a romantic person,' she reminded him. 'I thought

I'd made that clear. I hope that won't be a problem. I assumed you wouldn't want that.'

What if he did?

Perhaps he was expecting her to fall instantly in love with him and she knew that was never going to happen.

The heat in the tent was stifling and he was standing close to her. *So close she could feel the heat and power of him.* The breath was locked in her throat and Layla had no idea what she was supposed to do next. Was he expecting her to kiss him? Was he supposed to go first or was she? Both together?

Layla desperately wished she'd had time to study the various options.

She wished she'd read *that* book long before now, instead of grabbing it as an afterthought on the run from the palace and her old life.

The gaps in her knowledge were glaringly obvious. For a start, she was confused by how long he'd stood there just looking at her. She'd assumed it would all be over quickly. Instead he seemed to be taking his time. His hand had migrated from her hair to her cheek and the slow, exploratory stroke of his fingers unsettled her.

Her tummy tightened into a knot and her pulse leaped and pounded.

She wanted to look away but his gaze drew her to him, holding her eyes with his. And then his eyes flickered to her mouth and that made her feel strange, too. As did his next words.

'So what *did* you dream about when you were growing up in the palace?'

How was she supposed to answer that? Every day had been focused on survival. On protecting her sister. 'I didn't really dream. I prefer to focus on things that are real. Tangible.'

'You had no wish for the future?'

'If I did then it was a hope that the future would be better than the present.' She saw him frown slightly and felt his thumb slide slowly over the line of her jaw.

'The present was hard for you?'

What could she say? However hard it had been for her, she knew it must have been so much harder for him. He'd lost his father and the woman he'd loved. 'I had my sister.'

A faint smile touched the corner of his mouth. 'You're being evasive, but I'll overlook it for now because the past has no place in our bedroom.'

Our bedroom.

Her heart was pounding furiously and she found herself trapped by his dark gaze as he slid his hands into her hair and tilted her face to his.

'If I do anything you don't like you must tell me,' he breathed.

She'd just had time to think that was a very strange thing to say, because she had no expectation of liking any of it, when he lowered his head.

Anticipation held her rigid.

That sensuously curved mouth hovered close to hers, prolonging the moment of contact. Just as Layla was beginning to wonder whether there was a reason he was taking so long, whether there was something she was supposed to be doing that she wasn't, he slanted his mouth over hers and kissed her.

The gentleness threw her. Braced for something quite different, she found the slow, deliberate movement of his lips on hers shocking. Equally unexpected was the sudden tightening of her stomach and the warmth that rushed through her body and into her limbs. The feelings intensified but still his mouth moved over hers while his hands, buried in her hair, held her head trapped.

She felt his tongue trace the seam of her mouth, teasing, coaxing, and she parted her lips, shocked to feel his tongue delve into her mouth.

Something—*nerves*?—made her shaky? and she closed her hands over his arms to steady herself, her fingers moving over the solid muscle of his biceps. His physical power was undeniable, and she remembered the way he'd controlled the stallion and lifted her out of the pool. But he used that strength lightly now, his hands gentle as he smoothed her hair away from her face and kissed her mouth, all the time watching her through slumbrous dark eyes that made her aware of every part of herself.

Layla had never felt anything like this before, and she felt a flash of panic because she was a person who liked to understand things and rationalise them. But there was no understanding the searing heat that shot through her body and pooled low in her belly.

Releasing her head, he curved one arm around her back, slid the other around her waist and pulled her into him. She felt the strength and power of his thighs and the hardness of him. Pressed against the evidence of his masculinity, she discovered that the works of Michaelangelo didn't tell the whole story.

Layla was confused by the torrent of sensation that flooded her skin and seeped into her nerve-endings.

'Kiss me back.'

His husky command was spoken against her lips and she stared up at him, unable to see him properly in the darkness but knowing her mouth was just a shadow away from the dangerous curve of his.

Kiss me back.

Wishing she had more knowledge of technique, Layla tentatively touched her lips to his. She wanted to ask, *Is this right?* But then she felt his arm tighten around her waist, drawing her closer. Pressed this close to him, she felt hot and unbalanced in every way. She knew her cheeks were flushed, knew he could taste her confusion on her lips, but still he kissed her and the slowness of it, together with the long drawn-out ache of anticipation and something else she couldn't name, was agonising.

He kissed her until their surroundings faded and the only thing in her vision was him, and then he lifted her in his arms and carried her to the bed. The practical side of her prompted her to tell him she was capable of walking, but she thought it might be a lie so she kept silent and wondered how nerves could weaken limbs.

The light in the tent was dim, but not so dim she couldn't see his face, and she remembered Yasmin dreamily telling her how handsome he was—how he was *'hot'*. At the time Layla hadn't understood how a word used to describe temperature could be used as a positive indicator of visual appeal, but now she realised that looking at him made her *feel* hot. Burning hot. Her skin, her lips and other more sensitive parts of her that she rarely had reason to think about. And while he was kissing her he extracted her from her clothing. The ease with which he accomplished that feat was almost as embarrassing as being naked in front of him.

Grateful for the semi-darkness, she somehow resisted the desperate urge to cover herself. Never in her life had she felt so out of her depth and inadequate, and she lay there, her breathing shallow, staring up at him as he wrenched off his shirt, all the time watching her with eyes almost black in the candlelight.

Layla held her breath because even she, with her limited experience and previously limited interest in the masculine form, could see that his was perfectly proportioned.

Unable to help herself, she let her gaze slide over bronzed, muscular shoulders, down over his chest with its haze of dark hair, and lower still to his board-flat abdomen. She didn't look lower and he slid his fingers under her chin and lifted her face, forcing her to look at him.

'You're scared.'

'No.' Her voice was a whisper. 'But I wish I'd read more.'

'Not all the answers can be found in books.' His thumb brushed the corner of her mouth and his fingers slid into her hair, cupping the back of her head. 'Perhaps you know more than you think you do. Follow your instincts.'

As he drew her head down to his she wanted to tell him that she didn't have any instincts when it came to men, but her tongue wouldn't form the words. Instead it tangled with his, and she heard herself moan into the heat of his clever mouth.

And she discovered she *did* have instincts, because it was instinct that had her sliding her hands into his hair, clutching his head, meeting his hot, seductive kisses with her own. And instinct had her pressing herself closer to him. Later, she'd wonder how a kiss involving her lips could have an effect on her whole body, but right then she wasn't capable of wondering about anything except what was going to happen next.

'Next' was his mouth on her neck—slow, lingering, as everything he did was slow and lingering—and she lay still, hardly breathing as the warmth of his tongue traced the line of her shoulder and moved lower, to her bare breasts.

Her nipples were standing erect and she watched in tense fascination as he paused with his mouth close to that sensitive part of her. She felt the warmth of his breath brush over her skin, followed by the slow, deliberate flick of his tongue as he skilfully teased and toyed with that part of her that had never been touched before. Sensation shot right through her, pooling in her pelvis, until she found it almost impossible to keep still, until the urge to cry out was so powerful she had to bite her lip to stay silent. And what he did to one nipple he did to the other, and when he finally lifted his head and looked at her she found it impossible to look away.

For a moment they stared at each other.

There was a hardness in his eyes, a coldness she wished

she hadn't seen, and then he leaned across the bed and blew out the candle, sending the tent into darkness.

She could no longer see, but she could feel, and the feelings became more acute because everything was focused on that one sense—touch.

The warmth of his palm rested low on her abdomen and she wondered if he knew how much she was aching, just how badly she needed—needed *something*. But of course he knew. She remembered Yasmin's breathless statement that he was supposed to be a skilled lover and knew now that it was true.

No wonder he hadn't bothered returning her book.

I will teach you everything you need to know.

The fact that he knew her body better than she did embarrassed her, but nowhere near as much as when he gently spread her thighs and shifted lower on the bed.

Shocked, and feeling intensely vulnerable, Layla gave a soft gasp as his hand moved with sure, leisurely ease over her abdomen and lower still. He took his time, but whether that was out of respect for her inexperience, patience or just a maddening ability to know how to ramp up the tension until she was at screaming pitch, she didn't know. All she knew was that she was moving her pelvis against his hand, and then his fingers were there, sliding skilfully over that part of her, exploring her with slow, knowing strokes of strong, clever fingers, until her breathing was shallow and her hands fisted in the sheets.

She hadn't known it was possible to feel this.

She couldn't see his face, couldn't see anything except darkness, and that darkness intensified feeling because she never knew what was coming next. She felt him shift above her, then move lower, and this time he put his mouth on her *there*. Shock rocketed through her and her hands moved to push him away, but he caught both her wrists in one hand and held her securely, so that all she could do was lie there and let him do exactly what he wanted to do. And what he did was sinfully good, and he did it again and again, until her body quivered and heated, until she was slippery wet and sensitive, embarrassment blown away by sensation. And with each erotic slide of his tongue the feelings intensified, until the heat of it was so maddening she thought she'd explode.

She knew there was something more, that her body was trying to reach something, somewhere, and she squirmed and shifted, trying to relieve the unfamiliar feelings, and then he shifted position in a lithe movement and came over her, his hand under her bottom.

'I will try not to hurt you...'

His voice was husky and he slid his hand down her thigh, encouraging her to wind her legs across his back. Like this, she was open to him and she was once again grateful for the darkness as she felt the silken power of him against her and the warmth of his breath against her mouth as he lowered his head to kiss her again.

He licked at her lips, kissing her gently as he stayed still, letting her grow used to the feel of him against her. It was shockingly intimate with her legs wrapped around him, and for endless moments he held himself still. Then he eased forward and entered her slowly, gently, holding himself in check with ruthless control, taking it so slowly that the discomfort seemed minimal in comparison to the building frustration. Pain and pleasure mingled. Layla felt herself clench around the hard thickness of him, felt the heat and power of him stretching her, and when his hand tightened on her bottom she lifted herself against him and heard a low sound rumble in his throat as he sheathed himself deep. Her breath caught. The intimacy of it shocked her and she curled her fingers over his biceps and then up to his shoulders, aware that he was holding himself still and knowing that he did it for her.

'Are you all right?'

His voice was low and very male, and she opened her eyes, even though she couldn't see him, and said yes, even though she wasn't sure it was true.

She wasn't all right. With him so deeply inside her she felt shaken and unbalanced, as out of her depth as she had in the pool. Only this time instead of drowning in water she was drowning in sensation.

She didn't know what was happening, but she knew she wanted this, *needed* this, and when he lowered his mouth to hers and kissed her she kissed him back, her tongue tangling with his.

He eased back slightly and then moved into her again. She felt her body yield against the male thickness of him, discovered that if she relaxed it was easier, that when he shifted his angle the pleasure intensified and poured through her in long, wicked waves of ecstasy. He was deep, deep inside her, his hand locked in her hair as he controlled the rhythm, all the time kissing her. And she recognised nothing that was happening to her body, *knew* nothing—but he did, and he used that skill and experience to drive her higher and higher, until something strange happened, something unfamiliar and intensely exciting, until screaming ecstasy exploded into an almost unbearable shower of sensation that made her cry out despite her attempts to stay silent.

He trapped the sound with his mouth, kissing her through it as she felt her body tighten around the smooth, hard length of him. She felt the sudden tension of his shoulders under her fingers and then heard him groan deep in his throat as her body drove his over the edge. It was the most thrilling, explosive, intense experience of her life and afterwards Layla lay still, crushed by the weight of him and the knowledge that she had lived with herself for twenty-three years and yet not known herself at all.

She'd had no idea she was even capable of feeling that way.

Her illusions about herself had disintegrated. She'd never thought of herself as romantic, nor particularly physical. Nothing in her past had prepared her for what she'd just experienced. And she realised that delving into a book for information wouldn't have made a difference, because there were no words that could adequately describe what she'd just experienced.

Nothing she'd read could have prepared her for pleasure.

Shattered by the experience, her expectations blown apart, Layla lay there, not knowing what words were appropriate. They'd shared the ultimate intimacy and yet outside the silken haven of his bed they were strangers.

She lay rigid, feeling as if she should say something, trying out various sentences in her head. But before she could utter any of them she felt him rise from the bed. Her burning skin chilled instantly and that chill spread through her bones as rapidly as the heat had done.

Shattered and confused, Layla lay still in the darkness, listening as he dressed. Was this normal?

Was it usual for a man to stand up and leave the bed afterwards?

Or did his response have something to do with his wife?

Was that why he'd blown out the candle? Had he been imagining that he was with someone else? Or was it that he couldn't bear to look at her?

It sounded as if he were going to stride out of the tent without looking back, but then he paused, his hand on the heavy fabric that protected them from the heat of the sun and the cold of the night. Moonlight shone through the slit in the tent and in that moment Layla saw him. Saw the hard, savage lines of his handsome face and the emptiness in those cold eyes that were as black as a starless night.

She stared at him in silence, trying to read him, trying to understand what was going on and failing.

She had no idea what that look meant. No idea what was going through his head.

And now she wished she'd kept her eyes closed. Pretended to be asleep. Anything, to avoid a situation in which she was clueless.

Should she speak?

Was he waiting for her to say something?

And then, before she could decide whether to speak or not, he turned and strode out of the tent, leaving her alone.

CHAPTER FIVE

HE RODE RAJA deep into the desert, trying to escape the weight of his feelings but failing, because wherever he went they followed. His mouth was dry with the bitter taste of betrayal, the past a deep ache inside him that wouldn't heal.

There were so many issues demanding his attention, but the only thing on his mind was Layla.

He'd felt nothing but contempt for her family for so long that when she'd arrived in his camp and offered herself to him he'd treated her proposal with suspicion. Even when it had become clear to him that her life had been very different from the one he'd imagined for her, his feelings towards her hadn't warmed.

But now?

The scent of her clung to his skin and her soft gasps echoed around his head, refusing to be silenced by his own vicious conflict.

As if sensing his tension, the horse under him stamped impatiently. Raz soothed him gently with his hands and his voice until Raja calmed and stood still.

He had a sudden vision of Layla smuggling the *Kama Sutra* from her father's library before leaving the only home she'd ever known. He thought of her climbing onto a horse, even though she didn't ride, and then going in search of him even though she knew exactly how he felt about her family.

And then he thought about her standing still and straight next to him, speaking her vows in the hope that the union would ensure the safety of her sister, and writhing under his hands as he'd shown her what her body could do.

The thought of it sent heat rushing through him and he cursed softly.

He told himself that respect and powerful sexual chemistry didn't change the fact he wasn't ready to feel anything for another woman. Nor did it change the fact that he didn't want her feeling anything for him.

Nothing changed the fact that this marriage politically motivated.

Was she all she seemed to be, or was she a clever opportunist who had the sense to change sides for her own protection?

His suspicions were deep-set, rooted in a lifetime of bitter feud.

So why did the knowledge that he'd hurt her rub at his nerves like sand wedged in his boot?

Staring at the sunrise, he told himself it was a good thing.

He told himself that anger was a thousand times safer than those softer emotions that could fell a man faster than a samurai sword.

'Your Highness.'

It was Abdul, never far from his side and as much a father to him as his own had been.

'You should not be out here alone.'

'I don't appear to *be* alone.'

Ignoring the irony in his voice, Abdul touched his arm. 'This is hard for you, but you did the right thing marrying her.'

'Did I?' He heard the harshness in his own voice and winced, because he wasn't in the habit of revealing his weaknesses to those around him. 'We need to keep an eye on Nadia.'

'Yes. I can imagine she is very upset. But no doubt Her Highness will deal with that sensitively. She seems like a very sensible young woman.'

Sensible? Raz could have agreed with him, but he knew it wasn't her logic or her ordered thought-processes that teased and tormented his brain.

It was something far more intimate and a thousand times more dangerous.

Layla awoke slowly, aware of the sounds of animals, the laughter of children, the hum of voices. None of them belonged to Raz.

The side of the bed where he would have slept was cold, the pillow smooth and untouched.

Her body ached from her night with him, making it impossible to blot it out or forget.

He'd come to her in darkness and then he'd walked away.

Had he known how his touch had made her feel?

Of course he had. His expertise had never been in question. From the first touch to the last, he'd known exactly what he was doing to her.

Layla rolled onto her back and stared up at the roof of the tent.

But as for the rest of it—as for how she felt inside and in her head...

How could he understand that when she didn't understand it herself?

She'd thought she knew herself very well but it turned out she didn't know herself at all, because she hadn't known she was capable of feeling like *that*.

Sheltered by the silk sheets, she slid her hand over her breasts, still tender from the touch of his mouth and the roughness of his jaw. He'd touched her *there* and then he'd—

'Your Highness?' Nadia stood in the entrance to the tent,

her expression frozen as she saw the clothes piled on the floor. 'I have instructions to help you dress and fetch you anything you need.'

What did she need?

Layla had no idea. She felt like a jigsaw someone had dropped. She had no idea how to fit the pieces back together because she no longer recognised the picture. And she had no idea how to make peace with Nadia. It didn't feel good to watch the other woman's pain and know she was somehow the cause.

It was the first time they'd seen each other since the incident in the pool, but Layla decided that Raz had already said whatever needed to be said so didn't raise the topic.

'There is nothing I need, thank you.' She watched as Nadia moved around the tent, placing food on the rug and laying out fresh clothes. She wanted to ask where Raz was, but didn't want to reveal how much she minded his absence— especially not to this girl, who clearly resented Layla's presence and wished she were anywhere but there.

Layla wondered again if she were in love with Raz herself. Was that the reason for the rigid expression and the fact she didn't meet her eyes? Or was it because of who Layla was?

In the end concern for him overruled pride.

'Have you seen His Highness?'

Nadia paused in the entrance of the tent. 'The rumour is that he has gone to find Hassan and talk to him. If he is killed it will be *your* fault.'

The girl blurted out the words and then left the tent, leaving Layla alone with nothing but her conscience to keep her company.

The news that he'd gone to find Hassan disturbed her—not because she underestimated Raz's strength, but because she knew just how duplicitous Hassan could be. He was neither honest nor honourable, and she knew better than most that he was at his most dangerous when he was cornered.

Should she have voiced her suspicions to Raz?

Weighed down by her worry, the hours dragged past. Without access to the library Layla had nothing to distract her from her thoughts, no hope of reaching a state of relaxation. She would have loved to talk to someone but no one came near her. Even Nadia stayed away, and Layla realised that when she'd suggested this marriage she'd given no consideration to how others would feel about it.

Did they all think she'd put Raz at risk?

What if Nadia was right and by coming to him she'd created trouble?

What if Hassan found them here?

It felt like the longest day of her life, and she spent most of it alone, sitting by the oasis, aware of the unfamiliar soreness and aching in her body.

Several times she heard children laughing and the sound reminded her so much of her sister that a lump wedged itself in her throat. Where was she? Had Salem found her? Was she in trouble? *Dead?*

If Hassan had found her before Salem then the chances were she was already in America.

As darkness fell the noise of chatter faded, leaving only the sounds of the desert at night.

Layla lay still on the bed, staring at the single candle that had been lit for her, so tense she could hear her own breathing in the silence of the tent.

Would he come?

Would it be like the night before?

The question swirled around in her head until eventually she fell asleep. When she woke it was light, his side of the bed was still cold, and she had her answer.

He hadn't come.

She was still alone in the bed and she had no idea if Raz had even returned.

Seriously concerned, she swallowed her pride and sought out Nadia once more.

'I do not know where he is, Your Highness.' Her voice was frosty and hovered on the edge of rude. 'He never reveals his plans. And now he's brought you here the risk to him personally will be even greater.'

With no hard evidence with which to refute that challenge, Layla bowed out of the conversation. Guilt gnawed at her, driven by anxiety that Nadia could be right. Had she increased his problems? Had she made things worse, not better?

Or did his unexplained absence have nothing to do with Hassan?

What if it were driven by something even more personal?

Something to do with the night they'd spent together.

Was he thinking of his wife?

Layla spent a second day alone, with only her imagination for company, and was beginning another night the same way when she heard the sound of horses and knew it was him.

The rush of relief was quickly followed by other, more complex feelings.

All day she'd wanted to see him, but now he was here she wished she were on her own again. She had no idea what to say or what to do. She was hardly in a position to play the role of concerned wife, but still she *was* concerned.

Embarrassed, uncomfortable, and burning hot at the thought of the night before them, Layla sat rigid, wishing that there was a rulebook she could follow, an instruction manual—*anything* that might give her clues about how she was supposed to behave.

She heard his voice, deep and instantly recognizable, as he responded to people around him, but still he didn't appear in the tent. It seemed he had time for everyone except her.

Or maybe he was once again waiting for darkness. Maybe he just couldn't face looking at her.

As that explanation occurred to her embarrassment turned to humiliation.

Everyone would know the Sheikh had stayed away from his new bride.

That indisputable fact was a stark reminder that physical intimacy didn't mean emotional intimacy.

Curled up in a ball under the covers, Layla felt more alone than she ever had in her life.

At least back in the Citadel she'd had Yasmin. Her life had been wretched, but familiar. She'd known the rules, known what was expected of her and been able to rationalise every one of her thoughts and feelings.

Here, she was totally isolated, living with a man who apparently loathed her so deeply he couldn't bear to set eyes on her, tormented by emotions and feelings that were totally unfamiliar.

She heard a splash from nearby and assumed he'd gone for a swim in the oasis.

The fact that he hadn't even greeted her first upset her more than she could rationalise. She shouldn't care, should she? She wasn't *allowed* to care.

Layla hesitated for a moment, but then slid quietly out of the bed and peeped through the slit in the tent. It was dark, but without the pollution of the city there was sufficient light for her to make out powerful shoulders as he swam.

She stared at those bare, powerful shoulders, fascinated and shocked in equal amounts. If anyone had told her days ago she'd be hiding in a tent in the hope of getting a glimpse of a naked man she would have laughed at them. But this wasn't any naked man, of course. This was Raz. And because he'd blown out the candles she had yet to see his body.

And she couldn't really see it now—just the occasional

tantalising hint of male muscle and power as he swam with smooth, steady movements.

He reached the far side of the pool and turned. Layla shot back into bed, terrified of being caught.

By the time he walked into the tent she was safely under the covers with her eyes closed.

She heard his soft tread, then silence, and she knew he was looking at her although surely the lack of light would restrict his vision.

Feeling as if someone had set fire to her, Layla kept her eyes closed and tried to breathe evenly. She stayed completely still. Even when the mattress moved under his weight she didn't move.

She lay rigid, churned up inside by his reappearance, shocked that he'd stayed away for two days and then not even greeted her on his return, and shocked that such an action on his part could hurt so badly.

'A tip for the future. No one is that tense when they sleep.'

His voice was deep and soft and she turned, giving up the pretence. *What was the point?*

She saw that he had lit a single candle. Not much, but enough to send a golden shadow of light across the bed. *Enough for her to see his face.*

'Where have you been?'

Shock flared in his eyes. 'I'm not in the habit of disclosing my plans to anyone—least of all to a woman I met for the first time only three days ago.'

She wanted to point out that it might only have been three days but that he knew her more intimately than anyone, had revealed a part of her she hadn't even known existed, but she realised there were dark depths to him she hadn't begun to uncover.

'Has there been any news of my sister?'

His gaze was shuttered. 'None.'

Just one word but it made her feel sick, and suddenly all the daydreams were blown out of her head and replaced by stark reality. 'That's bad, isn't it? We should have heard something.'

'If she is alive then Salem will find her.'

'If?'

'Do you want false hope? Because I won't give you that. Lies destroy trust and create nothing but confusion. But until we have evidence that something has happened to her I urge you to stay positive. We have to hope she will have found a way to survive.'

'How? Neither of us spent any time in the desert when we were growing up.'

'And yet Tazkhan is ninety-eight percent desert. How can you serve a country when you are ignorant of the life its people lead?'

Thrown off balance by that unexpected attack, Layla sat up, clutching the silk sheet to her neck as she rose to her own defence. 'That is an unfair accusation. You know nothing of the life my sister and I led.'

'You were in a position of power and lived a life of luxury. There must have been something you could have done.'

Luxury? 'There was, and I did it. I came to you.'

Cold black eyes met hers. 'I am supposed to believe that was an altruistic act on your part? How do I know you didn't just have the sense to move to the winning side?'

It was like being slapped.

'If you believe that, why did you marry me?'

'Because your motivation has no impact on my decision. I am doing what is best for Tazkhan. My personal wishes have no part in this.'

'So when we were in bed you had to force yourself to do those things to me?'

His jaw clenched and his eyes narrowed. Two streaks of colour highlighted the hard, savage lines of his cheekbones.

'For a virgin whose first glimpse of a naked man was from behind a curtain, you suddenly have a great deal to say for yourself.'

She had the distinct impression that he was trying to pick a fight, and suspected she knew why. It was logical, wasn't it?

'You're angry,' she said softly, banking down her own feelings to try and understand his. 'You feel guilty and it's making you angry.'

'You know nothing about my feelings, Princess.'

'And you know nothing about *my* feelings, either. I may be inexperienced, and I admit I'm shy, but don't *ever* assume you know what my life has been. The reason my sister and I have no knowledge of the desert is not because we weren't interested but because we were unable to leave the city walls.'

'Did you ever try?'

Her heart was pounding. 'Yes.'

'And what happened?'

Her mouth was dry. The sudden emergence of a memory she'd squashed down brought sweat to her palms. 'There are some aspects of our past neither one of us wishes to revisit. I think we should both accept that and move on.' Her desperate statement earned her a long, questioning look.

'If your sister is in the desert then Salem will find her.'

He blew out the candle, there was a rustle of clothing as he undressed, and then he joined her in the bed.

Rigid with discomfort, heart pounding, Layla shot to the furthest end of the bed and lay still, hardly daring to breathe in case breathing brought her into contact with him. 'You think I came here to guarantee the continuation of some glittering lifestyle you've imagined for me and yet, feeling that way, you still want to share the bed with me?'

'We're married.'

'But you don't trust me.'

'Sharing a bed doesn't require trust, Princess.' Reaching

for her in the darkness, he hauled her against him. 'It simply requires sexual chemistry, and fortunately we have plenty of that.'

Layla wondered if he could feel her shivering. Wondered if he could feel the heat of her skin and the rapid beat of her heart.

She wanted to ask why he had to blow out the candle before he shared a bed with her, but before she could form words his mouth slanted over hers and his hand slid into her hair. As a concession to the desert heat and the sand she'd tied it back, but he freed it instantly and it tumbled down over her shoulders.

She felt his hand, warm and strong against her bare back, as he pressed her down onto the soft mattress and shifted her underneath him. She felt the weight of him, the strength and the power. Felt his lips move over hers in a kiss that created an instant response. It started deep inside her and then exploded outwards.

Intense excitement shimmered over layers of despair.

Was this how their relationship was going to be?

Days where they saw nothing of each other and nights spent in the dark?

Intimate strangers?

She wondered how his kiss could make her melt when her emotions weren't involved and tried to control her response to him, but her nerve-endings were already on fire and the erotic skill of his mouth left her with no choice but to kiss him back.

His mouth closed over her nipple and Layla moaned. Just like before, he used all his skill and knowledge to drive her crazy, until she was hot and desperate. The only difference was that this time she *knew*. This time she knew what was to come. And when he surged into her with sure, deep strokes she climaxed instantly, and again and then again, while he possessed and controlled her totally.

Afterwards Layla lay there, numb. Maybe she should be grateful for the protection of the darkness, but she wasn't. The knowledge that he could only make love to her if it was in the dark hurt her more than she would have thought possible.

She turned her head, plucking up the courage to talk to him about it, but before she could speak she heard a high-pitched cry coming from close by.

Layla sat upright, heart pounding. 'What's that? It sounded like a child.'

And then the screams began.

Raz moved quickly, his hand on the knife he kept strapped to his belt whenever he was in the desert.

The screams sliced through him, ripping his composure into shreds, because he knew who screamed.

His strides fuelled by a primal need to protect, he tore open the entrance of the tent next to his and saw the child sitting upright, eyes staring in terror, forehead glistening with sweat, as she screamed while Nadia stood there helplessly, hopelessly out of her depth.

'I can't get her to stop.'

In seconds he had the child in his arms, folding her tightly. 'What is wrong with her?'

He heard the raw edge to his tone but the girl simply shrugged defensively.

'She's awake but she won't respond to me. It's as if she's having a fit or something.'

He smoothed the child's hair, gazed into those staring eyes and felt an anxiety so acute it slowed his thinking. He prided himself on the speed and accuracy of his decision-making and yet now, when it was so important to get it right, his brain was motionless.

'Her breathing is fast. Her pulse is fast. Get someone medical in here immediately.'

A calm voice came from the entrance to the tent.

'It isn't a fit and she isn't awake.'

He turned his head and saw Layla, dressed only in a thin nightdress, her hair tangled and tousled from his hands. Her gaze was fixed on the child. 'She's having a night terror. My sister had them all the time at the same age. You shouldn't wake her.'

"She's already awake. Her eyes are open.' Nadia's eyes were cold and unfriendly.

Raz ignored her. 'You have seen this before?' Fear made his voice harsh, but Layla seemed calm and unflustered.

'Many times. It's very unsettling to witness, but I can assure you she will remember nothing of it in the morning. Who is closest to her? Who does she know the best?'

Her gaze flickered expectantly to Nadia and Raz drew a deep breath.

'Me.' The confession was dragged from him, because he hadn't yet decided how to broach this topic and this wasn't the way he would have chosen. 'I have the closest relationship with her.'

Was she shocked?

If so, she didn't show it. Nor did she question what that relationship was.

'In that case you should be the one to tuck her back into bed. Snuggle the sheets around her to make her feel safe. Talk to her quietly. It's not what you say that matters, it's the way you say it. You need to hold her securely. Blow out all the candles except one. Darkness helps. When she goes back to sleep, stay with her for about ten minutes. Once she is deeply asleep it's unlikely to happen again.' Having delivered that set of instructions, she looked at Nadia. 'We should leave. The fewer people the better.'

The other girl's expression was stubborn. 'She knows me.'

'It's better that way.' Layla's voice was firm. 'She needs quiet and just one person she trusts.'

'Do as she says.' Raz lowered his voice and eased the child back under the covers. She was quivering and shivering and it broke his heart to see her. His urge to call a doctor was powerful, but for some reason he was inclined to give Layla's suggestion a try, all the while wondering why he was following the advice of a woman he had no reason to trust.

She'd said it was the tone that mattered, so he spoke non-sense, reciting poetry from his childhood, his hand stroking those fragile shoulders until gradually the little girl calmed and relaxed under his fingers.

Her breathing slowed. Her pulse slowed with it. And as hers did so did his.

Her eyes fluttered shut, those eyelashes dark shadows against cheeks swollen by crying.

Raz sat until the change in her breathing told him she was deeply asleep.

His shoulders ached with tension. His head throbbed with it. Responsibility pressed down on him until he felt not as if he had the world on his shoulders but the universe.

Satisfied that she really was asleep, and unlikely to stir, he rose carefully to his feet and left the tent in search of answers.

Nadia was hovering outside, her expression defensive and defiant. 'I could have settled her. You should not have asked *her* advice.'

'How long has this been going on?'

Her hesitation told him everything.

'A while.'

That reluctant admission did nothing to ease his stress levels.

'*Why* wasn't I told?'

'You were away.'

'But everyone knows I wish to be told of anything that affects my daughter.'

'I didn't think it was significant. She doesn't remember it in the morning.'

Holding onto his temper, knowing that he needed time to cool down before he spoke what was on his mind, Raz clenched his jaw and gestured to the tent he'd just left. 'Stay with her.' Ideally he would have stayed himself, but he needed information so he strode back into his own tent and found Layla standing still in the middle of the room, her hands clenched into fists by her sides, stress evident in every rigid line of her body.

She'd lit the candles and the tent was bathed in a soft, gentle light that revealed sheets still rumpled and twisted from the wild heat of their lovemaking.

She turned as he entered the tent and their gazes locked and held.

Awareness rushed between them and sexual tension crackled like static in the air.

Now you're a woman, he thought, and then blocked that out because he knew this was not the time to address the other issues that were piling up.

'Thank you for your help. You knew what was wrong? You called it a night terror?'

'Yes.' Her confidence reassured him, because he was far from convinced he shouldn't have called for medical assistance.

'You have seen it before?'

'Many times.' Her voice was tight, her eyes shadowed by ghosts and darkness. 'My sister Yasmin started having them when she was five and it carried on for over a year. It might have been longer. I don't really remember. Every night, about an hour after she'd fallen asleep, she'd wake screaming, eyes wide open. She seemed to be awake, but she was asleep. The first time it happened I was just like you—I thought she was awake.'

'But she wasn't?'

'No, and it's very unsettling. It took me a while and some research to realise she was actually asleep.'

Of course she would have researched it. He knew virtually nothing about her, but he knew that much. 'And did your research suggest a cause?'

'There is no single cause, but there are different triggers. A fever, extreme tiredness, and—' She licked her lips and turned her head away so that he could no longer see her eyes. 'And stress. Stress can cause it.'

Guilt twisted inside him, because he knew without a doubt that the trigger in this case was very likely to be stress. And he knew the cause of the stress. 'And in your sister's case?'

'It was definitely stress.'

Still she didn't look at him, and he remembered her reaction to their conversation earlier.

You know nothing of the life my sister and I led.

Raz looked at the tension in those slender shoulders and realised he was looking at far more than a reaction to what had just happened in the tent next door. 'What was she stressed about?'

'This isn't about my sister.' She evaded the question. 'This is about the little girl. Has she been through a bad experience?'

How was he supposed to answer that?

The truth lodged somewhere behind his ribs, Raz turned away and paced to the far side of the tent.

It occurred to him that their relationship was already turning into a minefield of things they didn't talk about, issues they didn't address. The complications were endless.

'How did you stop it happening?'

'I couldn't stop it. I could only deal with it. And I tried to make her feel more secure so that she didn't go to bed scared.'

'She was scared?'

They were exploring two parallel lines of conversation and he was aware that she was avoiding his questions as skilfully as he was avoiding hers.

'They say overstimulation of the central nervous system can cause it. The temptation is always to shake them awake, but it's better if they can just go back to sleep.'

'So there was nothing you could do?'

'I tried very hard not to let anything frighten her.'

There are some aspects of our past neither one of us wishes to revisit.

He caught the bleak look in her eyes and realised just as there were layers to him she hadn't even glimpsed, so there were layers to her. And they were dark layers.

How could it be otherwise, growing up with a man like her father?

Only now did it occur to him how little he knew about his new bride.

An uncomfortable feeling spread down his neck and across his shoulders. 'Did she have reason to be frightened?'

'I started sleeping in the room with her. Sometimes that helped.'

'Layla, why was your sister frightened?'

It was only the second time he'd used her name and he saw her still.

Then she turned her back on him and picked up a robe, slipping it on and covering herself, shielding herself from him in every way. 'If you want to deal with the night terrors, the best thing is to talk to her family and find out what is likely to be causing them.' She fastened the robe around her waist. Her hair poured down her back, thick, shiny and as dark as a starless night. 'That shouldn't be a problem as you seem to know her well.'

Was that the second or third time she'd ignored his question about her life in the palace? Every time he raised it she deflected it. And suddenly he knew this relationship was going to be impossible if they shared nothing.

One of them had to make the first move.

'I do know her well. I know her better than anyone.' He had to push the words past his own natural reluctance to confide. 'She's my daughter.'

CHAPTER SIX

'YOUR *DAUGHTER*?' UNPREPARED for that revelation, Layla simply stared at him. 'You have a daughter?'

'She is six years old.'

He had a daughter.

She sank down onto the bed, her legs shaking, racking her brain for the information she had on him and discovering it to be depressingly sparse. 'I—I didn't know. I had no idea.'

She muttered the words to herself, examining this further piece of evidence to support her suspicion that it was possible to be intimate with someone and yet still know nothing about them.

It didn't make any difference that she'd shared something with him she'd never shared with anyone else. He was still a stranger.

'There are few who know, and those who do know better than to speak of it.'

His voice was flat and she looked at him blankly, shocked into silence and shaken by the enormity of it.

'Why don't people speak of it? Why would you hide the fact that you have a child?'

'I lost my father. I lost my wife—' He didn't finish the sentence. He didn't need to.

Layla knew her face matched the colour of his.

'No.' She shook her head in instinctive denial of that hypothesis. 'That wouldn't have happened.'

'How can you be sure?' His tone was raw. 'You insist on having evidence for everything—show me the evidence that my daughter would have been safe. Did your father live by a code of honour? Did he have boundaries beyond which he wouldn't go? If so, then please enlighten me, because I have seen nothing like that in my dealings with him.'

The shame of it covered her like a filthy, dark sludge. She wanted to dive into the oasis and scrub her skin clean. 'I can't show you evidence. I understand why you kept your daughter's existence a secret. But when I suggested marriage I would have thought—'

'What would you have thought? That I would have confided in you? You arrived in the desert out of nowhere. I married you because I saw the sense in what you proposed but let's not pretend that this marriage is a union of trust.'

His words shook her because in her head she'd started to spin a different scenario. When she looked at him all she could see was the burning heat in his eyes and all she could think of was his body, hard and hot against hers. Out of bed they were strangers but *in* bed? In bed they were as close as it was possible for two people to be and what they did in bed had started to dominate her brain. The craving inside her had intensified to the point that she found herself wishing the daylight hours away because at night there was a chance they'd be together. She found herself hoping desperately for the dark because it was only in the dark that he came to her. Swept away by the darkness and the wildness of the passion she'd started to imagine that this was real but now she realised she'd been deluding herself.

'That is all true, but I am your wife now and that also makes me—'

'Do not say the words.' His voice was thickened with emotion. 'Do not even think of yourself as my daughter's mother.'

The words slid under her ribs like a blade.

She tried to ignore the sharp pain that made it difficult to breathe. Used logic to remind herself that his response was understandable in the circumstances.

The fact that he would kiss her, touch her, didn't mean he trusted her with his daughter.

And she really couldn't blame him for that, could she?

Right now he was the powerful protector, ready to shield his daughter from any threat, and it was clear he considered that threat to be her.

Feeling his struggle to suppress the emotion that threatened to overwhelm him, Layla groped for the best way to handle the situation. 'At least tell me her name.'

'Her name is Zahra.'

'That's a pretty name. Does she know you have married me?'

'No.' He was brutally frank. Everything about him was designed to repel her gentle attempts to ease closer. 'There is no easy way to tell a child I have married the daughter of the man responsible for the death of her mother.'

The knife in her ribs twisted. 'Had I known you had a daughter I never would have suggested this marriage. I had no idea there was a child involved. It changes everything.'

'It changes nothing. This marriage was never personal so what difference would it have made?'

'I would not have sacrificed your daughter's happiness for—'

'For the future of Tazkhan? And what about your sister's safety? What about your own marriage to Hassan? Because that's why you came to me, isn't it? You wanted my protection.'

'Yes, that's all true. I was honest about that right from the start. But I didn't want those things at the expense of a little girl's happiness. A little girl who has already suffered a major trauma in her life.' Layla was shaking so badly she wasn't sure her legs would hold her. 'There is no way I would have foisted myself on her as a stranger. At the very least I would have suggested I take time to get to know her. To gain her trust.'

'That would have created a delay we could not afford, and this was never about building a relationship. And you are assuming you would have gained her trust.'

'I would certainly have worked hard to do that. I have experience with children. Give me the opportunity and I will prove it to you.'

The shutters came down on those eyes. 'No. We will wait and see if the night terrors settle and then re-evaluate.'

'Perhaps they would settle if she had someone she could bond with. Someone she is close to.'

He turned slowly, his eyes like ice. 'My relationship with my daughter is very close.'

'Yes, I can see that.' She thought about the way he'd soothed the child. About the anxiety and love on his face and the patience he'd shown. It had warmed her because she'd never seen a man like that with a child. 'But you're away a great deal. You have your business interests—'

'That is an inevitable part of life. When I can, I take her with me, and when I can't I make sure I return here as quickly I can.'

'But when you are away who looks after her?'

He didn't answer immediately. 'She is with Nadia, who loves her very much.'

Nadia?

Layla felt as if she were walking on eggshells. This wasn't the time to point out that Nadia had seemed out of her depth at the moment of crisis. 'How have you kept Zahra's existence a secret?'

'I have the support of many people.'

'But I don't.'

He glanced at her with a frown. 'What does that mean?'

'No one speaks to me. This marriage has not been welcomed by the people who love you.' Suddenly she felt overwhelmed by it all. By the distance that couldn't be closed by physical intimacy alone. 'How can this possibly work even on the most basic level? If you don't trust me, why would they?'

'Because this union was never about trust.' He towered over her, powerful and imposing. 'Most of them understand why we did this. They know it is the right thing.'

But not all of them.

Layla thought about the hatred she sensed in Nadia and wondered again if the cause of it didn't go deeper than dismay at seeing the Sheikh marry the daughter of his enemy.

'So what happens now? You have a daughter. Are you saying you don't want me to meet her?'

'For the time being, no. She is already having night terrors. I don't want to risk making those worse by introducing you to her.'

His belief that she might make it worse hurt more than she would have thought possible, but how could she, of all people, blame a man for wanting to protect his child?

She'd never had that and she felt the loss of it keenly.

'Of course, if that is what you prefer.' Layla's jaw was stiff, her thoughts a mess of pain as she thought what she would have given to have a father who fought so fiercely to protect her from harm. 'But I don't think it's the right decision.'

'You think you know better than me what is right for my child?'

'No, what I think is that you don't know me at all. You married me with a set of preconceived ideas of who I am, and I don't blame you for that, but we're married now and for this to work you have to start seeing me. The real me. I may not be able to swim or ride a horse, but I am good with children. I think if we are to become a family we need to start somewhere.'

'We have started somewhere.'

His gaze shifted to the rumpled sheets and then back to her and she felt a tiny shiver run through her. Right now he was distant and intimidating but she knew it wasn't fear that made her knees weak. Looking into those brooding black eyes, gazing at the dangerous curve of his sensual mouth, all she could think of was how it felt to have those lips on her body, how it felt when he filled her, possessed her, drove her mindless. Her skin still burned from his touch. Her head was dizzy with the memory of how he made her feel and she slid her fingers into her hair and shook her head in frustration.

'A relationship cannot just be about sex.'

His eyes held hers, hard and unsympathetic. 'It has to be, because I can give you nothing else.'

In the morning he was gone again.

If she'd thought their shared confidences would have moved their relationship forward, she was disappointed.

And this time when she heard children laughing she knew one of the voices belonged to his daughter.

It felt unnatural not to approach her and build a relationship, but he'd made his wishes clear on that matter so Layla sat in the shade on a smooth rock by the oasis and forced herself not to initiate contact with the little girl. And she seemed happy enough, playing with her friends, laughing as a child should laugh. Laughing without fear that the sound might draw unwanted attention.

The child laughed until darkness fell over the desert.

And then the screams started again.

Instinct drove Layla from her bed. Heart pounding, she came to a screeching halt outside the entrance to the tent.

He didn't want her near his daughter, did he?

Unless she wanted to create a rift between them she had to respect that decision.

Torn, she stood there, waiting for the child's screams to settle, telling herself that Nadia was there and would comfort the girl.

The screams grew louder and more desperate.

Sweat beaded on Layla's forehead. Just listening to it stressed her so badly her heart raced. The sound reminded her so much of Yasmin in the early days, and to stand there and do nothing demanded a self-control and thick skin Layla didn't possess.

Pressing her palm to her forehead, she breathed deeply and tried to calm herself. She told herself it wasn't her concern, that if she suddenly appeared in the tent it would probably just frighten the child even more. But none of that reasoning did anything to ease her urge to do something.

Why didn't someone else go to her? *Where was Nadia?*

Her will-power stretched taut, she lasted another five seconds before giving in. If Raz never spoke to her again, so be it. He hardly spoke to her anyway so it wouldn't be that much of a loss.

As she pushed aside the flap she expected to see Nadia, but the tent was empty apart from the little girl who sat alone in the enormous bed, shuddering and screaming at some imaginary terror. At her feet lay the two Saluki, whimpering and looking at the child in alarm and confusion, as if they sensed a threat but couldn't identify it.

Mouth dry, Layla stared at the dogs. Nothing but a screaming child could have propelled her forward.

Her heart was kicking at her ribcage—not just because to get to the child meant stepping over fur and teeth, but because the sound of the screaming brought back so many memories of Yasmin, terrified and clinging to her.

She threw one last glance over her shoulder, in case there was someone else who could do this, but there was no sign of Nadia or the bodyguards who were supposed to be in attendance.

Trying to look confident, she stepped over the Saluki as gracefully as a ballerina, braced to feel those sharp teeth close around her ankle.

The dog closest to the bed growled, a menacing rumble low in its throat, but it didn't move from its position.

Taking that as a good sign, Layla crawled onto the bed and snuggled down with the child, stroking her back and talking to her, hoping desperately that the tone of her voice would do the trick and the child wouldn't wake and realize that the comfort came from a stranger.

'There, you're safe now—and you need to go back to sleep.' She talked nonsense, and then decided a story might help. 'Once upon a time…' She told the same stories she'd told her sister at the same age, remembered them word for word, and the familiarity of the ritual soothed her as well as the child. She talked quietly until the little girl's breathing suggested she was deeply asleep while all the time the two Saluki lay by the bed, heads on paws, watching her.

Afraid that if she moved she'd wake the child, Layla stayed still, her fingers tangled in the dark curls that belonged to Raz Al Zahki's daughter. Looking down at that sweet, vulnerable face, now smeared with tears, she felt her heart twist.

What had she been through?

What had she suffered?

She'd stay just a while. Until she was sure the girl was asleep.

Then she'd return to her bed and he wouldn't be any the wiser.

The red ball of the dawn sun was rising up behind the mountainous dunes when Raz rode back into the camp two days later. His eyes were gritty from lack of sleep, his head pounding following long days spent in meetings with senior tribal members.

He needed sleep, but nowhere near as much as he needed a swim.

It was still early and everything was quiet and still. No one was stirring.

Having handed over his stallion to one of the waiting grooms, he made straight towards the tent where his daughter slept, noticing with a frown that there was no sign of the guard.

Fear for his daughter fuelled his stride.

Entering quietly, he stood for a moment on the threshold, his eyes adjusting to the dim light, relieved to see the dogs sprawled protectively at the foot of the bed.

The familiar sight of the lump in the bed brought relief rushing down on him—and then he realised that the lump was bigger than usual.

Stepping closer, he saw that there in the bed, with her arms wrapped around his daughter, was Layla.

Shock and surprise were replaced by anger, and then another, darker emotion he didn't dare examine too closely.

The dogs sensed the change in his mood and growled, and those growls woke the child. Her expression brightened as she saw her father and she sat up sleepily, the movement waking Layla.

Her eyes opened and her gaze met his, blank at first and then alight with consternation.

Sitting up, she clutched at the sheet. 'We weren't expecting you so early.'

'Evidently.' His tone was silky soft and he saw the colour return to her cheeks as she met his hostile gaze.

'I'm *pleased* you're early.' Zahra slid out of the bed, paused to hug and kiss the dog closest to her, and ran across to him, arms outstretched. 'Has Shakira had her foal?'

'Not yet.' Raz scooped her into his arms. Her hair brushed against his jaw and he felt his insides knot with love. It was a love that overwhelmed every emotion he'd ever felt. A love that made a strong man vulnerable. And he felt that vulnerability now as he held her and felt those slender arms tighten around his neck.

'When can we go and see her?'

'Soon.' He hugged her protectively, his eyes still on the woman in the bed. 'Zahra, I want you to play with your toys for a minute while I speak to Layla.'

'Can't she stay?' Zahra was openly disappointed. 'She hasn't finished the end of the story. We both fell asleep.'

'I can finish it later.' Without meeting his eyes, Layla slid out of the bed.

He saw her hesitate before allowing her feet to touch the ground and saw her hold her breath as she stepped carefully over the dog blocking her path, as if doing so required nerves of steel.

Oblivious to the atmosphere, Zahra smiled at her. 'When you've finished talking, can we play in the sand like yesterday?'

The news that she'd been spending her days with his daughter was the final straw. 'No, you cannot, because we are going riding.'

'Together?'

'Together.' Touched by her expression of delight, he put her down gently. 'Play with Isis and Horus for a moment.'

She needed no encouragement to play with the dogs, and they in turn fussed around the child, proving themselves better guards than the people he'd paid to stand over her and keep watch in his absence.

Keeping his anger in check, he left the tent, noticing that

one of the guards assigned to watch over his daughter was now standing outside, having no doubt taken a badly timed bathroom break.

Deciding to deal with him later, Raz followed Layla to the edge of the oasis, noticing that she stopped a safe distance from the water's edge.

'You deliberately went against my orders.'

'Yes, I did.'

She turned to face him, her expression calm. She made no excuses. Nor did she apologise and that surprised him.

'I thought I'd made my wishes clear on this matter.'

'Would you rather I'd left your daughter to scream, Your Highness?'

The news that Zahra had been screaming again sent ice down the rigid length of his spine. 'If she was screaming then it would have been better for someone familiar to comfort her. That was your advice.'

'And I stand by it. But there was no one familiar. She was alone.'

'My daughter is never alone. She is under twenty-four-hour guard and Nadia is with her at all times.' Even as he said it he remembered that the guard had not been present when he'd arrived, and her next words confirmed that.

'She was alone last night. And the night before. And the night before that. There was no guard and there was no Nadia.' She seemed more annoyed than intimidated. 'You weren't here. I made the decision I thought was best, Your Highness.'

'My name is Raz,' he said tightly. 'I think we are now sufficiently well acquainted for you to use it.'

'Evidently not, since you don't see me as fit company for your daughter.'

Raz breathed deeply. 'Nadia is supposed to stay with her at night.'

'Then no doubt that is something you will wish to explore with her.'

Listening to that calm appraisal, Raz realised just how much he'd underestimated her. He'd mistaken silence for a lack of opinion, and shyness for a lack of forcefulness, but it seemed his new wife had a layer of steel, visible only if someone pressed hard enough. On this she wasn't budging.

'Nadia would not have left her alone.'

'Are you accusing me of lying?'

'Perhaps it was a simple misunderstanding. Perhaps she went to fetch Zahra a drink or something to eat.'

'There was no sign of her at any point during the night, nor of the guard. I understand that as her nanny you believe Nadia to be the best person to care for her, but I'm providing you with evidence that she left the child alone. Why would you doubt me?'

'Because Nadia isn't Zahra's nanny. She is her aunt.' That confession was met by a tense silence.

For a moment she said nothing and simply stared at him. Then her mouth moved and finally words emerged.

'Her *aunt*?'

Raz stayed perfectly still. 'Nadia is my late wife's sister.'

'S-sister?' She stammered the word, visibly shocked. Again she said nothing, and then she shook her head briefly. 'And you didn't think that was worth mentioning? You let me turn up here in my wedding dress and you didn't even *warn* her or tell me who she was?'

'When would I have had the opportunity to warn her? We were married only hours after you appeared unannounced at my desert camp. Then we arrived here and she came out of the tent before I had a chance to speak to her privately.'

'It is no wonder she can barely look at me.' Her words were barely audible. 'It explains so much.'

'It does *not* explain why she would leave Zahra unattended.'

'Maybe it does. Maybe…' She frowned slightly and then stared at the still surface of the oasis. 'You should have told me. There is *so much* you should have told me.'

'Why would I tell you?'

'You really have to ask me that?' Her head was turned towards him, pain and accusation in her eyes. 'Because keeping secrets is doing nothing but harm. I understand that this is hard for you, I understand that you have to make love to me in the dark because touching me makes you think of your wife and that makes you feel guilty, and I understand that you don't want to be here during the day because it's like a slap every time you look at me. I understand that, given the way you feel about my family, you are reluctant to trust me with your child. I don't blame you for that. But it wasn't Nadia who comforted Zahra in the night, Your Highness. It wasn't Nadia who read to her and played with her. For the past two days it hasn't been Nadia who has cared for your daughter. It has been me.'

Raz was stunned into silence by her interpretation of the facts, but before he could respond she took a step closer to him.

'Do you think I'm not a caring person? Is that what you think?' Her voice vibrated with tension. 'Do you think I would have crossed a desert I didn't know, on a horse I had no idea how to ride, to find a man who hates me, if I weren't a caring person? Just in case the facts don't speak for themselves, let me tell you I'm a *very* caring person—and if you looked at the facts you'd be able to see that. And, yes, I was thinking of my sister and my future, but I also care about the people of Tazkhan. And before you dismiss that, based only on my bloodline, let me remind you that we can choose many things in life, but whom we are related to isn't one of them. I chose to go to your daughter in the night because I couldn't sit there and listen to her distress. And I chose to step over those horrible, scary dogs in order to comfort her. So *never* imply I'm not trustworthy enough to care for you daughter.'

The stillness of the baking desert heat intensified the silence.

Raz stood still, her words stinging as they sank into his flesh. 'Why do you find the dogs scary?'

'After everything I just said to you, *that* is the question you choose to ask?' She gave a choked laugh—a sound loaded with disbelief—and he frowned.

'Layla—'

'No. Enough.' Her voice was shaky as she backed away from him. 'This conversation is going nowhere. You don't want to come anywhere near me and you can't bear it when I come anywhere near you, so just leave me alone.'

CHAPTER SEVEN

LAYLA PACED THE width of the tent and back again, so upset she didn't know how to calm herself. Once again she was ripped apart by emotions new to her and she tried desperately to rationalise them.

Why *would* he trust her? He didn't know her. Of *course* he'd be reluctant to allow her near his child—a child whose existence he'd taken great care to keep secret from her family. It was a sign of his love for his child, and she was the last person ever to criticise a father for loving his child.

So why did his attitude towards her hurt so badly?

And why couldn't she share the same space with him and not think about sex?

Hyped up and unsettled, she picked up a ripe peach from the bowl on the table and then put it down again, knowing that she was already in possession of the answer. And the answer was that it hurt so badly because it *felt* as if he cared. When his mouth was on hers, when his hands were holding her face and his body was buried deep in hers, it felt as if he cared. And it felt incredible. So incredible she wanted more. And in wanting more she also wanted it to mean something.

The whole thing was turning her brain into a churning mess. She was used to using logic, but the feelings inside her defied logic.

With a murmur of frustration Layla turned and paced back

again, trying to filter out the facts, but even the facts were confusing. To be so intimate in bed and so distant out of bed was muddling her brain. In bed, the signals were that he cared. Out of bed, it was clear he considered her on a level with the life forms occupying the bottom of the oasis.

Having admitted that to herself, it horrified her when he strode into the tent and closed the flap between them and the rest of the world.

'Go away—' Her voice cracked and she stepped back from him, still reeling from their conversation and feelings that were new to her. She wanted to turn them off and had no idea how. 'Don't say anything else. I can't take any more right now. I got the message. If you really don't want me near your daughter I won't go near her, but please make sure that *someone* does because I can't lie here listening to her screaming.'

'And that is very much to your credit.' His voice was low, his expression guarded as he watched her pace from one end of the tent to the other. 'I came to tell you that you're wrong.'

She couldn't focus.

She couldn't concentrate on the conversation because she wanted to look at him all the time. Not just because he was a man who naturally commanded attention, or even because he was sensationally good-looking—although that had to play a part—no, it was something so much more personal. It was because he knew her in a way no one had ever known her before. Whenever he was near she felt as if they were being pulled together. She had to fight the impulse to walk up to him and touch him. And because she had no experience of feeling that way she had no idea how to cure herself.

She'd never felt like this before and it was driving her mad. They had huge issues, but all she could think about was the feel of his hands on her and the way it felt to be kissed by him.

Layla pressed her fingers to her forehead, trying to clear her brain, trying to harness her old way of thinking. *Trying to push out thoughts she didn't want in her head.* Her stress levels were running into the red, her grip on control so loose she was afraid the whole thing was going to slip from her grasp. She knew the only way to pull herself back together was not to be near him. She needed to be on her own so that she could rebalance herself.

'I probably am wrong. You know Nadia much better than I do. I don't have all the facts. If you think she's the right person to care for your daughter, it's not my place to disagree with you.'

'I don't mean that you're wrong about Nadia. I mean that you're wrong about the other things you said.'

She was so aware of him standing there that the whole conversation blurred in her head. 'What things?' Was this the ultimate in humiliation? To know a man could do those things to her and feel nothing and yet still her head could be full of nothing but him? Why couldn't she detach the physical from the emotional as he evidently could?

The intimate atmosphere suffocated her, and the way he was looking at her made her feel as if he'd touched her skin with the flame of a candle.

'I make love to you in the dark *not* because I am thinking of my wife, but because you are very shy and I am trying to be sensitive to your feelings. On that first night you would not even remove your robe to show me your bruises, so I assumed you would want to take that side of our relationship very slowly.'

Slowly?

Layla felt as if she were burning up inside. She thought about what they'd shared. *Was that slowly?* Trembling, she hid her damp palms behind her back. 'Oh.'

'You came to me clutching a copy of the *Kama Sutra*, but you hadn't even glanced between the pages and clearly had no idea of what lay ahead of you. I decided you might be less self-conscious if you were in darkness.' He paused to draw breath. 'I don't spend time with you during the day, that is true, but it's because I have a million and one demands on my time—not least the upheaval in Tazkhan. I have spent the past two days meeting with certain members of the council in secret. Hassan has disappeared. That is another reason I am particularly concerned about my daughter's safety right now.'

Still dealing with the news that he'd been thinking of her feelings, Layla felt her stomach lurch. 'Hassan has disappeared?'

'Yes, and until we know his whereabouts I don't want my daughter left alone.' He hesitated. 'Or you. He is a desperate man. Who knows what he could decide to do, given that he now has so little to lose? He has lost any chance of taking your father's place and he has few, if any, supporters among the people. Speaking of which, I have been learning a great deal of interesting information about you in the past few days.'

'You have?'

'I spent some time with the people. I visited hospitals and local schools—including a school where you apparently help out.'

'I love books and I like to help the children who struggle with reading. The school doesn't have enough staff to offer that sort of help.' Layla stammered over the words, horrified that he'd found out with such ease. So much of her life had been conducted with discretion, if not secrecy. 'Who told you?'

'Apparently the staff don't feel the need to keep it a secret any longer as your father is dead and Hassan missing. There is no shortage of people willing to tell me how good you are with the children and what an excellent decision I made in marrying you.'

She stood rigid, thrown by that news. 'But *you* don't think that. I know you don't. On that first night you left the tent because you felt guilty about what we'd done.'

'No. I felt guilty because the sex was incredible. I agreed to this marriage because of what it meant for Tazkhan, but what we shared that night went well beyond duty and I couldn't pretend otherwise.'

Shocked into silence by his honesty, Layla tilted her head and stared up at him, feeling a shift in their relationship. 'I didn't know—'

'That I felt that way? I would have thought it was obvious.'

His dry tone made her blush and the look in his ebony eyes made her stomach flip.

'Your Highness—'

'Raz.'

He was standing so close to her she could hardly breathe. She lifted her hand and placed it on his chest, feeling the steady thud of his heart under her fingers. 'Raz.' It felt strange to say his name. Strange to be this close to someone.

He cupped her face in his hands. 'Do you realise that, despite the intimacies we have shared, that is the first time you have spoken my name?'

'It felt wrong to use your name. You were a stranger.'

There was a prolonged silence. His eyes dropped to her mouth. 'But I'm not a stranger now.'

His self-assurance was in direct contrast to her own mixed-up, tangled emotions.

'You hate me.'

'No. But I admit it's a complicated situation.' A wry smile tugged at his sensual mouth. 'You are a person who likes facts, so I will tell you that the facts in this case are that nothing is going the way I thought it would go when you turned up at my camp that night.'

She wanted to reach up and sink her hands into that glossy dark hair. She wanted to pull his head down to hers and see if his kiss felt as good in daylight as it did in darkness. She wanted to give herself up to the emotion and the confusion and stop trying to rationalise the mess in her head.

'It's not going the way I thought it would go, either.'

'I owe you an apology for ordering you to stay away from my daughter. You should know that I am very overprotective where she is concerned and the past week has been a particularly unsettling time.'

Standing this close to him, it was a struggle for her to concentrate. 'I would never criticise any father for being over-protective.'

'Please understand that my reluctance to allow you near her was less about you as an individual and more about my determination to keep life as stable as possible for her. I thought Nadia was the perfect person to care for her. It seems I may have been wrong.'

'Maybe you weren't. As you said, there is probably some perfectly reasonable explanation for her absence.' What right did she have to comment on the behaviour of another person when she didn't even understand her own?

'Possibly, but at the current time we are unlikely to find that out.' There was an edge to his tone. 'She has gone missing, along with one of my guards. I suspect that when they both should have been with Zahra they were together. We are trying to find them. In the meantime I must thank you for being so incredibly kind to my daughter when she was upset.'

His apology was as unexpected and unsettling as it was touching.

She'd craved distance, but instead she had closeness and a new sense of understanding that simply intensified the feelings inside her.

'She is very sweet and good-natured. And I love her sense of mischief. She reminds me so much of Yasmin.'

'The people here have noticed your kindness to her and it

has done much to make them warm towards you. What are these stories you've been telling Zahra that make her so desperate to go to bed at night?'

'*One Thousand and One Nights*. I read them to my sister.'

His eyes glittered. 'So now you think you are Scheherazade?'

'Hardly. But I thought if I could relax Zahra before she sleeps she might be less likely to wake.'

'It was a good plan. Did it work?'

'It's too soon to know. I just wish I'd brought the book with me instead of leaving it at the first camp.'

'That was the other book you brought with you?'

'Yes. It's one of my favourites. I decided I could only carry two, because of the weight, so I picked that one.'

His hands were still on her face, his gaze intent on hers. 'And the *Kama Sutra*.'

'It was a matter of priorities.' She knew her face was hot against his palm. 'And ignorance.'

'You have no need to explain yourself to me and no need to feel embarrassed.' His eyes darkened. 'These last few days have been a terrible strain for you. The threat of marriage to Hassan, whom you clearly fear and loathe, escaping from the palace, losing your sister in the desert and then being picked up by my men. Marriage to a stranger, a near drowning, and then living with a husband with whom you've barely shared a conversation but are expected to undress for.'

Layla tried to smile. 'When you put it like that, it's no wonder I'm a little wound up.'

'A little?'

'A lot. I'd be a lot better if there was news of Yasmin.'

His hand dropped from her face. 'So far there is none, but that does not mean you should worry. Salem is renowned for not communicating.'

Remembering the dark, forbidding profile of the man she'd

seen only briefly on that first night, Layla found that of little comfort. 'What if he can't find her?' She blurted the words out, seeking reassurance.

'If anyone can find her it will be Salem.' Raz hesitated, as if he were deciding how much to tell her. 'He has a special set of skills.'

'But what if Hassan has already tracked her down? What if he has her right now?'

'Then Salem will find *both* of them and you can safely feel sorry for Hassan.'

Layla hesitated, because to make an accusation unsupported by solid evidence felt wrong. 'I have nothing but instinct on which to base this suspicion, but I think Hassan may have played a part in the death of my father.'

His expression didn't change. 'I'm sure you're right.'

The relief that came from having someone to discuss it with was overwhelming. 'You suspect it too?'

'Of course. The moment I heard about the Sheikh's sudden illness it was the first thing that came to mind. We have no proof, but we believe it was Hassan who ordered someone to tamper with the brakes of my car two years ago. I don't believe it was his intention to kill or injure my wife, because that would have brought him no political benefit. There is little doubt I was the intended victim, but sadly she chose that day to borrow my car.'

His voice was thickened with a mix of regret, guilt and anger, his pain so powerful she felt it as if it were her own.

'I'm sorry.'

'I do not hold you in any way responsible. But it is true that Hassan would do anything for power. He and your father were cut from the same cloth.'

She knew that, but it was the first time she'd heard anyone else say it. 'If he finds my sister—'

'I would trust my brother with my life and we must now

trust him with your sister's life.' He turned to look at her, the lines of his handsome face set and serious. 'When did you last eat?'

'I'm not hungry.'

'You've barely eaten in the whole time we've been together.'

'I've eaten.'

'We may be in the dark for much of the time, but that does not make me blind.' His tone was dry. He hesitated. 'Zahra is keen for me to take her riding today. I know your experience with horses to date has been less than encouraging, but if you would like to learn to ride it would give me pleasure to teach you.'

The thought of spending yet more time on a horse horrified her, but she could tell he was reaching out to her and didn't want to do anything that could be considered a rebuff. 'Teaching a beginner would drive you mad.'

'I have been teaching Zahra since she was able to sit unsupported. Believe me when I say that nothing you throw at me can be more of a challenge than putting an overexcited toddler on a horse.'

'You taught her to ride that young?'

'It is the best age. She has grown up around horses, as I did. It wouldn't surprise me if she chooses to make that her career in some way in the future.'

Career?

'You see her having a career?'

'Of course. And I can't see it being diplomacy, because my daughter is as outspoken as your sister.'

That fact clearly amused him, and Layla thought about the times she'd had to haul Yasmin away from a situation before her comments created havoc.

'You're proud of your daughter.'

'Very.'

The contrast between his love for his daughter and her own barren childhood was so vividly accentuated that the breath caught in her throat. Wondering what was wrong with her that she could envy a child, Layla stepped away from him.

'Thank you for the offer of riding lessons, but I don't want to intrude on your time with Zahra.'

He curved an arm round her waist, trapping her. 'You're still upset?'

'No.' All she had around this man were uncomfortable feelings. Feelings about him. Feelings about herself. She'd arrived here thinking she knew herself well and had discovered she didn't know herself at all. It was like being inside the body of a stranger. 'I just don't want to intrude on your relationship with your daughter.'

'You were the one who pointed out that you should be part of my relationship with my daughter.'

Did it make her a bad person that it was almost too painful to watch? 'You have a very special bond.'

'A bond that will not be threatened or broken by the presence of another person.' His eyes narrowed. 'But that isn't the issue, is it? Tell me what's wrong.'

'There is no issue. Nothing is wrong.' She tried to walk away but he locked his arm tightly around her waist.

'Your father wanted you to marry Hassan, so I assume from that your relationship with him was difficult. You don't have to hide it from me. I want to know. All of it.'

'Why? What difference does it make?'

'As you just pointed out to me, keeping secrets isn't going to do anything for the progression of our relationship.'

Did he see a progression? This was a man who had loved his wife totally and completely. A man who had vowed never to love again. What progression could there be? She could have asked, but she wasn't sure she could cope with the answer. They were together now, and nothing could change that.

'My relationship with my father wasn't just difficult, it was non-existent. You're so proud of Zahra and you want the best for her.' She stared at a point in the middle of his chest, trying to contain her emotions and relate only the facts. 'My father was never proud of me. His interest in us extended no further than how useful we could be to him. He met Yasmin just four times in his life.'

Shock flared in his eyes. 'Four times? That is all?'

'Five, if you count the day he died, when we were both hiding behind the curtain in his rooms.' Layla was surprised by her sudden need to confide when she'd lived her life relying on no one.

There was a long, tense silence. 'I had no idea. I assumed—' He broke off and rubbed his fingers over his forehead, apparently struggling for words.

'I cared for Yasmin. We've never been apart. She's the only person in the world I've ever been close to until—' She stopped, feeling her face burn. *Feeling his eyes on her.*

'Until me.'

'I know we're not close in *that* sense,' she said quickly. 'I know what our relationship is.'

'Do you?' His voice was soft and his eyes didn't shift from her face. Slowly his hand dropped. 'Then you're making more progress than I, because I truly have no clue what our relationship is.'

The air was thickened with a tension she'd never felt before.

Something changed when she was with this man. Something she couldn't put a name too, and didn't understand.

She wanted desperately to reach out to him, to touch him as he'd touched her, but she wasn't sure he'd want that and didn't have the confidence to risk being rejected.

'You should go to Zahra.'

'You will come too. It would please her if you were to join us.'

'I really don't—'

'And it would please me, too. Get dressed and meet us outside. Zahra's favourite treat is to have breakfast by the oasis, so we will do that and then fly the helicopter to Bohara—my home.'

'You have a home?' It was something else she hadn't known about him. 'All the rumours are that you live in the desert and move around for your own safety.'

'I do live in the desert, and I do move around—because how else is a man expected to know his people if not by living among them? But I also have a place that is mine. A stud farm just inside the border with Zubran. On paper it is owned by the Sultan of that country, who just happens to be a friend of mine.' When Layla stared at him he flashed her a smile. 'I don't spend all my nights in a tent. After the last few days I think you deserve a taste of luxury.'

'Just practise everything I taught you. I will keep you on a leading rein so there is no way she can run away with you.'

'That's comforting to know.' Layla sat rigid on the calm, placid mare and Raz hid a smile, oddly touched by her determination to ride even though she clearly found the whole experience uncomfortable and unnatural. So far she had fallen three times, but each time she'd insisted on getting back on the horse.

'If you want to give up, just tell me.'

'I don't want to give up. I won't give up.' Her jaw was set, her wrists inflexible as she gripped the reins.

'Relax,' Raz said mildly. 'If you relax you will not fall.'

'We both know I am going to fall whatever I do.'

But still she got back up again. He wondered if that was a skill she'd developed during her loveless childhood. But it hadn't been completely loveless, had it? She'd had her sister. The sister who was now missing.

He made a mental note to try again to contact Salem, even though he knew such persistence would irritate his brother. 'Relax your wrists and lower your hands slightly.'

She did as he instructed. 'At least it isn't as far to fall as it is from your stallion.'

'I promise I will not let you fall again. Don't grip the reins so tightly—you're pulling on her mouth.'

'I am?' Dismayed, she immediately loosened the reins and rubbed the mare's neck by way of apology.

He watched, intrigued by her and wondering how such gentleness could come from so much evil.

In all the rumours that had oozed from the corrupt walls of the Citadel there had been little about the princesses and most hadn't thought to question the detail of their existence.

'You're doing well.'

'We both know I'm not doing well, but I will learn. Just as long as I don't hurt an innocent horse in the process.' She balanced herself carefully and then risked a glance at him. It was the first time she'd taken her eyes off the horse's ears. 'Thank you for being so patient.'

'You are very easy to teach because you listen. Sit up straight. Sit down in the saddle. That's good.'

Her jaw was rigid and he could see her concentrating, going through his instructions one by one. The mare walked forward without fuss, as accommodating as he'd known she would be.

'She's very pretty. Is she pure Arabian?'

'Yes. She is brave, spirited and intelligent, like all of her breed. And very strong. She could carry you for days in the desert and not tire. It's the reason we choose this breed for endurance racing.' It occurred to him that she shared many of those qualities. 'The Arab horse is surefooted and agile in difficult terrain and bred for stamina. It can withstand the daytime heat of the desert and the cold at night.'

'You bred her?'

'My father bred her. He gave her to me as a foal but I am too heavy for her now. She taught Zahra to ride.'

'You mean *you* taught her.'

'The horse did most of the teaching.'

'Did your wife ride?'

She asked the question quietly and he realised how sensitive the situation must be for her.

'She didn't ride, but she was an artist and she loved to paint the horses. She spent hours studying equine anatomy and her attention to detail was astonishing. Her mother was an artist, too, and she always hoped that Zahra would be equally artistic. But Zahra only ever wanted to ride the horse, not immortalise its image on paper.'

'The greatest gift a parent can give is to allow a child to be who they want to be.'

Her wistful tone caught his attention.

'You have told me about your father, but nothing about your mother.'

'My mother died just after I was born.'

'So your sister—?'

'Yasmin is my half sister. Her mother was a model who caught my father's attention for a short time. She left when Yasmin was five and we haven't seen her since.'

It was a brief delivery of the facts, devoid of emotion, but he could imagine how much emotion was simmering below the composure that seemed to be part of her. *She'd learned to hold it all in*, he thought. *Learned to feel without expressing the feeling.*

'But you said *you* cared for your sister. How is that possible?'

She sat without moving, her gaze focused on the horse's ears. 'It's possible.'

'You were seven and she was five.'

'We learned what we had to learn.'

The mare, perhaps sensing the sudden tension of her rider, threw up her head and he saw Layla's fingers whiten on the reins.

'She is the most reliable horse in my stables, but if you feel unsafe you can always grab a piece of her mane.'

'It doesn't seem fair to make her suffer just because I'm nervous.' But her fingers closed gently and carefully around a hunk of the mare's mane.

Watching her, Raz felt himself harden. His gaze focused on those slim fingers. Heat shot through him as he remembered how those fingers felt against his skin.

He lifted his gaze from her fingers to her face, studying the curve of her cheek and the sweep of her inky lashes, and she must have felt his scrutiny because she turned her head and her eyes met his.

Raz felt that look all the way through him.

'Can she gallop yet?' Zahra cantered up, disturbing the moment, glued to the back of her horse as if she'd been born in the saddle, Isis and Horus running by her side. 'I want you to learn fast, Layla, so we can ride together. Isis and Horus can come with us too. They love it when we gallop.'

Layla had switched her attention from the horse to the dogs and Raz frowned.

'The dogs make you nervous?'

'I'm worried they might upset the horse.'

Her response made perfect sense, but he sensed something more and wondered if she'd been bitten as a child. That would certainly explain the fear he saw in her eyes whenever his dogs were nearby.

'Did you keep Saluki as pets when you were young?'

'No.' Her lips were bloodless, her slim fingers clenched in the horse's mane. 'Not as pets.'

'Layla…' He rode closer to her, his knee brushing against hers. 'If the dogs are a problem you must tell me.'

'The dogs aren't a problem. Zahra adores them and they adore her. They also guard her, which can only be a good thing.'

Her response was neutral and composed but he glimpsed something in her eyes—a shadow of something so dark and bleak he wasn't sure he even wanted to explore it further. He wondered again what her life must have been like. What it would have taken to drive someone like her to cross the desert to seek out a stranger.

The more he knew her, the more he realised that such impulsive behaviour was completely out of character. She was a woman who thought everything through, who relied on evidence to make decisions, and yet she'd chosen to risk everything to find him. She'd known nothing about him, and yet she'd preferred to commit herself to the unknown than spend another day in her old life. *So what did that say about her life?*

'When can we gallop?' It was Zahra who asked the question, circling her pony like a polo player as she waited impatiently for her father.

'Later,' Raz told her. 'I don't want to leave Layla.'

'Don't worry about me. I think I might have had enough for one day and so has this poor horse.'

Apparently relieved to have an excuse to finish, she rode the mare to a halt the way he'd taught her.

'You two gallop and I'll go back. See you at the stables. But I think I'll walk and lead her, if that's all right.'

Before she could dismount, Raz reached out and covered her hand with his.

'You are doing well.'

Her mouth twitched at the corners. 'We both know I'm doing terribly,' she said dryly, 'but thank you for saying that.'

'It's always harder to learn as an adult than as a child because your awareness of danger is more sharply focused.' And he suspected her awareness of danger was even more sharply focused than most. He watched her face, searching for clues, but her expression didn't change and he released her hand. 'Go and relax. Abdul will show you my library.'

'You have a library?' Her face brightened but Zahra shuddered.

'Who wants books when they can have horses?'

CHAPTER EIGHT

LAYLA SAT CURLED up on a low ottoman covered in rich red silk, a stack of books awaiting her attention and a chilled fruit juice on the table in front of her. Of all the rooms in Raz's beautiful home—*the home she hadn't known existed*—the library was predictably her favourite. Not just because of the walls lined with books, but because of the views. The doors opened over a courtyard with a central fountain that sent cooling water flowing over a majestic statue of a horse. And now, with the sun setting over the distant dunes, the courtyard was floodlit with a warm golden light.

It was the most beautiful place she'd ever seen.

On their arrival Raz had been called away, so it had been Zahra who had shown her round, predictably lingering in the stables and introducing Layla to every horse in the yard. The stables were beautiful, arranged around shady courtyards, and everywhere the sound of running water from fountains that offered a cool contrast to the parched desert.

After all the rumours about his Bedouin lifestyle she'd been surprised to discover that Raz owned a place like this, but what had really surprised her was the almost military efficiency with which it was run.

Here, horses were bred and trained in what was clearly a highly successful business. Smiling staff ran the place with smooth efficiency, allowing their elusive boss to come and go as security and his responsibilities demanded.

Used to the oppressive atmosphere of her rooms at the Citadel of Tazkhan, Layla felt a sense of peace and freedom she'd never experienced before. It wasn't just the ability to wander freely, but the absence of her father, Hassan, and all the others who had made her life so stressful.

She'd stood up, intending to explore the books on the higher shelves, when one of the dogs came bounding into the room, ears pricked.

Layla stood without moving and seconds later a woman rushed into the room and ushered the dog out, closing the door firmly behind the retreating animal.

'I apologise, Your Highness. I was feeding them and Horus went exploring. Please forgive me.'

Relieved that the overenthusiastic Horus was now on the other side of a closed door, Layla relaxed slightly. 'It's fine.'

'No, it isn't. His Highness left orders that the dogs weren't to be allowed near you. He was very strict about it. All the staff were informed.'

Layla stared at her. 'They were?' *He'd done that for her?*

'Yes, and I'm so sorry for what just happened.'

'Don't be.' She sank back down onto the sofa. She'd never given him an explanation for her fear of dogs, but he'd seen it and responded. She hadn't asked him to act, but he'd cared enough to instruct his staff to keep the dogs away from her. Realising that the girl was looking at her anxiously, Layla managed a smile. 'Don't worry. It's me, not the dogs. I'm sure the dogs are trustworthy.'

'Horus and Isis have had the run of this place since they were puppies, so it isn't always easy to keep them contained.'

'Keep who contained?'

Raz strode into the room at that moment wearing an exquisitely cut dark suit that suggested he'd come straight from meetings. His sudden appearance shattered her calm and sent her spinning straight back into that state of nervous tension that never seemed to leave her when he was around.

It was the first time she'd seen him since they'd arrived at his home but that didn't surprise her. She was fast coming to realise how hard he pushed himself and how seriously he took his responsibilities. Wherever he was, he rose before dawn, worked way past sunset, and still somehow managed to spend time with his daughter. Admittedly that time was usually spent galloping like two crazy people across the desert on horses that seemed half wild to her inexperienced eyes. His energy levels seemed limitless, his physical power, strength and stamina as much a part of him as those fierce black eyes that appeared to see under the surface she presented to the world.

And those eyes were on her now, stripping away her armour, seeing right through her. He saw her fear, knew how deeply that fear went, and the fact that he held that knowledge seemed as intimate as anything they'd shared in the darkness of the desert night. Somehow he'd accessed that most private part of her—her thoughts—and apart from her sister she wasn't used to sharing her thoughts with anyone. She wasn't used to revealing weakness. To do so made her feel as vulnerable as if she were standing naked in a crowd.

But he hadn't taken advantage, had he? He'd used the information, but he'd used it to her benefit not his. He hadn't mocked or ridiculed her response to the dogs. Instead he'd responded with gentleness and kindness. He hadn't just understood the depth of her fear, he'd tried to help.

The girl responsible for keeping the dogs under control was profuse in her apologies. 'I'm so sorry, Your Highness. Horus ran in here when my back was turned. I followed immediately,' she said quickly, 'and he didn't get farther than the door.'

Raz spoke in a low voice. Layla couldn't hear exactly what was said, but she saw the girl whiten and give a rapid shake of her head before backing away and leaving them alone.

'What did you say to her?'

He closed the door firmly. 'When I give an order I expect it to be obeyed, and I gave express instructions that the dogs were *not* to be allowed in the library or into whichever space you choose to occupy.'

'It's fine, really.'

His eyes held hers. 'But it isn't fine, is it? We both know it isn't fine even though you don't talk about it.'

Layla tried to steady her breathing but she knew it was a hopeless quest.

The moment it was just the two of them the atmosphere shifted.

She knew what sexual attraction was now. She knew it and she felt it right through her, from the tips of her fingers to the depths of her soul. It was the quickening of her heart when he walked into a room, the power of a shared look full of intimate promise. But most of all it was the constant longing to touch—the need to put her hands on his hard body and feel his hands on her. The craving was so intense it was almost visceral, and it surprised her because she wouldn't have thought the physical could have so much power over her. The feelings thrilled her and scared her because they were unfamiliar and uncontrollable.

Ignoring his reference to the dogs, Layla struggled to respond as her old self. 'Did you have a productive afternoon?'

'Yes, but the downside was that I neglected you on your first day here.'

'Zahra showed me round. We had fun together. And you don't have to worry about me—I'm used to occupying myself.'

'In the past, yes, but I don't want your future to be like your past.'

She put down the book she was holding. 'I love books. I'm always happy to read.'

'Because it's an escape? Do you feel the need to escape when you're with me?'

'No.' Her mouth was dry. She had no way of telling him how much her feelings unsettled her because she could barely articulate it to herself. 'I don't only read to escape. I read because I love the rhythm and flow of words. A good writer can create images with prose in the way an artist does with a brush.' And it was a good job she was a reader, not a writer, because she couldn't have found the words to describe how being with him made her feel.

'Then hopefully you can pass on some of your love of books to Zahra,' he said dryly, removing his tie and undoing his top button. 'To her, reading is an activity that takes her away from horses, which makes it something to be loathed and detested.'

'So we need to start by finding her some horse fiction.'

'Horse fiction?' His brows rose. 'Does such a thing exist?'

'Of course.' It was a relief to have something to focus on. She dragged her eyes from the addictive curve of his mouth and tried not to think how it felt when he kissed her. 'There are talking horses in *The Horse and His Boy* by C.S. Lewis, and I always loved *Black Beauty* because the story is told from the horse's point of view. I'm sure I can think of more.'

His eyes gleamed dark, his gaze disturbingly compelling. 'In that case you are now officially responsible for Zahra's reading—or lack of it.'

'It will be my pleasure. It's just a question of finding something to engage her interest. She is enjoying the stories I'm telling her at bedtime.'

'And on that topic...' He strolled across the room to her

and handed her a package. She unwrapped it cautiously, wondering how she hadn't noticed that he was holding something in his hand.

'Oh!' As the packaging fell away she felt her breath catch. 'It's my copy of *A Thousand and One Nights*. I thought it was lost forever.'

'It came with us when we travelled on that first night. I should have given it to you before now but I didn't think of it.' He was standing close to her. So close it would have taken nothing to reach out and touch him. 'I'm sorry I've neglected you today.'

'You didn't neglect me. I understand the pressures on your time.' What would happen if she touched him? She had no idea of the etiquette and no idea how to subdue the feelings that threatened to overwhelm her. 'I hope your meetings went well.'

'Very well. What did you do this afternoon?'

'I read. Explored a bit. Enjoyed the surroundings. I've never been this close to the border with Zubran before. It's beautiful. You've known the Sultan and his wife for a long time?'

'Mal and I have been friends since childhood. I often stayed in his house. His father and mine were close—' He broke off but she read his mind easily.

'United against a common enemy,' she said quietly. '*My* father.'

'We are not going to talk about that now.'

He cupped her face in his hands and the touch of those strong fingers on her skin made her go hot inside.

Was that really all it took? One touch. One touch and she was hopelessly lost. Suddenly all she wanted was more. Just how badly she wanted more was embarrassing to contemplate.

'I moved Zahra into the room next to ours so that if she wakes we will hear,' she said.

His finger traced her jaw. 'That was thoughtful of you.'

'And I met your cousin,' Layla said desperately. 'The one who manages this place. She is very impressive. And she was welcoming. I didn't know you had business interests. Hassan has no idea you own this. No one does. No one knows you have a home here.'

'Have you finished?'

'Finished?'

Those dangerous dark eyes burned into hers. 'You are chattering and I've never known you chatter before. You're nervous.'

'I'm not nervous.'

'You can be honest with me. I *want* you to be honest.'

How honest? Was he waiting for her to admit she thought about him every moment of every day? Did he want her to say she just wanted to tear off his suit, his tie, his perfect white shirt and everything else he was wearing until the only thing between them was bare skin? What would he say if she confessed that night had become her favourite time? That she wished away every hour of daylight in the hope he might come to her?

'I'm not nervous.'

He stared down at her—held her eyes with his as if he were drawing all her thoughts inside him so that he could read them and know every detail.

Terrified of what he'd find inside her head, Layla tried to pull away. But his free hand slid behind her back and he locked her against him with a strong arm.

She felt the hardness of his powerful body against hers and goosebumps raced down her spine.

'Raz—'

'My daughter is asleep,' he said softly. 'We should probably move this conversation to the bedroom so that we can hear her if she wakes.'

The bedroom.

'Yes.'

Except that it felt so good being this close to him she didn't want to move. Didn't want him to let her go.

Fortunately when he did it was only briefly, and then he took her hand and drew her close to him as he led her from library to bedroom. She was aware of every movement he made. Aware that he shortened his stride to match hers, aware of the brush of his arm against hers as he stepped back to allow her through the door first, aware that he drew her closer as they passed the door of Zahra's bedroom and the sleeping forms of the ever devoted Isis and Horus.

'They are very protective of her.' She followed him into his luxurious bedroom and he closed the door behind them.

'It has been that way since she was a baby. I believe they would give their lives for her, but I am conscious that you are uncomfortable around them so I have given orders that they should not be allowed to roam freely.'

'Zahra's safety is more important than the fact I'm a little nervous with dogs. They must be allowed to do as they have always done.'

'A *little* nervous?'

His eyes were gently mocking and she gave a half smile.

'Terrified—there, I admit to being that pathetic.'

'*Not* pathetic. Nothing about you is pathetic.' His expression serious, he pulled her towards him. Tension shimmered between them. 'You accused me of turning out the lights so that I didn't know I was with you, but the lights are still on and if you want them turned off you're going to have to say so.' His eyes were dark on hers and the hunger she saw in him shocked and thrilled her.

'I don't want you to turn them off.' She wanted to see him. *All of him*.

'You're sure?'

'Yes.' Just as she was sure if he didn't kiss her soon she'd be the one to do the kissing. In fact she was close to doing just that when he cupped her face and lowered his head to hers.

His mouth was hot on hers, his kiss sure and clever, and just like every other time the explosion of sensation was instantaneous and all-consuming. Just like every other time her mind blanked. She felt dizzy with it, and the fact that this time there was no doubt he knew who he was kissing somehow intensified all those feelings.

As his mouth seduced hers she felt his palms on her shoulders, easing off the simple, modest dress she'd selected earlier that day, felt the skilled glide of his fingers down her spine. And this time, whatever happened to her, *whatever she felt*, she was determined not to close her eyes.

Perhaps he sensed it because he took her hand and placed it on his chest. 'Undress me.'

His soft command made her pulse sprint.

She felt the steady thud of his heart under her palm and then her shaking, useless fingers fumbled with first one button and then another. But the speed of her fingers wouldn't match the desperation building in her and she gave a murmur of frustration and tugged at his shirt, sending buttons flying.

Layla froze. 'I'm sorry.'

'For what?' His eyes glittered down at her. 'For wanting me as badly as I want you? That isn't something to apologise for.'

Releasing her briefly, he wrenched off his torn shirt, leaving her face to face with his muscular male chest. She stared at the dark hair that shadowed the centre of his chest and then narrowed down and disappeared below the waistband of his trousers.

She wondered if he was going to make the next move. Felt his eyes on her as he waited.

Face hot, Layla reached for the fastening of his trousers.

She heard the sharp intake of his breath, felt his board-flat abdomen tense against her fingers, and paused.

'Do it.' His tone was raw. 'Do what you want to do.'

She was too self-conscious to do *exactly* what she wanted to do, but she undid the button and slid down the zip, freeing him. The only sound in the room was the harsh rasp of his breathing and she heard the sound change as she took him in her hand and stroked him.

He felt hot and hard, and the thickness of him in her palm made her own body heat. It was the first time she'd touched him like this and for a moment she stood still, unsure of herself, and then he covered her hand with his and showed her, guiding her movements, teaching her what no man had taught her before. And she learned fast what pleased him, discovered the instant high that came from hearing the sudden intake of his breath or feeling the bite of his fingers in her flesh as he struggled for control.

Her palm cradling the most intimate part of him, she lifted her face to his. 'I'm sorry you have to teach me.'

'That proves how little you know about men, because I'm *not* sorry.' His tone was rough and his features were as tense as his shoulders. 'I am traditional enough to be pleased that everything my wife has learned in bed she learned from me.'

Layla hid a smile. 'That's not very progressive, Your Highness.'

'In some areas progress is overrated.'

'It's your own fault. If you'd let me keep the book—'

'You will not need a book.'

His tone thickened, he pulled her into him, taking her mouth in a hard, burning kiss before he tumbled her back onto the bed. Dispensing with the rest of his clothes, he came down on top of her, his weight pressing her into the soft mattress.

'Tell me if I'm too heavy for you.'

'You're not. I like it. I like the feel of you. All of you.'

His gaze darkened and he shifted slightly so that she felt the roughness of his thigh against the smoothness of hers. 'I promised myself I'd be patient.'

'You don't have to be patient.' Layla gazed into his handsome face, so hungry for him she ached in every part of her body. She slid her palm over the smooth skin of his powerful shoulder and felt the tension there, felt his own struggle to hold back. 'I don't need you to be patient.'

'If anything I do makes you uncomfortable—'

'It won't.'

She was about to say that nothing he did could make her uncomfortable but he was kissing her again, the slide of his tongue against hers driving all rational thought from her head. He kissed her with slow, deliberate expertise, and although he'd kissed her like this before she discovered that the light changed everything because now she could see. She kept her eyes open and so did he, and she could see the fire in his eyes, the flare of heat as he looked at her, the raw hunger that she knew was mirrored in her own gaze.

She needed to see him.

Needed him to see her.

And if she'd been worried he couldn't look at her she wasn't any more, because it was soon obvious he couldn't *not* look at her as he slid down her body, exploring every shivering, trembling inch while the lamps threw golden shadows over her skin.

Layla watched as his fingertips grazed her nipples and then felt the skilled flick of his tongue. And then he took her in his mouth and the delicious heat of it intensified the ache in her pelvis until she was only able to stay still because the weight of his body was holding her down.

Her only outlet was to moan, and moan she did as she felt the brush of his erection against the soft flesh of her inner thigh. He eased away from her and slid his hand down one bare leg, parting her.

It was possibly the most intimate action of their relationship so far.

It was the first time he'd seen her. The first time any man had seen her. And she realised that the light offered no opportunity for modesty or concealment. Spread and exposed, there was no hiding, and when his gaze lifted to hers she knew her cheeks were burning.

'It makes me feel—'

'I know how it makes you feel,' he said softly, 'but you can trust me. I want you to trust me.'

Light shone from the two lamps positioned right by the bed. His eyes shifted from her flushed face to her breasts and lower still. To that part of her that lay between the shadows of her thighs—that part of her that now lay open to him. And if she were embarrassed it soon became clear that he wasn't. Nor did he intend to allow her to hide. Trembling with anticipation, she felt the warmth of his palm on the inside of her thigh, the gentle slide of skilled male fingers against her wet, sensitive flesh, and then he moved again and the next thing she felt was the scorching heat of his clever, knowing mouth.

Layla closed her eyes. He'd done this before but she was discovering that in the dark it was different. She knew how wet she was already, and then she felt his tongue on her and in her, parting her, exploring her in the most intimate way possible, until she was writhing against the silk sheets, only his firm grip on her hips keeping her still.

He drove her to orgasm again and again, and when he finally hauled her under him and thrust deep Layla was so dazed and disorientated, so weakened by pleasure, she could do nothing but move with him, lost in this new version of reality.

* * *

'Tell me about the dogs.'

He'd picked his moment carefully. Picked a time when she was at her most vulnerable. A time when she was more likely to trust him with those secrets she'd buried inside herself. Because she was wrapped in the curve of his arm he felt the tension ripple through her slender body as she tried to roll away from him.

'I can't.' The fear in her voice was so sharp it was almost visible.

'Try.'

'You don't understand—'

'I want to.' He wondered how far he could push before she shut herself down and refused him access. 'Were you bitten?'

Without warning, she pulled away from him and sat up. She stared blankly ahead of her and then drew up her knees and hugged them with her arms, as if giving herself comfort. 'When we were young Hassan used to make us play a game called Hide.'

'Hide and Seek?'

'*His* version of Hide and Seek. We were given an hour to hide and then—' The words seemed to jam in her mouth so he prompted her.

'Then they tried to find you?'

'Then they sent the dogs to find us.' Her voice was flat, the words factual, as if it were only by stripping out the emotion that she could bear to speak them. 'Saluki. Four of them. Although people keep them as pets, the Saluki is a hunting dog. But I'm sure you already know that. The Bedouin use them for hunting hares, gazelle, and foxes and other prey. In this case we were the prey.'

Shock stunned him into silence. When he finally managed to speak, he found himself devoid of words, because there simply were none. What could anyone say in response to a revelation of that magnitude? 'Layla—*habibti*—' The endearment flowed off his tongue so naturally he didn't notice. All his attention was focused on her.

'A Saluki is the fastest dog there is—did you know that?' She swept her hair away from her face with a shaking hand, her face ghostly pale in the dim light of the room. 'Some claim it's the Greyhound, but over long distances the Saluki is faster. Its paws are padded so they absorb the impact. Believe me when I say that no child, however terrified, could ever outrun a Saluki. I know because we tried.'

She was speaking quickly now, her breathing shallow, as if she were remembering what it was like to run with fear in her heart and menace at her heels.

The image she painted was so vivid Raz felt nausea settle in the pit of his stomach. He sat up slowly, staring at her frozen profile. 'You are saying he sent the dogs to hunt you?'

'It was Hassan's idea of entertainment. Yasmin was terrified—just terrified.' Her teeth were chattering as she remembered. 'Her little body used to shake so badly she couldn't run, but it didn't really matter because running was pointless. And they didn't want us to run. They wanted us to hide. Do you know how terrifying it is, waiting for the moment when they find you? Because they *will* find you. And you hear them before you see them—you hear them panting, and the muffled thud of their paws as they pick up the scent and follow your trail. And you brace yourself for that moment, never knowing if this time they'll rip you apart before the humans call them off. All you can do is close your eyes and hope.'

For the first time he noticed a mark on her upper arm— an old scar, a silvery twist of damaged flesh that ran from shoulder to elbow. Lifting his hand, he touched it with his fingertips and felt her flinch. 'They did this?'

'I used to lie on top of her...' Her voice whispered over the pain. 'And the dogs used to try and pull me off. And she was screaming and screaming and it drove the animals crazy and I kept telling her not to move, to try and keep still, because it made it worse. But it was impossible to lie still when you could feel the heat of their breath on your neck and hear that horrible, rumbling growl—'

It explained her behaviour whenever Isis and Horus were around. She was always still. She never moved. It explained her behaviour on that first night in the tent when she'd been frozen to the spot and he hadn't understood why.

Now he understood, and his anger was black and lethal as he pulled her into the circle of his arms, holding her as she shivered and shook. 'I will find him,' he vowed in a thickened voice. 'I swear to you I will find him and he will pay for what he did to you both.'

'He is already paying. What he wanted was power and he's lost that. Between us we've taken that from him and it feels good.'

'I will not allow Isis and Horus near you again.'

'I don't want that. I want to get used to them.' Her voice was fiercely determined. 'I *need* to get used to them. They're good dogs. I know they are. Nothing like the others.'

Her lips were bloodless, her eyes dark and bruised in the soft light. She was so pale he felt guilt rip through him

'I shouldn't have made you talk about it, *habibti*.'

'You were right to make me talk about it. Why should I expect you to share things with me if I share nothing with you? On that first night you asked why a woman would cross a desert on a horse she couldn't ride to find a man she didn't know. Now you know the answer.'

'Your father knew what Hassan did?'

'My father had no interest in us beyond our use to him in his political games.'

'I am starting to understand the reason for your sister's night terrors.'

'That was just part of it.' She eased away from him, her eyes wide with anxiety. 'You don't think Salem would use dogs to track her?'

'No. You can rest assured that Salem utilises far more sophisticated methods than dogs. By now he will have tapped his many contacts in various shadowy government organisations and be using the most up-to-date technology that exists.'

'I let her down. I was the one who made the decision to leave the palace, and because of me she is lost and alone.'

'You made the right decision. By leaving you took control away from Hassan.' He smoothed her hair with his fingers and lay down in the bed again, taking her with him. Keeping his arm round her, he pulled the covers over them. 'You're safe. I'll never let him touch you again. This is your life now. This is your home.'

'But when everything settles in Tazkhan you will have to move there. The people will expect it.'

Her voice was muffled against his chest and Raz stared up at the ceiling, the scent of her hair winding itself around his senses.

'It's what we do that matters, not where we live. We will sort something out that works for everyone. And in the meantime I'm going to make you forget that life. This is your life now and, yes, there is responsibility—but there should also be fun.'

'Fun?'

She sounded unsure, doubtful, as if she had no idea what he meant, and he realised how little thought he'd given to her life and just how wrong he'd been in the few thoughts he'd had.

'Dancing? Talking to new people? Wearing nice clothes?'

'I've never danced. I'm not sure I'd be very good at it if my experiences on a horse are anything to go by.'

'You've never danced?' His arms tightened around her. 'Then that's something else I need to teach you. Now, go to sleep. You're safe now, I promise.'

CHAPTER NINE

SHE WOKE ALONE and the level of disappointment that followed that discovery was shocking. And then she heard the sound of the shower and realised he was using the bathroom.

He hadn't left.

For once he hadn't walked away once the sun had risen.

Layla rolled onto her back and stared up at the ceiling, her head full of the night before. And not just because of the discovery that she had an unsettling capacity to enjoy sex.

He'd called her *habibti*.

It was the first time he'd called her that. She subdued the sudden lift of her mood with cold, calm logic. She'd been upset. Whatever lay between them, Raz Al Zahki was a decent human being. The endearment had been spoken out of comfort, not affection, and she'd be deluded if she pretended otherwise.

But it had been the first time in her life anyone had held her like that. The first time anyone had offered comfort.

And it had felt good.

And strange. She'd never shared her thoughts with another person. Not even Yasmin. Because her role had been to protect her sister, so she hadn't wanted to frighten her by revealing her own fears. Part of her felt vulnerable that she'd shown him so much of herself, that he knew so much about her.

'Layla?' Zahra hovered in the doorway, clutching a book, unsure of her welcome.

When Layla sat up and stretched out her arms the little girl bounded into the room, closely followed by the ever-protective Isis and Horus.

Despite her best efforts Layla felt her throat close and the fear spark inside her.

'*Bas!* Stop!' Raz thundered the command from the door-way of the bathroom and the dogs skidded to a halt, crashing into each other like clowns in a circus. There was something almost comical about the dopey way they looked at him but he didn't smile. 'Sit and stay, or tonight you'll be sleeping in the desert.'

The dogs gave a whine and obediently sank down, heads on paws.

Layla felt her heart-rate slowly normalise.

Raz transferred his gaze to her and she knew he was think-ing about her confession of the night before, so she smiled and tried to keep it light. 'They know who's boss.'

'My dad is the boss. Everyone does as he says except me.' Zahra climbed onto the bed, still holding her book. 'Can we finish the story you started last night? You stopped at the exciting bit.'

Layla shifted across in the bed, relieved she'd thought to put her nightdress on in case Zahra woke in the night.

She was desperately conscious of Raz watching her, his bare chest still damp from the shower, a towel knotted around his waist.

'You can read for a while but then you need to pack.'

'Pack?' Zahra lost interest in the book. 'We're going on a trip? Can we ride?'

'Not this time. We're flying to Zubran for a party tonight.'

Zahra's face fell. 'A party? That means I can't come.'

Raz strolled across the room and scooped his daughter into

his arms. 'You can't come to the party but you can come to Zubran. I need you there. I want your opinion on a mare I'm thinking of buying.'

Watching the two of them together, Layla felt something soften inside her. The fact that a father could care so much about his daughter's feelings and opinion was a revelation. It was something she hadn't witnessed before because she'd had no relationship with her own father.

Aware that Raz was looking at her with question in his eyes, she smiled. 'You are buying another horse? How many animals can one person ride?'

'She won't be for riding. She'll be for breeding,' Zahra told her seriously. 'I'm going to have a foal of my own to take care of. I'm going to pack right now.' Squirming out of her father's arms, she sped from the room.

Overwhelmed by emotions so intense and uncomfortable she could hardly handle them, Layla rescued the book from where it lay as the little girl had left it, in danger of snapping its spine.

'Layla?' His voice was soft. 'Talk to me.'

What was there to say? 'You're a good father.' The words were thickened by the lump in her throat. 'And she adores you.'

'You think that's a bad thing?'

'Oh, no! How could I? A little girl *should* adore her daddy.'

There was a tense silence. 'But it doesn't always happen that way, does it?'

'No. But life is full of things that shouldn't happen—as we both know.' She closed the book carefully. 'If you want me to encourage her to read, it's probably best not to mention the word *horse* while we have a book open.'

'I know, but in this case it was intentional.' The corners of his mouth flickered. 'I wanted her out of the room. I need to talk to you, *habibti*.'

Habibti.

Her stomach flipped. What reason did he have to call her that this morning? Or did he think she still needed the comfort? 'What about?'

'I want to make sure you are comfortable about tonight.'

'The party? What exactly does it involve?'

'It is a fundraiser for a children's charity supported by the Sultan of Zubran and his wife, Avery. I think you'll like her. She used to run a highly successful party planning business and her events are always spectacular. This one promises to be no exception.'

'A fundraiser?' Layla felt no excitement. Just pressure. 'What exactly is my role at an event like that?'

'Your role is to enjoy yourself. Something I suspect you haven't done anywhere near enough in your life.' Droplets of water clung to his powerful shoulders and his hair was still sleek and damp from the shower. 'Did you never attend formal functions at the Citadel?'

'Never. My father never raised funds for anyone except himself and neither did Hassan.' Thinking of Hassan made her feel sick, and this time her concern wasn't just for herself and her sister. 'If you appear in public at a high-profile event like this one, won't you be a target?'

'The only people who know in advance that we will be there are the Sultan himself and his wife. I would trust them with my life. *Have* trusted them with my life on more occasions than I care to count. And although I take sensible precautions I don't live my life in hiding. I am easy enough to find if someone knows where to look.'

As they both knew.

Their eyes met briefly and she felt a new intimacy—and something she hadn't felt before. A warmth. *A new level of understanding.*

And something else. A chemistry so intense it thickened

the air and created a tension that unsettled her. They were talking about serious issues and yet part of her just wanted to place her hand on the hard swell of his biceps and her lips on the dark haze of hair at the centre of his chest.

'What about Zahra?' Somehow she managed to speak. 'What will she do while we're at the party.'

'She will be safe in Zubran. She has been there many times and it is sufficiently familiar that hopefully her night terrors will not return.' His gaze lingered on her face. 'Since you started reading to her at night and settling her down there have been no more bad dreams.'

'I know. And I'm pleased.'

'I can't thank you enough.'

'No thanks are needed.'

'And now it is your turn,' he said softly. 'We need to replace those bad dreams of yours, and those memories, with something much happier. Starting with this party.'

'But if Hassan guesses where you are going—'

'I don't anticipate that Hassan will pay us a visit, but if he does then it will save us the bother of finding him.' His gaze held hers for a moment. 'So, how do you feel about the party? I don't want to overwhelm you, and I know how anxious you are for news of your sister, but I would very much like you to have fun and enjoy yourself.'

Layla couldn't imagine enjoying herself in the company of a large number of strangers but she didn't want to say so. 'I'm already looking forward to it.'

'I've promised to take Zahra riding this morning. Will you join us?'

Was it her imagination or had those dark shadows she saw in his eyes lessened? Was it wishful thinking on her part to think he seemed happier and more relaxed?

'I think the two of you should ride together.'

'Join us.' He brushed her cheek with the backs of his fingers. 'Abdul will stay with you and we will all ride slowly.'

But of course he didn't know the meaning of *slow*, pushing his animal to the limit as he sped into the distance in pursuit of his young daughter, who seemed to embrace their extreme ride with the same enthusiasm as her father. The horse's tail was lifted high and trailed like a banner in the wind, his curved neck betraying his enviable lineage. Even Layla, whose knowledge of horses came entirely from books, could see the animal was beautiful.

It made her sick with nerves just watching, but she had to admit it was good that Zahra didn't seem afraid either of horses or the Saluki who ran next to them.

If her childhood had been different would she have been the same?

Would she be the one galloping across the sand and whooping with excitement?

'You are doing so well, Your Highness.' It was Abdul, as kind and solicitous as ever as he rode by her side as Raz had instructed.

'We both know I'm not, but thank you for the encouragement.' She stared enviously at Raz and Zahra, now just specks in the distance.

'We are all born with different gifts,' Abdul said quietly. 'His Highness has a particular gift with horses, but he has also had the benefit of many years of experience. He was virtually raised on horseback. The moment he could sit unsupported he was put on a horse—I think he was about six months old. He rode with his father every day until he could control the animal himself. Then he rode alone. And he has a tendency to take what many would see as appalling risks, so I would beg you do *not* aspire to emulate him.'

'Not much chance of that.' She felt a pang that she wasn't confident enough to share that interest with him, but she knew that even if she rode each day and every day for the rest of her life she'd never be as good as Raz.

'You have your own gifts.' Abdul reached across and showed her how to shorten the reins. 'And those are to be valued every bit as much as His Highness's skills with a horse. You have courage and patience, as you have shown on numerous occasions over the past week. His Highness is growing more relaxed by the day and we have you to thank for that.'

'You think so?' Perhaps it hadn't been her imagination. 'Will you be coming with us to Zubran?'

'Yes, because His Highness will have talks with the Sultan.'

'And will you be at the party, Abdul?'

'Sadly, no, Your Highness. But I feel sure you will enjoy it.'

'Will I?' Layla wasn't convinced. 'I have no idea what I'm supposed to wear.'

'On that topic I have taken the liberty of contacting Her Royal Highness the Sultana of Zubran. She has generously agreed to assist with your wardrobe needs as there has been no opportunity to provide what you will require for such an event.'

'I don't want to put her to any trouble.'

Abdul cleared his throat. 'Perhaps it is indiscreet of me to say this, but I can assure you that there is nothing Her Highness enjoys more than dressing people in clothes of her choosing. Zahra loves going to see her for that very reason. And you will find Her Highness to be a very warm and caring person once she has finished organising your life and telling you what you should be doing.'

Layla was amused and intrigued. 'So she isn't dominated by the Sultan?'

'It is very much a marriage of equals,' Abdul said dryly, and Layla felt her heart squeeze as she watched Raz ride into the distance.

Theirs wasn't a marriage of equals, was it?

She couldn't ride. She couldn't swim. She was terrified of his dogs. She had no idea what was expected of her at this party.

What exactly *did* she have to offer him?

The realisation that she was hopeless at all the things that were important to him disturbed her, as did the thought that tonight they would be making their first public appearance together.

Never having been allowed to mingle with her father's guests, Layla felt as if she were back in the oasis with the waters closing over her head.

'I'd be delighted if Her Highness would help me with my wardrobe.'

If it came to a choice between inconveniencing the Sultan's wife and embarrassing Raz she'd pick inconvenience every time. But as it turned out Abdul was correct in his summation that their hostess would be only too delighted to take responsibility for her wardrobe.

'You've been hiding out in the desert together? I have never heard anything more romantic in my life! But romance can only take a girl so far and then she needs a decent spa day.'

Avery was the most elegant, capable, efficient person Layla had ever met, and within minutes they were curled up on a low sofa in an opulent room hung with beautiful tapestries and sipping tea.

'Mmm. Whenever we're in the desert Mal makes me drink the Bedouin variety, which is delicious, but you can't beat Earl Grey. Now, tell me all the details and leave nothing out.'

'Details?' Layla sat stiff and formal on the edge of the sofa, but Avery slipped off her shoes and curled her legs under her.

'I'm going to give you a tip, because once you and Raz are back in your rightful place in the palace at Tazkhan you're going to be throwing open those gilded doors and entertaining the whole world and your legs will feel as if they've been trapped between clamps: whenever you can before a big event take the weight off your feet. And now tell me if it's true that you escaped from the palace and rode into the desert on your father's wild stallion? It's too romantic for words.'

'It wasn't romantic. It was horrible in every way. And I don't think the horse was wild, precisely—at least not until we climbed on its back. Then it was certainly less than impressed—'

After a moment's hesitation Layla told Avery the whole story, and by the end of it she felt so relaxed she'd even removed her shoes.

'So you married for the good of Tazkhan, but now you're in love? That is the happiest ending I've heard in a long time.'

'Oh, no, that isn't true!' Startled, Layla stiffened. 'I'm not in love.'

Avery's brows rose. 'No? So when you say "Raz this" and "Raz that" in every sentence it's just because you're—' she waved a hand in the air '—sorry, but I only know one reason to mention a guy in every single breath and that's l-o-v-e. Either that or obsession, and you don't strike me as the obsessive type.'

Love? Layla stared at her blankly. 'I can't be in love. I'm not that sort of person.'

'Trust me, love is indiscriminate. It strikes all types without mercy. I didn't think I was "that sort of person" either and now look at me. I'm someone who has to control everything around them, but take it from me that love can't be controlled. Believe me, I've tried.'

'That's different. You and His Highness knew each other for a long time before you were together. Whereas Raz and I—' Her skin heated as she thought about the intimacies they'd shared. 'We are strangers. We have known each other only a few weeks.'

'I actually find that quite erotic.' Avery leaned back against the arm of the sofa. 'Strangers forced together. I presume you've actually...?' When Layla coloured Avery smiled. 'Mmm, and I'll bet it was good. Raz is super-hot. But don't tell Mal I said that.'

'He was so in love with his wife.' The words fell from Layla's lips before she could stop them and she saw Avery's eyes narrow.

'Yes, and that was tragic. But it happened. Stuff happens.' The laughter had gone and her husky voice hinted at layers of depth beneath the sophisticated social skills. 'It's called life. Sometimes life delivers a steaming pile of crap right in your lap, and when that happens all you can do is keep moving forward. You keep walking. You get out of bed, you move, and eventually you start living again. And that's what he's doing.'

'But this marriage wasn't his choice. It was mine.'

'Raz Al Zahki has never done anything that wasn't his choice. He is tough, single-minded and as stubborn as his brother and my husband.' Avery reached across and squeezed her hand. 'And he made a *good* choice. I'm thrilled we're going to be neighbours.'

'I'm nothing like his wife. I can't take her place.'

'Would you want to? Personally, I'd hate to be a clone of another person. You probably don't want my advice, but I'll give it anyway because I can't help myself: don't try and replace her.' Avery unfolded her long legs and slipped on her shoes. 'Be yourself. Be *you*. If you want to learn to ride, then learn. But only if it's what you want to do. You should probably learn to swim, but only so that his psycho sister-in-law can't have the pleasure of drowning you. The point I'm making is that if you are *you* then any relationship you form together will be real.'

Layla felt her mood lift for the first time in days. Maybe even longer. 'That makes sense.'

'Of course it does. I only ever talk sense—as I'm forever telling my husband. Now, drink some tea and tell me about your sister.'

At the mention of her sister Layla felt her happy mood evaporate. 'She's still missing.'

'Yes.' Avery's expression was sympathetic. 'Everyone is looking for her. And Salem is exactly the right person to be in charge of that.'

'Everyone says that, but he didn't look particularly friendly when I saw him.'

'I didn't say he was friendly.' Avery swept a sheet of blonde hair away from her face. 'No, he definitely isn't friendly. Dark. Moody. A bit scary, I suppose. But in a totally hot way. Exactly the right person to find your sister.'

'Why? Why does everyone keep saying that?'

Avery put her cup down carefully. 'You don't know?'

'All I know is that Raz seems to trust his brother with his life.'

'As well he would. Salem isn't just his brother—he's ex-Special Forces. After everything that happened in their family he left to set up his own private security firm. He handles *our* security—although I'm convinced that's just Mal trying to monitor my movements when I'm buying shoes.'

Layla laughed, but her mind was picking over what she now knew of Salem. On that first night he'd stepped in front of his brother to protect him, even though Raz was obviously well able to defend himself. 'He hasn't been in contact.'

'He's a man.' Avery selected a date from the bowl on the table. 'Men never call when they're supposed to, and Salem keeps everything close to his chest. Which isn't a bad place to be, I have to say, because he's all muscle and very sexy.' Catching Layla's expression, she grinned. 'Sorry, I'm trying to cheer you up. I honestly do believe that Salem will find her. He's the best.'

'But if she were alive surely he would have found her by now?'

'Maybe he has. Maybe he's lying low for some reason—such as the fact Hassan is a crackpot and no one knows exactly where he is.' Avery nibbled the date. 'Is she a resilient girl?'

Layla thought about her sister and everything she'd endured. 'Yes.'

'Shy? What would she do if she were picked up by a Bedouin tribe, for example?'

'Talk them to death?'

Avery's brows rose. 'It sounds as if Salem will have his hands full when he finds her. You don't know him, so you'll have to take it from me that he's very serious. And everything he does is top secret so he's not much of a talker.'

'Then how do you know so much about what he does?'

'Just one of the perks of being married to the boss, sweetie.'

Layla sifted through the information at her disposal. 'But if Salem is really as serious as you say he is going to strangle my sister.'

'Yes, it does sound like an interesting match. I predict that she will be a pleasant interruption from his usual life. Now, have some more tea. And eat something. Because it's ages until dinner and I'm always too busy mingling to eat much at these things.'

Avery topped up the cups and Layla breathed deeply.

'I have no idea what is expected of me tonight.'

'You're our guest. All we expect of our guests is that they enjoy themselves. In fact I insist on it or I'll assume my party is a dismal failure.' Seeing the expression on Layla's face, she gave a warm smile. 'Just enjoy the time with Raz. Sounds as if the two of you haven't had much time to get to know each other outside of a crisis situation, so this is a perfect opportunity to explore a whole different side to your relationship.'

'But I knew what was expected of me in the crisis. I knew I had to stop the wedding, find Raz, find my sister—it was stressful, but there was a purpose to it. I don't understand the purpose of a party. That isn't what our relationship is about.'

'Maybe it should be. Maybe you just don't know how to relax because you've never been allowed to. The purpose of tonight,' Avery said, 'is for you to spend time together. Be a couple.'

'I've never been part of a couple. I don't know what I'm doing.' Layla's desperation to talk to someone overrode her natural shyness about the topic. 'Raz is—experienced. I'm worried I'm not the woman he needs.'

Avery stared at her for a long moment and then gave a slow smile that transformed her face from beautiful to pure seductress. Suddenly Layla saw exactly why the Sultan had fallen so hard for her. She was strong and independent, but never at the expense of her femininity.

'Trust me, you are *all* the woman he needs,' Avery said.

Layla gave a helpless shrug. 'I don't know myself anymore. I thought I had such a clear idea of who I was and what I wanted, and then suddenly it turns out I'm wrong.'

'Not wrong, but people change and adapt according to their circumstances.' Avery sipped her tea. 'People grow and learn. Or at least the people worth knowing do. For the record, I'm glad Raz found you. He deserves someone like you. And you deserve him.'

'He was forced to marry me.'

'Stop saying that! Did he marry you kicking and screaming? I didn't think so. Now, finish your tea—we're going to make sure that by the time you and Raz make it back to the bedroom tonight he is going to be a desperate man.'

'I won't be comfortable wearing anything too revealing.'

'Don't worry. The true secret of allure is not to show all but to hint at what you are hiding.'

Layla gave a choked laugh. 'You want him to unwrap me?'

'Well, that's one alternative.' Avery stood up. 'Personally, I have a preference for a scenario where you unwrap yourself and make him watch but not touch. The theme of tonight's ball is Desert Nights. It has so much potential, don't you think?'

CHAPTER TEN

RAZ PACED THE length of the royal rooms that had been allocated to them for their stay and glanced at his watch for the sixth time in as many minutes.

Of Layla there was no sign, and he wondered how she'd coped with being plunged into the centre of a big working palace with people she didn't know. From the little he'd learned about her past he knew she'd had little exposure to glittering social gatherings such as the ones run by the Sultan and his wife. And he'd known Avery long enough to be sure she would have extracted every last scrap of detail from Layla, and suddenly wondered if it had been unfair of him to leave them together for so long.

The Desert Nights Ball—an annual event organised by Avery as a fundraiser for disadvantaged children—was about to begin and their presence was expected.

He pulled out his phone and was about to call Avery when Mal appeared in the doorway of his suite, flanked by his security team.

'I have been sent by my wife to tell you that they will meet us downstairs.'

Raz slid his phone back into his pocket. 'I expected Layla to be here.'

'She's spent the day shopping and lunching with Avery, so expect to find her exhausted.' Mal dismissed his guards with a discreet gesture and walked into the guest suite, closing the door behind him. 'Apparently they want to surprise you. And by that I mean that my wife has taken over, as always. I hope that isn't a problem?'

'I appreciate Avery's help. Layla isn't used to large social gatherings and she's quite shy. I'm worried she'll find it overwhelming.'

Mal gave him a speculative look. 'You care about her?'

'Does that surprise you?'

'Does it surprise *you*?'

'Yes.' Seeing no reason not to be honest with his friend, Raz paced over to the window. 'Yes, it surprises me. She is nothing like I expected her to be. I admit it. I made an assumption about who she was based on what we know about the rest of her family.'

'Most people would have done the same.'

'Perhaps, but it isn't something I'm proud of.' He knew now how desperate things must have been for Layla to choose to ride a strange horse into the desert with no fixed destination. She was careful, cautious—and with reason. Those were the qualities that had kept her alive. 'I suspect her life was hell.'

'Now, that comes as *no* surprise to me.' Mal's voice was hard. 'If you want my honest opinion, she is lucky to now be married to you and is probably feeling nothing but relieved.'

Was she? He realised he knew very little about what she was feeling because she kept her thoughts to herself. Except for that single occasion when she'd lost control and spoken out about the secrets he'd kept from her, she'd made no comment on her new life. He knew that much of what she did was driven by her desire to please him, to compensate in some small way for the sins her father had committed.

'She is very brave. She rides even though she hates it, and although she is scared of the dogs she insists they are allowed to roam free. She refuses to be beaten by fear.'

'Then hopefully it will not be long before she realises that with you there is nothing to fear.'

'I think tonight might be stressful for her.' And he realised he didn't want it to be. He didn't want it to be another task she had to endure, another challenge. He wanted her to relax. He wanted her to have fun and enjoy herself without constantly looking over her shoulder.

Mal was watching him. 'And what about you? This is the first time you have made a public appearance with another woman.'

It was something else that hadn't occurred to him. 'I don't care what people think, but *she* will care.' And people would be speculating about their relationship, his feelings about being married to the daughter of his enemy.

'We will all ensure that she is protected as much as possible. She will receive a warm welcome from all of us and that will help.'

But would that be enough?

'She isn't used to crowds.'

'If you sense she is bothered by it then of course you must leave early,' Mal said immediately. 'No one will be offended. Come up here and spend some time alone. My staff will serve you dinner—anything you need, just ask. You are like a brother to me. I hope you know that.'

Quiet words, but spoken with such sincerity that they unlocked something inside him.

'I do know that. For the past decade you've—'

'You would have done the same for me.' Mal cut him off before he could express his thanks. 'I am glad you've found Layla.'

'She's never danced before. Can you imagine that?' His tone raw, Raz lifted a hand and pressed his fingers to his forehead. 'Her life was *nothing* like I imagined it to be.'

He thought of two small girls, huddled together while they

listened to the dogs approaching. Had an image of the scar on her arm where those dogs had come too close. Knowing how hard it had been for her to share that with him, he had no intention of sharing it with anyone else.

'Having met both her father and Hassan on a few occasions I prefer to forget, I have no trouble believing you.'

'She has no idea how to enjoy herself. I don't think she knows who she really is.'

Mal hesitated and then reached out and squeezed his shoulder. 'Give her time. Her life has changed overnight. She has lived with people she couldn't trust, so it will inevitably take a while for her to realise she can trust *you*. It must be a relief to her to be living with you after the life she has led.'

Was it? He realised that since this whole thing began he'd barely thought further than his own needs. 'I have no idea how she feels about living with me,' Raz said honestly.

Mal raised an eyebrow. 'Don't take this the wrong way, but I think you underestimate your qualities. Not that I claim to be an expert on the minds of women, as my wife is always swift to point out.'

His wry tone made Raz smile. 'Your wife is an amazing woman.'

'She is pregnant.' Mal spoke the words in a rough tone tinged with male pride and then gave a half smile. 'I wasn't supposed to tell anyone that.'

'Congratulations.' It was Raz's turn to reach out. 'I'm pleased for you both.'

'I'd rather you didn't—'

'I won't mention it.'

'Good, because I would be in serious trouble. There will be a public announcement in due course.'

'I shall look suitably surprised.'

Mal glanced towards the door. 'I am the host. I should go downstairs and greet the early arrivals. Join me?'

They walked into the opulent ballroom together and Avery immediately walked up to Raz and kissed him on both cheeks.

'It's good to see you, my friend.'

Dressed in ivory silk, she looked stunning and Raz smiled. 'And it is good to see you. Thank you for looking after Layla.'

'I love her,' Avery said simply. 'She's the kindest, most sweet-natured person. And very, *very* beautiful—but of course you've already noticed that because you're a man. She's nervous, so please say the right thing when you see her. And if you need help working out what that is, don't be afraid to ask.'

Raz didn't respond. He was looking over Avery's shoulder to Layla, who was dressed like something from the *Arabian Nights*. Her dress was midnight-blue shot with silver, high at the neck, cut narrow at the waist. Her hair fell in a smooth sheet, dark as ink over the shimmering fabric. Her beautiful eyes were accentuated by subtle make-up.

'And just in case you're that guy who never asks for help, the word you're looking for is *stunning*,' Avery murmured, and then took Mal's arm and guided him towards the arriving guests, leaving Raz alone with a shimmering, dazzling version of Layla.

She looked at him through the dark sweep of those thick eyelashes that had caught his attention from the first moment he'd seen her.

'Did your meetings go well?'

She sounded composed but he saw the uncertainty in her face and knew that Avery was right about her being nervous.

His mouth on those lips, Raz struggled to focus. 'Very well. And I see you and Avery had a busy afternoon.'

'We had fun. We talked and then we shopped.'

Her eyes sparkled and there was an excitement in her expression he'd ever seen them. It was as if someone had switched on a lightbulb inside her. She had a new confidence.

She carried herself differently. He wondered what had brought about the change.

Was it just the dress?

'You look stunning.'

'She told you to say that. I heard her. But thank you, anyway.'

'I said it because it's true. And I would have done so without prompting.' He looked into her eyes and then reached out and drew her against him, his hand resting on the dip of her narrow waist.

'Can I ask you something?'

'Anything.'

'You mentioned dancing—' Her gaze slid to the dance floor, which shimmered and sparkled under clever lighting. 'I'd really like to try it.'

Hiding his surprise, Raz took her hand. 'Then let's try it.'

Intrigued by the change in her, he led her towards the dance floor, exchanging only the briefest of greetings with people as they moved through the crowd, all his attention focused on her.

He noticed Avery in the centre of the dance floor with a man Raz recognised as the French ambassador while Mal was deep in conversation with the man's wife.

When she spotted them Avery immediately escorted the dazzled ambassador back to his wife before grabbing Layla by the hands.

'Don't you *love* this song?' She swirled and shimmied, arms above her head, and Layla watched her curiously for a moment and then joined her, following Avery's lead as she danced, her movements more subtle, more discreet as she learned to match the flow of her body with the beat of the music.

It was a skill that seemed to come naturally too her. Raz felt tension throb through him as he watched her move with sensual grace, her long hair flowing like liquid silk around her shoulders as she discovered a love of dancing. Her happiness at that discovery was evident from the smile on her lips and the unselfconscious way she twirled with Avery, her enjoyment as infectious as the rhythmic beat of the music.

Raz watched her, hypnotised by the change in her, knowing he was witnessing the transformation from unsure girl to sexually aware woman.

Avery caught his eye and gave him a knowing look before twirling Layla into his arms.

She landed against his chest with a gentle thud, off-balance from the dancing and laughing in a way he hadn't heard her laugh before. And he found himself smiling too, because it was impossible not to smile with her eyes sparkling into his and her arms wrapped around his neck as she tried to balance herself.

'I'm dizzy.' Her fingers closed over his biceps. 'Did I embarrass you?'

Was this the first time in her life she'd done something for herself without thought to others? 'No.' His mouth was close to hers, his gaze locked on hers. 'You could never embarrass me.'

By chance, or more likely because the ever-observant Avery had organised it, the rhythm of the music changed from loud and throbbing to soft and smooth and Raz drew her against him, his hand pressed low on her back.

He felt her body relax against his, knew people were watching curiously and tightened his grip on her protectively, hoping she didn't notice the interest and lose that sudden burst of unselfconscious enjoyment that he was finding as addictive as a drug.

Her enchantment with dancing reminded him of that magical moment when a newborn foal staggered to its feet for the first time, balancing on shaky legs as it realised there was a whole new world to explore.

His grip on her must have tightened, because those exotic, beautiful eyes lifted to his in silent question.

Raz felt as if someone had kicked his legs out from under him.

Sexual energy crackled between them, scorching hot and intense. His hand was on her back and he felt the change in her, felt her response to the chemistry as her eyes dropped to his mouth and lingered there.

This time there was no shyness in her gaze, just curiosity, and something far, far more dangerous that came from the knowledge she'd acquired over the past week. Her eyes darkened like the sky before a storm, those eyelashes a silky veil of temptation. And then her lips curved into a happy smile and she leaned her head against his chest, the softness of her hair brushing against his jaw, the scent of it yet another drugging assault on his senses.

Fighting the impulse to drag her from the dance floor, Raz closed his eyes and gathered her close, blocking out everyone around them.

Time passed unobserved until the pace of the music increased and she tilted her head back and looked up at him.

He slid his fingers into her hair, pleased that Avery hadn't suggested she wear it up. 'Do you want to carry on dancing or would you like something to eat? Maybe a drink?'

'The beat has changed.'

'It's a different dance. I can teach you.'

'You must be tired of having to teach me everything.'

Her eyes were soft on his and he tightened his grip on her, pressing her closer until their bodies touched from waist to thigh.

'No, I am not tired of teaching you.' His arm was curved around her and the contours of her body fit perfectly against his. Sexual arousal slammed into him and he felt the answering tremor of her body and knew she felt the same. Her fingers dug into his shoulder. 'You're enjoying yourself?'

'Yes. Very much.'

'Did you have fun with Avery?'

'Yes. I've never talked to another woman before. Not like that.'

'What did you talk about?'

Colour streaked along her cheeks. 'Life.'

'Your life, *habibti*?'

'Not specifically. She talked a bit about you and Salem. She is obviously very fond of you both.'

'Those feelings are returned. Mal has been a friend for as long as I can remember. He and I were at the same party the night he first met Avery. It was like watching two asteroids collide. Everyone in the vicinity was hit by the explosion and the subsequent fallout.' They both glanced towards the edge of the dance floor, where Avery was deep in conversation with Mal, their connection so close it felt like intruding to watch it.

'They're perfect together.'

There was a wistful note in her voice and Raz tilted his head so that he could see her face.

'I thought you weren't romantic?'

Her eyes were fixed across the room on Avery and Mal who were indulging in a last brief exchange before greeting their guests. Remembering what Mal had told him earlier, Raz could guess what the exchange was about.

'I'm not. Not for myself. That doesn't mean I can't be pleased when other people find love.'

He looked down at the glossy curve of Layla's mouth and suddenly wanted to be alone with her, away from the curious glances and the speculation.

'Let's get out of here. The Old Palace is famed for its water gardens. They were a gift from Mal's father to his mother on their marriage.' Keeping his arm around her, he guided her outside.

'Should we be doing this? There are people waiting to speak to you.'

'Then they can wait. I have been doing nothing but speaking to people. Tonight is for us.' He wondered how often before in her life she'd been able to please herself and decided he probably didn't want to hear the answer.

'It's peaceful here.' Tilting her head back, she stared up at the stars. 'I love the sound of the water. It reminds me of your home.'

'*Our* home.'

She hesitated, then pulled away from him and sat down on the low wall that surrounded the bubbling fountain. 'Did your wife love it there? Was it her favourite place?'

He stiffened in instinctive rejection of the personal nature of her question and then saw the anxiety in her eyes and realised how much courage it had taken on her part to ask it. 'Nisa preferred the city. She grew tired of moving around. She was made impatient by the restrictions placed on our movements. She wasn't always careful.'

'I shouldn't have asked.'

But she *had* asked, and emotion settled in his stomach like a solid lump. 'The day she was killed—she wasn't even supposed to be in the desert. She had been staying in the city but had come out to surprise me. I had ridden one of the horses and she climbed into my four-wheel drive. They had tampered with the brakes and she was inexperienced at driving in the desert. Had I been the one at the wheel then perhaps—' He broke off, knowing that 'perhaps' was a useless word. 'She couldn't control the vehicle. It rolled and she was crushed.'

He felt her arms slide round his waist.

'I'm sorry. I'm sorry you lost her. I'm sorry for any part my family played in that. For all of it.'

'An individual is responsible for his own actions. I have never blamed you.' But he understood how hard it must be for her and knew he was the one making it hard.

'It hurts you to talk about it.' Her voice was soft in the semi darkness. 'I apologise. I shouldn't have asked. I've spoiled the moment.'

'You have a right to ask, and you've spoiled nothing.'

'I have no rights, Your Highness. We both know that.'

Sadness shadowed the dark depths of her eyes and Raz pulled her to her feet and took her face in his hands, forcing her to look at him.

'You are still calling me Your Highness after everything we have shared? Have we not moved further on than that?'

'You married me because it was the right thing to do for your people, and in doing so you ignored your personal wishes.'

'Maybe that was true at the time of the wedding, but it isn't true now. Do you think I was ignoring my personal wishes last night? Do you think what we do together has anything to do with my responsibilities?'

'Raz—'

Her hand was on his chest, her eyes on his, and he lowered his head, his mouth hovering above hers.

'Do you think this isn't personal? Does this not feel personal, *habibti*?'

Layla felt everything inside her tighten and spin out of control. Staring into his dangerous black eyes, she felt the world around them fade to nothing. The distant sound of chatter was replaced by the pounding of blood in her ears and her vision was filled with nothing but him.

She felt the roughness of his cheek against the softness of hers, the warmth of his breath and the bite of his strong fingers in her hair as he held her head for his kiss. But he didn't kiss her. Not quite. And the anticipation was electrifying. She felt his tension as powerfully as he evidently felt hers.

'Do we have to stay?' She almost whispered the words. 'Would it be possible to leave?'

His dark brows met in a concerned frown. 'You're not happy? Then we will leave.' Without pressing for further explanation he took her hand and led her towards some steps that led past a cascade of fountains to the rear entrance of the Old Palace. 'We can reach our rooms from here.'

She walked with him through an arched entrance, up spiral stairs, along opulent corridors with gilded mirrors and ornate tapestries, past uniformed staff and the odd exotically clad guest until they reached their private suite.

'I should not have taken you this evening,' he breathed. 'Forgive me.'

'Why do you say that? I had fun. Such fun.'

'You wanted to leave.'

'But not because I wasn't enjoying myself.'

'Then why?'

Layla hesitated, and then stepped forward and placed her hands on his chest. 'Because of this. Because of what I want to do.' She felt him tense. Saw the shock in his eyes as he realised her reasons for abandoning the party were not the ones he'd assumed they were.

'Layla—'

'Don't speak.' She wanted the illusion. No matter what lay between them, tonight it was all about the chemistry and she didn't want to shatter that with words. Whatever emotional hurdles they faced, physically there were none.

This time her fingers were swift and sure as she undressed him. Within seconds he was naked from the waist up, his trousers riding low on his waist, revealing a gloriously masculine chest, every line of muscle clearly delineated as he stood in front of her. Her fingers slid up his chest to his shoulders and then lingered on the hard swell of his biceps. His physical strength fascinated her, and she traced the shape of his muscles with the tips of her fingers, hearing his breathing change, feeling the tension in him as he held himself still and let her explore. She took her time because she wanted to discover and memorise every inch of him. After her fingers she used her lips, her tongue retracing the line her fingers had taken. And still he stood still, although she sensed the effort it took him to do so.

Candles flickered in all corners of the room, sending shafts of shimmering light across them, turning his chest from bronze to gold.

Without hesitation she undid his trousers and dropped to her knees in front of him, her hair falling in a sweep of dark silk over her shoulders.

She glanced up at him and his gaze clashed with hers and held.

Then slowly, gently, she took him in her mouth and saw his eyes close, his jaw clench. She felt the thickness of him in her mouth, tasted the silky, salty heat of him, until he groaned deep in his throat and closed his hands in her hair, easing her away from him.

'Give me a minute—'

His voice was thickened, his eyes dark with something she hadn't seen before, and then he pulled her to her feet and their mouths came together at the same time. This time there was nothing gentle about the kiss, no tentative exploration or patient instruction, just raw, undiluted passion. His hands were locked in her hair and then ripping at her dress as they kissed, so hungry for each other they staggered slightly and sent a lamp flying from its place on a table.

Raz caught it in his hand and she laughed against his mouth. 'Good catch, Your Highness.'

'If it had fallen we would have had Security swarming all over this place.'

Without lifting his mouth from hers he replaced the lamp and urged her back towards the bed, but Layla twisted at the last moment so that this time he was the one on his back on the bed and she was the one on top.

Her hair fell forward onto his chest and he slid his fingers into it.

'I love your hair.'

Smiling, she licked her way down his chest, heard him groan deep in his throat as she moved lower again, exploring him intimately, until his hands closed on her hips and he shifted her over him, his impatience evident in the hard bite of his fingers.

His hair-roughened thigh brushed against the softness of hers and she lowered herself onto him, watching his eyes turn deep, dark black as he drove deep into her. Layla moaned with the sheer pleasure of it, moving instinctively, until he locked his fingers over her hips to control her movements.

'Give me a minute—'

His tone was raw, right on the edge of control, and she leaned forward to kiss his mouth, licking at his lips until he muttered something unintelligible and caught her head in his hands. They kissed like wild things, the heat a pulsing, pounding force, his body hard in hers as they drove each other to the same peak and over the edge. She felt him pulse inside her, watched his face as he lost control, as pleasure gripped them both and spun them into ecstasy.

Afterwards, she curled against his chest and felt his hand come up to touch her hair.

He didn't speak and neither did she, because she'd learned how easily words could destroy and she wanted to preserve the moment. Preferably forever, but if not forever then at least for now.

And in the aftermath of their loving, while they both lay bathed in intimacy, she knew that Avery had been right.

She loved him.

The realisation was overwhelming, terrifying and puzzling all at the same time.

But most of all it was shocking. Shocking to learn yet another thing about herself. When she'd made the decision that marriage to Raz was the best solution, she'd braced herself for living with a stranger, but she was fast discovering that the stranger she was living with was herself.

She realised that her life before him had been as dry and empty as the vast desert. Because she'd never known anything else she'd assumed that was all there was, but now she knew differently. She'd thought she knew herself well, but had discovered she'd only known one small part of herself. And as for knowing *him*—

They say his heart is frozen into ice.

She knew that wasn't true.

She lifted her head and looked at him, staring down into the fierce black of his eyes. To describe him as handsome was to do him a disservice, because his appeal went so much deeper than that. Etched in those striking features was a strength that was more than surface deep.

Something flickered in those ebony depths and she saw all her own questions reflected back at her.

Without speaking he lifted his hand and pushed her hair away from her face. It was impossible not to react to his touch because it seemed everything she felt about this man was exaggerated and out of her control.

She felt a stab of envy for his wife, whom he had loved so deeply, swiftly followed by guilt that she could feel that way about someone no longer alive.

A few weeks ago she hadn't known anything about love. She'd felt disconnected from the poets' description of the agony and heartache that came with love and loss. She'd never seen any evidence to support the theory that hearts could break, shatter or be frozen into ice.

She'd been willing to believe in love, but had never expected to experience the reality.

But now she had both experience and evidence. She felt the pain of it heavy in her chest, the ache behind her ribcage growing by the hour.

Raz frowned slightly and just for a moment she thought he was going to say something. Then he gathered her close and pulled the covers over them both.

'That was amazing. *You* are amazing.'

Layla said nothing because she had no idea what to say.

When she'd made the decision to suggest marriage to him she'd been prepared to live in a loveless partnership. Any alternative hadn't occurred to her, because although she'd been willing to believe love existed for other people she'd had no evidence to suggest she was capable of it. All she'd wanted was respect and kindness. She'd been ignorant of the impact of sexual attraction and ignorant of the power of love.

But now she knew about both.

And she knew love hurt.

'Do you have to go away, Daddy?'

Raz turned at the sound of his daughter's voice and saw her standing watching him, her expression forlorn. Layla hurried towards her, trying to distract the little girl with the promise of a swim.

Raz noticed she didn't look at him.

It had been two weeks since the party in Zubran, and since their return Layla had been withdrawn and quiet. So quiet he was becoming increasingly concerned.

He made a mental note to talk to her about it immediately on his return.

'I have to go, but it's only for one night.' He scooped Zahra into his arms. 'When I come back we will ride together, I promise.'

As if realising that she should say something, Layla roused herself. 'Where are you going?'

'I have another meeting with the Tazkhan Council—this time to discuss arrangements for formalising my position.'

'So will we be moving to the city?'

It was Zahra who asked the question, but he wondered if that was what was bothering Layla.

'We will live there for some of the time, but not all.' He watched Layla's face but her expression didn't change.

As his security guards made the final preparations around him he drew Layla to one side. 'You are very quiet. Is something worrying you?'

'Nothing. I hope your meeting goes well.'

She was detached and formal and he knew this wasn't the right time to push her. Not with his daughter watching and his security team hovering in the background.

'I will be back tomorrow.' He lifted his hand to her face, intending to kiss her, and then let his hand drop, shocked by the impulse. They were in public, their exchange witnessed by a dozen other people.

Before he could say anything she stepped back. 'Safe trip.'

CHAPTER ELEVEN

LAYLA LAY AWAKE in the bed, sleep chased away by the ache in her chest.

Maybe a heart *could* break.

She'd read about people who lost partners only to die themselves.

Maybe such a thing was possible. Just one more thing she'd been wrong about.

It was almost a relief that Raz was away for a night because she didn't know how to be with him any more. She didn't know how *not* to show him that she loved him, and she didn't know how to stop herself falling harder and deeper.

Unable to sleep, she decided to read for a while and pressed the switch for the light by the bed. Nothing happened. Assuming the bulb had blown, she leaned across and tried the other one. When that didn't work either she pulled on a robe, slid on her shoes and walked out of her bedroom and onto the terrace. Stars twinkled in the sky and everything was quiet.

Too quiet.

Lights should have been burning in the house and outside on the terrace, but everything was in darkness and the fountain was silent. There was no sound of running water, no sounds at all.

It was eerily quiet.

Layla wondered if there had been a power cut and was

about to go back to her room and find a torch when she realised that there were no security guards outside Zahra's room.

Her heart stopped and she ceased to breathe for a few seconds.

No lights. No guards.

Grateful that there was enough moonlight for her to see the way, she walked quickly to Zahra's bedroom, adjacent to hers. There was sufficient light for her to see Isis and Horus curled up on the bed next to the little girl, and for once she was relieved to see them.

Her heart was pounding hard and her hands were clammy, and she stood for a moment, trying to rationalize the situation. The most likely explanation was a blown fuse or some other electrical fault.

Was she overreacting?

Possibly, but all she could hear in her head were Raz's words.

Show me the evidence that my daughter would have been safe.

She didn't have evidence, and she knew better than to underestimate Hassan at any time—least of all now, when he was likely to be at his most desperate.

What if he had somehow discovered that Raz had a daughter?

What if he decided to use that fact?

No matter that she might be overreacting. She couldn't risk letting Raz lose someone else he loved.

'Zahra…' Keeping her voice soft, she reached out a hand towards the sleeping child.

Isis opened one eye and looked at her.

Keeping as far away from the dogs as possible, Layla gave Zahra a gentle shake. 'Wake up. We're going on an adventure.'

Zahra snuggled under the covers. 'It's dark.'

'I know. The dark is going to make it extra exciting. We're going to have fun.'

The child yawned sleepily. 'Where are we going?'

Where? It was a good question.

For a moment Layla's mind blanked, and then she knew exactly what she had to do. Something she'd done many times before. 'We're going to play a game called Hide.' Her mouth dried at the memory, because those games, too, had been played in the dark. Pulling back the covers, she tugged the little girl into her arms, trying desperately not to frighten her. 'We'll just put on your coat in case it gets cold.'

'It's night-time. Why are we playing a game at night-time?'

'That's the best time to play it. I used to play it with my sister when she was your age. There are rules.' She manoeuvred Zahra into the coat. 'First, you mustn't make a sound. Second, you have to do exactly as I say. If I tell you to keep still you have to keep still. If I tell you to run you have to run.'

'This game sounds like fun, but why can't we play it tomorrow?'

Layla caught a flash of light out of the corner of her eye and saw lights approaching in the distance. Torches? Headlights?

Sure now that the threat was real, she cuddled the little girl close. 'Because it's going to be more fun to play it now. We have to go.'

Still sleepy, Zahra glanced back at the bed. 'Can Isis and Horus come too?'

Already halfway to the door, Layla eyed the dogs, watching her from the bed. 'Yes. Good idea. But we have to move quickly.'

Zahra called the dogs and they bounded across the bedroom. 'But who are we hiding from, Layla? What's the point of playing Hide if no one is going to try and find us?'

'We will find a safe place and see how still and silent we

can be. We're going to practise and then, when we're really, really good at it, Daddy can play it with us when he comes home.' Layla knew she was making no sense, and she was so afraid she could hardly make her legs move. Half walking, half running, she kept chatting and pretending it was all a game, trying not to frighten Zahra.

Because she knew now that they were being hunted.

She *felt* it, and the terror rushed over her as familiar and terrifying as it had been when she was a child.

'Zahra, listen to me.' It was a struggle to keep her voice light. 'If you didn't want anyone to find you where would you go? Where is the *best* hiding place around here?'

'Dahl Al Zahki. The Desert Caves.'

Layla had a dim memory of Raz pointing them out to her on a ride earlier in the week. 'Are they close?'

'We can ride there in five minutes.'

Ride.

Layla closed her eyes and faced the inevitable. 'Let's do it.'

'If you really want to be fast we should take Raja.'

'Your father's stallion?'

'I can ride him. You can just hold onto me. I *like* this game.' Zahra was wide awake now and bouncing in her arms. 'I'm glad you woke me up.'

They reached the stables and Layla turned and again saw the flash of lights in the distance. *How long did they have?* 'We'll take Raja. It's a great idea. But how will we find the way?'

'I know the way and so does he. He was born here. My daddy had him from a foal. But you'll have to help me up because he's too big.'

Somehow Layla managed to get both of them on the enormous horse and Zahra giggled.

'His coat feels all warm on my legs. I've never ridden in my nightie before.'

Layla pulled the coat round the child and resisted the temptation to look down. It felt as if her life had come full circle. She'd begun this new chapter by stealing her father's stallion and riding it into the desert, and now she was ending it in a similar way. Only this time she was determined not to fall.

'Go, Zahra. Get us out of here.'

'You've never galloped before.'

'Then it's time I learned and I know you'll be the perfect teacher. Isis—Horus—' she hissed their names '—come.'

The stallion sprang forward, needing no encouragement to unleash all that restrained power. Layla's breath caught and then she was hanging on, trying to remember everything Raz and Abdul had taught her about relaxing into the rhythm.

It was the most terrifying, uncomfortable few minutes of her life, but with each long, pounding stride she knew they were drawing away from whoever was at the other end of the light, so she concentrated on not falling off and let Zahra do the rest.

'We're here.'

They arrived at the caves and Layla slid off the horse, landing with an uncomfortable thud on the uneven ground. Zahra slid into her arms and the dogs stayed close. 'We need to get inside.'

'No. We have to tie Raja up or he could wander off and Daddy will be angry.'

'We'll take him with us deeper into the caves. We need to be out of sight.'

She shone her torch once and saw several tunnels leading off the main cavern. 'Over there—that's a good place to hide.'

'Why are you so good at finding hiding places?'

'Because I used to play this game with my little sister when she was your age.'

But she'd made a cardinal mistake. The horse had provided a quick escape vehicle, but by bringing the animal there was no way they could disguise their presence. 'We have to let Raja loose, Zahra. We *have* to.'

With luck the people tracking them would follow the horse, thinking they were still together.

'No! We can't do that. Daddy will be angry.'

'I'll take the blame. I'll tell him it's all my fault. But we have to let him go.'

'No! I won't let you—'

But Layla had already removed the reins and given the enormous stallion a slap on the rump. Delighted to be free of his reins, Raja launched himself into the darkness while Zahra gave a sob.

'He will hurt himself. He'll—'

'He's going to be fine.' Layla grabbed the child in her arms and sprinted across the cave. Zahra was squirming so badly she almost dropped her.

'But, Layla, he doesn't—'

'Hush.' Layla slammed her hand over the child's mouth and pulled her behind the rocks. 'I can hear someone coming. Don't be frightened, but do not make a sound. Not a sound. Isis—Horus—*down*.' The dogs slunk behind the rock obediently and lay down with them just seconds before lights shone into the cave.

'Don't be scared,' Layla whispered, holding Zahra tightly in her arms. 'I've got you.'

'They cannot both have vanished.'

It was Hassan's voice, speaking the same words he'd spoken the night she'd last seen him. Layla closed her eyes, back in her father's bedroom on the night of his death, only this time the person she was protecting was Raz al Zahki's child.

She hugged Zahra against her, keeping her hand over her mouth as she had done so many times with her sister, and all the time she was wondering how Hassan could possibly have known they were here. How had he even found out about Zahra's existence?

'They have to be here. There is nowhere else they could have hidden.'

Recognising Nadia's voice, Layla felt shock punch through her.

So now she had her answer.

She felt Zahra wriggle and held her tighter, but the sudden movement had dislodged something and sent stones tumbling, the sound magnified by the cavernous walls of their hiding place.

Layla realised she had nothing with which to defend them both. No knife. No weapon of any sort with which to protect Raz's child.

'Stay there, and whatever happens don't move.' Whispering the words, she stood up and moved out from behind the rock just as torchlight swept across the cave and dazzled her eyes.

'It's *her*.' Nadia's voice was thickened with contempt. 'If she's here then the child will be with her.'

'Zahra is asleep in her bed. I left her there when I ran. I assumed it was me you wanted. Well, here I am.' Layla walked forward and saw the glint of Nadia's eyes.

'She's lying. She's never far from the girl because she thinks that's the way to get Raz to love her.'

Before Layla could respond Hassan stepped into the beam of light. She felt a shiver run down her body from neck to toes as she remembered all the occasions he'd stood over her trembling body when she'd run from him as a child.

Determined that Zahra wasn't going to know that same fear, she stood as tall as she could. But he simply smiled.

'The best way to look for something is to hunt it and I know just how to do that.'

He snapped his fingers and before Layla could work out

what he was doing she heard the sound of panting and four Saluki shot into the cave towards her.

Her knees liquid, she stumbled back towards Zahra, determined to protect her, the terror so acute she could hardly walk.

She should have anticipated that he'd use Saluki.

She could hear the dull thud of their paws as they raced across the cave towards her, heard the sharp patter of stones dislodged, the low whine and the panting of the dogs as they drew closer. And then she was on her knees beside Zahra, shielding her, covering her, determined to protect her even if it meant the flesh was torn from her bones.

She braced herself for the feel of hot breath on her neck and then pain, but the growling intensified and Isis and Horus sprang in front of them. And then there was nothing but the most terrifying snarling as the dogs clashed, swirling together in the darkness in some macabre dance that sent dust and fur flying.

'Isis!'

Horrified, Zahra tried to go to them, but Layla held her tightly, wondering helplessly how two dogs could possibly be a match against four. And even if she'd wanted to help she couldn't, because the dogs were wild as they fought each other and she couldn't make out Isis and Horus from Hassan's beasts. The best she could do was take advantage of the distraction.

'Is there another way out of these caves?' She spoke the words urgently but the little girl shook her head.

'Not without ropes.'

It wasn't the news Layla wanted, but just as she was about to carry Zahra deeper into the caves there was the sound of vehicles approaching at speed. The next moment the whole cavern was filled with light and there were shouts and something that sounded like gunfire.

Layla flattened Zahra down on the ground.

The snarling became a whimper.

And then she heard the harsh tones of Raz's voice and knew that the guns and the lights belonged to his security team. Almost melting with relief that she was no longer alone, she snuggled Zahra close, afraid to move until she was sure it was safe.

All around them was pandemonium. Layla kept low, knowing that the best thing she could do was not make the situation more dangerous by moving around.

'Layla? *Layla!*' His voice was raw and desperate, the emotion painful to hear, and she knew she had to reassure him.

'It's fine,' she called out. 'She's safe. She's here with me. They haven't touched her.'

Before she could stop her Zahra wriggled out from under her and started to run towards her father, but then she stopped dead.

'Isis? *Isis!*'

Layla saw that the dog was lying still, her blonde fur coated in blood, while Horus stood guard over her body, a sombre sentinel.

'Oh, no—' Layla ran towards Zahra but the little girl was already on her knees beside the dog, sobs tearing through her chest as she tried to cuddle her.

'Don't die, Isis. Daddy, don't let Isis die. Please *do something.*' She scooped the dog's head onto her lap, stroking, rocking, making a terrible keening sound.

Her distress was so painful to witness Layla felt tears on her own cheeks. She reached the child at the same time as Raz.

'Let me look at her.'

His voice was calm and steady, but Layla noticed that his fingers shook slightly as he gently examined the dog. He snapped a command over his shoulder and someone appeared with a flashlight so that he could take a closer look.

'She's been bitten. We need to stop this bleeding.'

'Here—' Layla ripped off the cord that was holding her robe together and dropped to her knees beside him. 'Make a tourniquet. That should do until we can get her back home.'

Her hands were over his and together they tied it firmly and then tightened it. It was the first time she'd touched a dog voluntarily, but she didn't even think about it until she felt something cold and damp nudge her palm and saw Horus standing next to her, looking at her with anxious eyes.

'Good boy.' Layla hesitated and then reached out and stroked his head. 'She's going to be all right.'

'No, she isn't. They saved us from that bad man,' Zahra sobbed, 'and now Isis is going to die.'

'She is *not* going to die.' Delivering a series of orders, Raz rose to his feet in a fluid movement and peeled his daughter away from her beloved pet. 'But we have to get her help, *habibti*. We have to get her home right now. And you need to come home, too. You need to be brave and put your trust in others.'

Zahra clung to him, her little body shuddering with sobs, and Layla rubbed the tears from her own cheeks so that she could help as Raz's men gently lifted Isis and took her limp body to the nearest vehicle, accompanied by a worried Horus who refused to leave her side.

Layla turned to Raz. 'Where is Hassan?'

'He has been arrested, along with Nadia, who apparently masterminded tonight's episode. They are both being taken to Tazkhan for questioning.'

Layla stared at him, still stunned by the discovery that Nadia had been involved. 'I assumed Hassan had forced her in some way. Why would she do that?'

'Jealousy.' Raz's mouth was grim. 'She was jealous of her sister. Apparently she had some deluded idea that I'd marry *her*. It is something I only discovered in the past few hours.

It explains so much about her behaviour and I am angry with myself for not seeing it sooner.'

'Why would you?' Layla shivered and rubbed Zahra's back gently. 'We need to get her home.'

His gaze lingered on hers. 'How can I ever thank you?'

'You don't need to thank me.'

Raz inhaled deeply. 'There is much I need to say to you.'

Layla was too exhausted to contemplate a conversation. 'It can all wait.'

'The vet says Isis will make a good recovery and Zahra is finally asleep.' His handsome face drawn and tired, Raz walked across the bedroom. 'I have put a mattress next to the dog and both Abdul and Horus are sleeping with her for now, along with four of my security team. It's like a menagerie down there. All I need is for Raja to join them and the circus that is our life will be complete.'

The fact that he'd said 'our' warmed her, as did the wry humour in his voice, but Layla wasn't fooled. She knew how raw he was feeling because she felt the same way. She was still so shocked by everything that had happened she felt disconnected.

The warm sunshine and the soothing sound of the fountain in the courtyard beyond the doors to their bedroom were a contrast to the long, terrifying hours of the night before.

Knowing that she wouldn't be able to rest, she'd taken a hot shower, scrubbed away the physical evidence of their flight through the desert and changed into a practical outfit of trousers and a loose shirt, intending to go and sit with Isis and Zahra.

'I'm so relieved Raja is all right. Zahra was beside herself when I turned him loose, but at that point I was still hoping they wouldn't find us. I'm sorry. I didn't know what else to do.'

'You did the right thing. I still can't believe you rode my

stallion.' Raz shook his head and looked at her in naked disbelief. 'How did you do that?'

'I didn't. I just sat on him. It was Zahra who rode him. It's a good thing she takes after you.'

There was a glint of anger in his eyes. 'They arranged for me to be away last night. They arranged for you to be alone. If you hadn't woken—' He raked his hand through his hair, visibly tense. 'Why did you? Did you hear something? Did they disturb you?'

'No. I wasn't asleep.' She didn't tell him she'd been lying there thinking about him. 'I turned the light on to read and nothing happened. At first I thought it was the bulb and then I realised the whole place was dark and there were no guards. Just like that night—' Realisation dawned and she felt the colour drain from her face. 'Just like that night in the desert a few weeks ago.'

'Yes. That was to have been their first attempt to take my daughter and use her as leverage against me, but you foiled that one, too, by climbing into bed with her. They didn't anticipate that. They weren't prepared for the two of you. But this time they were.'

'How did you find out?'

'I arrived in Tazkhan and had an illuminating conversation with the senior council members, all of whom were surprised by my arrival. As soon as I realised what had happened I returned as quickly as I could, but I was terrified I was going to be too late.' He pulled her into his arms. 'You were so brave. You took my daughter into the desert and you took the dogs with you, and I know how much you fear them.'

'Not any more. I took them because I thought they might protect Zahra and they did. They were unbelievably brave.' She shivered as she relived those awful moments. 'I didn't know how two could possibly win a fight against four, but now I do. Isis and Horus love her so much they would have died for her, and that love gave them ten times the strength of Hassan's dogs. I've never seen anything like it.' Remembering moved her so much that tears sprang into her eyes and spilled onto her cheeks. 'Sorry—I think I'm just very tired.' Embarrassed by her loss of control, she lifted her hand to brush them away, but he was there before her, his fingers gentle as he stroked away her tears.

'You must be exhausted, and *so* stressed after everything that has happened.'

'I'm just relieved. And worried about poor Isis.'

'I am assured by the vet that she is going to be fine. And, on the subject of being fine, I have good news about your sister. Salem contacted me half an hour ago, when we were with Isis. He has Yasmin safe.'

'Really?' The tears still flowed and Layla wondered what on earth the matter was with her that she couldn't get through five minutes without crying. 'You're sure? It's really her?'

'Salem says he has never met a woman who talks as much as she does.'

'Then it's *definitely* her.' Layla was laughing with relief and happiness as she hugged Raz. 'Thank you. You were right to have faith in your brother.'

'So now we have your sister safe, Hassan and Nadia off the scene and Isis recovering, perhaps we can finally focus on our own relationship, *habibti*. There are things I must say to you.'

Not now.

She kept her face pressed to his chest so that he couldn't see the change in her expression. She couldn't cope with any more trauma in one night. *Couldn't cope with hearing him tell her again that he couldn't ever love another woman.*

'There is nothing to say. And we ought to check on Zahra—'

'Zahra is fine for the moment.' He eased her away from him so that she was forced to look at him. 'I have never felt fear as I felt it tonight.'

Hearing the change in his voice, Layla pushed down her own feelings. It was selfish of her to think of herself when he was also in shock. 'It must have been terrible for you, being so afraid for your daughter.'

'I wasn't only afraid for my daughter.' He took her face in his hands and the expression in his eyes made her catch her breath.

'Raz—'

'*Don't* speak.' He covered her mouth with his fingers. 'There are things I have to say and I need to say them without interruption. I owe you an apology.' His words thickened. 'You came to me that night in the desert and I was cold, distant and uncaring. I was *so* hard on you and it shames me to remember it.'

'It shouldn't. I thought your behaviour was very restrained in the circumstances.'

'I should have asked more questions that night. I should have suspected that you had suffered great trauma. But I looked no deeper than the surface and I cannot forgive myself for that.'

'I probably wouldn't have told you even had you asked,' Layla mumbled. 'And you behaved very decently towards me, given everything my family has done to yours.'

'I pride myself on being fair and treating everyone as an individual. You are not responsible for the sins of your family.'

'But you didn't know that. Given everything that had happened, you would have been less than human had you not had reservations about me. You were protecting your family and you would not be the man you are had you not done that. It's one of the things I love about you.' The words slipped out without thought and she saw his eyes darken. 'Respect and admire you,' she said quickly. 'I meant that it is one of the things I respect and admire about you.'

'*Is* that what you meant?'

'Yes.' Trapped, she averted her head, but he caught her chin in his fingers and gently forced her to look at him. 'Raz—'

'You were the one who insisted on honesty in this relationship. You've never been afraid to tell me the truth before. You weren't afraid to tell me I was wrong to trust Nadia and that I shouldn't have kept my daughter's existence a secret from you. You weren't afraid to ask about Nisa, even though most people dare not broach that subject with me. Why would you be afraid to tell me the truth about your feelings?'

Why? Because she wasn't sure she could handle his response.

'Feelings were never part of the deal when we married.'

'That is true. But life does not stand still—as we have both discovered. People change. Feelings change. Pain we believe we cannot endure we somehow learn to live alongside. Although I am pleased to have your respect and your admiration, I would so much rather have the first thing you were offering, *habibti.*' His voice husky, he looked down into her eyes. 'Tell me why you were awake last night. The truth.'

'I couldn't sleep.'

'*Why* couldn't you sleep?'

It was clear he wasn't going to let it drop so Layla gave up, too wrung out to keep fighting him.

'Because I missed you. Because I *love* you—' It was a surprising relief to say it. A relief to finally acknowledge the emotions she'd been holding back. 'I love you. I didn't expect to, I didn't think I could, but I do. And I wouldn't have told you except that you forced the subject, and I hope it doesn't make things awkward because it really shouldn't.'

'Why would it make things awkward?'

Wasn't it obvious?

'Because I know you're not capable of loving another woman. Our marriage was driven by political necessity. We both know that.'

'It is true that it began that way, but sometimes it is less important how something begins, *habibti*, than how it ends.'

Ends?

It was shocking how quickly happiness could turn to misery. 'You want to end it?'

'No! I do *not* want to end it. Not ever. I'm trying to tell you that things have changed. Everything has changed. Including my feelings.' His tone raw, he hauled her against him. 'This is the most important conversation of my life and I'm making a mess of it. I'm *trying* to tell you I love you, too.'

Layla was pressed against him and she could feel the strong thud of his heart against her cheek.

His heart not frozen into ice but warm, healthy and capable of love.

Heat spread through her, driving away the chill that had been part of her since her flight through the desert.

Raz eased her away from him so that he could see her face. 'I loved Nisa. That is a fact and it will never change. We met as children—grew up together.' He frowned slightly, as if he'd never thought much about it before. 'She was always part of my life. I don't even remember either one of us making the decision to marry—it felt inevitable. And then when I lost her—'

Layla slid her arms round him, feeling his pain as her own. 'You honestly don't have to talk about this.'

'I want to. Since I met you it's been easier to talk about it. I was trapped in my old life, clinging to memories because moving on without her felt too hard. And then I met you.'

'That first night—'

'I felt guilty.' His voice was soft. 'It felt like a betrayal. Not just because I was with you, but because that night was so special. I didn't anticipate that what we shared would be so powerful. I rejected it precisely because the chemistry between us was so intense, *habibti*. I'd expected to feel nothing. Instead I felt deeply, and I didn't know how to handle those feelings.'

'I didn't expect you to love me. I didn't expect to love *you*,' Layla confessed honestly. 'I've never loved anyone except my sister. I've never looked at a man and felt anything until that night I met you for the first time. I'd never met a man like you. I'd never met a man who used his strength and power for good rather than personal gain.'

'You were so brave, arriving with nothing but two books.'

His eyes gleamed and she felt the colour darken her cheeks.

'You've taught me everything. It would have been nice to bring something to this marriage and teach you something in return.'

'You have.' Lifting his hand, he touched her cheek. 'You've taught me that life does not stand still. That love can come from unexpected places. That there is always hope. And you've taught me to love again, *habibti*. When you came to me I was so closed off. I couldn't even think about allowing another woman into my life. But instead of putting on pressure you just accepted me as I was and didn't try and change that.'

'I wouldn't want to change it. I know you loved Nisa.'

'Yes, but I've learned that loving you doesn't diminish what I felt for her. It took me a while to accept my feelings for you without guilt. She was part of my past, but you are my future. I consider myself fortunate to have fallen in love twice in a lifetime when many do not ever find themselves in possession of that gift.'

Layla swallowed. 'I didn't think I would. I didn't grow up with expectations of love and happy endings. It just wasn't what I thought about. When I came to you in the desert that night I wasn't thinking about love. All I wanted from this marriage was your respect. I used you as an escape from the life I had and because I knew that without me Hassan could not rule, and he is not a man who should be in a position of power. I didn't expect anything else. I didn't expect you to notice so much about me and be so caring. You think you were hard on me, but there were so many times when you tried to make life easier for me. You noticed I was scared of the dogs and tried to keep them away from me—' She choked slightly. 'No one has ever done anything like that for me before. No one has *ever* wanted to protect me.'

'I never cease to be impressed by your determination to confront everything you fear. Particularly riding my stallion!'

'He was remarkably tolerant. I wonder if he somehow knew he was part of our escape.' Layla gave a half smile. 'And Isis and Horus came too.'

'All your nightmares in one evening,' Raz said dryly, but his hand was gentle as he stroked her cheek. 'You are an example to all of us, *habibti*.

'My biggest nightmare was that something might happen to Zahra. I love her, too. She is so confident and trusting, and I hated the thought of that confidence and trust being crushed.'

'She told me you turned the whole thing into a game so that she wouldn't be scared.' He hesitated. 'When I saw her a moment ago she asked me if she is allowed to call you Mummy.'

'Oh—' Emotion wedged itself in her throat. 'But you—'

'One of the biggest sources of my guilt—and believe me there are many—is the fact that I told you not to think of yourself as my daughter's mother.' His handsome face was paler than usual. 'It was a terrible thing to say. I hope you will forgive me.'

'There's nothing to forgive. You were in the most awful situation, being forced to marry me and—' Layla broke off, her vision blurred by tears. 'Do you know what I think? I think I like what you said just now, about separating the past and the future. Can we do that? And if Zahra is thinking of me as her mother then the future is looking better all the time.'

He hauled her close. 'I didn't think I would ever feel this happy. I didn't think it was possible.'

'Me neither.' She hugged him tightly, feeling happier than she ever had in her life before. 'I love you. I love you so much.'

Raz slid his hand into her hair, his mouth close to hers. 'I will never tire of hearing you say that.'

'It was Avery who noticed the way I felt about you.'

The corners of his mouth flickered into a smile. 'Avery is a master at interfering in the lives of others.'

'But in a good way. She was the one who encouraged me to just be myself. I was very confused. I knew I loved you and I didn't know how to live with those feelings without sharing them with you. I didn't know how to be with you. She was the one who pointed out that I should be myself. Just me. That you deserved to know the real me.'

'And I fell in love with the real you.'

Raz lowered his forehead to hers and she slid her arms around his neck, dizzy with the feelings inside her.

'Could you say that again? Just one more time? I need to keep hearing it.'

'I will be saying it many times. I love you. I will love you forever and always,' he breathed, gathering her against him. '*Enti hayati*. You are my life, *habibti*.'

* * * * *

'I've given the press a story that will melt their cynical little hearts,' Dante said, knowing his tone was sending the temperature in the room into a rapid decline. 'The real thing.'

The frown in her brow deepened.

'The real thing?' Eva asked, her voice as softly decadent as whipped cream.

'Si. *Love.*' The word was like poison on his tongue, making it swell, and his next words sounded thick. 'I've provided them with a true romantic fairytale.'

Without looking up, Eva gave a little scoff of disbelief and began to scratch at the arm of the sofa, making patterns of what looked like love hearts. 'And who is the heroine in this fabricated tale?'

Dante smiled the half-smile that never failed to make women weak at the knees and tumble backwards onto a satin-covered mattress.

'You are, *tesoro.*'

Victoria Parker's first love was a dashing heroic fox named Robin Hood. Then came the powerful, suave Mr Darcy, Lady Chatterley's rugged lover—the list goes on. Thinking she must be an unfaithful sort of girl, but ever the optimist, she relentlessly pursued her Mr Literary Right and eventually found him lying between the cool, crisp sheets of a Mills & Boon®— her obsession was born.

If only real life was just as easy…

Alas, against the advice of her beloved English teacher to cultivate her writer's muse, she chased the corporate dream and acquired various uninspiring job titles *and* a flesh-and-blood hero before she surrendered to that persistent voice and penned her first Mills & Boon® romance. Turns out creating havoc for feisty heroines and devilish heroes truly *is* the best job in the world.

Victoria now lives out her own happy-ever-after in the north-east of England, with her alpha exec and their two children—a masterly charmer in the making and, apparently, the next Disney Princess. Believing sleep is highly overrated, she often writes until three a.m., ignores the housework (much to her husband's dismay) and still loves nothing more than getting cosy with a romance novel. In her spare time she enjoys dabbling with interior design, discovering far-flung destinations and getting into mischief with her rather wonderful extended family.

A recent title by the same author:

PRINCESS IN THE IRON MASK

Did you know this is also available as an eBook?
Visit www.millsandboon.co.uk

A REPUTATION
TO UPHOLD

BY
VICTORIA PARKER

MILLS &
BOON

First published in Great Britain 2013
by Mills & Boon, an imprint of Harlequin (UK) Limited.
Harlequin (UK) Limited, Eton House, 18-24 Paradise Road,
Richmond, Surrey TW9 1SR

© Victoria Parker 2013

ISBN: 978 0 263 90701 8

Harlequin (UK) policy is to use papers that are natural, renewable and recyclable products and made from wood grown in sustainable forests. The logging and manufacturing process conform to the legal environmental regulations of the country of origin.

Printed and bound in Spain
by Blackprint CPI, Barcelona

A REPUTATION
TO UPHOLD

For Tony, who has developed a saintly patience with
regard to his 'missing' wife. For my amazing children,
Ben and Issy, who graciously accept when Mummy is
busy. And for Megan Haslam and Kathryn Cheshire
for their keen insights and endless encouragement.

Thank you all.

And finally, I dedicate this book to Nanna Beena,
Auntie Dot, Lynn, Helen and my beautiful sister, Phillipa.
To always remember that life is not about waiting for the
storm to pass…it's about learning to dance in the rain.
As my characters Dante and Eva are about to discover…

CHAPTER ONE

'DON'T DO THIS to me, Finn. Please. Not today.'

Over the din of society's elite, Eva St George crushed her mobile phone against the shell of her ear and sank a fingertip in the other. Hoping the snowy crackle was a particularly bad line and not an indication that her brother was still knee-deep in Switzerland.

'Damn.' Pushing off the oriental silk-covered wall, she swerved through the cliques—women dripping in jewels, adorned in the latest haute couture, and male powerhouses garbed in bespoke evening wear. And all the while her eyes were locked on the ornate double doors leading from London's most prestigious ballroom. 'Finn, give me a minute.'

Twenty-foot banners hung from the high ceiling in swathes of candyfloss-pink emblazoned with crystal love-hearts—the emblem for Breast Cancer United, the charity Eva and Finn supported. One night a year, together, they launched the fund-raiser in honour of their mother.

Right now, the omission of togetherness was the sting of a needle sinking into her heart.

Palm flat, she pushed the heavy oak and swept into the vast reception of the Royal Assembly Rooms, wobbling on her five-inch heels as plush fawn carpet gave way to sleek graphite marble.

'Okay. Talk to me. Where are you?'

'Look, sis, I'm really sorry. Every airport is closed. I've

even tried to pay some rookie half a mill to fly me there but he can't get clearance.'

Pain exploded behind Eva's eyes and her hand shot up to her temple. 'Oh, God.'

'You can do this, Eva.'

Eyes darting this way and that, she spotted an alcove and slunk into the small space, swallowing past the wretched knot in her throat. 'Finn. They're expecting both of us. How can I possibly…?' She stopped herself short. Inhaled long and deep, then pursed her lips, releasing the warm air in one soft stream. Knowing full well she *could* do it on her own; she just didn't relish the thought. Speaking in front of hundreds of people who were no doubt waiting for the 'Diva' to nosedive wasn't the nicest prospect in the world. Not only that, in a strange sort of way it felt as if they were letting their mother down. And, since her death, Eva had let her down enough. But the last thing she wanted was for Finn to worry or feel guilty.

'Don't worry, okay? I can handle this.'

'Of course you can,' he said with an encouraging bluster that said he wasn't entirely convinced. 'We're talking about the woman who has just won the admiration of Prudence West, the soon-to-be Duchess of Wiltshire. Congrats, by the way.'

Eva rubbed her temple, waiting for her brain to catch on to the change of subject amidst the escalating throb, as she mentally altered a speech for *two* speakers. Problem was, it was taking a while and, by the time she realised what she was doing, her fingers wore more make-up than her face.

Scrambling in her vintage clutch for a tissue before she ruined her best dress, she said, 'Thanks, Finny. Prudence West is lovely. She adored my gown designs.'

'So she should—anyone with an ounce of taste can recognise a star in the making. Westminster Abbey, huh?' His deep voice paused as if he were relishing every word. 'My little sister under the royal spotlight. I'm so proud of you.'

Eva smiled and thought, not for the first time, how much

she missed him. Finn was the only sane person in the family. Well, as sane as any jet-setting racing driver could be.

Tissue-hunting abandoned, Eva slipped her fingers from her clutch and leaned against the narrow ochre wall. 'I can see perfectly well what you're doing and I love you for it. And by all means give me an Abbey full of duchesses and I'll collude in the art of dazzling every one. Then sit me behind my machine or in my design studio and I'll make their every dream come true. But when it comes to this…' A heavy sigh gushed from her mouth, making her lips tingle with dryness. 'Dad's here too, playing devil's advocate over his flurry of ex-wives as they hurl daggers at each other. Honestly, Finn, the man would give Henry the Eighth a run for his money. He's half cut, making an utter fool of himself. Why can't he have more respect, especially tonight?'

'Head high, turn a blind eye.'

'Good in theory, lousy in practice.' With her free hand she rubbed her bare shoulder to ward off a sudden ominous chill. 'I've worked so hard for this, Finn. If something goes wrong tonight my face will be splashed on every tabloid in the country.'

'Nothing is going to go wrong. Listen…' she heard him inhale; the fact that her stoic-under-pressure sibling felt the need inched her tension levels as high as the opulent chandelier filling the reception '…I was worried about you. I know how much today means to you. So I sent…'

A group of guests hustled past and she turned her back to them to face a mural of the Angel Gabriel filling the inside wall of the alcove. She just hoped it was a good omen. 'Sent? Sent what?'

'He won't crowd you but he'll be there if you need him.'

Need? She didn't *need* anyone. To be continually let down? No, thanks.

Hold on… *He*? A thread of unease tightened around her

chest, then unravelled so fast her heart began to whirl. 'He? Who's he? You keep breaking up.'

'I've…asked Vitale…come in my place.'

Before her eyes the Angel Gabriel morphed into Lucifer, horns and all, while Eva went up in flames. '*Dante*? No way— call him off.'

'Call him *off*?' A dark chuckle hummed down the line. 'Despite his bloodthirsty reputation, he isn't a Rottweiler, Eva.'

'Oh, yes, he is.' Voice feathery, her hormones went on a rampage, tearing through her body, piping her veins with more heat. 'He's…he's a snarling, arrogant brute.'

'Hey, he's a good guy. I'd trust him with my life. He won't let me down.' That was exactly what she was afraid of. 'Dante wouldn't be the global success he is today if he purred like a pussycat. You don't know him, Eva.' She knew enough but she had no intention of telling Finn that. He'd ask why and then she *would* be in trouble.

Air whipped in and out of her lungs. Her breasts threatened to escape from the ruched bands of cerise satin and she pressed the flat of her hand to her stomach, begging the tremulous churn to subside. Except her fingers shook so badly her tummy began to swirl like a washing machine on full spin.

'I thought he was staying in Singapore, setting up his precious department store. Not that the man hasn't got enough of them.' That was another thing Finn was good for—dropping information on Dante Vitale without her having to ask questions. She liked to know when he honoured London with his presence so she could go into hiding. Ridiculous. How old was she? Too old. She thanked heaven Finn was trying to speak again before that line of thought took hold.

'He's back to get…' The line hissed. His voice faded in and out. 'I was speechl…'

'Finn! Are you there?' Oh, God. 'I'm going to kill you, Finn, you hear me? With my bare hands. I'll never forgive you for this.' A total lie. She'd forgive him anything. But *Dante*? Her nerves were already fraying like torn taffeta.

The line's-gone-dead tone resounded through her head like a death blow and her eyes shuttered. Trust Finn to pour petrol on the blaze without even realising it.

Breathe, Eva, breathe.

Okay. She had two choices. Stand. Or topple off her brand-new stilettos. And wouldn't the vultures love that!

No choice really. Standing tall, spine pin-straight, she sucked in air. *Get a hold of yourself. Remember why you're here.*

Of course she could face the upper echelons of society and make her annual speech. So she didn't have Finn by her side—so what? She was a grown woman who was forging her own way to success. She'd just landed one of the biggest contracts of the decade and she refused to let her inebriated father, his ex-wives or the mighty Dante Vitale witness her fall from grace.

It had taken years to climb from the depths of hell after her mother's funeral. Thankfully, the passage of time had washed the grime from her past. No longer was she faced with another hideous front page photograph every morning while every tacky tabloid in the country savaged her reputation. And she wasn't going back there. Ever. Unless it was to showcase her creations and prove to the world she was more than the daughter of a famous designer and a notorious eighties pop star.

Chin up, shoulders pinned, she sauntered back into the ballroom where the air was awash with cultured tones and the tinkle of feminine flirtation.

Turning a blind eye to her father's attention-seeking wave, she hit the wide mahogany bar and gripped the thick brass rail surrounding it.

Smiling sweetly at the bartender, she ordered her usual. 'Sparkling mineral water, please.'

She could do this.

Definitely.

Then it hit her—a deliciously warm musky scent embracing her body in cashmere and teasing her dormant senses to life. Dizzying need, long forgotten, popped her eardrums to bring his dark, rich, Italian lilt direct to her brain in high definition.

'Being a good girl tonight, are we, Eva?'

Skin erupting with a million pinpricks, her stomach wove a torrid sensual spell. It took every stitch of effort to stand tall, keep her head high and inhale enough oxygen so she didn't pass out.

'It's all in a good cause, Dante,' she said, proud of her strong, if a little sassy voice—the adage 'fight fire with fire' flaming to mind.

Ungluing her sexy heels, she forced an even sweeter curve upon her lips and turned oh, so languidly to face him. And realised the strength of Hercules couldn't have prepared her.

Air locked at the base of her throat as she collided with eyes the colour of burnt umber, gleaming with intelligent purpose and deeply set in a face that could only be described as pure Italian masculinity. Satin-sheen golden skin, an abundance of thick, glossy saddle-brown hair tumbling over his forehead and flicking over his ears.

Eva fiddled with the strap of her handbag to stop herself from tracing the curve of his gorgeous cynical mouth—a mouth she'd spent half her adolescence yearning to kiss.

There was something almost deadly about his beauty, she thought, as she skimmed the wide set of his shoulders, encased in the finest black evening-wear money could buy, the tuxedo only serving to lend his sophistication a ruthless, savage edge.

Eva licked her suddenly dry lips. 'Well, this is a nice surprise.'

'I doubt it,' he said, his fiercely intent gaze searing over her face.

The man saw too much and the idea that he could see inside her, her heart thumping full pelt, her blood rising to boiling-point, peeved her off. She was over this man—had been for years.

Although, in all fairness, it was perfectly natural to still find his dark magnetism so devastating. Right at this minute she knew every woman in the room had been enticed into a delirious state—staring at the forbidden, wanting past endurance. More fool them because never again would he hold power over her. Where her once vulnerable and innocent heart had been deceived, now she knew the difference between lust and love. And she wanted neither. From Dante or any man.

Picking up her crystal tumbler, she relished the cool condensation against her palm and used it to motion to an old client. 'Look, I'm not sure what Finn told you, but I don't need my hand held to speak to a few friends. I'm a big girl. I suggest you go home to your latest mistress. Business or otherwise.'

Renowned for his stupendous retail mind, his financial wizardry and his ferocious talent in the bedroom, Dante Vitale was a one-night wonder. With the exception of his wife, Natalia, of course. If she remembered correctly, that had been a two-month wonder. Almost as long as her father lasted with one of his fine specimens.

The worst thing was, she'd been so pathetically enraptured with him she would've taken one night. But his taste ran to sultry brown eyes, sleek brunettes with svelte sun-kissed bodies. Pure Italianesque. Little wonder he'd never given Eva a second glance. Until she'd literally thrown herself into his path. And even then…

Her face began to burn as the mortal humiliation came back to her in a torrid rush of heat. 'If you'll excuse me, I need to mingle.' Feet bolting, she managed two steps before a steel arm wrapped around her waist and hauled her back to the bar.

Eva shuddered from top to toe, the melting sensation back with a vengeance as a lock of his shockingly thick hair fell across one eye as he tossed her a 'stay put' look.

He ordered a finger of single malt and pinned her in place

with the wide span of his hand, only his thumb and forefinger touching her satin sheath. The tiniest contact enough to send all the heat from her face down to her knickers.

'Don't you think your dress is a little revealing, Eva?' he said with a satiric bite. 'This is a charity fund-raiser, not a nightclub.' He knocked back the shot and carefully lowered the glass to the polished mahogany bar.

'There's nothing wrong with my dress and you know it.' It was nun-like in comparison to what his usual dates wore. 'Why are you here, Dante? I understand what Finn was trying to do. He has no idea what happened. But you...' She shook her head. 'You should've refused. Especially since you can't bear to look at me for more than five seconds.'

As if to deny her accusation, he deigned to look at her— with such cold detachment he might well have tossed the whisky-coated rocks in her face.

'I'm here because I owe Finn, nothing more. As you've accurately pointed out, I have far more *pleasurable* things to do than babysit a loose cannon. But if you think for one minute I intend to break my word to him, you are sadly mistaken.'

She closed her eyes momentarily. 'People grow, people change.'

'No. They do not.' He leaned a touch closer and she went strangely woozy. 'Especially when they still have the power to stop traffic.'

Only Dante could twist a compliment into an insult with that cynical mouth. His dark eyes flickered down her body and she cursed her penchant for decadent ice cream.

Then he continued in that same thick, dark drawl, 'That was quite a pile-up you caused in Piccadilly Circus. Did you enjoy the world staring at your body?'

Distaste filled her mouth. 'That billboard was a campaign for—'

He waved her off with a dismissive flick and Eva sighed. What was the point of arguing with a man who saw everything in black and white? So she stuck with the facts, praying he'd just walk away. 'Go home, Dante. I don't need a chaperone.'

'Apparently you do,' he said, his caustic gaze dropping to the mineral water she held in a death grip. 'At least you're not plastered.'

She gasped. And to think she'd once thought herself in love with the guy!

'You're locked in the past. You don't know me. I drown in work these days.'

'Really.' One word, brimming with derision, and she wondered if he even knew what she did for a living. He'd been in Singapore for the past year or so, Italy before that, but he'd seen Finn on occasion. Maybe he didn't care enough to ask, but frankly she'd had enough of being dragged through the wringer.

Her mouth shaped for speech, ready to tell him what she'd achieved. All about her stunning new boutique, the new contract for the soon-to-be Duchess she'd fought tooth and nail for—

When suddenly he snorted like a displeased horse. 'And what work would that be, Eva?' Eyes glittering, he traced her décolletage, a look that turned almost cruel—a striking contrast to the velvet now stroking his voice. 'Slipping between the warm sheets of the morning papers...*hot* off the press. Now I'm back in London, what will I wake to find tomorrow? I wonder.'

Eva gritted her teeth and tightened her fingers around her clutch, the temptation to swipe the mocking look off his face far beyond her usual realm of control. Honestly, what was the point of defending herself? He'd made up his mind. It shouldn't hurt so much, it really shouldn't. And the only reason her insides felt as if they were being picked apart was because she wanted him gone.

Chin up, she was determined to stand her ground. This time there would be no regrets.

'Is this the support you promised Finn? To come in here, berate me, when you obviously have no idea what I've been doing for the past few years? Claw at my confidence before I have to go on stage? *Wow.* I'll be sure to tell him what a grand job you did. Now, get your hand off me and disappear into the night. That is your usual parting gift, after all.'

Dante tightened his grip on her warm stomach and felt the muscles clench under his palm, the tiny contractions spiking his pulse so hard his jaw set. It took no more than a second to convince himself he was misreading the pain in Eva's eyes. Then he snatched his hand back and set her free.

A wisp of her sultry scent drifted up his nose as she spun with the grace of a ballerina and sashayed through the clumps of dowdy patrons—a dark pink firework amongst a sea of sickly candy, her position as co-founder of the charity blatant in her choice of colour.

Dante tore his gaze from her sinful behind and ordered another shot of single malt.

Maledizione! He'd handled that *really* well. And she was right. He should've told Finn to find someone else. The crackling atmosphere was like a dark storm brewing in the room, threatening to rain destruction on them all.

Flawless, that was the word people used for her beauty. But it was a lie. Her flaws lay buried deep, hidden under dark lashes, lurking in the wary shadows of her mesmerising mossy-green eyes.

Assuming he'd buried his memories was his first mistake, because he could still feel the damp warmth of her blanched almond skin beneath his lips, the pure tone hinting at an innocent enchantment that was her dangerous allure. The only truth was her curves, which should, quite frankly, be illegal.

Heat, swift and decadently erotic, flooded his veins.

Eva St George. Wild child. Fantasy pin-up for every hot-blooded man.

Raising the glass to his lips, he downed the second finger of Scotch, the warm amber liquid lubricating his throat and inflaming the annoyance swirling in the pit of his stomach. He should *not* have touched her again. But if there was one thing Dante loathed it was a woman turning her back on him. He did the walking. He was in control. Always.

It didn't help that the only time he'd ever lost it was with Eva. No matter how many times he insisted he had merely been comforting her on the night of her mother's funeral, he couldn't escape the fact that sanity had slipped from his grasp. And he'd almost taken her...*Cristo*, on the floor of the pool-house!

And tonight. She must be hurting. *That* was the pain in her eyes. *That* was why Finn had asked him to come. Because he knew Dante would remember. For all her wild ways, she'd loved her mother and watching her struggle with remembered grief was not a sight he relished. That, he insisted, was because of his loyalty to her brother, his *friend*.

The thought of Finn brought him back down into the ballroom with an almighty thud. He had to forget the past, deliver on his promise to Finn and get the hell out of here. He could be nice. For at least twenty minutes.

Sliding a fifty across the bar, he turned to face the bustling glitterati, taking less than five seconds to find her, courtesy of the dress that smothered her luscious body as if poured with silken oil.

Eva now had a flute of champagne in her long slim fingers and curved those famous do-me-now lips to lure another man. *You don't know me. People change, she says!*

He didn't want to hear it. For the first fifteen years of his life he'd hoped, prayed, pleaded for such *change* from his equally wild mother. So he'd switched off years ago to Finn's ramblings about his precious little sister. Diverting conversation had quickly become an art form. Finn naturally had a soft spot for her and Dante liked the man too much to smash his rose-tinted view.

Shaking his head, he crossed the space between them, the stark light of the bar fading as the crowds parted and he moved deeper into the extravaganza; where butlers in black and white vintage garb enticed the waifs with canapés and tall glasses of pink froth, and the pianist seduced with classical opera which seeped through his skin and eased the tension from his spine. By the time he caught up, Eva sat alone at one of the huge round tables, washed in a soft peach hue courtesy of a thousand tiny crystal tea lights.

Sitting on the deep velvet seat beside her, he pinched the stem of her champagne flute and handed it to a passing waiter before ordering his senses to go on mute. 'Here we are again.'

Her dark blonde head snapped around, the long, luxuriant waves swaying about her bare shoulders. 'Can't you take the hint? I. Am. Fine. You need to. Go. Home.'

Dante leaned back, knowing full well he projected ennui. 'No.'

Her eyes glittered with the first sparks of her temper but he had to give her credit because she banked the fire, no doubt disinclined to cause a scene. 'What are you doing back here anyway? I thought Singapore had captured your full attention.'

'Impossible. Nothing is enough to capture my full attention.'

She leaned her perfect body into the back of the chair and crossed her arms, the action slow, controlled, pushing her breasts upward, affording him a delicious view of her satiny cleavage. He allowed his eyes to drop. That was what she wanted, wasn't it? His full undivided attention. It wouldn't last—it never did.

'How stupid of me to forget,' she said, her husky voice mocking. 'Guess I thought business was different.'

Dante tore his eyes from her. 'Singapore was a huge success. Two Vitale department stores in twelve months *and* one of the most lavish malls in the world.'

'You sound disappointed. That wasn't enough?'

'It's never enough.' Now he had his sights set on the biggest prize of all. The jewel in the Vitale crown would be the Knightsbridge store he'd wanted for almost a decade. He just needed to convince the seller that Dante was the superlative choice. Problem was, Yakatani, the staunch Japanese businessman, wanted a family man and that particular vessel had sailed four years ago. Flying the flag of treacherous betrayal.

A swell of rabid emotion, black and cold, inflated his chest and he fisted his hand where it lay on the pristine white tablecloth. When he caught Eva glancing down he stretched his fingers wide.

'So what now?' she asked, a small furrow lining her brow. 'Why come to London?'

'Why not?' he said with a careless shrug that tore at his stiff muscles as he tamped down on the dark current of unwanted, loathsome feeling.

'There's more to it than that. I can see it in your face.'

She saw far too much.

Dante cleared his throat and glanced around the room, content that she would drop the conversation when he wasn't forthcoming. Seconds blurred into minutes of warding off the waves of sensuality that poured effortlessly from the woman beside him, which only served to heighten his determination in what now felt like an enjoyable exercise in self-restraint.

So he focused on the towering glass vase taking centre stage on the table, overflowing with cream and dusky pink blooms, each rose delicately wrapped in ivory voile to cup the open bud, and streams of pearls cascading from a lofty hydrangea to pool upon the tablecloth. And, before he knew it, his mind's eye trailed those very pearls over every inch of Eva's body, skimming up those long satiny legs and teasing them between her thighs, where she was hot and wet—

Cristo, for the life of him he could not understand why fatal attraction still poured through his blood...scoring his cheekbones. For a second he wondered if he'd made a sound.

'Dante, are you okay?'

There, he had his answer, Dante noted, without allowing himself to react.

Lazily, he shifted in his seat. Turned and raised one dark brow. '*Sì*. Of course.'

'Well, you didn't answer me,' she said. And for a second he was thrown, his back nudging the velvet pad of the chair. When was the last time someone had the audacity to demand an answer from him? Then again, this was Eva and he should've expected nothing less. Any woman who could turn sweet grieving vulnerability into an all-out seductive war on mankind took daring to a whole new level.

Dante yanked at the sleeves of his white dress shirt until shards of diamond light bounced off his platinum cufflinks. He didn't suppose Eva would be a risk to his deal. She was more front page scandal than the business section type and he needed to talk about something before he touched her.

'I was considering your question: why London?' He drew his answer out. Waited until he had her rapt attention. Waited to feel the power of the word on his tongue, the weight of it lifting his spirits. 'One word. Hamptons.'

'Nooo,' she breathed, evidently interested. Although he guessed it was merely the conditioned response of a practised woman.

Still, he allowed himself a small smile. It was almost his. He could feel the power of ownership fizzing in his blood.

'Hamptons have the most beautiful departments I've ever seen,' her voice now wistful.

Dante cottoned on to the reason for her enthusiasm. Shopping. Every woman's idea of nirvana. To someone like Eva, he imagined the experience akin to an orgasm.

With mind-blowing speed and precision, his imagination

inflamed, offering him an erotic image of Eva exploding under his fingertips…beneath his mouth…coating his tongue. Her glorious body arching like a bow…

A loud female voice shot through the haze and Dante winced. *Maledizione*, he needed sex—to drive out the tension of the last few weeks that had slowly, surely pervaded his body. That was the issue here. It had nothing to do with *her*.

'Ladies and gentlemen, please give a warm welcome to our co-founder, Eva St George.'

Rapturous applause filled the air and Dante watched the rose hue drain from Eva's cheeks. Watched her throat work, the slender column pulsing.

'Eva? What is it?'

'Nothing. I'm fine,' she said with such ease that he realised his imagination was playing tricks on him. Again.

'Of course you are,' he said as he nodded towards the podium where the operatic beauty who was tonight's entertainment stood waiting. If the card she'd slipped him earlier was anything to go by, she was more than willing to *perform* personally at his request. 'Show them Eva St George, the Princess of the Press.'

She looked at him then. Properly. For the first time since he'd arrived. Her eyes were swirling tempests which spoke of barely concealed anger. Was she still vexed with him? Even after he'd sat and spoken to her for at least ten minutes?

Dante almost asked what more she expected of him, but each guest now stood waiting. Watching.

'You'll be fine,' he said. 'What are you waiting for? Go.'

'It's not that,' she said, scratching at her lower lip. His eyes narrowed on her short, unpolished fingernails. 'Dante, listen. If I only ever ask this one thing of you, will you do it?'

He didn't like the sound of this. Women and favours were a risky business. There were only three things to be certain of in this life. Ownership, power and control.

'Ask me,' he said.
'Will you leave? Now. Please.'

Eva stepped down from the podium, willing her ribbon-like legs to keep her upright. She'd never thought it was physically possible to want to cry and whoop at the same time but now she knew. All she'd had to do was stand on a stage—in front of *hundreds* of people—on her *own*, and pour her heart out.

But she'd done it. She'd actually done it!

Slightly deaf from a thundering show of hands, she gripped the hand rail and tottered down the steps from the stage. From the corner of her eye, she saw her father beckoning and the temptation to go to him was so strong her feet altered course. But the sight of Claire, wife number six, tugging on his arm stopped her mid-step and she feigned ignorance. There was a happy bubble floating in her chest and no way was that woman popping it.

After a few obligatory handshakes, Eva spotted the heavy gold brocade curtains shrouding the double doors leading onto the terrace. She'd prefer a hot bath and eight hours' sleep, but in her position leaving early was out of the question. So she'd take ten minutes' peace instead. Escape beckoned and, like a prowling cat, she edged around the room, slinking around the guests. She slithered through the small gap in the curtains onto the terrace beyond and quietly closed the door behind her....

And walked into a dense wall of nipping icy air. The fight left her body in one long rush and her shoulders slumped. 'It's over.' Done. For the girl who'd always found large crowds intimidating, she wished her mother could've seen her standing tall.

Wrapping her hands around her upper arms to ward off the chill, she tipped her head skyward, gazing at the beauty of nature's palette—the richest blue imaginable, sparkling with diamanté-studded brilliance. Focused on the biggest, the brightest star and revivified the words she spoke every year, only on this night. *'I miss you. I've made mistakes—so many mistakes—but I'm trying to move on. Make something of my life. Be the person you knew I could be. And I swear I'll make you proud if it's the last thing I do.'*

Closing her eyes, she became lost in time, remembering the sight of her mother teaching her how to work with her nimble fingers. How to stitch another beautifully perfect pearl on dense shot silk and create someone's dream, fill it with romance and beauty and love—all the things she would never have. Only gift. Just as her mother had for women the world over. Until the dark shadows had come knocking and the world went black, everyone left.

Dante.

Thank God he'd left earlier. The thought of him watching her. His beautiful, intense gaze was like a brain-wiping device—

'Eva.'

She flinched and spun around as her hand flew up to her chest to stop her heart bursting through her skin.

'Dante,' she breathed. 'I thought you'd gone. I asked you to.'

He stood in the shadows, face dark, body rigid, his hands stuffed deep in his trouser pockets. 'I gave my word to Finn. Let us call it a compromise.'

'So you sat out here the entire time?'

'Like I said, I promised Finn I would be here if you needed me.'

I needed you once. You left.

As if the last five years had disappeared, the same thoughts began to run through her head, the pictures replaying like an old black and white movie. *Hold me. Touch me. Take me.*

'I don't need anyone.' Not any more. Her warm breath filled the air like a puffy cloud but her voice, icy and brittle, didn't sound as if it belonged to her.

No words. He simply looked out towards the gardens where the cool mist lay like a thick veil, swirling as if beckoning its master back into the Cimmerian lair. And that air of danger seemed to thicken further still, become seductive in its intensity as Dante turned back and closed the short distance between them. Through the dim light she couldn't make out his expression but the heat pouring from his body wreaked chaos on her senses.

'It was a good speech, Eva,' he said, his deep voice imbued with warm sincerity—a hint of the man she once knew. *No, Eva, that man did not exist.* 'Your mother would be proud of you.'

Oh, God. Hold it together. Hold it together. 'Thank you,' she said, but it was a choked sound that tore from her soul and if he didn't leave right now, she was going to...

He growled, long and low, as if he understood, and hauled her into his arms. And the past crashed into the present with heart-stopping brutality. No thought, no hesitation, she buried her face in Dante's neck, drank in his expensive, darkly sensual cologne and luxuriated in the lashing strength of his arms around her, his long fingers fanning the bare skin on her back....yet he said nothing. He was just *there*. Where she needed him.

No. No! She didn't need him. She didn't need any man. Never had, never would. They let you down, left. Brought nothing but heartache and pain.

So pull away—you have to pull away.

Except...where once cold, she could now feel Dante's hot breath caressing the underside of her ear, whispering over the highly sensitised skin of her neck and she trembled from tip to toe. *Pull away, Eva—do it now.* So why did she ignore the screaming in her head and answer the flaming shrill in her blood to sink her fingers into his gorgeous thick hair and pull him closer still?

Another husky, cursing groan rumbled up his hard chest, vibrating over her aching breasts, and her heart began to thrash against her ribcage. This was not good. It felt good but it was a bad, bad idea. He hated her, for Chrissakes. And hadn't she already learned her lesson with this man?

Loosening her grip on his neck, she eased down from her tippy toes, her fingertips scoring down his sculpted shoulders, unfurling to push him away. But when her palms smoothed over red-hot silk and she felt the carved perfection of his body, heat splashed through her midriff, flooding her core, banishing all thought and she wanted... *More.*

Suddenly his lips were *there*, hovering over hers, and *oh*, the temptation to touch again, taste him, to see if he was just as thrillingly wonderful as she remembered, made her slide her lips across his in a gossamer-soft stroke...press a moist kiss to the corner of his full mouth...

Dante's entire body hardened to iron ore....

A flare of electricity danced across her skin and, right then, she knew her mistake. His power had undergone a seismic shift and increased tenfold over the years. Which made him even more dangerous than she'd ever thought possible.

As if he heard her question the force of his dominance, his large hands curved around her waist and cinched vice-tight until she could barely breathe. Then he lifted her entire weight from the floor as if she weighed nothing more than a spool of French lace.

Crushing her body to his, he murmured in her ear, so dark, so quiet, she almost didn't hear him. 'You cannot help yourself, can you, Eva? What is it you want this time? Another night—or shall I just take you up against the wall?'

What? Oh, oh, God. Hot and sharp, a prick of hateful regret stabbed her throat. So when her words came they were laden with biting precision. 'In your dreams, Dante.'

A loud throat-clearing from behind acted like a fist striking glass, shattering the moment. As soon as Dante slackened his grip she jolted back and slammed into the wall, wincing as rough stone bit into her skin.

Claire and her father stood at the top of the stone steps, just watching like a couple of bloody voyeurs.

'Well, well, well,' said Claire. 'What have we here?'

Eva stabbed her palms with blunt nails. 'Oh, I…' What on earth was she supposed to say?

She risked a look at Dante. He stood like cast bronze. Just staring at Eva. Eyes hard, jaw so stiff she fancied his teeth ached. He was angry. No. He was furious. With her. Well, he wasn't the only one!

'I was just saying to Nick, here,' Claire said, all innocence and light, catching Eva's attention, 'where has that *gorgeous* boy got to? I want to be the first to congratulate him.'

Eva felt Dante stiffen beside her and the air became so heavy she could feel it bearing down upon her shoulders.

Ohhh, something was not right. Anguish unravelled behind her breast and Eva knew in an instant that she was about to be very stupid. She was about to fall in the trap Claire was spinning for her. But she was missing something here and she didn't like it one bit.

'Congratulate him?' Eva asked.

Claire's ice-blue eyes glittered with venom. 'Didn't you know? Dante here is engaged to my old school chum, Rebecca Stanford.'

Eva blinked, sure she mustn't have heard correctly. He was getting married again? '*What*?'

'Yes,' said Claire. 'She came to see me yesterday after she flew in from Singapore.'

Eva sucked in air so quickly she almost lost her balance. This was *not* happening. But Claire hadn't finished hammering the nails in her coffin yet.

'We had a lovely lunch with Prudence West. I believe you're designing her gown. Such an honour.'

Eva felt Dante's gaze burning into her cheek. She couldn't look at him. She hated him right now. Years of hard work, clawing her reputation back from the brink. Working eighteen hour days to build the Eva St George brand. And then one look at this devil incarnate and everything was tossed to hell!

'I hope she forgives you, Eva. It's not nice to poach someone else's fiancé.'

Eva reached out for Claire's arm, knowing the violent quiver of her hand betrayed her inner state but she was too far gone to care. 'Listen, Claire, you're taking this all the wrong way. Dante is my...' What? *Friend*? Claire was too clever to fall for that blazing lie. And how much, if anything, had she heard? Brain reeling, Eva tried to think of their last words. Something about...*oh, God*—taking her against the wall! 'There is *nothing* going on here.'

'Didn't look that way to me. Oh, don't worry, my lips are sealed. Although I feel I should warn you.'

From the corner of her eye, Eva saw Dante shift his attention to the swell of her chest. Heard him groan in disgust.

But, before she had the chance to follow his gaze, Claire spoke. 'You haven't taken the microphone off your dress.'

CHAPTER TWO

DANTE'S HAND SHOT to the ruffled bodice of Eva's gown and he curled his fingers around the small black mike, warm from her—or should he say *their*—body heat and tore it free.

He dropped the plastic shell to the frosted stone and crushed it beneath his heel in a satisfying crack.

'Please tell me…' she whispered, standing tall, lifting her chin in the face of adversity '…that what just happened didn't really happen. I'm just in some nightmare. I mean, *you* are here, after all.'

Dante held up one flat palm to prevent another word until he'd at least shaved the edge off his volatile mood and figured out what the hell was going on.

Nick St George paused as his viper wife tried to tug him back into the ballroom and Dante fired the spineless man with the Vitale glare before they disappeared from view. How could he have stood there and let that bitch set Eva up for a fall? What she was hurtling into he had no idea, but he was determined to find out.

As for him…*Cristo*, he'd bet his Lamborghini that within five minutes Rebecca would hear of his *apparent* indiscretion. A shaft of unease fired through his gut, yet, as quickly as it flared, he thrust it away. Rebecca would be easily placated. The good old-fashioned way.

Eva smoothed her tight sheath over her curvaceous hips, brushing the wrinkles free. 'I have to get out of here,' she said. 'I have to think.' Head swiveling, she searched the floor. 'There's little point going back in there; Claire will have me hung, drawn and quartered by now.' She spotted her bag leaning against the old stone wall and bent over to snatch it up.

Dante's heart rate kicked up a few thousand beats per minute as the heart-shaped curve of her full derrière filled his vision and brought forth a multitude of sinful images.

Cristo, she was lethal.

He tore his eyes away as she straightened up and shimmied past him, heading for the stone steps. 'Well done, Dante; you've most likely just ruined me. At the ball in honour of my mother!'

Dante blinked. '*I* have ruined *you*? Forty minutes I've been in your company and already you have wreaked havoc in my life.' Every time. *Dannazione*, the woman never failed.

Pausing on the edge of the top step, she swung around, mouth agape. 'What exactly have I done to you? Just tell Rebecca Stanford the truth. I was…upset. You came for Finn and you gave me a…a…brotherly hug.'

Brotherly? He still had an erection that minus two degrees couldn't diminish. There was nothing fraternal about that!

'Siblings do not kiss each other,' he bit out.

He wished the lighting were better so he could see if the flush on her chest was real. Because he was sure the woman had just propositioned him. Again. She was no innocent. She knew where kisses led. Given another three minutes, he could have taken her up against the bloody wall.

Cristo, she was like a Venus flytrap. Luring, bewitching, with that sweet, grieving vulnerability, which she knew would beguile him. Because, in a once-in-a-lifetime moment of weakness—so she'd known she was not alone—he'd told her the brief details of burying his own mother. For two minutes of time he'd resurrected the fetid blend of conflicting emotions, only to bury them back into the depths. So the siren knew *exactly* how to play him.

'Well,' she said, 'obviously, I was of unsound mind. Because I have no interest in you. *Whatsoever.* In fact, you can rest assured hell will freeze over before I touch you again. Give me some credit, for heaven's sake, I've got some pride.'

Something close to affront clawed down his chest. It was as unsettling as it was idiotic.

'Just tell Rebecca you hate me,' she went on. 'Nothing but the truth. I promise you within seconds your stunning fiancée will tumble back onto your well-frequented bed!'

Dante almost laughed. Almost. 'My sleeping arrangements seem to bother you, Eva.'

Her head reared. 'Hardly. I couldn't care less what you do. But you could've told me you were getting married,' she said, her husky voice fracturing with a heartfelt anguish that made him pause mid-step, frowning at the contradiction between her words and tone. 'I was caught completely unawares. I could've at least come up with a better look than a shocked guppy for a retort.'

'Because appearances are everything, of course.' There was truth in that sarcastic inflexion and he knew it. She knew it. Any bad press would smash his deal to kingdom come if he didn't play it carefully. And, as for Eva…

Clip clopping down the steep stone slabs in those ridiculously high, sexy-as-hell stilettos, she continued to chatter incessantly. 'And now they'll all think the worst. That you…and I…' A husky groan poured from her mouth to wrap around his self-restraint and choke it near to death. 'That I'm a fiancée-poacher. A marriage-wrecker! Not the best marketing ploy, wouldn't you agree, Dante?'

'Which is why we need to talk,' he ground out. How could he take control of the situation if he didn't know what was at stake? His brain was still having problems processing what his ears told him. 'Is what Claire said correct? You make wedding gowns and you won the contract for the next Duchess?'

Screeching to a halt on the lower patio, she stood stock-still…then turned around eerily slowly, bristled and nigh on exploded in front of him, arms thrusting in the air. 'Why are you so incredulous?'

Why, indeed?

'Maybe I pictured you drinking yourself into oblivion and sleeping till noon. Partying yourself onto the front pages every day can be exhausting, so they say.' He gave her an unaffected shrug that tore at his spleen. Because suddenly his memories veered from Eva splashed across the headlines to his mother. Stumbling through the door half-dressed. Slurring her words. Polluting the air with the stench of whisky and vomit. Invariably with another man in tow.

'In all honesty,' he continued, the unwelcome memories making his stomach revolt, his voice bitter, 'I never thought you could manage a day's work in your life. So I am surprised. That is all.' Surprised? She might as well have stunned him with a laser gun. He did not like the feeling. It blasted his equilibrium to pieces.

Blinking, her stunned mouth worked around words. 'Oh, just *go away*, Dante, and leave me be. Go seduce your bride. I hope you'll both be very happy. Burning in hell.'

Then off she went, swerving around the cobbled stone path. Dante rocked on his heels, tempted to let her go. The more time he spent with her, the more frustration clawed his insides. She was the most disobedient, agitating woman he'd ever met. So why was he still standing here allowing the frost to travel up his limbs?

'Bloody woman.' With a growl, he caught up with her as she strutted beneath the ornate lamps illuminating the gardens, and the dim glow casting her body with a warm sheen.

Thought vanished. His guts pinched with a peculiar nip. '*Cristo,*' he burst out, making her pause mid-step. 'Your back!'

Unthinking, he reached out, dusting his fingertips across the raw, scraped flesh marring her beautiful almond skin…felt a shudder ripple down her vertebrae before she jerked away.

'Don't touch me.'

Dante set his jaw—she hadn't said that ten minutes ago. Or five years ago. But he was not going *there*. 'Your skin needs treating, Eva.'

She swirled around, scepticism widening her eyes. 'What do you care? If you didn't hear me the first time, I'll tell you again. I'm a big girl. I can look after myself.'

She was right. She didn't need his help. Eva St George, the Princess of the Press, knew exactly how to play the game. And let's not forget, she'd just stood in front of hundreds of people and made a speech from her very soul about the mother she'd adored. That kind of emotional strength was not indicative of weakness.

'Go home, Dante.' Chin up, Eva thrust her shoulders back with a lofty flounce. 'You're fired!'

A humourless laugh burst from his lips. '*Fired?*'

'Your job as brotherly stand-in is over. Quite frankly, you've been appalling. I hope I never lay eyes on you again.'

Fury bubbled in his blood. Why, he had no idea, because technically she was doing him a favour.

Dante stepped forward, close enough to make out the tiny freckles kissing her pert nose, and murmured, 'That makes two of us, *tesoro*.' And he meant it. The woman reminded him of cyanide. Troublesome. Deadly potent. She'd been toxic enough years ago and her seductive allure had somehow quadrupled with age.

'Good,' she said, stepping backward straight onto a patch of black ice.

Dante snatched at her arms, cupping her elbows to stem her fall.

Time stilled as he trailed his gaze over her exquisite face and, the chilly eve forgotten, he pictured laying her down on a bed of grass—the same lush colour as her eyes—curving his hands around her stunning body, feeling the weight of her heavy breasts in his palms, glorying in the sweet sinful taste of her skin. He wanted to cup her face. Take her breath away with his lips. He wanted to kiss her. Properly. No. He wanted to devour that impertinent mouth.

Dante swore he could hear her thunderous heartbeat echo his own. And he knew. Her entire body thrummed with a craving so intense she vibrated with the power of it. She had just lied to him outright. Of course she had. She still wanted him. More than ever.

His mouth twisted, even as he acknowledged the revelation. It was still there. Incomparable. Extraordinary. A ferocious desire that crackled the air with tiny fireworks and wreaked havoc on the exploding senses. His own control was barely leashed, his brain a fog…until she tore from his hold. 'Get your hands off me!'

Dante's jaw went slack. *Cristo*, the way she wielded her sexual power would render a lesser man witless.

'Next time you want to play games, *cara*, I suggest you choose a man unaware of your technique. Despite my reputation, I am extremely particular when it comes to the women I take to my bed. And the hot and cold routine turns me off.'

Her lips parted with a stunned smack and for one second he thought she was going to hit him. And the bizarre thing was, he wished she would.

'I wouldn't sleep with you if the future of civilisation depended on it,' she hurled back before she swivelled on her heel.

A noxious blend of rage, frustration and unadulterated desire swirled behind his ribs. 'Eva, I'm not done with you. Do *not* walk away from me.'

She didn't walk. She marched. He refused to bend to her will and go after her. He was in control. Always.

So instead he watched thick clumps of vaporous air swell in front of his face long after she'd disappeared from view. And, as the anger waned, unease flooded his psyche as he asked himself the very same question he'd asked Eva hours earlier…
What will I wake to find tomorrow? I wonder.

* * *

Slivers of daylight shone through the slits of her duck-egg curtains and, with one last look at the Sunday morning headlines, Eva tugged the top edge of her quilt and watched the mountain of newspaper scatter upon the parquet floor. Pulling the blankets up over her head, she nestled further into the lavender-scented warmth and closed her eyes, trying to block out the bold script etched on her brain like the tombstone of what remained of her career.

Soon-To-Be Duchess Threatens to Give St George the Royal Snip.

Is Diva up to Her Old Tricks?

Watch Out, Brides! Eva's on the Prowl.

'Thank you, Dante Vitale.' Writhing against the sheets, she kicked the blankets away from her over-warm skin, half-tempted to sue him for disclosure.

Then again, what on earth was she thinking kissing him in the first place? You would think the humiliation of five years ago had been enough to last her a lifetime. The only saving grace was that Dante's scathing one-liner about taking her up against the wall didn't appear in print!

Her pride was an ultra-fine thread stretched so taut it threatened to snap at any second.

'Enough.' She was quickly forgetting her new life motto: no regrets. Move on. It was time for a plan. A strategy.

Glancing over at the clock, she groaned when she saw that the small hand had only turned a quarter since the last time she'd looked. Eight forty-five a.m. Still too early.

She needed to call Prudence West. The serene soon-to-be Duchess had left a disarmingly polite message on Eva's answering machine last night before she'd even arrived home.

'Thank you, Claire.'

By then it had been too late to call her back and Eva knew what was coming—'You're fired', delivered with dignified, heart-cracking finality. After all, she knew how destructive bad press could be. She could hardly blame the woman, especially in her position.

The lump swelling in her chest made it hard to breathe. How many more clients would she lose? How could she ensure that business kept walking through the door? This wasn't anything like when she'd started out on her own. This time she had other staff to think about. Her seamstress, Katie, who had two little boys to feed at home. Her assistant, who would have a nervous breakdown if she couldn't go clubbing on Friday night. Not forgetting the rent for her boutique downstairs, which was colossal.

Responsibility tore her insides to shreds. What if she could persuade Prudence West to stick by her? Surely, everyone would follow suit. If she appealed to her, told her the truth…

The buzzer shrilled through her apartment for the hundredth time since seven a.m. and Eva yanked the blankets back over her head. 'Go away!' This was just like when her mother died.

Princess of the Press, Dante had called her. Four tiny words with the power to crush. Because, in all honesty, she felt ruled…almost owned by them. Blood-sucking creatures to whom decency was a foreign concept. This morning they didn't want the truth; they wanted sensationalism. In the past, how many times had she tried to give her version of events, only for her words to be twisted beyond recognition, ensuring she was as red and fiendish as the she-devil herself?

The phone shrilled, making her temples throb, and she waited until the answering machine kicked in.

'Eva, pick up the phone.' Dante's fierce bark filled the air of her apartment.

'Oh, *great.*'

'I am outside parked at the kerb, surrounded by reporters and I'm warning you, if you don't pick up—'

Thrusting back the covers, she scrambled across the wide

dark wood sleigh bed to retrieve her cordless from the bed-stand. Determined to be calm, composed and totally in control.

'*What*?' she snapped. 'What will you do, Dante? Haven't you done enough damage?'

'*Me*?' he said, incredulity and exasperation lacing his voice. 'May I remind you that your reputation precedes you? And do not speak to me of damage when I have just endured thirty minutes of female temper tantrums from my *ex*-fiancée!'

'Ex-fiancée?' she repeated, her mood lifting. And in that moment Eva knew she was a horrible, horrible person. The man undoubtedly brought out the worst in her. But why shouldn't he at least feel a smidgeon of the turmoil she was in?

A long sigh poured from her lips. 'For heaven's sake, just tell the woman you love her.' Where was the man's famed in-telligence? No wonder his marriage hadn't lasted long.

A stunned silence, then, '*Love*? What has love got to do with it?'

'Ah, well, say no more,' she said sardonically. 'It's usually why people get married, didn't you know?'

'In your world, maybe,' he growled down the line. 'Let me up, Eva, we need to talk. There's only one way out of this mess.'

'I don't want you here. It'll make things look worse.'

'Believe me,' he said. 'Things could not *possibly* get any worse.'

Oh, yes, they could—he could come up here and she could murder him for the unforgivable things he'd said to her last night. He could witness sleep-deprived Eva, eyes heavy with fatigue. But, more importantly, 'I refuse to provide the wolf pack with even more fodder.' And how could she approach Prudence then? *Oh, it's okay, he always calls for a friendly brunch early on a Sunday morning?* Yeah, right.

She heard him exhale and swore she could feel his warm breath trickle over her collarbone. Reaching up, she stroked the goose-pimples dotting her skin…and then yanked her hand away. What was wrong with her? How could she still crave the man's touch? A man so cynical. So savagely brutal.

'I have the answer to everything,' Dante said in a shiver-inducing low tone. A rich velvet she'd never heard before, didn't trust. It was luring, almost spellbinding.

'You do?' she asked, drawn in against volition.

'*Sì*,' he said, silky as sin. 'The perfect plan.'

'What, like a miracle?' And hold on a minute, why did he want to help her all of a sudden? Yesterday she'd been an alcoholic tramp. Goodness and hearts didn't generally figure in the Vitale phrase book. 'Did Finn send you?'

'No, I have not spoken to him since yesterday. The lines are down. It's either me or nothing.'

Lips parting, she almost told him *nothing* sounded wonderful but something stopped her. The business. Katie's two little boys. The rent.

She thrust her hands through her hair, tugged at the roots, tried to shake out the kinks.

If Dante could help with the press in some way, maybe she should hear him out. The man wore power as comfortably as other people wore shoes and thinking of herself was selfish, right? In reality, she had nothing left to lose.

Dipping her chin, she glanced down and winced at the cosy, ratty PJs. Hardly the uber-chic designer look.

Drat. There was that pride again.

'Okay. Give me five minutes.'

'Three,' he said before disconnecting.

Mouth agape, she stared at the phone…realised she was wasting valuable dressing time and tossed it across the pearly-pink throw. 'Odious, obnoxious, offensive snake. I must be mad.'

Gripping the thick knot of his dove-grey tie, Dante pushed the silk further up his throat and straightened the lapel of his black jacket. Tension pumped through his blood, making him hard all over—energised, taut, inordinately satisfied he'd given the press the perfect picture of ruthless determination by upending every last one of them from Eva's doorstep.

In one respect he questioned why she hadn't given them the boot herself but on the other hand he was grateful she hadn't unleashed her tongue. He had plans for Miss St George and the sooner he brought her round to his way of thinking the better. Obstinate to the nth degree, he knew he'd have a fight on his hands but the predator in him could already smell the scent of glory.

And why the hell was she taking her own sweet time opening the door?

A seed of a sinister thought detonated and a strange emotion settled in the pit of his stomach, curdling thick and black. Did she have someone in there? In her bed. Entertaining. Was that why she was ignoring the press?

Dannazione, he'd never thought of that. And for the man who was renowned for meticulous planning, that should've told him something. Yes, he assured himself, it told him his deal was hanging in the balance and if she…

Sweat bubbled on his nape and trickled down his spine at the thought of walking in there. Seeing another man in her bed. Her full do-me lips meshed with his.

Heart twisting, it tore from his chest and dropped into the well of his stomach.

The sound of metal sliding across metal filtered from inside and scored his suddenly sensitized skin like talons down a chalkboard.

Rolling his shoulders, he inhaled slow and deep. Yet when the solid oak door swung open he realised the intense lung workout had been an utter waste of energy resources.

There she was. Tousled. With that adorable sleepy look about her. The one he remembered from sleeping over at Finn's and watching an eighteen-year-old Eva tumble down the stairs on legs so long it had taken her an age to fathom the art of walking gracefully. It would've just turned noon and she'd mooch round the kitchen wearing huge earphones and skimpy cotton pyjamas, the small, tight shorts leaving nothing to the imagination.

For a moment he wondered what she wore to bed these days and then cursed inwardly as his blood pressure spiked through the roof.

So he focused on the now. This Eva. Twenty-seven years old and more beautiful than ever. All that gorgeous hair falling down around her face and caressing her bare shoulders. A tiny vest-top in a soft blush colour that threw her dense cleavage into stunning effect and a long dark pink skirt that reminded him of a gypsy. But *Cristo*, it was the bare feet that really snagged him. Perfect little toes painted pearly-white as if she walked on heavenly clouds. And there it was again. That hint of innocence he *knew* to be fake.

'Are you entertaining in your bed?' he asked, his voice so hard it almost cracked his skull. And, just to make sure there was no misunderstanding, he rephrased. 'Are you sleeping with anyone at all?'

'Did you really just say that?'

'Yes.' After all, it would ruin all his plans if she had a multitude of boyfriends all over the place. Was her rock star still on the scene? A man with a perpetual hangover. The perfect couple.

Dante ground his back teeth. 'Just answer my question, Eva.'

His don't-mess-with-me tone was met with an arch of her delicate blonde brows.

'Good morning to you too,' she said, hand braced on the door frame as if she was half-tempted to slam it in his face. 'You're in a lovely mood this morning.'

He smiled. It was an evil twist, he knew it. 'I'll be in an even better mood when you answer me.'

Firing darts of ire, her eyes drifted to the wall above the

door frame, breasts rising and falling as she grappled for control. 'No. I don't… I haven't…' Chin down, she straightened to her full impressive height. 'What exactly does my private life have to do with you, anyway?'

'Plenty, considering the newspapers this morning,' he said, striding past her, not entirely convinced by her claims to single status but willing to give her the benefit of the doubt. For now. 'Haven't you heard? We're the new golden couple.'

She laughed—a hollow sound that serrated his spine. 'There's nothing golden about *you*. Anyway, I haven't managed to get past the front page yet.'

'Then I assure you, you're in for a real treat.'

Dante heard the door click shut and her mocking remark, 'Come in, why don't you,' as he strode down the narrow hallway and found himself in a…cosy lounge flooded with light.

Cream muslin hung in swathes at the wide windows, softening the stark glare of December and bleaching the dark oak floors. Huge, squashy gold sofas—the curling up with a book type—framed a large coffee table and took centre stage around a black Edwardian fireplace. Frames in every shape and size covered the hessian-covered walls—large gilt mirrors and reprints of times gone by—brides of every era and the accompanying fashions. There wasn't a moneyed feel at all. It was tastefully eclectic with a subtle romantic ambience. But, *maledizione*, the clutter sent ants crawling across the back of his neck as if marching down a vine.

'You are still messy,' he said. It used to drive Finn insane. Between Eva and her mother, their family home had been a constant artistic chaos. It was a sure bet you'd be pricked by a sadistic pin or three from sitting on a perfectly innocent-looking chair.

'So shoot me.'

Reluctantly his mouth curved at the petulance in her voice, until his eyes fell on a dressmaker's dummy filling one corner of the room with a voluminous frothy tulle skirt tacked around the waist. Stepping closer, his breath snatched—the retail connoisseur in him enchanted by the sight of delicate pearls stitched into the weave.

'By hand?' he asked. Knowing it to be impossible because it would have taken her—

'Yes, of course. Took me almost a week.'

Every day he was shown a multitude of beautiful clothing, but this… 'It's exquisite. I see you have inherited your mother's eye for detail. Her unmistakable genius with fabric.'

Even as she stood behind him he could sense frank bewilderment that he'd complimented her work.

Having been subjected to his father's particularly vicious brand of criticism since the day he'd been torn from his mother's graveside, he had no problem with dishing it out. No longer did it make him angry to hear; it only made him strive to be harder, stronger, more powerful than ever before. But the beauty in Eva's raw talent stopped him dead in his tracks for there was not one fault in any stitch or placement of pearl.

'Why didn't you tell me the extent of your success last night? Your boutique?'

She gave a little huff. 'Oh, come off it, Dante. You had no interest in my life or anything I had to say.'

He didn't mistake the touch of hurt in her voice and he was man enough to admit he deserved it. One desperate phone call from Finn, one look into those dazzling green eyes and he'd known trouble was coming. Deflecting it, however, hadn't brought out the best in him and in the end it had been a pointless pursuit.

'I had no idea about your work.' Now he wished he hadn't closed his ears to Finn's animated renditions. Without them, he'd been left with one possible avenue.

So this morning he'd ignored every flammable headline and had his investigators expose her business interests. She'd built her small bridal couture company from nothing. *Nothing.* Laser gun time. Stunned would be an understatement. Where was her inheritance—her mother's legacy? Blowing millions of pounds within a few years on the party scene must've been one hell of a joyride. He assumed that when the money had run out she'd had to make a trade of some kind.

At first glance he'd thought Finn would have provided capital but no, she'd done it all herself, through banking loans and hard work. And he felt something he'd never thought he'd feel for her. A measure of respect.

'Now you do,' she said. 'Except do me a favour and lay off the congratulations regarding Prudence. She's already left one message and I shouldn't think the next royal wants an engagement-wrecker to bless her gown.'

The anguish in her voice sliced at his throat. He knew what it is was like to work night and day with recognition continuing to be far from reach. At twenty-three he'd fought for the chance to save the ailing Vitale empire. The battle had been endless until desperation had forced his father to hand him the reins. It had taken Dante almost six months of working 24/7 to operate back into the black. So he knew the determination, the frustration, the rage.

'Won't stop me trying to change her mind, though,' Eva said with a dose of grit that made his mouth tilt. Ah, there it was. The fight.

'So why are the shutters locked downstairs?' he asked.

'Luckily, I only open the last Sunday of every month. I wanted to contact some of my clients before facing the hounds.'

'It is best you do not speak with them until we get our story straight,' he said, hearing his autocratic tone ricochet off the walls.

A small frown creased her brow. 'Our story? There is no story, Dante, only the truth. If that doesn't set me free I'll just have to wait until the furore dies down. There'll always be other jobs.' But she wanted this. Desperately. Oh, she tried to hide it, but the stiff smile she tried on for size visibly cracked her composure.

She wanted it, just as much as he wanted Hamptons. Neither could afford tittle-tattle. Yakatani not only preferred committed family men but he was inordinately disturbed by tabloid fodder. With plenty of multi-billionaires in the running, he had his pick of the auspicious crop.

Dante considered the tartan wingback chair, decided not to take the risk and walked over to the windows to inspect the street below. Decent enough area for a boutique, he supposed. Mayfair or Bond Street would be better.

Rolling his neck, he breathed deeply. Truth time. Explanations he wasn't very good at because as a rule he answered to no one. 'I had an arrangement with Rebecca.'

He allowed her to soak up the admission, wrestle her thoughts into some kind of order. When her words came they were doused with intrigue. 'What kind of arrangement?'

'I needed a fiancée to close the Hamptons business deal.' And with that one strategic purchase he would make Vitale the biggest retail phenomenon in the world. Then his father would have no choice but to acknowledge his first son—his bastard son—as the rightful heir. Finally he would prove to the old man that he was worthy of the Vitale name. That he was no longer a dirty stain on a virtuous thousand-year legacy. That he wasn't tarnished by his mother's bad blood. That he was strong enough to live only for Vitale and nothing, *nothing* would stand in the way of his success.

Fingers delving into his hair, he thrust the memories back into the dark depths. Locked down his emotions with ruthless efficiency.

'I had no intention of marrying the woman,' he said. One stab at the marital state had been enough to inoculate him against the institution for life. 'I only bumped into her a couple of weeks ago in Singapore.' Dante had known Rebecca from Cambridge days. A striking brunette who had a tendency to flirt with him outrageously. But she had chosen the wrong day and the wrong man to play with.

She'd cornered him and while he'd been sorely tempted to take what was on offer that night, to lose himself, drive out the anger, something had stopped him. Despite her overt sexuality, she'd turned him to stone.

While he'd never been the small-talk type, he had listened. To dampen his fury. To forget his father, his half-brother. It soon became apparent she was neck-deep in debt and needed funds—astronomical amounts. She was desperate. And, like a shark smelling bait, Dante's killer instincts had kicked in and within seconds he'd pounced on that weakness and a business arrangement had been born.

'Oh,' Eva said, 'you must want Hamptons very much.' Warm, understanding, her husky voice wrapped around him, taking the edge off the chill that had been pervading his bones for so long.

And, before he knew it, need hit him with the force of a jet, tearing through his body. It took all of his restraint not to walk over there and slide his fingers across her deep silken cleavage, over her décolletage, up the sweet column of her throat. He wanted to sink into that gorgeous thick blonde hair, tilt her head for his kiss and drown in the sinfully erotic taste of her tongue.

Which was inconceivable for so many reasons; his brain refused to wrestle one to the fore. Putting her troublesome tempestuous nature and loose morals to one side, Finn would never forgive him for slaking his lust on his little sister. And this, whatever *this* was, had turned into business and never the twain shall meet.

So he narrowed his focus, his desire, on the only thing that mattered to him. 'I need this deal, Eva. Except now my business relations with the owner are heading for the toilet. Rebecca claimed it is embarrassing enough for me to be seen embracing '*the likes of you*' without her friends believing her a fool in unrequited love.' She'd even hinted that she'd fallen for him and such lies inflamed his gut.

Dante turned from the view, leaned against the sill and caught Eva stuffing some letters under the plush cushion of the sofa before she sat down. The hunch she was hiding something expired as she curled her long legs under her bottom and writhed to find comfort.

How different she seemed in her own surroundings. She looked sumptuous and snuggly and… He shook his head. Appearances meant nothing. *Business, Dante—focus.*

'I assume all her friends thought it was a love-match?' she asked.

'Her words. Certainly not mine.'

'So what do you plan to do now?'

Crossing his arms over his chest, he locked on his target. To eyes narrowing warily. He responded to that glimpse of suspicion by raising a dark eyebrow. 'I've already done it.'

'Of course you have, Action Man. Care to elaborate?'

He ignored the sarcasm; she'd thank him soon enough. Instead his mind drifted to earlier that morning. When he'd stood in his office listening to Rebecca's histrionics, mouth shaping to quieten her with a lucrative financial bonus. And all the while his eyes kept drifting to the front page headlines. To Eva. And he knew. Even if Rebecca took another cool million and stood by him, Eva would suffer. A good business reputation was something money couldn't buy and, regardless of fault, of the past, they were in this together. Finn had always stuck by him, whatever the storm, and Dante owed him. He could help Eva while ensuring Yakatani remained happy.

There had been moments; *Cristo*, there still were moments of doubt, of reason—telling him not to trust her. Putting her business acumen to one side, he wasn't convinced she would come over as 'wife' material in front of Yakatani. His investigators might have failed to unearth any recent inflammatory stories but that meant nothing when her weekends could be made up of secluded private parties and dangerous liaisons.

Slowly, inexorably, his gaze roamed over her apartment,

the blatant romanticism of her career choice. Something didn't make sense. *She* did not make sense.

Dante scrubbed his jawline with the back of his hand. He'd just have to keep an extra-close eye on her. If only to ensure she played by the rules. *His* rules.

The tension in his midsection eased, just a touch. This plan could work. It *had* to work.

They could have it all.

'I've given the press a story that will melt their cynical little hearts,' he said, knowing his tone was sending the temperature in the room into a rapid decline. 'The real thing.'

The frown in her brow deepened, even as she focused on the fireplace. As if she were somewhere else. In thought so deep her expression was almost dream-like in its intensity.

'The real thing?' she asked, her voice as softly decadent as whipped cream.

'*Sì. Love.*' The word was like poison on his tongue, making it swell, his next words sounding thick. 'For surely there is only one reason I could be torn from the bonds of an engagement. The fact that I've fallen madly in love with someone else. I've provided them with a true romantic fairy tale.'

Without looking up, Eva gave a little huff of disbelief and began to scratch at the arm of the sofa, making patterns of what looked like love-hearts. 'And who is the heroine in this fabricated tale?'

Dante smiled. The half smile that never failed to make women weak at the knees and tumble backward onto a satin drenched mattress.

'You are, *tesoro*.'

CHAPTER THREE

Eva's head snapped up so fast a spasm shot up the side of her neck and exploded in her ear.

'*What*? Are you *crazy*?'

Fairy tales? Her and...*Dante*?

He hitched those broad muscular shoulders, all lazy insolence, and the dark silk lapels of his jacket rippled over the stark white shirt adorning his chest. 'It's perfect,' he said.

Perfect. He was perfect. From his yummy, thick, overlong tousled hair all the way down to his high-sheen voguish shoes. Perfect to look at. Detestable inside. A bit like Christmas cake.

Her mouth worked around words, trying to free her stunned vocal cords. How dare he? How *dare* he!

He, who just stood there. Wielding a half smile that was nothing short of a weapon of mass female destruction sending her body into nuclear meltdown. A smile that said *roll over and take it*.

Then there was that arch of one sleek dark brow. Expectant. As if waiting for her to thank him. For what, exactly? Digging her a bigger hole to bury herself in?

'Let me get this straight. You've told the press that you've fallen in love with *me*,' she said, jabbing her index finger into her chest before turning it back on him. 'To save *your* business deal?'

'*Sì*. And your deal with the next Duchess.'

His words tore at the tower of her indignation, making it

wobble precariously. Would Prudence West be pacified by such a story? She supposed a woman in love, about to marry the man of her dreams, would understand such a predicament.

'But we'd have to feign a relationship,' she said, sounding horrified even to her own ears. 'In public.' She couldn't do it. It would kill her. Bad enough he was in her apartment. Touching things. Sucking the pleasure she'd always gained from her soothing space and replacing it with wretched visual pictures sure to taunt her for days. But what was worse, far worse, was that while she'd been counting down the minutes until he would leave, he'd been planning on staying for the foreseeable future. With her. A woman he abhorred. So really, 'Who would ever believe us?'

'It is done, Eva. Everyone already believes,' he said, his voice hardening to steel. The self-satisfied look of earlier being replaced by dark irascibility.

Understanding dawned. He actually expected her to jump aboard the Dante freight train to hell. Without so much as a quibble. In effect, she'd require an industrial-strength fire retardant suit!

'You didn't think to ask me first?' she said, her indignation now fully stoked, voice high octane, ready to smash every glass object within a ten-foot radius. She was in control of her own life, dammit! 'You're so…so arrogant.'

He stood to his full six-foot-three, eclipsing the sun and sucking all the air from the room. And Eva held her breath until she nigh on asphyxiated.

'I am taking control of the situation and fixing it. What have you been doing all morning? Lying in bed painting your pearly toes and rewriting your social calendar?'

'Oooh. You just can't resist, can you?'

The devil-may-care shrug he gave her made her angrier still.

Eva sighed, rubbing her temple. When was he going to start taking her seriously? 'If you want me to admit to something then I'll admit to fretting. Fretting my little heart out and thinking of what to do next. But do you blame me? There is nothing wrong with being concerned about my business. It may be small fry compared to your whale of enterprise but it's mine and I've worked hard for it.' Her business was her life. For however long she had. The only joy in a sea of uncertainty. She'd do anything to keep it afloat, but feigning a relationship with Dante was sailing into depths unknown and she wasn't ready to drown just yet.

'If it is so important to you, where is the problem?' he said, now irritated to the point of explosion.

'I don't like the idea,' she said, risking another glance at him, voicing the only argument she could think of without the need to purge her life story. 'It's lying.'

Frank bewilderment widened his beautiful deep umber eyes. 'Funny how naive has never been a word I associate with you. You want to be successful, Eva? You have to play the game. You want to save your career? Get ruthless.'

The only thing ruthless about her was the way she haggled with her suppliers for a measly two per cent and dashed to the supermarket when her favourite ice cream was on special. She preferred to play fair. And she loathed lying. Blame it on the tales she'd heard spouting from her father's tainted lips as her mother lay sick in bed. Blame it on the press for painting her as an alcoholic, drugged up, sexual assassin. Whatever. Lying to the world, to the soon-to-be Duchess, with Dante, made her feel…dirty, somehow.

That must be why she was scratching at her neck. Why her skin felt too tight. It had nothing to do with his presence filling the room with a dark feral aura that made her feel equal parts aroused and scared witless. How could she possibly hide this ridiculous, malapropos attraction when *he* wanted it on full show? For everyone to see…

She gripped the squashy arm of the sofa until her knuckles screamed. 'Whoa, hold on. What's Finn going to think?'

Dante rubbed over his lips with the flat of his hand and Eva fancied she'd just taken a chunk out of his invincible armour.

'I will explain everything and he'll realise that such a story is in our mutual interest. I will *not* risk losing Hamptons and it's clear to me you've worked hard to gain your professional standing. So let us make the most of a bad situation.'

Why was one more department store so important to him? Was he so power-hungry? She understood ambition but, heli's bells, he was one of the richest men on earth. It was said he could turn one dollar into a million within an hour. Sell noodles to a Chinaman, green grass to the Irish.

It was seriously tempting to use that power for her own ends. If she lost custom, she would never meet next month's rent. Her staff would be out of jobs. Life as she knew it, the success she'd fought for, would end.

Could it really work? She was so desperate she wasn't sure she was thinking straight. He made everything sound so simple but simplicity had never figured in her life. There was always a black figure lurking around the corner. Ready to pounce.

'Rebecca will know the truth,' she said as needles of doubt began to pop his plan. 'What's to say she won't pull the plug? Next Sunday she may have sold her story to the papers and we'll be right back to square one.'

The look he tossed her made her feel ten kinds of a fool. 'Ah, *tesoro*, so little faith. Rebecca was the first to know of our affair.'

Never mind thinking on his feet, the man was two steps ahead of time!

'We haven't had time for a love affair,' she said, flinching as the words *love affair* tripped her heart to miss a beat. 'I only clapped eyes on you last night for the first time in years.'

'Precisely. One look and we knew. Rekindled love affairs are the sweetest, so they say.' His voice was jaded silk as he turned away to peruse the flea market knick-knacks on her Edwardian mahogany occasional table.

Rekindled. Right. That made perfect sense. Oh, God. His sharp, cunning intellect sliced her every objection to shreds. But, looking at it another way, he'd clearly thought it through and decided it could work. Still…

'I don't imagine she was very happy.' She'd bet her best sewing machine the woman was neck-deep in love with him. Women with broken hearts could be problematic. Make the most impulsive, illogical decisions…

Digging her blunt nails into her palms, she slammed the brakes on her reminiscences and shifted on the sofa, desperate to stand but knowing she'd only pace and Dante was making her dizzy enough.

Picking up an antique mother-of-pearl trinket box, he ran the thick pad of his thumb over the inlay and she'd swear she could feel that very touch glissade down the sensitive skin beneath her ear and she shivered wildly.

'She was beginning to lose perspective,' he said, voice hard, dark. 'Blending fable with reality. I wanted a business arrangement, not a twenty-four-hour migraine.'

In that moment Eva had no idea what she ever saw in him. Or why her body craved his touch. He was despicable.

'Obviously the poor woman fell head over her stilettos,' she said, remembering the shattering pain of hurtling into mindless oblivion for this man. 'I almost feel sorry for her.'

'Save your pity,' he said, lowering the small trinket back to the table with a surprisingly gentle touch. 'Women are incapable of love. Unless it comes with a million-pound price tag.'

'Good grief, you're abnormally cynical.' What made a man think in such a demeaning way of women? All women?

'Realistic, *tesoro*.'

'So how come you trust me?'

'I don't,' he said in a casual tone that completely belied the tension radiating off him. 'It is dangerous to place faith in another. Especially when the outcome is of the utmost importance.'

Slumping back into the soft embrace of the sofa, she said, 'Oh, charming.'

'The difference is you have just as much to lose as I. This is not just about money to you.'

Good point. And did it really matter if he trusted her or not? Her heart ached for him to believe in her but, then again, her heart had always been on the stupid side where he was concerned.

Business—she had to focus on business. He was right. This was the only way. On her own it would be hard, maybe impossible to fix such catastrophic damage. They had a far better chance together.

'Okay. What would I have to do?'

A small smile lifted the corner of his mouth. The victorious type. In truth it didn't matter what type it was, it was just as lethal as the rest of him. Also highly premature. She hadn't *technically* agreed to anything.

'Go out,' he began in that silky sinful drawl. 'Attend a few dinners with Yakatani. Play my loving *devoted* fiancée.'

Fairy tales.

Everything stopped. The room morphed into a black and white blur as her vision began to swim as the enormity of his suggestion hit her with the thwack of a hammer-blow to her head.

An unseen hand gripped her heart, the fingers spreading to her throat, squeezing relentlessly until her pulse thudded in a rapid beat. Yet somehow, knowing his fierce shrewd gaze watched her every move, she managed to choke out a laugh. 'Ah, well, there we have our first problem. I don't do devotion.' Nothing but the truth. She didn't want a relationship of any sort—never even *had* a real relationship before.

'Ah, yes,' he said. 'Eva, footloose and fancy-free. Why does that not surprise me?' Dark, savage and wickedly sharp,

Dante's tongue was like a blade slicing across the room, lacerating her skin, gashing open another wound. It took every shred of strength she possessed to lift her chin and affect a careless shrug that almost ripped her shoulder blades in two.

It didn't matter to him why she felt so strongly. He was here to save his deal. She was a means to an end. But Eva knew the limitations of her life.

The script had been written years before by one of the most renowned specialists in the world. The moment she'd heard 'high risk' she'd known with bone-deep clarity she would never experience love or the joy of having a family of her own. She couldn't tempt fate. Her mother's death was a living, breathing thing inside her, reminding her of the destruction one woman's demise could cause. Eva refused to take the risk. Refused to expose herself to such pain.

And what exactly was she missing out on anyway? She doubted true love even existed outside the imagination of youthful naivety.

She'd never forget the day her father had left. After her mother had endured another dose of chemo. For twenty years Libby St George had devoted her life to her husband, gave him two children, curbed his alcoholic tendencies and sang like the proverbial groupie at his every concert—whilst building a successful career of her own. And the day his wife needed him more than ever was the day he'd left.

It was Eva who'd picked up the shards of their fragile world. Eva who'd stroked away every tear. Eva who didn't make it to design school that term or the two long, heart-shattering years that followed. Eva who hid every newspaper showing her father on another drunken binge, invariably wrapped around a leggy brunette.

If that were payment for love and devotion—if *that* was true love—such utter heartbreak—she'd rather live her life out completely dependent on herself.

Clearing her throat, she directed her voice to sass. 'Yes,

Dante. Footloose and fancy-free. That's me. So, you see, I can't possibly feign a relationship with you. I wouldn't know where to start. And, as for attraction…' A *ppff* vibrated over her lips. There'd be no feigning *that*.

The air shifted, tilting the room on its axis, as he prowled across the room towards her. She felt hunted and it was a dazzling, terrifying experience. Each lithe stride was a thump of her heart and a beat of heat through her blood, until everything melted when he braced one large hand on the sofa arm and the other across the high back, caging her in.

Brooding and fierce, he leaned forward and her brain was attacked by the infusion of his expensive scent. Raw enough to strip away the layers of her anguish.

'Are you saying it is impossible, Eva? To *fake* it.'

'Not impossible,' she said, air stuttering in her lungs as her internal organs went on strike. 'Just a bit of a stretch.' *Push him away, Eva, push him away.*

'Do not lie, *tesoro*, even to yourself. I can hear your heartbeat from the other side of the room.'

Exactly. How mortifying was that?

She stared at his full, dark red lips, unable to move. Her entire body was liquid. A boneless, quivering mass of thrumming desire.

'That would be the clock, Dante. Your welcome in my home is coming to an end.' He had to leave now. Before she did something very, *very* stupid. For the second time in the last twenty-four hours.

His breath trickled over her face, warm and alluring. Spellbinding. He dipped his head and lightly grazed his jaw up her cheek, the friction a delicious firework of sensation. And all the willpower in the world couldn't have prevented the mini explosions in her midriff, the ripples that danced up her body. Piping her veins with heat. Making her breath hitch.

'Ah, Eva, we have enough chemistry to blow up a small country.'

Blinking over and over, she said, 'We do?' *Oh, boy*. Was he saying he felt the same way?

She would laugh if she had the strength to fight through the painful irony. Of all the times she'd wanted him to crave her, only her, he finally desired her when it was too late. 'Explosives are dangerous, Dante.'

'Very dangerous,' he murmured, his deep voice sliding over her, dark and sensuous, like a physical touch.

And then, *oh*, he did touch. His lips shimmied over the soft spot between her neck and shoulder and her lashes fluttered to a close.

'Therefore not to be trifled with,' he went on, before flicking her earlobe with the tip of his nose.

A moan threatened to trip from her lips but she caught it in the nick of time. Determined to stay strong. Not to cry out for more. More pleasure. More pain.

'Eva…' he said, her name another caress, sliding off his tongue with all the practice that had once made her name an endearment. When she was young, stupidly naive, she'd fancied he said it as if she was the most special thing in his world.

The past blended with the present as his heat surrounded her, drawing her in. Without conscious thought, she reached up…touched the smooth satin of his jaw. Satin over steel, his skin smouldered, scorching her fingertips. And Eva—now a moth to a flame—turned her face until they shared one breath. Until he licked her lower lip with the devilish accuracy of his tongue. Leaving it burning. Tingling.

'Need more proof, *cara*?' he said, drawing back, his eyes the deepest, most sensual hazel she'd ever seen. Hot. Heavy. Glittering. The same way he'd looked at her last night. In the gardens, when he'd held her tight to his body to stem her fall and she'd convinced herself that look was antipathy. That he couldn't bear to touch her.

Suddenly the room revolved once more, spinning their situation in another direction entirely.

Dante was attracted to *her*. He felt the same way. And suddenly she was less of the girl she used to be and more Eva, the older, wiser woman on an equal footing. The woman who'd made peace with the strictures of her life. The woman who didn't need love. Nor passion. Especially with a man masterful in the art of devour-and-discard.

Oh, she'd read the tales of his jar of tattered hearts, seen enough pictures of Dante with his glamorous brunettes to fashion the ultimate armour. She may not want a relationship but hell would freeze before she slept with a man no better than her father.

So, if she was going ahead with this spurious soap opera, losing her grip, her head or her pride was not an option.

She'd been thrown for a loop yesterday, unreeling like a spool after the fund-raiser. Missing Finn, her mother. But, today, everything had changed. She had her business to save. Be the woman she'd fought to become.

If she could rise from the ashes of destruction and build a business to be proud of she could go out and be his date for dinner. Easy. Two or three dinners in a nice, controlled, professional atmosphere—deal done. Her beautiful little boutique, her new life saved. His deal saved. Everyone happy.

Some of the stress knotting her nape unravelled. Of course she could do it. She met clients over lunch, knew how to talk the talk.

There was really no need for the words *fairy tale* and *relationship* to bring on a migraine of epic proportions. It wouldn't resemble a real relationship at all. No lovey-dovey stuff. This *was* Dante they were talking about, after all.

'And this is strictly business. Right?' she asked, just to make sure they were pulling the same thread.

'*Strictly* business,' he agreed in a low, deep growl that sent a shudder the strength of 7.0 on the Richter scale on a direct course to her pelvis.

Oh, boy, if this was going to work the man *had* to keep his distance.

Conviction enhanced the adrenalin pumping through her body and Eva pushed at his chest with all her might. He didn't budge one inch. 'What are you made out of—granite? Will you back off? You've proved your point.'

He stayed right where he was and demanded, 'So your answer is?'

'Yes. I'll do it.'

'Good,' he said, pushing his weight off the sofa, the outrageously expensive silk of his suit rippling over his hard body, his face a picture of that-moment-didn't-happen dispassion as he strode towards the door. 'Get your coat—we're leaving.'

Gripping the curved lip of the sofa back, she twisted at the waist, swivelling towards the door, brow furrowed deep with suspicion. She didn't like the sound of that command. There was nothing businesslike about going out on a Sunday morning. 'What do you mean, *we* are leaving? To go where?'

'Shopping. I'm going to buy you the biggest diamond you have ever seen, *cara*. Let the fairy tale begin.'

CHAPTER FOUR

THUMB FLYING OVER the screen with speed and dexterity, Dante tapped a reply to an e-mail on one phone and pressed his second phone to his ear. Fluid French streamed from his lips as he spoke to one of his directors in Paris, conscious to the point of aggravation of the woman sitting beside him.

Quiet, subdued, Eva had barely said two words since leaving her apartment. It unnerved him. Made him want to climb into her brain. Quite a change from thinking about climbing inside other parts of her.

His thumb paused as he ruthlessly tamped down the ferocious heat pumping through his blood.

Cristo, he'd seriously miscalculated this side of his proposition. Attraction.

If he'd thought the skimpy top and gypsy skirt of earlier was synapse-scorching, it was nothing compared to what had greeted him when she'd finally deigned to exit her bedroom.

Skin-tight black jeans, knee-high boots with a kitten heel, a white polo neck clinging to her gorgeous breasts and the sexiest little brushed suede jacket he'd ever seen, the colour of peridot. Zesty and fresh, the lime-green was a distinctive signature found deep within the earth under tremendous heat and pressure. It suited her volatile temperament and his inner state to perfection.

Jacques, his Director of European Operations, fell silent as if waiting for Dante's reply. To what he had no idea. And another flicker of annoyance sparked in his gut. With ruthless precision he ended the call and attempted to douse the flames of his ire. He didn't need this kind of distraction. What was it about the woman that made him so hot? And why did his body insist on replaying that moment back in her flat when she'd reached up…touched his jaw and sent a bolt of lightning shooting through his body?

Glancing across, he found her biting her ring finger nail as she stared out of the limousine window, a deep frown pleating her brow.

Dante tucked one finger down the back of his tie knot and gave a good tug. 'What is it, Eva?'

Hand falling from her lips, she began to stroke the leather door panel with the tips of her fingers. Without turning to face him, she said, 'I don't understand why you have to buy me an engagement ring when this isn't real.'

Dante ground his back teeth. 'To everyone else it is real. Let us not forget I was engaged to another. For this to work we are talking undying love here. The sweeping-off-your-feet variety. For this to work I cannot introduce you to Yakatani without one.' Affecting a careless shrug, he forced his voice to become neutral. 'When it is over, you may take the ring as a token of my appreciation.'

Shifting on her bottom, she turned sideways and her eyes speared darts of disgust. 'Is that what you say to all your women?'

'I'm a very generous man, *cara.*' Often he sent jewellery as a gift. They were a fond *arrivederci*, not a love token.

Cristo, he'd never given a love token in his life. Even Natalia, his father's idea of the perfect bride, had chosen an engagement ring from the Vitale collection.

The memory brought his head up from the screen. Why was he escorting Eva himself—or frog-marching her if the displeasure on her face was anything to go by? And right there he had it. Even if he gave her an unlimited credit card she wouldn't go. The woman wore sheer obstinacy for skin and she didn't *do devotion*. But at least she was honest. If he could admire her for anything today, it was the truthful delivery of that statement. Any other woman would have lied or at least tried every trick in the book to play heart's desire—such lies inflamed his gut.

While he was in no doubt that his dark, brooding looks drew them in, it was the drugging scent of bank notes—the aphrodisiac of power—that dropped them before his feet.

Eva's eyes began to sparkle brighter than the winter sun slashing through the black leather interior. 'Hold on… I have my mother's ring at home—we can use that.'

'No,' he said in a firm tone, brooking no argument. Or at least it would have, if it wasn't Eva he was speaking to.

'Why not?' she tossed back. 'It's a good idea. Why waste your money on me?'

With no intention of telling her his body simply rejected, rebelled and downright screamed *no way*, he kept the strength of his response leashed. 'I am not wasting anything. It is insurance. Suppose someone recognises it? Your father. His latest viper wife.'

'You're right. Good point.'

Dante blinked wildly in mock horror and slapped his hand over his heart. 'Say that again, *Tesoro*. I shall record it for future reference. May even convert it to a ringtone.'

'Ha bloody ha.' Turning to face front, she wriggled back into the plush padding and he noted the tiny smile she tried to stifle. One that vanished with her next thought. 'I wouldn't give her the satisfaction.'

'Ah, yes. Which number is this?'

'Sixth.'

'Has your father never heard of sex outside of marriage?' For the life of him, he couldn't fathom why Nick St George kept returning to the snake pit time and time again.

'Oh, I'm sure he has,' she said, directing her gaze back to

the sweeping view of Knightsbridge, the hurt in her voice unmistakable.

Dante had never given the man much thought. Only remembered the subtle weakness that hovered over him. But sitting here, now, hearing the anguish in Eva's words, he began to question Nick St George's untimely departure and how it had affected Eva, a girl so close to her mother.

Before he knew it, his voice softened, 'I do not blame you for being hurt by the events of last night. It was beneath him to allow it.'

A new emotion burst through the sultry static crackling in the air. 'You don't know anything about my dad,' Eva said, her temper bubbling to the surface. 'So please keep your opinions to yourself. He has no control over the actions of his wife, therefore he can hardly be held accountable.'

It wasn't so much the words as her tone that threw him. She was *defending* him!

'As you wish,' he said. 'The woman certainly took great enjoyment in setting you up. No matter. The joke is now on her.'

Eva snorted. 'Oh, yes, until we break up. Then I'll be a laughing stock.'

'A *laughing* stock?'

'Oh, come off it, Dante. Everyone will think you've thrown me over for a new improved model. Who on earth would believe otherwise?'

For a moment his thoughts derailed with the nonsensical idea that she harboured a lack of self-confidence. *Improved*? How was that even possible? In the beauty stakes, she was untouchable. And hold on...

'*New*? I very rarely date women under—' He couldn't remember the last time he'd had a date, never mind her age. No wonder his legendary control was tauter than a tightrope and just as hazardous.

'You were saying?'

'I do not consider age when I take a women to my bed.' He

didn't. Did he? 'The only thing I ensure is that they know the rules.' His rules. And he supposed women in their early twenties were less complicated. They were perfectly happy with what he offered. Good sex and a lucrative farewell.

'In any case, I am older than you. Four years at least,' he said, wanting to get off the topic of sex and beds before he grabbed her small waist and hauled her atop his lap to straddle him. Then she'd know exactly what age, make and model he was currently lusting after.

'It's different for men,' she said, warming to her topic, hands wafting in the air. And Dante felt a small smile tug at his lips. She'd always been expressive. At least some things were still the same. 'Look at George Clooney. Or Sean Connery. The older they get, the yummier they get.'

His lips flattened with the speed of an express train.

Yummier? 'You find older men attractive?' What was the black emotion swelling in his chest, pinching his ribcage, making him shift in his seat? 'But you have only just turned twenty-seven.'

'I…' Head whipping round, she searched his face. 'You remember my birthday?'

November fifth. Bonfire night. How could he forget? She was born to cause havoc. 'I remember your eighteenth birthday party. The Masquerade Winter Ball.'

'Oh. No wonder you remember the season. You brought that dark-haired French actress who went skinny-dipping in the lake and almost contracted pneumonia. What was her name again?'

No idea.

'My point, Eva, is no one will believe our break-up is due to upgrade requirements. We will give a short statement to the press claiming irreconcilable differences and we only wish to be friends.'

She '*pfff*'d, the vibration rippling over her lips. 'Irreconcilable. How very apt. Except friends tend not to hate each other.'

'*Hate* is a strong word, *cara*.' While he felt a hyperbolic spin of emotions, not all of them were of the hostile variety. 'Haven't we just had this conversation?'

'Lust is different,' she said huskily. 'We're ignoring that bit. This is business. Safe.'

How long would she last without sex? If her sexual appetite were anything like his today, she would be hungry by Wednesday, famished by Friday. And on Saturday…

A flashback seared his retinas and he glanced at the blinding sun in an attempt to burn the image from his mind. Utter waste of time and effort. For still he could see her as if it were only yesterday. Eva locked in the arms of her rock star…his filthy hands fanning the upper curve of her ass. His Tequila-drenched mouth buried in her neck. Mere hours after Dante had done the exact same thing.

Bitter acid flooded his tongue. *Maledizione*, what was it with women? Why couldn't they honour one man? But hadn't his father told him this from the day Dante had walked onto the Vitale estate, no more than fifteen years old? That his own mother had been a whore just like any other.

Dante hauled air into his tight chest. He wasn't used to this wild emotional state. He was calm. Nothing rattled him. Except *her*.

Keeping his voice steady and even, betraying none of the tumultuous churn of his thoughts, he turned on her. 'It's time we discussed the rules.'

She visibly stiffened before him. 'Rules?'

'*Sì*. Rules,' he bit out. 'No provocative dress. *No* drinking. And, most important of all…you will remain faithful to me, *comprende*?'

Eva drew back, blinking over and over. And he wondered then how much of the darkness was showing on his face. 'F…faithful?'

'*Sì*. Completely. Utterly. Faithful.' Diving into her eyes, he attempted to curb the lash of his tongue but it was a useless pursuit. 'When the furore settles and we separate, you may sleep with whomever you wish. In the meantime, do not betray me. You will not like the consequences, *tesoro*. This may be business but I will not be made a fool of. Even in appearance. No boyfriends. No. Sex.'

Hot, heavy and sticky, the air clogged her throat, seared her skin and evaporated the moisture from her mouth as they faced off in the rear of the car.

For the briefest second she thought she saw pain in his eyes but this was Dante they were talking about—all cold, ruthless determination and closed off to the power of ten. Otherwise she would think the idea of her sleeping with another man bothered him. And maybe it did. Not on an emotional level but on the playing field of pride. Eva knew all about pride.

'This from the man who specialises in one-night stands and two-month marriages,' she said, wincing at the bitterness in her voice. Still, 'I would *never* embarrass you in such a way. I thought the whole point of this charade was to protect our reputations, not crucify them. Honestly, Dante, I've had enough. I am sick and tired of your caustic references. I do *not* sleep around. Never have, never will.' And wasn't *that* the understatement of the century! If he only knew... *Don't go there, Eva. Just don't go there.*

Time stretched paper-thin as he searched her face for the sincerity she prayed was there. Eventually he drew back, nodded.

The jerky reluctance in that movement didn't fill her with confidence but it was a start. 'And do I have your word that I will gain the same consideration from you?'

'*Sì*, of course,' he said, voice coated with umbrage.

'Oh, you're offended by that demand? Well, now you know how I feel. Neither of us truly knows the other, so can we stop this? Call some kind of truce. Please?'

Because surely the only way to get through this wretched

charade with her soul intact was to try to get along with him. Maybe they could be friends. *Oh, yeah, when he thinks you're a bed-hopping harlot who carouses on the dance floors at night?* Like that was going to happen.

Well, she decided, she'd just *make* it happen. While he claimed not to trust her, he *was* taking a leap of faith. So this was her chance to prove to him that she wasn't the Diva, party-girl-extraordinaire. That she'd pulled her life around. And maybe, just once, he would look at her, converse with her with something other than derision. Was that really too much to ask?

Maybe it was, if the assessing scowl on his face was anything to go by.

'Dante, listen, I—' The car rocked to a stop and her attention veered to the stunning black and white façade of *the* most exclusive jewellery store in London.

Thump, thump went her heart as she soaked in the sight… the dim interior. And relief zigzagged through her body. 'It's in complete darkness. Oh, what a shame,' she said, sounding suitably disappointed. 'It's closed.'

'Good,' Dante said, face now schooled into impassivity.

Eva frowned, then jolted as the car moved forward, negotiated a tight corner and pulled down an alleyway, coming to a dead stop outside a large, ominous black door. Oh, *hell*. 'Is this the tradesmens' entrance?'

'I believe so,' he drawled with a self-satisfied smirk she wanted to swipe off his face. He was enjoying this, she realised. The sadistic snake.

A phalanx of bodyguards walked from the car behind—a car she'd had no idea was following them—and took up position standing sentinel either side of a vault-like doorway, which began to open with eerily slow precision. Eva felt as if she was watching some horror movie from behind a cushion and this was the moment where the heroine lost every brain cell she was born with and walked headlong into the temple of doom.

'Let's go,' said Dante, unfolding his long muscular frame from the car. Standing tall, he swept one broad hand down the front of his jacket as he waited for her to alight.

Except her bottom was adhered to the leather, making her feel all kinds of stupid. What on earth was wrong with her? You'd think she was walking down the aisle to wed the devil himself, not buying a *fake* engagement ring.

'Eeeva?' he ground out.

'Yes, I know. I know.' Swallowing around the lump lodged in her throat, she shimmied across, took Dante's proffered hand and plastered a smile on her face that would place the Cheshire cat in the unemployment line.

A rotund grey-haired man hovered at the open doorway, bowing to Dante with a smile almost as big as hers. Although she doubted it was costing him the same extortionate price—three years' worth of facial tightness at least. When Dante squeezed her hand with hot, virile strength and stroked a seductive circle over the plump ball of her thumb a ripple danced along her veins and she boosted that estimation to ten.

'Good morning, Edward,' Dante said. First-name terms. She should've guessed.

'Sir, it is an honour to see you again.'

Again? Oh, *great*. He must've brought Rebecca here for her *fake* ring too. Humiliation nipped her cheeks and she wished there was a crack in the paving to slither through. Being one of many was not a condition she'd ever strived for. And for some reason she wondered if her father had taken all his wives to the same shop for multi-purchase discount.

Edward welcomed them into his dark lair with quiet aplomb and Eva twisted her wrist this way and that, attempting to wriggle her hand from Dante's hold. *Nada*. So, with her free hand, she grabbed the sleeve of his jacket, tugging him back a little so she could hiss a violent whisper. 'We should've gone to a different shop. The man's going to think you're a serial fiancé!'

'I could not care less,' he said, his dark voice booming down the hall, making her wince.

'Shh.'

'Why?'

'Because…well…' Yes, Eva, *why*? If he didn't care what people thought of him, why should she? He was so unapologetic. She should hate that, she really should. Her brain was obviously warped because she found it hot. Sexy as hell. Not a good sign. 'You're right,' she muttered so only he could hear. 'Who cares if you escort two fiancées here in one week?'

They were shown into a large lounge area, the walls adorned with sensual boudoir-type prints that sent heat, fast and furious, coursing through her body. *Oh, boy.* What with the erotic red walls, enormous black velvet couches, seductive mirror-top tables and the low crystal chandeliers bouncing shards of shimmering light off every surface, she began to wonder if this place sold more than jewellery. Never in her life had she seen such carnal opulence. It was seriously evocative, yet bizarrely romantic. Dizzyingly so.

'I want a diamond, Edward.' Dante's unyielding command knocked the air from her lungs so, by the time he encouraged her to sit upon a velvet sofa, she could do nothing more than obey with a slump. Dante shot her a quizzical glance as he sat beside her.

Too close. *Oh, boy*, was he trying to sit on top of her?

'I want the most beautiful diamond in the world, Edward. For the most beautiful lady, wouldn't you agree?'

'Absolutely, sir.'

Oozing deference, Edward slid a small tray in front of them and Eva's eyelids fluttered as sweat prickled behind her knees. She inhaled a deep stuttering breath.

'Eva?' Dante said, a tinge of concern in his voice colouring the question. And still she kept breathing, trying to work out what was bothering her so much. The room? Dante?

Then his scent—so dark, so rich—drifted up her nose,

wrapping around her senses, so when he nuzzled her neck she curled her face towards him with a basic instinct. Wanting to be closer. To relieve the need pulsing through her body, thrumming against the lace of her knickers.

Dante dropped an open-mouthed kiss on the sensitive skin between her neck and shoulder…tugged gently on her earlobe with his front teeth—flooding her core with liquid heat—and whispered in her ear, 'You are the first woman I have ever brought here. I often buy specialist stock from Edward for retail. There is no need to feel embarrassment, *tesoro*.'

Heart thumping, she eased back a touch, slowly opened her eyes and locked them on to his beautiful dark depths, glittering with sincerity. His recognition of her embarrassment was around ten minutes too late, but it was something, wasn't it? 'Okay.' *Pull yourself together, Eva. Think temporary torture, long-term happiness.*

Content she was back in the game, she moved her attention to Edward's small smile, to his assistant—a pretty, elf-like blonde—who heaved a long blissful sigh behind him.

'See anything you like, madam?' Edward asked.

Eva scanned the selection of diamonds. Huge, whopping diamonds. Ovals, squares, pears, hearts—blurring into one huge white nothingness, much like the pit of her stomach. Where were the price tags? How did she know if he could return it?

'No.' Dante's unimpressed voice shot through the haze. 'Too plain.'

Edward nodded his assent, lifted the tray from the table and swivelled on his heel.

Dante slipped his hand between the tight slit of her clenched thighs and she nigh on jumped off the couch. Had to bite her tongue to stop from yelping. Because, honest to God, she was sure that awesome body of his could fuel the energy supply for an entire nation.

'Relax,' he said, silky, sinful. 'You are too tense. Choose what calls to you.'

Another tray. Another pad. More diamonds. More carats than Lexi, her old precious mare, would munch through in a week. None of them called anything except *run*, gallop for your life. 'You choose. I don't care.'

Dante's fingers bit angrily into her inner thigh for one, two, three beats of her cantering heart.

'Scharrt,' he ordered with a calm severity that fired another burst of hot tingles through her bloodstream.

A small feminine gasp rent the air and Eva glanced at Edward, whose eyes lit with unabashed delight. *Scharrt.*

Excitement enhanced the crackling atmosphere, so she knew it had nothing to do with spreadsheets—they were the most boring things in the world. Whereas Dante, the financial genius probably got off on them. Another difference. Another divide. Another reason she'd never have been enough for him all those years ago. Compared to Finn and Dante, Eva's B grades made her intellectually challenged.

The elfin blonde began to vibrate as a crushed velvet pad the colour of midnight appeared in front of Dante. One fleeting glance and Eva's heart stopped. Dead.

Edward's voice came to her as if spoken from the other side of reality. 'The stunning emerald-cut yellow diamond with trilliant-cut white diamond shoulders. Totalling thirty-eight point one carats. One of rarest diamonds in the world, sir.'

Dante picked up the ring, took her hand from where it lay fisted on her lap and uncurled her fingers with a gentle stroke. *This is not happening. This is not real*, she repeated inwardly, fighting the tremble starting in her toes and meandering up her legs, spiralling through her midriff.

Dante slid the heavy platinum band along her finger, nudged it over her knuckle and embedded it deep. 'Perfect fit,' he murmured.

Perfect. It was perfect. From the cool platinum band to the sparkling diamonds flanking the shoulders to the biggest, most beautiful stone she'd ever seen—the most gorgeous rich shade of yellow. It was the ring of fairy tales. Of handsome princes and happy-ever-afters. It was the ring a man gave to the woman he loved beyond reason. It was for her clients. It was *not* for her. Because the gesture was as cold and empty as her stomach, whose pangs she felt every time she looked at it.

Breakfast. She must be starving. That was what this was all about. She needed to eat—

'We'll take it,' he said.

'No!' Hand shooting to Dante's thigh, she gripped his honed flesh, felt it tense beneath her fingers. Felt the answering fizz in her blood. Ignored it.

The notion that she was supposed to be play-acting came a second too late and she scrambled for a ditzy *oh, gosh* look and turned towards Dante with a flirty coyness she hoped she remembered how to pull off. 'What I meant was…it's too much. You don't need to prove your…' She couldn't say it. Love. It was a total, utter lie. She, who loathed lying, was living a lie. Lying to everyone around her. 'It's not right.'

Dante gave her an admiring glance that said her *performance* was Oscar-worthy and sank his hand into the nape of her neck. The touch of his fingertips against her scalp… The way he tugged her to him with ferocious need… *Oh, boy*. And then his breath shimmied over her tongue as he spoke against her lips, just loud enough for everyone to hear. 'Nothing is too much for the woman of my heart, *tesoro*.'

Another blissful sigh came from…somewhere. Realisation hit and her eyelids fluttered closed. *Oh*, he was seriously good. And she'd never hated him more. Or maybe she had. Yes, yes, of course she had. When he'd left her in the pool-house, promised he would come back. Swore he wouldn't leave. Yet he'd disappeared into the night like a dark phantom. When she'd needed him the most. Just like her father had left her mother.

Self-preservation knocked the pain from her chest and she twisted her head to speak low in his ear. 'I'll get you for this, Vitale.'

Drawing back, he loaded up that mouth with enough sex appeal to slay half the female population, snagged her hand and swooped up from the couch.

'Send me the bill, Edward.'

Yank, he tugged her down the hall in his wake. As far as social development went, it was one touch away from clubbing her over the head with a mallet and tossing her over his shoulder. Not that she cared. Speed was definitely of the essence.

Fresh and crisp, December stung her face but it was sheer bliss to Eva and she tore her hand free and darted towards the car door being opened before her.

From nowhere one steel arm blocked her way and suddenly Dante stood smack bang in front of her. 'Ready?'

God, yes, she wanted out of here. Away from him. What planet had she been orbiting when she'd agreed to this loony scheme? It was possibly the stupidest idea in the universe. *Temporary torture. Long-term happiness.* Just remember what type of man he is—a predator who devours and discards.

'Yes, I'm more than ready,' she said. 'And if you think for one minute I'm going through this again—'

'Good.'

Slam went that full sexy mouth over hers, obliterating her every thought and dropping her headlong back into the inferno. Heat doused every inch of her, soaking her in his blistering formidable power. The ground whipped from beneath her feet, her heart flipped over in her chest and, with one touch of his warm tongue against hers, she was riding a demon wave of scorching lava.

Anchoring herself, she reached up, vaguely noticing the strange weight on her left hand as she speared her fingers into his gorgeous thick hair. And, *oh, boy*, he tasted of sex and sin and dark bitter chocolate. He tasted of Dante. Of everything she remembered and more. More power. More strength. More passion. More. More. More.

Lips slanting, firm and lush, he devoured her mouth with long, leisurely licks, leaving her restless, breathless.

Maybe she closed the gap, maybe he did, but suddenly they were flush-tight, silken-clad iron crushing her breasts, steely fingers dominating…gripping her nape, keeping her to him, as if he never wanted to let go. As if he wanted her, wanted her so much.

And suddenly, with the same speed he'd lunged for the kill, Dante loosened his grip and Eva rocked back on her heels, swaying on her feet as the earth spun and lights exploded behind her eyes.

'Perfect, *cara*,' Dante said in a voice that solidified the heat in her midriff to a block of ice. 'That should do very nicely. Now we can be *certain* of what we will wake to find tomorrow. And let's have no more talk of the need to *fake* anything.'

CHAPTER FIVE

'ARE YOU HAPPY now, Vitale? Once again, there I am. Smack bang on the front page!'

Eva's voice shot down the phone line and would've easily burst his eardrum if he hadn't been holding the phone ten inches away. 'Good afternoon to you too, *cara*.'

'Don't *cara* me. You set me up!'

No, what he'd actually done was set *himself* up for an endless night of physical torture.

Dante surged from his leather chair and, palm flat to the chilled glass, braced his weight against the vast window of his UK headquarters. The unrivalled views of a festive Mayfair were doing an abysmal job of assuaging the tension snaking through his ribcage.

Where the hell was the Princess of the Press? Why wasn't she revelling in the attention? It was almost as if she hated it.

'What is the problem, Eva? It worked, didn't it? Are the reporters free from your doorstep? *Sì.* Have they soaked up every drop of exaggerated mulch? *Sì.* And let us not forget how you appeared to get into the spirit of the thing.'

Cristo, that was an understatement. The woman was a siren, hell-bent on his destruction!

'Yes, well, anyone would've got into the spirit of the thing when dealing with an expert in the field. Just *look* at me.' He was looking at her. Filling the front page. All long black sculpted legs and thick caramel hair cascading down her spine, five seconds away from having sex on the pavement. 'I'm all over you like a sticking plaster. Finn is going to get the shock of his life. Please tell me you've spoken to him, explained that it's all a…a lie.' What was it with the woman and lying?

'There are no lies between us on that page, Eva.'

'I'm not talking about the lust and you know it. I'm talking about the engagement.'

Dante paced the fifty-foot length of his office. 'No, I haven't spoken to Finn. His line is still down.' And, knowing his best friend, he'd be taking advantage of being snowed-in with the latest starlet to fall for his charms. At least one of them was getting some kind of satisfaction, he supposed.

'Oh, God, I hope he's okay.' The concern in her voice snagged at something deep inside him.

If there was one thing he could say about Eva, she adored Finn with all her heart. At one time that sibling loyalty had made his chest clench with envy. For, after being wrenched from his mother's pitiful grave and dropped into the opulent world of Primo Vitale, his father's legitimate heirs had been consumed with hatred.

Not that Dante had cared. After a childhood spent in a squalid, debauched hell, he'd been darker than sin himself and ready to take on the world. Little had they known it would be Dante who would save them all from financial ruin. It would be Dante who now held power in the palm of his hand, able to crush their world at will.

'Dante, are you still there?' Eva's voice, rich and decadent, washed over his taut, hard body in soft lulling waves.

'Sì, cara, I am here. We are talking about a man who drives at the speed of light. It will take more than snow to knock him off course.'

Her soft breath whistled across London as if she tried to be calm, to believe. 'You're sure?'

A small smile curved his lips. 'I am convinced Finn is safe

and well. But, if it makes you feel any better, I will contact one of my men in Zurich to search for word of his team.'

'You will? Oh, well, I'd really appreciate that. Thank you.'

Dante stiffened his spine, smoothed his hand down the front of his tailored jacket and hauled his thoughts back to order.

'Good. Now that is settled and you have calmed—'

'I have not calmed. And I'm not finished with you yet either.' Ah, there it was. The tongue of a vixen. That husky voice. Every sex-dripping syllable wrapping around his groin and pulling tight.

'I see you have found your voice today.'

'My brain is what I've found. First off…no more kissing,' she said, more than a little breathless.

It was a good idea. Also impossible. For two reasons. One, this charade must go on. And two, it was becoming impossible to keep his hands off her. Luckily, this time next week, Hamptons would be his, her deal with Prudence West would be saved and he'd be jetting to the Far East. Out of sight, out of mind.

'Are you listening?'

'To every word,' he replied, scrolling through his e-mails to see if there'd been any word from Yakatani.

'I don't believe you. Put your phone down. I do realise I'm a mere female but I want your undivided attention when I say this.'

'Say what?' he murmured, distracted by the incoming fist to his gut in the form of a text from his half-brother, Lazio—one he deleted without reading and moved on.

'No more fake loved-up flower arrangements. No. More.' Her voice cracked and his eyes sprang up from the screen. For a second he imagined she was struggling to breathe, to talk, but when she spoke again her sass was full throttle. 'It's one thirty and my boutique resembles the Chelsea Flower Show.'

'You do not like flowers?' he asked incredulously. Women adored flowers. Usually in every colour and variation. Maybe she was a lingerie girl… He stopped before crashing into another wall of lust. Never in his life had he bought a woman lingerie and he wasn't about to consider the notion now. Especially with a woman he'd never get to see modelling it. Torturing himself with self-denial he was not.

'Hate them,' she said tightly. 'Although I must admit it's a recent development.'

'How recent?'

'This morning recent.'

Dante settled back in his chair, the leather cushioning the blast of affront. So she didn't want his ring. She didn't want his kisses. And now she hated flowers because he'd sent them. A unique state of play, to be sure. Still, he assured himself, if Eva was so opposed to romance that was her problem, not his.

'Now that's sorted,' she said, 'I have to work. So I'll see you Wednesday for dinner with Yakatani?'

Leave her *alone*? For two days?

'I think not, *tesoro*. Until my name is on Hamptons' deeds, think…sticking plaster.'

Eva smoothed her satin sheath down her front, snagging on her oddly heavy left breast and winced.

Hormones. Nothing more. Nothing less. What with the ring and the lust, and the flowers and the lust, and the kissing and the lust she was in a volatile state. Add in the fact the man couldn't seem to leave her alone and she was a wreck!

Monday evening, Dante had demanded dinner at a fancy hotel, where he'd spent half the time on his phone with some Russian oligarch. Tuesday evening was the Scottish Ballet premiere, which in any other circumstances she would've adored. But she'd fallen headlong into the inferno on the red carpet beforehand and the flaming heat had burned bright for the entire performance. By this morning she'd learned her lesson in the art of submission and tied herself up in so many appointments he couldn't demand lunch.

Now all that was left was dinner tonight. Yakatani, Dante

and Eva. Easy. Private. No kissing. With a bit of luck he'd close his deal and leave her in peace.

Sucking in air, she pressed the flat of her hand to her stomach. Stomach ache. Every day. All day. *It's hormonal. It's the kissing. You know this.* But, *oh, boy*, the kissing. Made her want more. Of him. Of that sinful mouth. Not only humiliating, considering the man was made from the same cloth as her father, but it was all for show.

Oh, yes, the devil had the entire British press wrapped round his pitchfork. Every day there they were, front page headlines. It was awesome to behold and, though she was loath to admit, it was far nicer seeing captions professing devotion than detailing the latest 'Diva Scandal'. Even Prudence West had agreed to meet her on Friday to discuss 'everything' and she was *not* blowing it.

Grabbing her long crushed-velvet coat from the back of the couch, she checked the clock before sinking her arms into the cool silk lining and buttoning from neck to knee. The long hand clicked to the hour and Eva heard the rumble of a machine so loud the building shook as if she lived beneath an airport.

Lights off, she walked to the living room window to see... *wow*, a blood-red Lamborghini Aventador parked outside the boutique. The coveted super-car, named after a famous bull, riding double yellows.

The air whooshed out of her lungs as the sexy-as-sin machine open its jaws and Dante unfolded his tall muscular frame from the low-slung seat.

Thump, thump went her heart when, with a deft flick, he shut the car door and fingered his yummy hair. More with frustration than for appearance's sake.

Then her knees turned to water as he ate the pavement like a black panther, all deadly, lithe masculine grace. Dynamic. Energised. And *outrageously* sexy.

Mouth dry as hessian, it took her a few seconds to realise what his intentions were.

'Oh, no.' The place was a tip!

Quickly, she grabbed her vintage ruby-red clutch, rushed to the front door, swung it wide, moving forward a pace, and slammed straight into his chest.

'Miss me *that* much, *tesoro*?' he said, voice dripping with sin as he curled his fingers around her upper arms to steady her.

'Like a hole in the head.'

He pursed his lips as if containing a smile and before she remembered the sinful flavour of that mouth she backed up a pace, clutching her handbag to her chest. 'Shall we leave? Don't want to be late for the big event.'

His hot gaze trailed down her body, lingered on the flare of her hips…her bare calves until she felt positively giddy.

'What have you got on under there?' he drawled, for what felt like the hundredth time this week. 'And…' his eyes lit with fury '…*where* is your ring?'

Oh, *great*. 'I forgot, I was in a rush—just give me a second.'

'You *forgot*?'

Eva breathed deep, fighting off the need to punch him in the arm. Knowing her luck, she'd break her knuckles. 'What are you getting into a tizz about?' If she didn't know any better she'd say he was offended. 'It gets tangled up in my hair in bed and…'

Eva glanced at the crimson plaster wall of her hallway, seriously tempted to bang her head off it.

'You—' he croaked, before clearing his throat '—you wear it in bed?'

She couldn't look at him—she just couldn't. 'I tend to play with—' *Oh, boy*, was it too much to hope the floor would crack open about now?

'Play with…?'

Eva swallowed. 'My hair. In my sleep.' This was awful, awful, awful. 'I'll get it.'

About turn, she headed for her bedroom, his footsteps echoing on the oak behind her, the snickity-click of the front door closing. 'Just stay there. I'll be one minute.'

In she went, out she came. Took one look at his dark, thunderous face. 'I'll check the lounge.'

'*Cristo*, I realise it means very little to you, but how can you lose a ring in a day?' Was it her imagination or was there a thread of hurt in his voice? 'When tonight is the night you need it most!' No. Not hurt. He was angry as hell.

Light splashed over the room and she winced at the ivory threads worming across the carpet, the sewing paraphernalia littering every surface.

'*Maledizione*! You expect to find it in *here*?'

'Of course I will. Come on, don't you ever put things in a place where you'll never forget? Then forget?'

'Oddly enough, no.'

After a few minutes, Dante joined in and from nowhere the memory came to her and she strode over to the black mantelpiece. Halfway there and she snagged on Dante digging his hands down the sofa cushions in case it had fallen from the arm. And her stomach plummeted to the floor. 'Stop!'

Dante froze, slowly straightened to his dizzying full height.

'There it is,' she said, one unsteady finger pointing to the mantelpiece. 'I remembered. Told you I would.'

Insides shaking, she prayed he'd walk away. He could *not* see those papers from the specialist. He'd want an explanation and she couldn't lie and he'd tell Finn and Finn would worry and maybe tell Dad and *oh, God*, she had to get him out of here. Distract him somehow.

'Come on, I'm starving,' she said, practically shoving him out of the door. 'Where are we going, by the way?'

'Takumi,' he murmured, distant, suspicious.

'I think I read about that in the papers.' *Keep talking, just keep talking.* 'Some spectacular star-studded opening.'

'It's Yakatani's new venture. Or should I say his son's. Takumi is the Michelin chef taking the country by storm. Tonight is the opening.'

Eva stalled halfway down the hall. 'I thought this was dinner. Me. You. Him. Private.'

'It is dinner,' he said, now exasperated. Which was fine. It was better than being suspicious. 'And getting to private is the goal here. It is an honour to be invited. Meeting informally is the perfect launching pad.'

Yeah, to fire her off to the moon.

'Think you could refrain from kissing me on the carpet tonight?' It was a stupid request. Because, from the look on his face, she'd just waved a red rag to a bull.

CHAPTER SIX

A LINE OF super-cars and limousines snaked a path to Drathon Tower, sitting on the bank of the River Thames, soaring into the sky, all black tinted glass and subtle curves.

Dante watched Eva lean forward, head tilting to peer up through the windscreen as the parking attendant waited for his signal.

'What were you saying about this meeting being the perfect launch pad? It looks like a rocket, don't you think?'

It looked phallic to Dante but he was beginning to think his mind was continually in the gutter these days. Or at least since Saturday when this little missile had projected into his life.

Cristo, never had he spent so much time with one woman—*hell*, with one person. And the sight of his ring on her finger, stamping his possession all over her slender hand, only made him even more aroused. Knowing she wore it to bed, that she touched herself, caressed all that beautiful almond skin with *his* ring on her finger only turned up his internal temperature gauge.

Any other woman and she would have been flat on her back by now. But she was still Finn's little sister and there was no way he was crossing that line for a fling, however heady, however sexually gratifying it would be.

What was more, she was hiding something. Being secretive. Sneaky.

And, just like that, his temperature dropped through the

red leather bucket seat. He'd missed the signs with his ex. Although he often wondered if he'd cared enough to look. But right now, with Eva, there was too much riding on this deal.

After motioning the parking attendant to open his door, he walked round to Eva's side and took her small hand in his.

'Wow, I'm getting the full treatment tonight,' she said.

Whether it was her sassy mouth that sparked his fire or her repeated request not to kiss her, he wasn't sure. But his mood darkened with the desire to put on a real show. The devil in him wanted proof that she could no more resist him than he could her.

Gripping her hand, he hauled her from the seat—knowing every lens was focused upon them, that thousands of eyes would see the stamp of his possession—and brought those lush curves flush against his hard body.

Fisting his jacket lapels, her wide green eyes shot up to his. 'Dante,' she whispered frantically, 'what are you doing?'

'Not on the red carpet, Eva, that was your request.'

Plink. Plink. Bright white camera bulbs saturated the air in a dazzling display and Dante plastered her against the glossy carnal-red paintwork and took her mouth on a joyride she'd never forget.

It took him a good few seconds to think past her brazen lips frisking over his and the heat pervading his groin, to realise his fatal error. This was Eva and the woman kissed him as if he was her last breath. All sex and desperation. So he tangled with the uneasy notion that it would be *him* who would never forget. When business should have his undivided attention. That Hamptons was the goal here.

Even the imprint of her hot mouth refused to leave him as they rode the glass express elevator, zooming up forty-two floors in complete silence, Eva refusing to meet his eyes and Dante fighting the destructive animalistic need to pin her against the steel cage. *Business, Vitale—focus.*

By the time they were greeted by the maître'd he had the

hunger leashed…until Eva's long black velvet coat slipped from her provocative body and his heart stuttered in his chest.

Cristo…

Swathes of golden silk sheathed her body like a second skin, from the high slashed neck to the straight cut knee in an understated oriental elegance, the wide band cinching her waist embroidered with delicate pink orchids and tied at her back in a huge gold bow.

Sensually extravagant. Yet oddly demure.

He had to swallow in order to speak. 'Eva, *cara*, you look…'

'What?' she asked warily.

'Stunning.' Like thwacked-over-the-head stunning. 'Breathtaking.'

Her high cheekbones flushed crimson. Another hint of innocence. As if she'd never been given such a compliment in her life. Which was ludicrous to imagine in a woman with a trail of ex-lovers in her wake.

And thankfully, before that thought took hold, they were ambushed by Takumi and it was back to business. To safety. To total control.

Together they worked their way through the throng of foodies, TV personalities and society's usual glitz, nibbling on sushi and tempura, while Eva sipped an odd concoction of lime and lemonade—to satisfy her sweet tooth, he was sure. And, when they were shown to the private cordoned-off table of Yakatani, Eva dipped her head and greeted the older man in stilted Japanese. Making Dante rock back on his heels. And that was just the beginning of tonight's stun-gun attack.

Every time their upcoming marriage was mentioned she blushed that intoxicating rouge that swept down her neck and all he could wonder was if it covered her gorgeous full breasts. Yakatani was smitten with her apparent innocence. But the more Dante watched her, the more he suspected it was untruths. At one point she stumbled so hard, Dante had to catch her fall.

Turning to his host—a small man in his greying years who reeked money and intelligence—he asked, 'So tell me. Are you looking for a quick sale?'

'Yes. The quicker the better. It is time for retirement. My wife informs me she would like to see her husband before he meets his maker. As you can see,' he said, encompassing the glass and steel extravaganza with a sweep of his hand, 'my children all have their own interests.'

'It's spectacular. You must be very proud of your son.'

'Immensely.'

Dante couldn't mistake the sincerity and a fist of envy punched him in the gut. One he stiffened against. Pushed past. Moved on.

'Any issues with the store I should be concerned about?' Dante asked.

'Just the usual. Concessions getting complacent. Staff issues. Nothing that a man of your reputation cannot handle, Vitale.'

'New blood.' Eva's voice drifted across the table and, when Dante looked up, her attention seemed divided between their conversation and Yakatani's daughter-in-law, who'd just settled into the chair beside her, all long straight ebony hair and sloe eyes. Or was it the baby in her arms—a boy, if the blue sleep suit was anything to go by.

'You were saying, *cara*?' he said.

Her head snapped around, soft blonde waves swishing about her shoulders. 'Oh, sorry. It was just when you said…concessions.' He could feel her reluctance and it reminded him of the times she used to put herself down in the intellectual stakes during conversations between themselves and Finn. Not that Finn helped one iota. Without realizing, he'd used to make Eva feel as if her opinion didn't matter. It aggravated Dante. He knew too well the frustration of not being good enough, worthy enough to be heard.

'Go ahead, *cara mia*. We wish to hear.'

'Well…in my opinion, you need new blood. A better mix of class and sass. In the ladies department especially. The problem is your rents are too high and so you're not allowing the up-and-coming designers a chance to exhibit their raw talent. London is the place they want and they can't afford it.'

Dante blinked.

Yakatani's smile reached his deeply lined eyes and he said, 'What would you suggest, Eva?'

Warming to her subject, her hands joined in the party. 'Free rent for six months to get them established. Then off they go into the big wide world. Or they have the money to start paying *you* rent. Now, before you get all hot and bothered—'

Hot and bothered? *Cristo*, he was burning up.

'—about the words *free rent*, think about what you would gain. Respect in the industry. The opportunity to showcase new stars, thereby bringing in new custom, and satisfaction that you helped a fledgling company. Everyone's happy,' she said with another little shrug as her eyes flickered back to the baby.

Eyes that melted at the sight. Almost…longing.

With the back of her finger, she reached up and smoothed down the baby's soft cheek. Once. Twice. Dusted over his dark mop of hair with a loving touch.

Then, as if she sensed he watched her, she turned towards him and curved her beautiful lush lips. Untutored. Pure. *Affectionate*?

No. Impossible. Women didn't look at him with affection. They looked at him with lust. Lust for sex, money, inordinate power.

So Dante didn't want to think about what that smile did to him. All he knew was Eva belonged on the stage.

All too soon, her lips fell, together with her eyes. 'Excuse me,' she said. 'I must use the powder room.'

It was Yakatani's voice that tore his gaze from her lush hair and curvaceous behind.

'She is more than ready, Vitale. You will not have to wait long.'

Dante frowned. 'For what?'

The man laughed as if they shared some private joke—one which Dante wished he was in on—and said, 'That has certainly made up my mind. It is time we brought this discussion around to its lucrative assets. I fly to Tokyo on Friday and will not be returning for two weeks, so time is the issue. I prefer a quick sale, if you can manage it.'

Dante eased back into his chair, back in control of his world. 'I also fly east on Friday morning to Phang Ton.'

'They say it is truly a sight to behold. The most luxurious private domain in the world.'

Dante's killer instinct snarled and sniffed the scent of victory. 'I say you should see for yourself. Come. Be our guest for the weekend. Eva would love to meet your wife. One hour of business, the rest pleasure. I guarantee you'll fall in love with my slice of paradise.'

'We would be delighted.'

Dante smiled on a swell of gratification.

Come Monday morning, Hamptons would be his.

Eva stared at the first fall of snow dusting every step, every paving stone, like crystal sparkling, blazing like diamonds beneath the glare of streetlamps, as snapshots flickered in her mind. The beautiful baby boy. Dante staring at her with a dark, fierce intensity. One of his stunning ex-lovers kissing him on the cheek as they'd left. All reminding her of the naive, foolish girl who'd once made castles in the sky. Making her feel as fragile as the snowflakes kissing the heated windscreen. *Don't do this, Eva. Just walk away.*

'…so I agreed to fly out at ten a.m.,' Dante declared. 'I'll pick you up at eight. A warmer climate will suit.'

Warmer climate? Eva whipped around to face him. Noticed the car was parked outside her boutique. 'I'm not with you.'

'Have you listened to a word I said?'

She gave her head a little shake. 'Sorry, I'm tired. Tell me again.'

'Which is why you need a break, *cara*. Yakatani has accepted an invitation to my island this weekend. We fly out Friday morning.'

Eva blinked, her bones freezing despite the warm gush of the air-con. 'I can't go anywhere on Friday. I have a meeting with—' Her brain clicked into gear in the nick of time. She had an arrangement to see Prudence West. To save her deal. Her business. *All* she'd ever have. But she couldn't tell Dante that. Because all week he'd been insistent on meeting Prudence with her and she knew it would be an unmitigated disaster. Not only couldn't she think straight around him, this was her deal and she was saving it by herself. *Her* way. So, instead, she said, 'With a client.'

'Eva,' he said, the first flicker of annoyance firing his words, 'if all goes well, Hamptons is mine. It is one weekend. That is all.'

An entire *weekend*? No. *No*! No more. She couldn't take any more. 'I can't fly anywhere, Dante. I have a meeting at nine-thirty.'

'So change it.'

Eva locked her teeth, breathed deep. They'd made a deal. Yes, she wanted him to get Hamptons. Of course she did. But she was also sick and tired of him controlling her every move. 'No. I can't and I won't. Why don't you change your flight?'

'*Cristo*, cease with being difficult, Eva! I cannot go back on my word.'

'Oh, but I can? So it's okay for me to look unprofessional but not you.'

'I did not say that,' he bit out, raking his hand round the back of his neck.

'Yes, you did. Can you stop thinking of yourself for one solitary second? That,' she said, pointing one unsteady finger at the façade of her shop, 'is all I have. While you stockpile billions, that little boutique is all I have.'

'So you intend to go back on your word to me? For a prospective client who you could meet when we return? *Cristo*, I knew I shouldn't have trusted you.'

'You can trust me! But we're supposed to be in this together. You never consult me or I would've told you. I couldn't think of anything *worse* than spending the entire weekend with you but I made a deal and I intend to stick to it. We'll just have to compromise. Okay?' Even as she said the words, her stomach cramped with dread. An entire *weekend*?

Two whole days of kissing and touching. Craving the impossible.

Dante just looked at her as if she'd lost her marbles. Maybe she had.

'*What*?'

'Have you ever heard of the word *compromise* before?'

'I do not think so,' he said sardonically. 'It makes my brain slur, which leads me to believe it is a foreign language.'

'And here I thought you were multi-lingual.' She ignored the insolent arch of his dark brow. 'Compromise is when each side gives up something in order to reach a consensus. It is not me kowtowing to you. I'm quite happy to try and move my appointment back to nine but anything before that is a downright unsociable hour to call on someone. So, Mr Control Freak, if you'd like to engage in the foreign concept of compromise, you know where I am.'

And with that Eva burst from the car, slammed the door and held her head high as she negotiated the slippery foundations that were now her life. Another two days of this charade would bleed her heart dry.

Once inside, she tore her coat off, slung her bag on the sofa and paced. After two lengths of the room, an angry shrill broke her stride and she glanced down at her phone. And let loose a sigh.

Snatching the phone, she plunged into the wingback tartan chair. 'Hello, Dante.'

'Is eleven-thirty enough of a compromise?' he said, frustration lacing his voice with that yummy accent.

Eva closed her eyes. Her body at war. Brain screaming she was getting in too deep. Heart demanding she stand by her word. 'Yes.'

'Then you'll come with me?' he asked, a little huskier.

'I will.'

Silence stretched her already fragile composure and her head fell back, pillowed, comforted by the soft warm cloth. 'Goodnight, Dante.'

'*Ciao, cara,*' he said, low and delicious. Bone-melting to the point of exasperation.

Tossing the phone back on the oak coffee table with a resounding clatter, she released her breath in a long calming rush.

Why did he keep throwing her off balance? Why couldn't he stay arrogant and unbearable? Why did he have to tell her she looked exquisite when there was no one around to hear him? No audience to play to. Encourage her to speak, hang on her every word as if he truly cared what she thought.

A sweet sharp ache pierced her chest.

Lies. All lies. He was playing the perfect charade.

And yet, for several beats of her heart, they'd shared one long loaded look and she was eighteen again, her mother well and life was wonderful because Dante had burst into their world like a dark storm to whip her body and mind into a frenzy of want and need. And she'd taken every look, every innocuous word and spun them in the spinning wheel of her mind to weave the perfect spell—dreams of a forever kind of love. Where he'd be her first, her last, her everything.

Dante Vitale had been The One.

Then…suddenly her world had begun to fall apart. Suddenly her mother had been fighting for her life. Suddenly they'd been crushed by lies and betrayal and Eva had been catapulted into reality. Where women were fleeting diversions. Disposable. Dispensable. Where Dante soared to stratospheric heights, indulging in one-night-stands with his striking svelte brunettes, Eva knowing she could never compare.

A groan—pained, hers—echoed through the room. Because all it had taken was his warm hand reaching for hers as her mother's coffin was lowered into the ground and she'd forgotten all about how she was *nothing* like his other women. Only craved his touch, ached for him to still be her first, knowing it was her last chance…

Disaster. One she couldn't bear to remember. Because she'd start asking herself questions. Like: why? Why kiss her with the fervour she'd longed for, only to stop? Disappear. She must've disappointed him. Somehow.

Much like her second attempt at a physical relationship.

After that, she hadn't needed any more proof that she wasn't made for sex. So, in reality, when she'd been told she was high risk, the decision to avoid men altogether had been easy enough to make.

But now he was back.

Dante Vitale, the only man who'd ever made her feel true desire, was back.

And if he'd been disappointed five years ago, God only knew what he'd think now. Now she was broken. Racked with fears even she struggled to comprehend.

She didn't want to want him. To lie in his arms and be held, desired, made love to with a dark thrilling intensity. So why, every night, when her flesh was stone-cold and the silence was a physical ache, was she dreaming of that with him? *Still*, after all this time.

Impossible.

It was all too late.

One more weekend. Then this charade would end and she'd find peace. The desire would wane. It had to.

She'd forget him again. She must.

Right now it was time to save her business. All she'd ever have. And she was doing it *her* way. The only way she could live with herself.

She was telling Prudence West the truth.

CHAPTER SEVEN

SLEEK, SOPHISTICATED, AND as sexy as its billionaire owner, Dante's white super-yacht sliced through the mangroves, trailing ribbons of white froth in its wake.

Hair whipping about her shoulders, spray slapping against her skin in a refreshing cool mist, Eva basked in the endless beauty before her—towering rock faces on either side scored by the hands of time, the rugged façades sprawling with greenery and delicate ivory flowers she couldn't quite place.

The sun was sheer bliss, a blazing orange, rich and soothing against a sky so blue it could only be described as God's blank canvas.

Paradise on earth.

'Comfortable?' Dante asked, a savage edge still lingering in his tone. A censure she ignored. Yes, she'd been running late for the flight but the man was lucky she was still standing after the week she'd had.

'Very comfortable, thank you,' she replied, all sweetness, determined to lighten the mood, if only to get her over the next two days, as she lounged back in the buttery white leather chair.

Despite his dangerous aura, Dante leaned insolently against the back of the dark wood helm facing her, his tall muscular body draped in tailor-made trousers the colour of crème bisque and a navy blue polo shirt—all suave class and sophistication.

Arms crossed over his glorious wide chest, her eyes seared

over the densely corded muscle of his forearms before gliding to the open neck. Navy collar flipped high; the crisp edges flirted with his hair but it was the aviators wrapped around his face that almost tossed her over the edge.

Even after all these years, working with models, hanging out with the most handsome men in the world, Dante was still the most savagely beautiful picture of masculinity she'd ever seen.

Tearing her eyes from virile perfection, to her glass of freshly squeezed passion fruit juice, to the sheer beauty whistling by, she said, 'Oh, how the other half live.' It was meant to be a joke, a compliment. Instantly, she knew her mistake.

Dante's lips twisted. 'You've been cushioned by wealth all of your life, Eva. Still would be if you hadn't blown your mother's legacy on the party scene.'

Hand tucked into her side, Eva clenched the folds of her white sundress. 'How do you know about my legacy?' Blown on the party scene? My God, he really had a low opinion of her. Insides twisting, it took every ounce of effort to hold his slashing glare.

'Finn told me,' he declared.

'I forget how close you two were. Still, I'm surprised he told you something so personal yet you had no idea about my business.'

Something close to guilt washed over his bronzed complexion as he glanced to the east. 'It was a long time ago. The information was not freely given. I asked him if you were provided for. That is all. We have never spoken of you since.'

Grateful for the huge sunglasses covering half her face, she tipped her face towards the sun. *What were you hoping for, Eva?* That he would ask about you because he cared? That he couldn't help himself. Just as you couldn't resist the temptation of hearing one word about him?

Silence stretched, pulling her nerves every which way, until the boat swerved around the rugged edge of a cliff face…

'*Wow*! That's your island?' Clear aqua water lapped at sand so white, so fine, it reminded her of icing sugar. Shallow beaches framed with lofty palms swaying to and fro in the slightest breeze. And, set back within dense foliage, an enormous multi-level mansion, stucco walls, wide panoramic windows. 'I've never seen anything like it. Anything so stunning. So…dramatic. Dropped smack bang in the middle of paradise.'

'Welcome to Phang Ton.'

The way he said it… 'Phantom.' Like a dark shadow disappearing into the night. 'It suits you.' One minute here, gone the next. Leaving a hole as huge and devastating as his home. But not this time. This time there'd be no shadows lurking in her world, taunting her at night.

After the longest flight of her life, she was back in the game. He would have Hamptons in his hand even if it killed her.

All she wanted was for him to look at her with respect. True respect. If they could be friends, she would have closure on the past. Move on. This was her last chance. Because after this weekend she could never risk seeing him. Ever. Again.

The boat veered into a wide private dock where a phalanx of security and staff lined up on the highly polished deck. Dressed in white, they stood to attention, welcoming their master back into his powerful lair. And in that moment she felt a ripple of unease curl around her vertebrae, shimmy down her spine at the thought of the days to come. A role she'd never undertaken before—the role of hostess to a man who demanded perfection—and Eva was far from perfection. If this past week had stretched her acting abilities to the point where her nerves were fraying under the pressure, she just hoped this weekend didn't tear her apart.

Two long, hot days of sailing and scuba-diving in the glorious depths of the Andaman Sea blurred into nights of cocktails, laughter, dinner and dance. And by Monday evening, as Dante stood on the deck and waved Yakatani and his wife goodbye, a tidal wave of satisfaction washed over him.

Knowing Eva was waiting for him out back, he swivelled on his heel and jogged up the tiled steps, swerving into the staff entrance at the side of the house. After snagging a bottle of champagne and two platinum-lipped flutes, he headed back outdoors, this time veering left to skirt the balcony to the rear where the fresh scent of the island's jungle-like interior hung in the vaporous air.

One look and Dante took the usual swift kick to the guts.

There she was. Standing beneath the terracotta-tiled canopy gazing at the lush foliage, one hand twirling the tiny pearl at her lobe, the humidity clinging to her almond skin. Dressed in a white short-sleeved broderie anglaise shirt and a matching knee-length flirty skirt, she appeared angelic. A vivid contrast to the untamed danger surrounding her.

Lowering the chilled bottle to a small table, he noticed the pensive expression on her face and his heart did a strange pang.

Clearing his throat in warning, Dante watched her spin around, her face brightening as she walked towards him.

'Well?' she said, coming closer, caramel locks bouncing about her breasts, her gaze darting over his face. 'Stop teasing me. What did he say?'

Either she was emotionally invested in this deal or her acting skills were outstanding. Because he wasn't sure, he tried for an unconcerned shrug. 'Sign in two weeks.'

Fire, fierce and instantaneous, lit those stunning green eyes. 'Yes!' she whooped. And flung herself into his arms, or maybe he picked her up—*who cared?*—because he locked his arms tight around her and swirled around the floor. 'I'm so happy for you,' the words unnecessary because the way she kicked her feet into the air as he took her lush weight said it all.

Dante buried his face in her hair, inhaling the scent of camomile, so pure, so soft, so innocent.

A mass of emotions assailed him. That was why he held her tighter still, rocking, trying to block the image, the memory, the sudden question in his mind—one he'd *had* to stop asking himself a long time ago…

Why? Why had she run straight into the arms of another man mere hours after they'd parted in the pool-house? He wanted to know. Why? Why she'd acted so desperate for one night with him when any man would've done? But what was the point of dredging up the past, only for her to deny what he knew to be the truth. He wasn't even sure he could say the words without showing the unwelcome force of his emotions. What a fool she'd almost made of him.

Arms going slack, he gently lowered her to the floor and when she'd gained her footing he took a giant step back.

No matter the past, there were things she deserved to hear. 'You were amazing, *cara*. Made quite the impression. Yakatani has invited you and me to stay in Japan whenever we wish.'

Cheeks pinking, she smoothed the hug-wrinkles from her blouse with unsteady hands. 'Oh, dear. How did you get out of that one?'

'I didn't. I had more important things on my mind.'

'Like?' she asked.

'Thanking you.'

A warm smile—small and sweet, untutored and beautiful—curved her lips. As if he'd reached to the sky and plucked a star, just for her. 'You're welcome,' she said quietly, that sense of melancholy returning—one he couldn't understand, one he wanted to erase.

'Come,' he said. 'Let's celebrate. I have a bottle of the finest fresh from the cooler.'

While Eva held the glasses up, Dante had to force his eyes to do their job until the amber effervescence bubbled to the platinum band, in one, then the other. After sliding the bottle back to the table, he took one glass and toasted, 'To the future of Vitale. The biggest retail phenomenon in the world.'

'Congratulations, Dante. I hope it brings you much happiness.'

Happiness? Hell, no, his memory was too good for that. Still…

Clink went the flutes as the finest crystal collided in midair. 'Grazie, *cara*.' Years of hard work to ensure Vitale was crowned the world leader. To prove he was worthy of the name. That he, the bastard heir, had succeeded in doing what no other man had.

Tart and smooth, the cool liquid fizzed over his tongue, popped and crackled down his throat as he watched Eva from the corner of his eye. Simply cradling the glass. The exact same thing he'd watched her do all weekend.

'Why aren't you drinking?'

'I don't drink alcohol. But that doesn't stop me toasting your success.'

Dante's face twisted in disbelief. 'Eva. Come, now. I spend very little time in London but your antics were enough to reach news-stands the world over. Photographs, too many to count, you and…' *Your lover.* What was wrong with him? Why couldn't he even say it? '…Van Horn. Other male friends besides. Drinking. Partying. *Exclusive* clubs.' The words began to fire out of his mouth like bullets because suddenly it wasn't Eva he could see. It was his mother. Stumbling through the door, yet another man in tow. Another noise from her room. Part pain. Part pleasure. Dante covering his ears with the palms of his hands…

Bile rose in his throat and he swallowed, over and over.

'I know how it looked,' she said, her hesitant voice pulling him from the depths to meet a sense of shame hovering in the air. 'Believe me, I know. And I can blame the press for exaggerating my every move. For painting me the Diva. But I was the maker of my own downfall. I put myself in their path. I knew what I was doing at the time. Or at least I thought I did. In hindsight, I think I was…lost. Searching for what, I don't know.'

Dante blinked, bringing her face back into focus. There she was. The Fallen Angel. But at least she could stand tall and admit her mistakes. Had his mother ever done that?

'The paparazzi bothers you now.' Because she had a reputation to protect. So the Diva he'd expected had failed to make an appearance.

Now she lived only for work. Just as he did. She'd turned her life around and he admired her for that. Yet, there was more. Beneath. Secrets. A contradiction in her life he couldn't grasp.

'It always has. But this week, for the first time in my life, I haven't felt controlled by them.' One side of her lush mouth curved and the temptation to lick and taste made his mouth water. 'No, instead I've been controlled by you.' She placed her glass of amber fizz on the table. 'Reminds me of that adage: from the frying pan into the fire.'

'Too much heat, *cara*?'

'Way too much,' she said, edgy, breathless. Avoiding it. Fighting it. All they'd done all week.

And, *Cristo*, this weekend. Sweat-drenched nights of wanting, knowing she was in the bedroom opposite his. Those long satiny legs tangled in his sheets. That creamy almond skin smothered in his finest silk. Her breasts pushed into his soft mattress. His ring on her finger.

Of course the constant craving only served to heighten his frustration and fury. How could he still want her after she'd betrayed him?

Eva sat on the top wooden step leading down to the tropical interior. 'Anyway,' she began, slipping the black wedges from her feet and poking her toes into flimsy white tennis shoes, 'you promised me a walk on the wild side and, before I leave in the morning, we need to decide when we'll officially break up.'

The flute froze halfway to his lips. He watched the golden bubbles nudging, popping against the glass while his lungs remembered how to breathe. The reason, he assumed, was because they were nowhere near done.

Dante drained the glass in one smooth swallow. 'Let us not think of that now. We have two weeks until I sign and Miss West to contend with.'

Eva's foot froze mid-wiggle and she tilted her head until thick caramel hair tumbled, veiling her face.

A loud drum beat throbbed at his temple. '*Eeeva*? What are you not telling me?' Secrets—he could feel them lingering, putrefying, thickening the air like poisonous gas.

Eyes wide, determined, obstinate, locked on to his. 'My meeting on Friday morning was with Prudence West. She's going elsewhere for her gown. I lost the job.'

'*What*? I've a good mind to call the woman and tell her what a disastrous mistake she is making. Why did you not wait for me?' *Cristo*, why would the woman not let him take control?

'I can fight my own battles,' she said quietly, padding down the wooden steps to negotiate the beaten path snaking a trail through the wild tangle of palms, ferns and towering tree trunks.

He almost told her she hadn't fought this one very well but in that instant something dawned on him. Something so profound the earth revolved three-sixty. Pretty much the same way he felt every day this woman had been back in his life!

'And yet,' he said hoarsely, launching down the steps, his loafers crunching the woody undergrowth, curling his fingers around her upper arm, he tugged her to a stop, to face him, 'you came here regardless. When I could do nothing more for you. For two days you have entertained, been the perfect host, bewitched Yakatani at every turn to persuade him to sell to me. *Why*?'

'Because I gave you my word. You wanted Hamptons

so badly and I wanted you to have it. Why shouldn't one of us win?'

Bang—another shot from that stun-gun of hers—like a poacher's bullet straight between the eyes, making his head jerk. Never in his life had anyone done anything so selfless. Only for him.

Rendered dumbstruck, he found himself in the unique position of not knowing what the hell to do about it. And yet… as his eyes dipped to where she licked her full lips, there was one thing he'd never been more certain of in his life.

He wanted—*needed*—to kiss her. More than his next breath.

Except wasn't it more likely that Eva *needed* something more important than a taste of the man beneath?

In that moment Eva wouldn't have changed the last week for anything and, considering her entire life, her career, her business was hanging in the balance, that was saying something. But it was glorious to see derision replaced by a bud of admiration and a whole load of shock.

There was something else, too. An incredible force of will tautened his hard frame as if he leashed raw power. And the air began to pulse and moan as blood rushed through her veins.

Before she did something very stupid, like jump back into his arms to be held deliciously tight, beg him to kiss her and never stop, she stepped back and resumed her walk down the rutted pathway, shaded by the lush green overhang.

Without the Duchess, she had no idea what would happen next. All she knew was that she needed to wrest back control, call a halt to this charade, fly back to London and try to rebuild her world pre–Dante Vitale. Again.

Goose pimples flurried up her arms and she shivered violently.

Dante snapped out of his odd stupor and fell into step beside her. Voice controlled, so dark she sensed a danger in him, 'I'll make up what you lost on the job. It is the least I—'

Heat flamed from within, licking her insides, firing her voice. 'Don't even say another word. I wouldn't take a penny of your money. It was my choice to go it alone. Anyway, I had every intention of telling her the truth—'

He coughed an incredulous bark. 'The *truth. Maledizione!*'

The reason for his outburst suddenly dawned on her and her feet screamed to a halt. Swivelling to face him, she reached out a placating hand, careful not to touch, knowing she was at the very edge of her control. *Don't touch him, Eva. You'll lose your mind.* She knew. Just looking at him set her body on fire. *Oh, boy—focus, Eva, focus.*

'Hey, don't worry, okay? I realised at the last second how it may affect your deal and I didn't tell her in the end.' There she'd been, sitting in Prudence West's morning room being congratulated on her and Dante's engagement, and Eva had frozen, lies clogging her throat. Knowing there was a good possibility she would be risking his deal. So she'd sat there and told more lies for a man. One thing she'd *sworn* she'd never do after her father's antics.

In the end it had been pointless because, 'The decision had already been made.' And Eva had no doubt the soon-to-be Duchess had been pressurised by the cliques. One of which was fake fiancée number one—Rebecca. Eva had known from the start the power of a woman scorned. But Dante had his eyes on the prize and what would a man know of such humiliation, such pain? Nothing. 'My point is, I either make it on my own to swim or—'

Whoosh, he was off, dark, primitive and perilous, garbed entirely in stark, uncompromising black, pacing in front of her like a predator at home in his habitat. 'Are you telling me you will sink without it? So why will you not take my money? What the hell kind of woman are you, Eva? *Cristo,* first it is the ring, then the flowers, now my money! Am I not good enough for you, is that it?'

Good enough? Was he serious? Did he even know what he'd just said? No, surely not, he was too angry.

'Calm down. It's not personal. I won't be bailed out by anyone. I have new consultations lined up.' She just hoped they still came off when the novelty value of her and Dante wore off. And she didn't even want to think of what would happen when their break-up was announced. 'I won't sink. I've made it this far without help.'

Punching his fists into his pockets, he sent bark flying into the air with the toe of his loafer. 'Bank loans,' he growled, as if he knew. But she guessed his financial brain just connected the dots.

'One or two,' she choked out, trying to make light of her situation around the block in her windpipe. If he knew the true astronomical amounts involved he'd be…well, much like he was now—exasperation oozing from his every sinuous pore as he held her with an intense slashing glare. But that was ludicrous. He couldn't possibly know.

His pulse-thrumming physique towered over her. 'Are you telling me, you actually frittered over eight million on the party scene, to be left with *nothing*?'

So much for avoiding this topic of conversation. 'Don't be silly, Dante. On a couple of club memberships and a few parties? Only you could think that way in the first place.'

'So what happened to the money?'

The first prick of a migraine stabbed behind her eyes and Eva rubbed her temple. 'My dad remortgaged the house over and over. We almost lost it. I couldn't bear to see my mother's pride and joy being sold. Funny thing is, I can't even bear to go there now. To watch his latest wife tear another room down. Another strip of silk from the wall. By the time he'd settled on wife number four, my legacy…my car, Lexi…was gone.'

'*Maledizione*! You sold Lexi, that pampered mare, the love

of your life, to keep your father in that house? Finn *allowed* this?'

He was practically ranting. She couldn't help but smile. 'Finn was racing in the F1 World Championship at the time. When he came back he was furious, but it was too late. In all honesty, he doesn't know half of it. He already worries. Feels guilty. So don't you *dare* tell him. It was my choice to bail my dad out. And I'm sure you realise how much ex-wives cost.'

A thick, turbulent storm clouded his beautiful eyes. '*Sì*. I know this.'

Eva questioned how wise it was to pursue such a conversation. She couldn't bear to imagine him with his ex-wife. It physically hurt. The svelte brunette must've been infinitely special to coax Mr-One-Night-Wonder down the aisle. 'I'm guessing once was enough for you.'

'More than enough,' he said fiercely. 'And no, I do not wish to talk of it.'

Meaning there was an underlying hurt. Strange to imagine a mere woman having the power to hurt him.

'So you loved her?' she asked, wincing inwardly at the crack in her voice.

Dante choked out a laugh. A horrid, mocking sound that sent the tree-dwellers into a flurry of squawks and scuttles. 'I am incapable of such a thing. Love is for the weak and needy and I am neither.'

No, he was neither of those things. He was all indomitable strength and power. Always had been. Always would be.

Dante scrubbed his hands over his face, raked his hair with his fingers. 'Eva, I refuse to stand back and watch you struggle.'

'You have no choice,' she said with a hard undertone he couldn't easily miss.

'*Cristo*, there must be something else you want. What if I buy your lease? Move you to Mayfair. Buy you a house. *Whatever* you want. As a thank-you for closing this deal for me.'

Growling, she flung her arms wide. 'Is that your answer to everything? *Money*?'

He gave an insouciant shrug—an act that completely contradicted the sudden tension emanating from his powerful frame. And words, *his* words, began to prick her psyche. *What the hell kind of woman are you, Eva? Why will you not take my money?*

That was exactly what he thought. Women only wanted him for his money. It was the most harebrained notion she'd ever heard and yet he *actually* believed it.

A sweet, sharp ache pierced her chest. How must that feel to him?

In truth, she knew. How many times had she wished people would see past her notorious pop star father, her uber-talented mother, even Finn, the dashing, death-defying racing driver and see *her*, Eva? Want to spend time with *her*, Eva? Not that she could get them backstage passes or get them smack bang on the front page, or even a longed-for introduction to Finn. And to think that all this time Dante—*the* Dante Vitale—felt something similar, just boggled the mind. Cracked her heart.

Forgetting about all the reasons she wasn't to touch, Eva reached up, brushed the back of her fingers down the side of his savagely beautiful face, cupped his unyielding jaw. Felt the heat and need trickle through her veins. Ignored the desperate surge of self-preservation to pull away. Because he *needed* to hear this.

'Oh, Dante, I don't want your money. I knew you when you had nothing.' *I wanted you when you had nothing.* 'And still I don't want or need anything from you.'

Brow scrunching, he gave a flummoxed shake of his head, eyes never leaving her gaze, those haunted, almost tortured umber eyes boring into hers as if searching for veracity.

Veracity he must've found because that look morphed into something hot and heavy and thick. Clouding his eyes with hot, devilish intent. Clawing the air with ferocious need. 'Now *that* is a lie, Eva, and you know it. You wanted something from me then and you still do…'

Daunting and more than a little dangerous, his voice incited a weft of excitement and a warp of unease through her body.

'…A taste of the dark side.'

Oh, boy. Hand slipping from his face, she took a tentative step back, heart thundering so loud she'd swear a herd of elephants were stampeding towards them. *Run, Eva, run.*

Except his deep gaze held her captive as he towered above her in an unmistakable pose of sexual dominance. Then his big strong hands shot to her waist and yanked her flush against his hardness.

'Let me go,' she panted, even as she gripped his upper arms, felt the dense muscle flex beneath her fingertips, sending a deep tremor through her core, exploding in a feverish flurry.

A ghost of a smile played about his sinful mouth. 'Say it like you mean it, *cara*, and I will consider it,' he said in a voice thick and syrupy with hot, sweet intent, sucking heat from her every pore to gather and pool low in her pelvis.

Oh, hell, did he have to be so…so horridly, deliciously male?

Eva cleared her throat, tried again. 'Let. Me—'

Pounce—the fiend jumped straight in for the kill and nipped the words from her bottom lip with his front teeth. And when he soothed the tingling flesh with a sinful flick and lap of his tongue the jungle vanished behind her eyelids. *Think, Eva, think.*

'Explosives. Dangerous. We're ignoring this bit, remember?'

Except now he was doing that nuzzling thing that turned her brain to a cotton puff ball. That delicious, delirious, nuzzling thing, where he brushed up the side of her face with his roughened jaw and the erotic friction made everything go maddeningly wild inside her.

Breathe, Eva, breathe.

'I've had enough of ignoring it,' he growled. 'It makes me angry.' He licked the sensitive skin beneath her ear and inched his way down her neck, tasting her skin with delicious, dewy, open-mouthed kisses, and the sensory overload sparked the need to thrust her fingers in his hair and hold him to her. So tight. So close.

His big hands curved around her waist and moulded to her bum before he yanked her tight against him and slanted his mouth over hers in a kiss of seduction and fire. And, *oh boy*, she could feel him, hard against her stomach, and she rolled her hips against the thick ridge of his erection, desperate now, mewling against his lips.

His answering groan coalesced, fogging the air with a carnal cloud. '*Cristo*, I *must* have you, Eva.'

The thought that she was in the jungle, being ravished by the king of all predators, should have had her scrambling up the nearest tree but, *oh boy*, she'd never felt so alive. He really, truly, seriously wanted her. And she wanted him to take her, devour her. With all that dark, delicious, smouldering power. Just this once.

Her heart wasn't at risk. She wasn't that girl any more. As long as he didn't stop; she couldn't bear it if he stopped again.

'You kiss like a flaming siren, you know that?'

She did? Ah, well, it didn't take a genius to work out what he'd expected. A siren to drag down, down, down into his inferno. Such heat, she would surely burn.

Eva. A siren. If she wasn't on the scorching cusp of the mother of all orgasms she would laugh. Because surely she would disappoint him again. Of course she would. *Oh, boy*, what was she *thinking*?

'Dante, I…should go pack. I leave early and…' *I'm scared. In case I can't be the woman you want.*

But this is your last chance, Eva, your only chance to have him. Inside you. To know what passion truly feels like. To know what Dante Vitale feels like.

His grip tightened with a sharp possessive nip as he thrust one hand into the hair at her nape, curled the other underneath her bottom and lifted her into his arms, encouraging her to wrap her legs around his waist until her lace knickers snuggled against his hard, thick length and a helpless plea poured from her throat.

'The only place you are destined to be, *cara*, is in my bed.'

CHAPTER EIGHT

Up the sweeping grand staircase they went, while Eva snatched kisses, nibbling, biting her way across the scimitar curves of his hard cheekbones and jaw. When she thrust her hands in the hair at his nape and tugged at the silky strands, Dante sucked air between his teeth, his low baritone a sonorous boom, '*Cristo*, Eva.'

Stumbling awkwardly, Dante paused on the first landing and crushed her against the wall to deepen the kiss and press hard up against her. *Yes, kiss me. Kiss me. So I can't think. Don't stop. Please don't stop.*

The notion that it would be quicker to let her walk filtered through her lust-deranged mind but thankfully he seemed to share her urgency because off they went once more, down the wide picture gallery hallway to their suites, lips locked, banging into the walls, first one side—knocking a priceless painting off its perch, the clatter caroming around the cavernous space—then the other, time and time again.

Slam went her bedroom door against mink plaster, then *slam* back it went, before Dante loosened his grip and Eva slithered down his body, luxuriating in every wickedly hard inch of him.

Lungs screaming for air, their lips tore apart but the onslaught never stopped, not for one second.

For a seamstress, her fingers were failing miserably, fumbling with his shirt buttons and after a good five seconds she tore it wide.

'Hungry, *cara*?' he rasped.

'Famished.' She could do this. Definitely. Be everything he expected and more. Hadn't she read enough steamy books in her time? Of course she had. Hadn't she been Oscar-worthy this week? Of course she had. With any luck, enthusiasm would more than make up for the fact that she was about as practised as a nun. Because there was no way on earth she was disappointing him again.

Eva smoothed her palms over his chest, the thin dusting of hair over his honed pecs, her palms burning. 'You're so hot.' Feverish.

'Always for you,' he said. Injecting her bravado with another shot of intensity.

Snap went the button on his trousers and Dante kicked them to the floor—*don't look down, don't look down, you're bound to blush like a gauche fool*—before he curved his big hands around her waist, stopping at the small of her back to whip down the zip of her skirt.

Eva felt the cool fabric swish down her legs, his fingers curl under the waistband of her knickers, and fought another bout of antsiness that she was nothing, *nothing* like his skinny other women by crushing his mouth with hers, tangling with his tongue in a raging sensual dance of wills. Thrust, parry, back and forth, heads slanting for a deeper connection that spoke to her very heart.

'Next time we go slow, *sì*? I've waited for you too long,' he said, unsteady hands back at her stomach, fumbling with the thin belt of her blouse. '*Cristo*, it feels like an eternity. I want you, Eva. In my arms. In my bed.'

Eternity? Eva closed her eyes, knowing he didn't mean it, but it sounded so wonderful she took every word, locked them in her mind. Just as she'd used to all those years ago. Little meaningless things he'd said to her or the way he'd said her name. She'd store them all. Knowing it was wrong, bad for her soul.

'It's okay,' she said breathlessly. 'Whatever you want.' Because the way he wanted her, with such desperation, drowned out the voices, warning, whispering.

He whipped off her belt and unsnapped the tiny hooks down the centre of her blouse, opening the material wide and smoothing his hands to ease it over her shoulders until she stood only in her white lace bra.

Before he could even think about taking it off, she lunged back to his mouth, lips clashing with a hunger he returned tenfold.

Dante backed her towards the bed, his hands around her back, reaching for her bra clasp and, dammit, she felt her shoulders stiffen, her stomach pull with a fear she'd never been able to understand. But it was so strong, she undulated her torso, rolled her shoulders to dislodge his hands.

Thank God he didn't seem to notice and they plunged atop the bed, Dante's glorious weight pushing her deep into the sumptuous, luxurious swathes of satin and silk.

'Eva, what the hell do you do to me? *Cristo*, I cannot think.'

His hands were everywhere. In her hair, fisting. At her waist, gripping. At her thigh, lifting her leg high over his hip. Wildfire trailing. Skimming over her bottom. Then she felt him. Hot and, *ohh boy*, he was huge and thick, and she widened her legs, hoping…hoping…

But then his hand followed the dip of her waist to cup her breast and her insides chilled, grew taut. No. *No*! She tried, she really tried to breathe, to relax, but at that moment she realised her mistake. She should've told him. Told him everything. And that realisation made her tense even more. Because he would never have believed her. Never.

Too late. Too late, she knew.

Lips locked, he groaned into her mouth, his huge body

flexing and then *slam*, he drove inside of her with one powerful thrust.

Her insides tore as if wrenched with a red-hot darning needle as he embedded himself so deep she'd swear he crushed her heart. Arching her spine, she couldn't stop the high-pitched cry spilling from her lips, pouring over his tongue.

Blackness hovered at the edges of her mind, dancing around with her vision, skewing her pulse. And she tore her mouth free. Dragged air into her lungs. Gasping. Gasping. *Don't you dare pass out, Eva, don't you dare. Breathe. Breathe.* In and out. Slow and even.

Glimmers of warm sensation—like dust motes—fluttered inside her. A heady feeling of rightness—blissful, halcyon rightness—seeping, easing, until she grew lax and smoothed her hands over Dante's shoulders.

Shoulders that were locked. His honed body the epitome of a cast bronze god.

Eva prised her eyes open, eased back, looked up…

And her heart stopped. Dead.

Horrified. He was utterly mortified. 'Dante?' she whispered, hating the tremble in her voice.

'No,' he choked before cursing thickly, words slurred by his heavy accent, '*No*! Impossible.' His damp dark hair clung to his temples as he shook his head, lifting his weight, his warmth, his protection, from her body.

'Stop!' This man was *not* doing this to her again. 'Dante, *please*. Don't do this.'

The past slammed into her, throwing her back five long years, and there she was, lying on the sofa in the pool-house, clothes torn in haste—*Stay with me, just tonight.* If not to give her the night she'd always dreamed of, then just to hold her. Tell her everything was going to be okay. That the pain would diminish somehow. And he'd stood up. Left. Walked away. And she'd lost him too. Leaving her so alone, so lost, she'd drifted mindlessly for months, years.

A tear slipped, unchecked, trickled down the side of her cheek into her hair. 'Please don't go.'

Same look on his face—stupefied, stunned, blinking as if waking. As if someone or something else had taken over his body and he was fighting it. Fighting it with all his might. Struggling. Struggling for control.

'I… *Maledizione*, Eva, I cannot.' Same words, same darkness falling into his beautiful eyes as he withdrew, disappeared into the black of night. Never to be seen again.

Palms flat, Eva pushed his chest. 'Just go, Dante,' she said. 'Just…go.'

A deluge of feeling, as if he'd been doused, plunged into a thick, turbulent whirlpool of emotion, had Dante yanking at the mocha satin sheet and draping it delicately over her body as she buried her face in the pillow and curled onto her side in a defensive ball.

Scrunching his eyes shut, his guts twisted so hard the muscles in his stomach gave way. Abs crunching, he flinched.

Cristo, he'd hurt her.

Control obliterated, he'd been riding on the atavistic need to take her, make her his, stamp every other man from her mind. Mindless, desperate, he hadn't even removed her bra and he'd taken her with the civilised finesse of a savage barbarian.

Dante tore his eyes from her, whipped his hipsters up his legs and took another swift punch in the gut when he saw pale red smear the white cotton.

An innocent. *Maledizione*!

Another swirl of thick black emotion curled in the pit of his belly, one he'd never known, and it made him feel sick and his heart ache.

He stalked through to the en suite bathroom, bent over the tub and twisted the gold taps until water gushed, hot and steamy, pooling generously at the base. Tearing through the mirrored wall cabinets, he found the bath soak he'd ordered especially for her, tried one squirt, gained ten little bubbles, so he tore off the lid and upended the entire bottle with a satisfying squelch.

Plumes of neroli flower and gardenia wisped in the air and Dante strode back into the bedroom, around the side of the huge bed, sank his arms underneath her prone form, swept her up in his arms, holding her tight, so tight to his chest as he carried her through.

'Dante?' she breathed, tensing, struggling for a few heart-tripping seconds until she burrowed into him, curled her arms about his neck. 'Wh...what are you doing?'

Slowly, inexorably, he eased her into the water, wincing inwardly as he waited for her pained cry. Yet she just looked at him. Green eyes sparkling with *amazement*?

She'd expected him to walk away. To leave her. As if he cared nothing for her.

Rubbing over his chest with the palm of his hand, he asked himself: could he really blame her for thinking such a thing? *You're cold, Dante, hard, just like your father, how can anyone love you?*

Brow lined with pain, Dante watched her lift her knees and hug them to her chest. And it was right then he noticed the soaked white straps...

'*Dannazione, cara*, your bra, I forgot.'

'Oh, it's okay,' she said, her attention drifting to the mass of scented bubbles rising around her. 'I have another one.'

'Here,' he said, bending over the roll-top to reach her back. 'Take it off.'

'No!' Jerking her shoulders to stop him. Dante swallowed hard. She didn't want him touching her and could he blame her for that either?

'*Cristo*, Eva, why didn't you tell me?'

She shook her head in a sweet, naive kind of sadness and the ground gave a peculiar tilt. It was like looking at young

Eva. As if the clock had been turned backward. As if the last five years had never happened.

'I thought you wouldn't believe me,' she said.

And that feeling came back. Made him want to do strange things. Like get in that bath. Snuggle up behind her and hold her and rock her and wash away the blood, the pain. But she didn't want his touch, did she? No. So he rooted his feet to the floor, knowing he didn't deserve to assuage his own needs, and stood firm, his every muscle aching, burning under the pressure.

'I'm okay. Honest. It was just a flash…at first. It was almost gone.'

'It was?' he said, releasing a breath he was unaware he held.

'Yes. There's no need to feel guilty. It wasn't your fault.'

Guilt. Yes, that was what he felt. Guilt. Fault. Because it *was* entirely his fault.

Wasn't it?

Maledizione! A lightning bolt shot down and every muscle in his body coiled with murderous intent.

'*Cristo*, that bastard told me he'd had you six ways till Sunday.' Lies. Lies. Lies Dante had believed.

Eva's head snapped around. 'Who? Who told you that?'

Dante thrust his fingers through his hair. 'I cannot have this conversation with you naked.' Except for the bra. There was something…something not quite right about that bra and he couldn't work out what.

And *hell*, all he wanted to do was get in that bath. He'd be lucky if she ever shared one word with him again, never mind water. And just the thought of never touching her again, tasting the sweet delicacy of her skin, devouring her lush mouth. *Cristo*, what was wrong with him? He was losing control, dammit! 'Ten minutes. Then I will be back.'

'*What*? You can't drop that bombshell and then leave me. Dante, wait!'

Ignoring her sassy mouth that said if he walked out he

wouldn't get back in again, Dante stormed to his bedroom, showered, donned some black lounge trousers and stalked back to her room. Half-expecting it to be locked.

The door was ajar; he eased it open, his chest clenching as he found her standing in front of the dark wood dressing table, tearing her hair out with a soft paddle brush. 'The only reason you're back in here is because I want the truth. I deserve it. Then you can leave.'

Slap went the brush to the dresser as she turned to face him, sparks firing from her eyes, swamped in a fluffy white robe, arms crossed tight over her breasts in self-defence.

Dante cleared his throat. 'Are you sore? Do you need pain-killers?'

'I'm absolutely fine. I want to know who said that about me.'

Raking his hand round the back of his neck, he said, 'Van Horn. The night of your mother's funeral. After you and I... parted in the pool-house.'

Silence seeped into every crack, every fibre, except the corners of his mind, where he could still hear Van Horn's vile words. Still feel the blistering fury that had almost smashed the other man from Kent to kingdom come.

Expecting her temper to flare, instead he found the green depths of her eyes swimming in hurt. 'And you...you *believed* him?'

Truth. Always truth. '*Sì.* Every word. He told me you'd been an item for weeks.'

'Weeks?' she said. '*Weeks, Dante?* You actually believed that I'd had the time or the desire or even the inclination to have secret trysts and slum it in his seedy hotel rooms on tour when my mother was ill? When I'd put my life on hold to look after her night and day?'

He nodded, well aware that, for the first time in years, he was feeling something close to shame. 'I never thought of it that way. I was angry.'

'I don't care how angry you were. How could you think that of me? I asked you to spend the night with me. I—' Stricken eyes flaring with dismay, her arms fell to her sides. 'Oh, my God. You must've thought I wanted one night with you, just so I could go on sleeping with him too. That...that's sick. Disgusting. Please tell me you didn't think me capable of that?'

'I thought exactly that, Eva.'

Crushing her lips together, her thick eyelashes fluttered closed, brow pinching.

Within seconds he was padding across the mahogany floor towards her, swerving round the foot of the bed...when she snapped out of her sombre state and held one palm flat, breaking his stride a couple of feet from her.

'Why? Why did you think the worst of me? Or is every woman a conniving wretch?'

Dante faltered. He didn't suppose he'd had the greatest example of women from the start. His mother could never have been termed a paragon of virtue and admittedly his father gave him little chance to forget it. Toss in a glut of women who had their third eye focused on the scintillating lure of his billions and his cynicism had been nailed. Of course, as she'd rightly pointed out earlier, Eva had come along before he'd made his fortune. And since the moment he'd first seen her till the night he'd walked away he'd truly believed she was an angel. So why? *Because just looking at her scared the hell out of you*, his conscience whispered.

Locking on to her gaze, he said, 'I saw no reason for him to lie.' As the past unfolded in his mind, he felt a stab of retaliation. 'And don't you *dare* play the innocent with me, Eva. At the time I didn't think you knew your own grief-stricken mind. You were Finn's little sister, for Christ's sake. I came back to explain why you and I could *never* happen and what do I find? You and Van Horn locked tight in the garden, bringing new meaning to mouth-to-mouth. Before I left he took great pleasure in extolling your sexual escapades. So, from where I stood, you were quite happy to seduce another in my place.'

Her robe, so soft, so white, rose and fell on shuddering breaths and she stumbled back a step as if he'd slapped her with the sins of the past.

The usual lush green of her eyes turned bleak and she nodded. 'He found me in the maze. I was so upset. You just…disappeared. He hugged me. And yes, he kissed me.' The inner torment scouring his soul must've shown on his face because she reached out, her hand quivering in mid-air. 'But when I realised what I was doing, I pushed him away. Told him no. So I can't understand why he lied to you.'

'Come now, Eva. Can you not? The man obviously wanted you for himself. Let us not forget you were then pictured with him continuously during the year that followed.'

With one hand, she reached up and gripped both sides of the robe, closing the small gap—knuckles bleaching—hiding the thin sliver of almond skin.

'We hung around in the same crowd. Parties. Concerts. Perfectly oblivious. He persisted…hounded. Was relentless in trying to get me into bed.' Chin dipping, she looked to the floor, where she flexed her foot, rubbed her toes on the rug. 'Pity I wasn't worth the effort.'

Flinching on another swift kick to the guts, he tried to speak through the fiery knots in his throat. 'Things developed between you?'

Backing up another pace, widening the gap, she leaned against the wide panoramic window. The soothing rouge hues of sunset cast her in an ethereal light, picking up the golden strands of her beautiful long caramel hair, outlining her lush body to stunning effect.

'About a year after I last saw you…' Which would have been around the time he'd got married, he was sure. And why could she not look him in the eye? 'I decided it was time and I tried.'

'*Tried* being the operative word, *tesoro*. Because, right then—' he said, pointing to the rumpled sheets with an unsteady hand, 'you were still just as innocent as when I first laid eyes on you.' And hadn't it always been there? A whisper of purity that called to him—a man who had seen the darkest, most tainted, debauched side of life.

'I struggled. He said I was...' Closing her eyes, her brow creased and she banged her head gently off the glass.

Crack went his knuckles as his fists screamed bloody murder. 'Eeeva?'

'Sexless. He found it quite amusing that men drooled over me. Over my chest.' Cheeks pinking with a heart-wrenching embarrassment, her attempt at a small smile bordered on apologetic. 'Problem is, I don't like them being touched. I didn't realise how strongly I felt until that night. So, as you can imagine, it was a disaster. But, looking back, I agreed to sleep with him for all the wrong reasons. I didn't want him. I wanted...'

'Wanted what, *cara mia*?'

'It doesn't matter any more.'

Frustration snaked through his chest. The need to push her for more coiling in his throat. But she was closing in on herself, withdrawing. Pain pleating her brow. Making him wonder if this was the first time she'd relived it.

'Speak to me, *please, tesoro*.'

Rubbing her temple, she said, 'It was my fault, Dante. Everything he said was right. That I was a tease. I didn't mean to be. I was just messed up. He said I was frigid and his face, my God, he was so angry and nasty and—'

Black and thick, fury poured through him. 'Did he touch you? Hurt you? Make you cry?' Teeth bared, he let out a low growl, struggling to leash his temper as he sorted through words, let loose a few Italian expletives. 'That bastard. I'll kill him.' Not even close. Doubting there was a vile enough word in the Dante vocabulary that could come close to satisfying the noxious mixture of frustration and rage that churned through his veins.

Eva's eyes flared wide and she pushed off the window with her bottom, laid her hand on his upper arm. 'No, no, hey, you can't do that! He just said nasty things. That's all. In all fairness, Dante, it was true. He couldn't even—' She looked down at his crotch. Seemed to stay there a while. 'You know.'

'He couldn't get it up, right?'

Tipping his head to one side, he snagged her attention from the thick ridge in his trousers. 'Let me make one thing abundantly clear, Eva. That excuse of a man was probably so high on drink and drugs that he could not stand up, never mind get *it* up.'

Insanely, he was grateful. She would've felt cheap giving herself to such a man. And, though it was a contemptible thing to admit, he wanted her only for him. To not have been touched, defiled by others. He knew what that made him—a hypocrite of the highest order. But she was his, dammit!

Whoa... His? No, she wasn't his. What the hell was wrong with him?

'So why did you stop?' she asked faintly. 'That night. In the pool-house. Didn't I disappoint you too?'

Dante raked his palm over the hard ridges of his aching stomach. 'You think you disappointed me?'

Cristo, what would that have done to her confidence? Then, after him, Van Horn. 'No, *cara*. No. You were grieving, it was not right.'

Disappoint him? *Maledizione*, she couldn't be further from the truth.

He wanted her to be confident in her body. Not for him. Only for her. All that passion seemed to be restrained by vulnerability and a lack of self-confidence he had engendered. Well, he was damn well fixing it. Right now. Her purity was gone and the devil would dance in heaven before he allowed her only memory of this night to be one of pain.

Dante slowly backed her up against the glass wall, unravelling the sash on her gown, unwrapping her provocative body to his eyes, unveiling a plain white bra and matching panties—which drove him crazier than any G-string or crotchless slip he'd *ever* seen.

'Did it look like I was disappointed, *cara*? Does this,' he said, curving his hands around her small waist, delving lower to cup her lush, round cheeks and hauling her against his pelvis, 'does *this* feel like you don't turn me on?'

A little shiver. A little shake of her head.

'You are the *sexiest* woman alive. I am no virgin, Eva, and I can tell you right now I have never *ever* been so desperate to get inside someone as I am you, *capisci*?'

She nodded. Chest rising and falling. Soft skin spilling from her bra.

'I want this lethal, gorgeous body naked,' he said, voice thick and husky with want. 'It is a constant craving. Like a ticking time bomb, one touch to detonate, one thrust to explode. And I am going to watch you explode time and time again until you cannot think of what that useless bastard said to you. Only what I am doing to you. With my fingers, my mouth, my wicked tongue and my painfully hard…' Brushing up the side of her face, knowing it drove her wild, he whispered the word in her ear—the dirty variation he knew would flip her trigger—and he felt her stomach scrunch, her spine hit the glass.

Resting his brow against hers, he luxuriated in the heat seeping from her body, oozing into his. 'Do you pleasure yourself, Eva?'

He heard her audible gulp. Knew that was the only answer she was capable of.

One hand still holding her mind-blowing curvaceous derrière, Dante caught hold of her left hand, raised it to his mouth and nipped and sucked her ring finger from tip to base, watching her cheeks flush and her thick hazel lashes grow heavy.

As he twisted her hand this way and that, her yellow diamond caught fire and that possessiveness was back with a vengeance, pervading his chest until his ribs cracked at the thought of her taking it off to walk away, to leave him. *It's only because you're her first; it will wane. It must.* 'And do you wear my ring, Eva? Do you think of me while you touch?'

Body visibly seething with desire, she could barely breathe. 'Yes.'

He felt her knees give way and he thrust his thigh up between her legs to stop her fall. Within seconds, she was rocking against him. And, *Cristo*, he could feel her hot, wet heat at his thigh, scorching his skin.

The notion he may lose it flashed through his mind, yet he discarded it just as quickly. This time he'd take it slow. Replace every imperfect memory of earlier with a night she would never forget. The first time she deserved.

Eva gripped his shoulders, fingered his hair. 'I need…'

'What?' he said, licking across her bottom lip, kissing the corner of her full mouth. 'Tell me exactly what you need, what you want. I will give you everything you have ever desired of me.'

Chin dipping, Eva glanced at her bra. He caught her meaning instantly.

Why dislike being touched there? An inkling that it pertained to her mother slithered into his mind and his stomach fisted. But now was not the time. He would fix it. Later.

'So we take it one step at a time,' he said. 'First time we leave it on and I will touch you everywhere but your breasts. *Sì?*'

'You can do that?' she asked, her eyes flicking up to his, striking green pools connecting to his like powerful magnets.

'*Sì*. Of course.' It would take every scrap of self-control but he would do it. For her. And, just so she could relax, he admitted, 'You will soon discover I am bottom-half kind of guy, *cara*.'

'Oh. Yes. I think I've noticed.'

With a half smile designed to make her bones liquefy, he said, 'Trust me.' And swept feather-light kisses down her soft stomach, revelling in her sweet moans and the gooseflesh that arose on her almond skin. Then he delved into her panties, deeper into her wet folds, stroking, probing and swirling.

The urge to replace his fingers with his mouth, bury his tongue to taste her sweetness, coursed through him, making his mouth beg, his pulse quicken. So much so, he gripped her waist to keep her upright, ready to fall to his knees. And *devour*.

But, before he did, she fisted his hair, undulated atop his hand and pulled him down for a kiss. His kiss. Only his. And all he could think was: mine. Mine. Mine.

For one night only.

Eva belonged to him.

CHAPTER NINE

OVER AND OVER, Dante pushed her to the wicked edge of oblivion and tossed her into the deep, dark realms of ecstasy. Until she was boneless. A boneless quivering mass of thrumming desire. Until the sky was velvet black and the moon waxed in fullness.

Heart pounding, blood rushed through her veins as they finally, *finally* tumbled upon the bed, Eva cushioned atop piles of luxurious silk pillows, while Dante braced his weight on his forearms either side of her head, caging her with his long, hard, muscular body—a body vibrating with arousal, stretched to its very limits by his infinite patience.

Silver ribbons of light spun through the windows and her heart stumbled at the sight of her dark phantom hovering above her—colour slashing his cheekbones, eyes black with desire. And she couldn't resist because the man was a primal male fantasy come to life, so she ran her fingertips over his washboard abs, down the sweat-slicked super-sexy V of muscle on his pelvis and curled her fingers around his thick satiny length…

Dante sucked air between his teeth, jerked from her touch. 'No, *cara*.' And gently pulled her wrist away. 'Give me a minute. *Cristo*, I cannot think when you touch me.'

'Don't think. I want you now,' she said, smoothing her fingers round the tight curve of his rear, which she cupped and squeezed to lure him inside her. So very deep. Until she felt whole. Wanted. Desired. By him. Only him.

'Eva,' he growled, slashing his mouth over hers, one hand diving into her hair, the other roaming over her waist and hip with a covetous, mind-blowing touch.

A touch he withheld from her breasts. Breasts that ached with an inexplicable heavy need. So sensitive, she fought with the sudden desire to be free of the white fabric encasing, clutching. But if she tried, took it off, he would see. He would know. And he could *never* know. So she leashed the need—something she sensed in him too. Leaving her vaguely aware that they both held something back.

It was the rapacious predator in him. Dark. Perilous. That savage intensity that made her feel truly alive. Harnessed by the brutal power that was all Dante Vitale. So virile. So heart-stoppingly male.

Yet as soon as the void bubbled in her brain, it popped on a red-hot pinprick of rapture as he traced over her knee before slowly, seductively gliding up the inside of her thigh, stopping short of her wet curls. Wet from his mouth, where his tongue had lapped and kissed, tearing orgasm after orgasm from her shuddering body.

And, right now, she could taste that very essence, her blood already addicted, thirsting for more, and so she held him to her, tangling her tongue with his, drinking *them* in. Knowing. Her dreams hadn't come anywhere near close to the divine reality of him.

'Eva…Eva…' he murmured—making her heart throb— as he eased one hand under her bottom to lift, to tilt, so he could snuggle hard and tight in the apex of her thighs. And, *oh boy*, the sensation of his thick length pressing shot her straight back to that wicked edge and she undulated, grinding her pelvis into him.

'Slow, *cara*. Only pleasure,' he said, voice hoarse as his

breathing escalated. 'You are so small inside.' His bronzed skin damp, big body trembling as if he feared hurting her.

'Take me… *Please*.' Just give me this. Memories to hold, to cherish, to remember.

As if she were made of the finest French lace, able to tear under the slightest of pressure, he eased the wide velvet tip of his erection inside her, so very gently. And her heart, *oh, God*, her heart ached. Ached so much she brushed the damp hair from his brow and stared into his dark eyes—watched them grow heavy, glaze out of focus with her every touch—as he finally took her. Because she didn't want to miss this moment. The one she'd been waiting for all her life. The connection so startlingly intense she felt tears clot her throat, prick the back of her eyes.

Panic seeped into her chest and in that moment she understood her craving for him to unleash. Because like this he posed more danger to her heart. He was almost making love to her. If she closed her eyes, she could pretend, dream as she used to so long ago, that this was her wedding night, *their* wedding night, and she'd saved herself for him. Only him. And such dreams did not belong in this bed. They were the dreams of a naive heart. A girlhood crush. Not the dreams of a woman who knew the limitations of her life. Knew the agony from loving another.

'*Cara*, tell me if you pain.' *Easy*, he entered her and her sheath tightened, pulled, sucking him in.

Her head pressed hard into the pillow and she arched sinuously. 'You feel *amazing*, Dante. So good. I want more. I want all of you.' *I always have. Your heart, your soul…* No. No! She didn't. Not any more. This was just sex, passion. Lust.

'Eva…' Pure animalistic, a groan, long and deep, came from the depths of his chest, calling to her, spurring self-preservation, refashioning it into recklessness, pulling him down for another kiss. A kiss to blow his mind, make him lose control. All heat and need and want as she writhed to take him deeper, curling her legs around his lean hips, hugging him closer.

'More.'

'*Cristo*,' he groaned, sinking in the last incredible inch until their bodies locked into place. Like two halves of a puzzle clicking together. And the relief, *oh*, the relief was unlike anything she'd ever known. It made her fall back into the mattress, nestle her face in his neck and just…breathe…in and out… breathe him in—all raw masculine power and dark desire.

Time stilled in a unique fragile trance as they lay that way, holding, clutching.

Dante murmured against the sensitive skin where her neck met her shoulder, his every hot breath enticing a shiver. 'You feel like heaven, *cara mia*, you taste like heaven. You are mine, Eva. Mine.' All possessive domination.

Even knowing it made her a fool, she couldn't help but luxuriate in the vibrant violence behind his words.

'I'm yours.' And she was. For this moment. The most amazing of her life.

'Kiss me,' she begged. Because the man could rock her world with just a kiss and he growled into her mouth, before his lips stole her breath.

Flexing his hips, he began to move in and out of her— slowly at first, focused solely on her pleasure, kissing her face, sucking softly on her neck, smoothing his hand down her thigh, caressing her bottom.

'Do you have any idea what you do to me? Do you, Eva?' His dark accent hummed over her skin, notching the heat to danger levels, and she pulsed and clenched with the force of another climax, her lower abdomen now a spool spinning faster and faster, wrapping in luxurious velvet…

'Dante…' She kept breathing his name and each time she did his rhythm grew fiercer as if hearing her chant his name fed his fire. So for the first time in her life she danced beneath a warm deluge of female power.

'Speak to me,' she implored. 'I love it when you speak to me.' Feet flat to the bed, she pushed up into his hard strokes, moaning when he swivelled his hips to lick her sweet spot with the base of his shaft, sparks flying with the friction.

'Eva, *tesoro*, slow, slow,' he groaned huskily, voice pained, body vibrating as he grappled with the reins of his control.

Dancing closer to the flame, she bit the flesh of his bottom lip, threw his thrusts off tempo and wrung a deep feral groan from his chest.

'Dammit, Eva.' Grabbing her wrists, he pinned her to the bed as if he owned her. Eyes glittering with fire as he towered over her. 'So much passion,' he said, voice gruff. 'Never have I felt anything like you.' His big body flexed above her, muscles bunching as he ground against her. Slowly. Deliberately.

Electricity began to nip her skin, sizzle in the air…

Then, *boom*, it was hands everywhere they could reach, lips clashing, moans coalescing, control obliterated.

'Yesss…'

Dante's voice dropped to a low thrum as he drove inside her in a hot, sensual rhythm, murmuring in his native tongue. A litany of thick Italian to maraud her senses. God, she wished she knew what he was saying because it sounded so wonderful, ignited all the colours in her heart, slamming her body past the point of no return.

'*Dante…*' A lightning crack of energy ripped through her core and she arched like a bow, shoulders digging into the downy pillows. Suspended. Captured on a sensually erotic plateau.

Dante's awed tone drifted from the other side. '*Cristo*, Eva,' as he stroked two blunt fingertips down her chin, swirled down the column of her throat, 'look at you. *Maledizione*, let go…' he demanded hoarsely. 'Let go, *cara*.' Lifting his torso just a touch, he rubbed her clit with the pad of his thumb rhythmically. 'Come for me, Eva. Come for me. *Now*.' And *whoosh*, the spool unravelled in hot, delicious waves of bliss, her entire body seizing in rapture while her world broke apart.

Suddenly fearful, a wild vulnerability quaked through her body until she shook—shook so hard she was petrified she'd never stop.

Anchoring, *needing* his strength, she wrapped her arms around him, vaguely aware she was murmuring in his ear, hoping he adored the sound of her voice when he came as much as she loved his. Telling him how amazing he felt inside her, how hard she wanted him, how deep, only him. Only ever him.

'*Eva*,' he said, like a plea. So she held him tight, so tight to her.

His big body was racked as he was tossed into the heart of the storm, spilling heat, hips pumping long and hard in a mind-blowing rush. The shuddering fever-pitch engulfing her with gratification that she did this to him. Gave him pleasure. It made her feel wonderful. Deliciously happy.

Then her heart screamed, stay. *Stay with me. Please don't leave. Hold me in your arms. Just tonight.* The night she wanted never to end. But of course it had to. Reality would puncture the hazy dream until only memories lingered like wisps of bliss. The truth of her life would rise with the dawn. Depart on his jet. But not yet. Even if he stayed until she slept. It would be enough.

Storing every last second to her heart, Eva drifted down from the glorious heights like a shower of rainbow confetti—her body fluttering, the place between her legs beating out a soft tattoo of lingered pleasure, as they lay in each other's arms, lips moving over jaw and throat, nuzzling, soothing, calming.

Dante brushed down the side of her face—reverently, tenderly—at odds with the sudden hard edge of his voice. As if the man who'd just delivered her to ecstasy was no more than an illusion. A dream. 'Sleep, *cara mia*. I must work.'

'Okay,' she whispered on a slumberous sigh that feathered

the aching wall of her throat as he gently unlocked their bodies, taking his glorious heat and strength with him. Leaving her cold. Empty. Bereft.

A heavy sensation that dragged the weight of her exhaustion and pulled her into the depths.

Until a thick curse burst from his lips and her eyes flew open. Connected with his. Then burned from the flames of fury she saw there.

Disgust twisted his lips, but it was the remorse hanging in the air that tore a seam up her midriff.

'Dante?' *Oh, no. No! Please, no regrets.*

Supple, agile, he lunged from the bed, throwing himself to his feet, anger crackling in every movement.

Standing like some bronzed god, he was totally, gloriously magnificent in his nakedness and she felt an astonishing twist of renewed heat–

'Are you protected?' he bit out. 'On the contraceptive Pill?'

And, with a deft push, she tumbled from heaven straight into hell.

Dante spun on a flaring blast of energy, spied his black silk lounge trousers and snatched them from the hardwood floor. Dragging them up the taut contours of his legs, he was vaguely aware that Eva did much the same at the opposite side of the room, snagging a white scrap from the back of a chaise, no doubt the closest thing to hand.

Swivelling to face her, he caught the white ripple of her linen sundress glissading down her sleek thighs, veiling skin that shimmied with pearlescent dew from an erotic fever the likes of which he'd never known.

Cristo, he'd always known she would be the death of him. Clearly, as soon as his angel hit the sheets her halo disintegrated. If he'd ever wondered if there was a creature who could unearth the dark passion that ran a black river beneath his skin, Eva was his answer.

Since when had he—Dante Vitale, the bastard heir—forgotten protection? Such loss of total control.

Since Eva.

Anger seeped into his brain like venom, swirling his vision in a black mist.

Cristo, one touch of that sinful body and he'd lost his mind. *Never* had he come so hard. Explosives being dangerous had been an ironic distortion. Detonation had obliterated every brain cell, and he doubted he would've sensed a tsunami thundering through the house, never mind the blatant lack of latex.

Weak. She made him weak. A condition he loathed. A condition that had just landed him in the dishonourable ranks of his father.

'Is it a safe time or...?' he asked, keeping his voice easy, modulated, despite the seething chasm opening in the pit of his stomach waiting to consume her answer.

Brow pinching with pain, she shook her head in tiny little jerks. 'It's probably the worst time.'

Horrified. She was horrified. Of course she was. The only thing she'd ever wanted from him was one night. Of sex.

Had his mother looked horrified when she'd suspected she was pregnant with him? So utterly mortified?

A look. A torture he could not physically bear.

Turning, he paced back and forth before bracing his hands, his entire weight, on the rounded lip of the dresser and bowed his head. Closed his eyes, trying to rid his mind of that look.

'Let's not jump the gun, okay? What are the chances?'

His famed forethought abandoned him. 'Of history repeating itself?' With their chemistry? 'Fairly damn high in my book.' It would be just his luck.

Then his conscience was a bloodying assault, one deft punch and kick after another. Cracking ribs, colouring his insides black and blue.

Not only had he stripped her of her innocence, he'd failed to protect her.

Maledizione! A possible child. One she didn't even want.

'History repeating itself?' she said faintly. 'What are you talking about?'

His insides writhed like a venomous snake pit.

Trudging in the mire of his parents' affair had never appealed to him—hell, he'd never given it a second thought—but there he stood, reliving his mother's drunken tales of woe and, before he knew it, the words were hissing from his mouth.

'My father took my mother's innocence,' he bit out. 'Slaked his lust. Used her up and tossed her out. Ruined her reputation by walking away when she was pregnant with me.' A heinous dishonour Dante had no intention of repeating.

'Oh, Dante, your mum must've been so scared, left alone like that.'

Head jerking upright, he watched his brow crease in the dresser mirror.

Not once had he thought about how it had affected his mother. Had she been scared? Knowing she'd had no choice but to bring him up alone? Had the wait been terrifying, just to find out? Alone.

He doubted it. But what was more telling was that Eva immediately empathised.

Dante spun on his heel to search her beautiful face.

Pale. So pale. A stark contrast to her lips, bruised crimson from the crush of his mouth. Was she scared? Was *that* the look on her face?

Cristo, of course she was. What was wrong with him? He needed a bloody instruction manual to read her.

'But that doesn't mean history will repeat itself,' she said softly. Was she was trying to make *him* feel better? 'I'm not your mum and you're not your dad.'

Too right he wasn't. And no, Eva wasn't like his mother. Old Eva had wanted children, hadn't she? Problem was, he wasn't sure which Eva he was looking at from one moment to the next.

Regardless, he had no intention of allowing her to worry alone. This was his fault and he was fixing it.

'You will stay here until we know, *capisci*?' he said fiercely. Maybe a little too harshly if the stunned arch of her blonde brows was anything to go by. 'If you are...'

Dante waited for the barbed wire to wrap around his guts at the thought of another marriage. So why the hell relief was a warm river rushing through his system he'd never know. *Because she will belong to you. No one else can touch her.*

Then, before he could even attempt to stem the flood, the fathomless depths of Natalia's betrayal sucked him down into the dregs. Where, instead of Natalia lying on the sheepskin rug in front of his hearth, entwined with another, it was Eva. Eva telling him he was cold, frozen to the core. Eva finding comfort in the arms of another while he was continually away on Vitale business. And where he'd felt naught but fury at Natalia's deceit, the mere thought of finding Eva with another...

A monstrous hand gripped his stomach and twisted tight. Black poison oozed through his veins, flooding his mind with corrupted toxic visions and he scrambled for the antidote.

Rules. His rules. He'd tie her up in a marriage contract so tight she wouldn't dare wriggle free by deceit or adultery. One false move and he'd take his child to the far side of the earth.

This time he'd have total control.

The black mist cleared from his vision and he focused back on Eva. Mouth working around a retort at his indelicate demand that she stay, her beautiful dainty hand fluttering around the dip of her waist and circling the linen shrouding her stomach.

Right then, the most spectacular sensation inflated his chest.

Hope. Strong. Unwavering.

Eva would carry the Vitale heir. Finally he'd have a son to pass on the legacy he'd fought so long and hard for.

'Dante, you can't be serious. I can't stay here. I have to work.'

Commanding every emotion in his body to shut down with ruthless efficiency, Dante rolled his shoulders and flexed his neck.

Knowing. His powers of persuasion were unequalled.

So he would tempt. Lure. And she *would* surrender.

'I am deadly serious, Eva. Because if you are, we will marry right here on the island and no one will ever suspect.'

So, until they knew for sure, he wasn't letting Eva out of his sight.

CHAPTER TEN

BRAIN IN LOCK-FUNCTION, it took Eva a good few seconds for the cogs to turn. '*What*?'

Marry? Her and *Dante*?

'Forget jumping the gun, you've pulled the trigger.' Of course he had. He was being Dante. Powering forward, two steps ahead of time. As if he could see into the future and wanted to control it *now*. 'Let's just wait and see. If I am p... pregnant we'll discuss the future then. Okay?'

Standing at the opposite side of the bed, washed in the silvery light of the moon, he looked like some Prince of Darkness. Staring at her. With a sinful smile that was a dangerous mix of cold-blooded ruthlessness and annihilating charm, eliciting an ominous sense of déjà vu.

Her spine smacked against the panoramic window with no idea how she'd retreated ten feet and still her eyes devoured him.

'And will you please put some clothes on.' Already the hot splash of desire was swirling in her midriff. Hungry. She craved him. Didn't her body realise they were in enough trouble as it was?

A ghost of a killer *knowing* smile hovered around his lips and she spun on her bare feet, gripped the door lever, wrenched the glass panel wide and burst into the midnight air—thick with tropical heat and just as cloying.

Marry Dante? *Oh, boy.*

Heavens above, her mind was still trying to wrap itself around the possibility of a baby.

So Eva was *not* envisioning a picturesque little church, crawling with ivy and pink roses washed in morning sunlight. And she most certainly was *not* designing an A-line gown with elbow-length sleeves layered with floating lace appliqué. She was not!

Pins stabbed the backs of her eyes and Eva scrunched them shut. 'I promise you, Dante. Whatever happens, you don't want to marry me. I'm a living nightmare.'

'I know this, *cara*,' he said dryly. 'But do not feel too badly. It makes life…interesting.'

A reluctant smile played about her lips. One that she crushed a wrenching heartbeat later. 'Interesting isn't always good.'

The soothing sound of cool waves lapping at the shore was like music to her ears and she veered towards the spiral staircase at the far end of her veranda like some kind of frantic Cinderella. Running before the clock struck twelve and Dante discovered the reality of her life.

'Eva!'

'Not now, Dante.'

Down and around she went, the cold metal balustrade biting into her palm, her bare soles pad-pad-padding down the smooth, blissfully chilled tiles.

'Eva, what the hell are you running from?'

My life. The truth. Because any minute now he would catch up with her and if she ran he would never know. Finn would never know. No more pain for her family. Not as long as she drew breath.

At the sound of his heavy footfall she jumped off the bottom rung and sank into the white icing-sugar sand, tinted pale silver from the stark glare of moonlight.

'I just want to be by myself. Okay?'

'No. It is not okay,' he ground out.

Catching up with her halfway to the water's edge, he curled his warm fingers around the soft flesh of her upper arm and tugged her to face him.

'I want your vow you will stay and if you're pregnant we will marry.'

'I can't stay. I have two weddings on Christmas Eve. Which leads me on to my second point. *I* don't want to get married. To anyone. *Ever.*'

Darkness descended as if the moon had been usurped by the blackest of clouds and she shivered wildly. There was something almost terrifying in his splintering gaze.

'Why?' he ground out with sarcastic bite. 'Because, let me tell you, you make no sense, Eva. Why does an innocent, who lives and breathes romance, not *do* devotion?'

The cynicism contorting his face was like pouring fuel on the petrol of her ire and sparked a retaliation that, quite frankly, had been a long time coming. The words exploded from her mouth without a single thought. 'Because I've seen enough heartbreak and pain to last me ten lifetimes. So I'm not willing to devote my life to a man who believes the word monogamous equates to one woman in every city. When I grew up with one who thought nothing of scratching his itch while his wife suffered and his children rotted!'

Heart threatening to burst from her heaving chest, Eva watched understanding relax his tight features. Unfurl his fists.

'*Cristo*, why didn't I see this?' Tipping his head back, he glared at the starlit sky and blew out a ragged breath. 'Eva, *cara*, not all men are weak.' Chin lowering, he locked on to her eyes and jammed his thumb in his chest. 'I am *not* your father.'

'Weak?' she said, wincing at the crack in her voice. 'That's what people call adultery and desertion now? A weakness?'

'*Sì*. It is a weak man who leaves his wife and children when times are hard.'

Eva slammed her hands on her hips. 'Or maybe it's a man

who believes one woman equates to eternal boredom. Let's face it, you have just as much staying power. Finn too.'

Nostrils flaring, she watched his wide chest swell. 'You know nothing of my staying power, Eva. Do not judge me without a fair hearing. I have never lied about my intentions or cheated on another. If you knew—'

Blinking, she pondered the pain marring his staggeringly beautiful face. 'Knew what?'

'I would *never* do such a thing to you.'

No one could dismiss the sincerity blazing in his fierce gaze and she wanted to believe him. Desperately. But the doubts lingered on. Maybe it was because she was *nothing* like his other women. Or maybe she realised he would soon tire of a wife who couldn't even make love with her bra off. How long would his patience last then? What if she lost her breasts altogether? Would he want her then? Of course he wouldn't. Not when he could have any woman in the world.

'We would always have truth, you and I. Always honesty. Without messy emotions overruling common sense.'

Messy emotions? Wasn't that just a typical Dante remark?

'I appreciate what you're saying, I do. But marriage is not the answer.' She refused to ensnare him in her life.

'Let me make one thing very clear, Eva.' Darkness, like demon shadows creeping over a soul, clouded his eyes with... *pain*? 'No son of mine will question his existence, no son of mine will be without his father's name.'

Eva blinked, his seething dominance shuttering in and out of view. Such normal words, yet the agony, the violence behind them.

Suddenly, the penny dropped. His father had never acknowledged him. Or at least until he'd had no choice. When his mother had died? Oh, God, what must that have been like for him? No wonder he was jumping ahead of time. Picturing the worst. *History repeating itself.*

Eva reached up. 'I promise you, *if* I am pregnant, he or *she* can still have your name. I swear—'

He jerked from her touch and her hand plummeted to her side. 'Forgive me if I do not trust your promises, *cara*. There is more to consider here than your obstinacy. We have business reputations to protect. Finn to consider. The happiness and well-being of a child. We *will* marry.'

Eva closed her eyes. He was right. She knew it. If they didn't marry, Dante would look all kinds of a louse and, as for her... *Ohh,* boy. She could see the headlines now: Diva Up The Duff! Who's The Father? Finn would murder Dante with his bare hands. In truth their child would need him. He was right. *If* she was pregnant, they would have to marry.

'Yes. Okay. If. If. Don't forget the *if*. Oh, God, this is awful.' Dante would be stuck with her for life. Or at least until she fell sick. How was she supposed to tell him? That one of his one-night-wonders might turn out to be his worst nightmare.

Stomach churning violently, she pushed the flat of her palm against her belly-button and breathed deep. How could the most amazing night of her life go so horribly wrong?

'Is marriage to me so distasteful, Eva?' There it was again. A sharp edge of something close to a sting. Oh, he tried to hide it, lighten it with a wry tone, but it was there, she knew. As if she'd offended him. 'Or is being tied down with my child so distasteful?'

'No,' she insisted, forking her fingers through her hair, pulling to redirect the pain shredding her heart. 'No!'

'Then speak to me, *cara*,' he said, frustration lacing his accent. 'You make no sense. *Maledizione*! One minute I am at the Gala, staring at the Diva, and tonight I am lying in bed with Eva. Beautiful young Eva, who told me she wanted three children. Two boys and a girl.'

Every muscle in her body froze. 'I...I told you that?' Grateful for the dark night sky, she felt heat flush up her cheeks at the untimely reminder of one of her more excruciatingly gauche attempts at figuring him out.

'*Sì*,' he said, unfazed.

A sharp, sweet ache pierced her chest. The kind where if she were alone she would be gasping for air, rocking to make the pain abate. So she had no idea how she found the strength to stand tall, to even speak. 'That Eva doesn't…' Exist any more. 'She's…she's…' Gone. Grew up in the real world.

Turning her back on him, knowing she was being a coward for doing so, she faced the lapping froth of the incoming tide, stared at calm waters rippled with the silver reflection of the moon. 'I decided a long time ago that life isn't for me.' *Tell him, tell him—it's the only way to change his mind.* 'Because there's a good chance, a *high* chance, I might get sick. Like my mother…and my grandmother.'

The clammy air grew thicker still, swirling around her with a tension she couldn't grasp. Then his voice came to her, dark as the sky above, smooth as the richest velvet, touched with warm understanding. 'Ah, Eva, finally I see you.'

Crushing her lips together, she squeezed her eyes shut and breathed in a deep shuddering breath, inhaling the fresh salty tang of the sea.

'Does Finn know this?' he asked.

'No. I don't want him worrying. He didn't take Mum being sick so well.' With one hand she pulled her hair over one shoulder and rubbed a silky strand between her fingertips. 'So *please* don't tell him.'

More silence. And still she couldn't turn. Look at him. For fear of what she might see. Pity? Or maybe remorse. For surely it was dawning on him that he might be stuck with a wife who waited for the axe to fall.

Heat. Scorching heat seeped into her back. As if he'd moved closer and she could feel the almighty strength he exuded rolling off his body in pulsating waves. Yet he didn't touch. Not once. Even as her heart begged him to take her in the lashing strength of his arms and tell her everything would be okay. Even as she hated that weakness. That need. Knew it was far safer not to need a living soul.

'Look at me, *cara*.'

She couldn't—she couldn't. 'Dante—' her voice was thick, clotted with tears, trembling '—I'm so sorry. I'm just as much to blame. I should have thought of protection myself.' *Oh, God.* She should *never* have succumbed to the temptation of him. 'I never want to put a child through what I went through.'

The touch of his warm fingers curling over the balls of her shoulders made her flinch. 'Look at me!' he demanded with a quiet, savage intensity, spinning her around to face him.

'I am not your father, Eva. I am not a weak man. I will be there for our child. I swear it.' Sincerity scored his face. 'I am strong enough and powerful enough to shield him from every storm and I will *never* let you down. You believe me, *Sì*?'

Eva nodded slowly, dazed by the ferocity of his declaration.

'Say it, Eva!'

Words burst from her lips. 'I believe you.' She did. Absolutely.

In that moment Eva had never wanted to touch him more. To kiss, to ease the stark pain haunting every angle of his riveting bone-structure.

And why was he looking at her in that way? As if he was about implode with the emotions pummelling his body. She'd do anything to know what he was thinking. Anything. Was he regretting every second of this night?

He reached up and brushed a damp tendril of hair from her brow before his gorgeous face came closer, closer. While her hopeful heart missed a beat waiting for his kiss. *Yes, please— kiss me, make love to me, show me you still want me, make me forget.*

Warm lips touched her brow. Tender. Amiable. The notion that this was the first kiss she'd ever hated spread through her mind like a blood-red stain. 'Stay until we know, *cara*.'

'I can't. The boutique is in enough trouble as it is and I have orders to go out. Dresses to finish.'

Frustration oozed out of his taut frame as he pulled back. As if he didn't want to let her out of his sight. Eva knew better.

All the times she'd dreamed of marrying Dante, his proposal was never sewn by the threads of honour. All the times she'd secretly dreamed of having his baby—all thick, dark, yummy hair and amazing deep umber eyes—it was never trapping him by the treacherous hands of fate. But back then she'd been living in fairy tales. But this? This was reality.

Tipping her head skyward, she gazed at the diamante-studded brilliance. Focused on the biggest, brightest star. *I've messed up big style this time, Mum. I just couldn't help myself. He's my weakness. But you always knew that, right?*

Thousands of pinpricks stabbed her clogged throat. A solitary tear escaped, trickled down the side of her face.

'Ah, Eva…' he said, sweeping her into his arms bride-style and enveloping her in his white-hot heat.

Weaving her arms around his shoulders, she buried her face in his neck as he carried her into the house. And the lashing strength of his arms was the final dent in her armour. Or maybe it was the way he peeled the white sundress from her body and made love to her with a slow, seductive, exquisite intensity she was powerless against. He made her forget, he made her feel alive, so gloriously alive. So by the time she shattered in his arms he had her oath to stay one more day.

One more day in paradise.

CHAPTER ELEVEN

DANTE LEANED AGAINST the door-jamb of his kitchen, crossed his arms over his naked chest and contemplated the pitfalls of an idyllic mansion while the frantic pounding of his heart slowed.

There she was.

Rooting through the cupboards, her caramel tresses rippled down her back and his eyes devoured her half-dressed state, her habitual bra smothered by a white silk vest and matching shorts laced with baby-pink ribbons.

Eva St George. Soon-to-be Eva Vitale if his hunch proved correct.

After receiving the marriage contracts through from London, he'd gone to check on her before returning to his own suite—one cold bed, blood freezing in his veins.

Although in hindsight he should've known where he'd find her. How many times had he caught her wandering the St George kitchen in the dead of night, hips swaying in a natural hypnotic rhythm, sensuality drenching her glorious body in a light sheen as she prowled to satisfy her sweet tooth.

So young. Happy. Carefree.

An astonishing contrast to the heartbreaking vulnerability he'd been faced with on the beach. A woman who virtually hid from the world. All sass and obstinacy gone. Replaced by a fragility so un-Eva-like he'd worn a dagger in his gut ever since.

An off-key humming invaded his thoughts and he focused back on Eva, now on her tippy-toes, stretching sinuously to reach the top shelf. 'A-ha!'

Dante smiled knowingly and eased back against the door-jamb to drink her in. Quench his thirst.

Pulse flipping into high gear, he watched her twist the lid from *his* jar of chocolate spread and delve deep with a long-handled café spoon. With a swirl of her hand, she plucked it free and popped the glob of chocolate between her pink lips.

Eyes closed, Eva moaned in sheer ecstasy.

That was it. Lust—white and hot—poured down his spine, pooling in his groin, and he growled long and low.

Time slowed as she caught sight of him, jumped nigh on a foot in the air and let go of the jar.

Dante jolted forward as the thick glass smacked the travertine with a dull crack, the splatter of rich chocolate and hazardous shards inches away from her bare feet.

Eva slammed her hand over her left breast, 'Oh, my God— you gave me the shock of my life, you idiot!'

Willing his heart to calm, his gaze jerked up from her perfect little feet. 'Did it satisfy your craving, *cara*?'

Cheeks pinking, she gave her head a little shake. 'No, not really.'

Dante lips curved in a half smile. 'I know exactly what will.'

'You do?'

'*Sì.*' He closed the space between them, coming to a stop at the outer edges of the jar disaster. Holding out his arms, he beckoned her with a flick of his curled hand. 'Come to me.'

His guts took a deft kick when she hesitated, those mesmerising eyes wary, guard up.

Heart thudding, he counted four beats before her chest swelled on a loaded inhalation and she leaned forward, holding out her arms.

Dante lifted her clean off the floor, swivelled and plonked her on the black granite island in the centre of the vast space.

'Do you have a brush so I can clean up?' she asked.

'Stay there.'

'It's a good job you have flip-flops on.'

He didn't bother telling her he'd learned long ago not to walk anywhere without shoes. Paved streets in the dead of night when his mother was entertaining had been sole-splittingly hazardous.

Within five minutes he'd cleared the debris and opened one of the wide cases lining the kitchen with a tug of the lever handle.

Kerthunk went the door, with a suction sound that brought a sexy-as-hell curve to her lips. 'Freezer.'

'And what do you think,' he said, 'I could tempt you with in here, *Tesoro*?'

Hands either side of her hips, she launched off the bench and shot to his side.

'Please tell me you have macadamia nut or…or chocolate cookies…or—' Trailing off, her brow furrowed as she looked up at him, sussing him out with eyes as warm as the rarest emerald. *Affection*? No, he must be wrong. *You're as cold and dark as your father, Dante. How can anyone love you?*

'Dante, did you hear me?'

He breathed through the twist in his guts. 'Sorry, *cara*. Say again?'

'Is your favourite still Tiramisu?'

'Naturally,' he said, grabbing all three, relishing the icy bite on his palms. 'Where would you like to feast?'

'Outside. My balcony. I have the most delicious view.'

'I guarantee the mosquitoes will find you just as tasty, *tesoro*.'

'Who cares? I feel like living dangerously.' Words so lightly voiced, yet he could sense an underlying meaning behind them. And for the hundredth time he asked himself how the weight of her health risk had affected her. For clearly she bore it alone.

Cristo, his soul ached for her.

Twenty minutes later they were ensconced on a soft-cushioned swing seat, the sound of the waves lapping, the palms swishing in the breeze, dawn hovering on the horizon, heaped spoons in hand.

Lips cold, his tongue laced with coffee creaminess, his apparent genius was trying to figure out a way to approach the bra subject when she coughed out a laugh—

'Hey, do you remember the night I persuaded you and Finn to drive me to a twenty-four-hour store for ice cream?'

Like a vault opening wide, Dante allowed the memories to slither through the cracks of his mind. Eva, all huge green eyes peering up at him from between thick, gorgeous hazel lashes, begging him and Finn to drive her.

'It was a disaster,' she went on. 'Finn got pulled for speeding, managed to dodge three points by promising Dad would sing at the policeman's wedding—'

The tension in his midsection eased with a smile. '*Sì,* I remember.' As if it were yesterday.

'It took us hours to find this store and what happens?'

'No ice cream,' he said.

'I was devastated. Then Finn scored with the shop girl and you were…' she swallowed '…stuck with me.' Was it his imagination or did she literally choke on the word *stuck*? 'Boy, were you furious. Then again, you always were. People used to say Finn was day and you were night. I saw you as more of a thunderstorm. Dark and ominous. So angry.'

If he'd ever harboured the notion that Eva might think differently from his mother, that statement quashed it in a nanosecond.

'I did buy you a box of chocolates, *cara*, so the night was not a complete washout.'

'Yes, you did. I can't believe you remember that.'

The sensation of her stunned eyes searing over his face made him turn. 'What?'

'Nothing,' she whispered, shaking her head, attention back to the deep tub.

Maybe it was the hot crackle in the air, maybe it was the tension pulling taut. Whatever it was, Dante scooped another spoonful of Tiramisu and got back to topic. 'Did your father ever sing at that wedding?'

Lapping the base of the spoon with the flat of her pink tongue, she smiled. 'Yes, I think he did. I think Mum made him.' Her brow pleated. 'I can hear her now: *Nicky baby, you have to, Finn promised.* The look on my dad's face.' Spoon hovering in mid-air, her lips flattened as she gazed out to the ocean, unseeing. 'Pure indulgence. I forgot how he used to look at her.'

'Maybe you buried the good memories, *cara*.' In a vault. 'Buried under a weightier memory of his betrayal.'

'Yes,' she said, nodding, still staring out to sea. 'So many broken promises. So many lies. Even I lied to her beautiful pale face and every time my heart broke a little more. I burned newspapers so she wouldn't see photographs of his women. Told her he was on tour. Told her *anything* to stop her heart from breaking while she was in pain. She'd given him her heart and he betrayed her—he betrayed us all when we needed him so desperately and I'll never forgive him or myself.' Her voice cracked, making his stomach tighten. 'I should never have lied to her, Dante. Wherever she is, I just hope she forgives me.'

Cristo, little wonder she hated lies. Couldn't even speak them without blushing furiously. No doubt in remorse. How hard this past week must have been for her. Living and breathing untruths.

'I am sure of it, *cara*. Your mother will know you did it out of love.'

Eyes glossed with grief, her gaze sought his. 'You think so?'

Dante reached over and brushed the hair from her brow, stroked down her delicate jaw. 'I know so.'

When she nuzzled into his hand he couldn't help himself. He leaned over and kissed the pleat from her brow. 'He let her down. He let you all down. But not through lack of love. He is not a strong man, Eva. Maybe it hurt him too much to see her that way. In so much pain.'

The thought of Eva in pain…

Maledizione, when she'd told him. His insides had quaked with so much emotion he'd feared eruption but she wanted, *needed* his strength. So she would have it. Always.

'It hurt me too,' she said. 'But did I leave?'

'You are stronger than him. You handled your pain, your grief in different ways. You submerged yourself in the party scene. Perfect oblivion. Surrounded by people who couldn't hurt you. Maybe that's why you tried to sleep with Van Horn. You told me yourself you felt nothing, so there was no risk to your heart.'

Eyes wide, she blinked up at him. 'You're right, I did. I don't even see those people any more.'

'I remember so many things about your home. The love. Laughter.' The claw of longing down his chest, one he stuffed down into the depths, knowing that life was not possible for him. 'Keep the good memories in your heart, *cara*.'

Dante had no good memories of his childhood. He didn't want that for her.

'What do you remember about your home?' she asked warily.

The pot crumpled in his hand, jaw locking tight while he pondered brushing her off. *Cristo*, was the woman telepathic? Now he remembered why he didn't talk!

He didn't want pity from her soft heart. But nor did he want her to back off from him.

Clearing his throat, he focused on the hazy line where the sea met the oncoming dawn in a soft wash of pink. 'I remember nothing more than veering mood swings and broken vodka bottles, *cara*.'

Quiet descended and his fingers bleached white around the handle of his spoon, body braced for the onslaught of pity.

'Oh. No wonder you snatched that wine bottle off me at my eighteenth birthday party.' She nudged him lightly with her arm. 'Your mum and my dad would've made a great pair.'

Then. Then he remembered exactly who he was talking to. Eva. Always thinking of others before herself. With a remarkable flair for knowing exactly how and when to lighten the mood.

He couldn't help but return her small, knowing sassy smile. 'A better choice than my father,' he said. 'He ruined her.' Why had he never seen that before? When he knew Primo Vitale could strip self-respect with one acidic glance.

'Maybe that's where she buried her pain. In the bottom of a bottle,' Eva said, her brow a deep V. 'Do you think that's why my dad's drinking is worse than ever?'

'I imagine he is not very proud of himself, *tesoro*. He has to live with such guilt. I noticed at the Gala he can barely look at you. He is ashamed.'

Her face scrunched in a pretty confusion. 'You're right. Here I'm having trouble forgiving him and he has to live with guilt every day. Oh, Dante, I wish I could help him.'

'Already you have done so much for him, *cara*.' For a long moment he thought of his mother's tears. The gluttony of men, the binges. How furious and frustrated Dante had become that no matter what he said or did, he hadn't been able to help her. Nothing he'd done was good enough. 'He needs to find his own peace.'

It wasn't until he felt Eva's fingertips dust the back of his hand that he realised his entire body had seized. Their eyes caught...held. With a warmth, a connection he couldn't grasp. One that shifted to a sensual bent to thicken the air. And Eva's gaze dropped to his mouth as she shifted on her hip to face him. Her bare thigh nudging his. The hot friction spiking his pulse.

'Can I try your Tiramisu?'

Dante licked the creamy dribble from the base of the spoon and raised it to her open mouth, the sight of which set fire to his veins. Her lush lips closed around the silver and Dante watched a droplet drizzle down the handle and plop upon the full curve of her left breast.

Evading the urge to lean forward and lick the sweetness from her skin, he wiped the glob with his thumb, raised it to her lips and watched her take the thick pad into her mouth to lick and suck as her pupils dilated.

Heat, swift and savage, flooded his veins, pooled at the base of his spine until his groin throbbed viciously. And the temptation to haul her in his lap and plunge into her hard and fast made his stomach quake. But her guard was low and this was his chance.

Fighting, fighting for control, he smudged his thumb over her full bottom lip…trailed it down the elegant sweep of her neck and slid a finger underneath one pure white bra strap. 'Do you ever take it off?'

'Sure I do,' she said, tucking a long caramel lock around her ear with an unsteady hand. 'In the shower.'

'Tell me why. Why dislike something so beautiful?'

'You mean apart from the fact they're big enough to fill a billboard and create carnage in Piccadilly Circus?'

Dante took the hit, remembering his quip at the Gala. *Cristo*, he'd been furious with her for doing it. But clearly, 'It bothered you.'

'Of course it bothered me. But I did it as a favour to Breast Cancer United. Then, after the pile-up, the hype was just humiliating. But I don't regret it. Apparently that ad raised millions in sponsors.'

'*Sì*. I am not surprised.' The thought of half the western world staring at seventy per cent of her breasts made the blood

freeze in his veins. 'But I think this is only half the truth.'
He knew it was. But he needed her to say it. To tell him. To
trust him.

'Honestly? I think it started with my mother. I remember
certain things so vividly. Her operations, when she lost them.
I'm not sure how to explain, but…I kept putting myself in her
shoes. Some days I could almost feel her pain.'

'Ah, Eva, you were so close to her, I am not surprised, *cara*.'

'It made me wish I wasn't a woman. And when…' The
smooth column of her throat convulsed as she ditched the
carton on the table beside her before she turned back to him.
'I've never spoken about this before, but I guess it's only right
that you know.'

Unease swirled behind his ribs—or was it undiluted
dread?—and he pushed his spine into the soft padded back.
Waiting.

'A couple of years ago, I had a scare. I found a small lump.
What with all the specialists and the tests and the biopsies
and—'

'Whoa,' he said, holding up one hand while he flung his
empty tub to the floor, arms aching to wrap her in his body.
Except he doubted he would let go. Ever.

Strength—he needed to keep strong for her. 'You were
alone?'

'Sure. I didn't *need* anyone.' Her slender throat convulsed.
'Turns out it was benign, so just a scare, that's all.'

Just?

Cristo, she must have been petrified. He could barely
breathe thinking about it. And, knowing Eva, she'd have gone
alone to protect Finn. To protect them all!

'Anyway, the long and short of it is—' she continued with
bravado that belied the nervous flutter of her expressive hands
'—I don't like them being touched and this…' she curled her
fingers around the top edge of the lace cupping her left breast
and tugged to reveal a white scar line about an inch long—a

giant fist gripped his heart '…reminds me. So I always wear a bra and I suppose you could say it's become a habit that I can't shake. But, more recently, what with the fake kissing and the…sex…even when you look at me a certain way they feel different and I want you to touch me there, but it's hard for me to let go. Relax.'

Dante set his jaw hard enough to crack a molar. Specialists. Tests. Biopsies. 'So whenever you have been touched there, it has been impersonal, intrusive. Cold.' He swallowed. Around a boulder. 'Painful?'

Suddenly, he was staring at the top of her head as she watched her fingertips stroke the hem of her shorts. 'A little.'

He closed his eyes for a beat. Her feelings made sense. If she'd never experienced any pleasure from them, why would she feel any different?

A vision popped into his mind, a place he'd never taken another living soul. 'Have you brought a bikini with you?' he asked.

Blinking, her face scrunched in confusion at the swift change in conversation. 'Y-y-yes.'

'Good. I want to show you something. Here comes the dawn—get ready and I'll meet you downstairs in thirty minutes.'

'We're going somewhere? But don't you have to work?'

Dante switched off the incessant voices in his head. Yes, Vitale would always come first, but he hadn't had one day off in fifteen years, so he was sure he could spare her one day for this. 'Not today.'

A beautiful smile curved her lips and he was filled with the inexplicable urge to keep it there.

'Come with me, Eva. *Per favore.* Let's have some fun, *cara mia.*' When was the last time she did that? When was the last time she shed the weight of an unknown future?

'Always, your mother smiled, Eva. Smiled and said, "Life is not about waiting for the storm to pass. It's about learning to dance in the rain."'

LIFE IS NOT about waiting for the storm to pass. It's about learning to dance in the rain.

For the first time in years, Eva wanted to dance. Because Dante Vitale had actually taken a day off work. It boggled the mind. There was not one phone in this canoe. Although she doubted there was even room for one. Narrow and precarious didn't begin to cover it.

But the distinct lack of cellphones wasn't the reason a giddy swirl of exhilaration and anticipation hummed through her veins. Nope. It was because she was happy. *Keep the good memories in your heart, cara.* Just reliving the good times gave her a sense of peace she hadn't felt in years. So alive, she wanted to have fun. Do crazy things.

Like allowing herself to imagine, after years of denying herself the luxury. To nurture the notion that there could be a life flickering inside her. To think about marrying Dante. Having him always. She wouldn't be alone any more. She didn't *want* to be alone any more.

After they'd made love last night, he'd kept touching her tummy as if he was envisaging. Already utterly convinced. And the gorgeous man had her doing the same. Dreaming up names and designing a christening gown. It was just absurd. Surreal. More than a little scary. Because she'd mooned over such things before. Could remember the bone-crushing pain of falling from magical clouds of happy ever after. *So don't expect more from him than he can give...*

'*Love is for the weak and needy and I am neither.*'

She just had to remember what they shared was passion. Lust that, when sated, he left to work or slip between his own cool sheets. In truth, making love was the only time she felt the power of his emotions. So, like an addict, she craved another fix. A higher dose of his lethal sexual dominance. Resistance was futile and she hated herself for the weakness.

Still, he'd taken a day off work for *her* and she wasn't wasting a minute.

Dante powered the oars from behind and the canoe sliced through the water, heading for a towering rock face. On approach, Eva could see the rock open up into a jagged split and streams of excitement washed down her chest, percolating inside her as the split swallowed them whole, plunging them into darkness.

'You still with me?' he asked.

'Absolutely. I love the dark.'

'You will not like it so much when your head collides with a stalactite, *tesoro*,' he said sardonically. Then his loud command, 'Lights,' echoed around her and the enormous cavern illuminated in a soft white glow, the lights flaring from the bottom of the lake.

Eyes adjusting, she inhaled sharply. 'Oh, *wow*! It's like something out of a fantasy. And those,' she said, pointing at the elongated straw-like formations hanging from the ceiling, 'look like crystals.' Huge rare chandeliers. Millions of years in the making. 'And the water,' she said, 'it's like a clear azure lake.'

'Duck.'

'Really? In here?'

Dante burst out laughing, the sound rich and throaty, drenched in masculinity, sending hundreds of tiny tremors through her core. *Wow*. She'd never heard him laugh before.

His laugh went on even as he pushed her head down between her splayed legs. 'Quit, Eva, unless you really want this boat to go over.'

'*Boat*? You call this a boat?'

'Right, that's it. You asked for this.'

Before she knew what he was about, he leaned over, rocked once…twice and *splash*, over they went, headlong into the water. Water so warm her bones dissolved and she went lax, in no hurry to resurface.

Then the hot hands of the devil himself curled around her waist, gripping—protective, possessive, lifting….until the air smacked her face as she broke the surface.

Gasping, she rubbed the water from her eyes. 'You're a bad boy, Vitale.'

'Enjoying yourself down there?' Voice raspy, he exhaled raggedly and that touch of concern sprang her eyes wide.

Brow lined, Dante searched her face, stared at the pulse she could feel fluttering at the base of her throat. Then he squeezed her waist for one, two, three beats of her swelling heart.

It was silly, pointless, but Eva began to search right back. Looking for something, anything that told her he truly cared. About *her*. Because there were so many little things that could mean something but she'd been here before, hadn't she? Misread every sign, every loaded glance. Searching. Hoping for more. Only to be crushed beyond repair. Ache until she could barely breathe. *So stop looking, Eva!*

Suddenly he blinked and spun her around until her back crushed into his front and thought vanished.

'See over there,' he said, pointing to a sliver in the rock wall where natural daylight peeped into the cavernous space.

'I see it.'

'That's your reward if you do everything I ask of you in the next twenty minutes. I will show you heaven on earth.'

A seam of unease tore up her spine while ruffles of exquisite elation spun up her midriff. 'Everything you ask?'

'*Everything* I ask. I swear I will not hurt you and if at any time you wish me to stop, you have only to say the word.'

'What word?' she asked breathlessly.

Flicking her earlobe with his nose, he whispered in her ear and her eyelids shuttered.

'And you'll show me heaven?'

'I'll show you more than heaven, *cara*.'

No thought, no hesitation. In truth, she'd never felt so alive. 'I'll do it.'

Dante exhaled harshly, his breath fanning her nape as he curled his arm around her waist and yanked her tight against him. Her bottom nudged his groin and if she'd been in any doubt as to what was on his mind, the hard length of his arousal quashed it with stunning effect.

With her back to his front, he moved them through the water until they reached a jagged lip. 'Up.' He lifted her clean out of the water and she stumbled forward a step. 'Don't turn around.'

So Eva waited. For his touch, for his command. Her heart a *bump, bump,* thumping beat, her hands trembling.

Slosh—she heard him leap from the water. 'Close your eyes,' and he came flush against her once more, steering her pathway with his hard body.

Jerkily they came to a stop and she was smacked with so many sensations she swayed uneasily on her feet. 'Can I open them?'

'No. Trust me, *cara mia*,' he said, voice smouldering as he gently took her hands and laid them flat against…a wall.

Then his fingers were at her nape and he slowly untied the sash of her bikini top. No wires, it wrapped around her breasts sash-like and tied at her nape. A tie he was languidly unravelling with practised hands. *Oh, God.*

'Breathe,' he said with calm severity and she inhaled long and low—the fresh scent of raw earth, Mother Nature at its finest weaving through her head, smoky like an image of opium mist. 'Do not be afraid of your body. Let it speak to you.'

Bones now lax, her other senses heightened, she felt the material give way, the heavy weight of her breasts pull on her shoulders. Then the soft material slithered around her face, vanquishing any remaining light behind her eyelids.

Blindfolded.

No fear. Just anticipation thrumming through her veins. Life beating in her heart.

'What can you feel?' he said in that husky murmur that made her heart thump faster, harder. 'Because you like to touch, don't you, *tesoro*.'

'Heat everywhere,' she said, her voice a quiver, rasping past her dry lips. 'As if…I'm stood in an inferno blasted from every angle. So hot. So sticky.'

'More—tell me more,' he said, breath ragged as he splayed her legs with his large hands.

'Sand tickling the soles of my feet. Cool and wet. Slipping, *sliding* between my toes. Rock biting into my palms. Coarse. Craggy. And now…' She gasped, shook with the force of his devilish touch. 'Your big warm hands curving around my waist, spanning, gripping…flaring wide over my stomach… sneaking under my waistband.'

Legs turning to water, she leaned forward, bracing her full weight on the wall. 'You're taking them off,' she whispered on a tremulous breath.

A thrilling ripple of wicked titillation sizzled over every inch of her skin, set fire to her veins. Sweat trickled down her spine. So hot. So very hot.

'I am. Slowly, teasingly, sliding the damp clinging fabric down your beautiful long legs. I dream of these legs, *tesoro*. Around my waist. My neck. And, *Cristo*, if they do not kill me, your lush firm behind just might.'

His long dextrous fingers shimmied down her legs, pushing her bikini to the floor and then he kissed, *oh*, he kissed and moulded his hands to her calves, lapped the backs of her knees with his velvet tongue.

A primal groan, long and deep, rumbled from the depths of his chest as he lapped and kissed the curve of her bottom, gently nibbled up her spine, pressing his lush wet mouth over every inch of her skin. Until she was boneless. Pliant. Completely at his mercy.

'That's it, *cara*, give yourself to me.'

Eva crushed her lips. Fearing it was too late. Far too late. She'd given herself to him long ago. Dante Vitale had owned her from first glance. *No, no, Eva. Don't even think it.*

Panic flared behind her left breast…but when his hand slid back around her waist, glissaded up her torso and gently cupped the heavy weight, panic was replaced by the fervour for pressure and she pushed into his hand. *Oh, boy.*

A guttural groan tore from his throat. '*Maledizione*, Eva.' His foot pushed the inside of her calf—first one, then the other—forcing her legs wider. 'More.' And she did exactly that, shuffling across the sand, widening her stance, bending more at the waist, the jagged rock now lancing her palms.

'You have the most beautiful back I have ever seen,' he said, his Italian accent now deliciously raw as if the polished exterior was being buffed away. 'Every dip, every curve, provocative perfection.' He scraped his blunt fingernails across her shoulders, down her vertebrae and Eva threw her head back, arching sinuously.

Perfection? Did he really mean that? She wanted to ask but it sounded so needy. And she hated need. Knowing the only person she could rely on was herself.

'What do you feel?' he growled.

'You. Everywhere.' And he was. Flush tight at her back, she could feel his thick erection, hard and demanding behind his swim shorts.

Without conscious thought, she lifted one hand from the cold craggy rock, reached behind her and smoothed down his sweat-drenched honed stomach to touch him. Hot. So hot. Hard. So very hard. He must be in agony. So she curled her fingers around his thick length, determined to entice, but he jerked from her touch.

'No,' he said, with his raw, unrelenting force of will. 'This is about your pleasure, not mine, *cara mia.*'

Before she could think of a retort to tempt him, he rolled her nipple between the pads of his fingers—gentle, hesitant—luring a moan from her parched throat.

With every touch, he waited for her reaction, testing, teasing. And her heart, *God*, her heart ached. Why was he doing this for her? Why did he care?

His thumb dusted over her small scar and Eva stiffened, waiting for the threads of tension to pull in her stomach. A tug that never came.

'So brave, *tesoro*,' he murmured. 'Do not let this remind you of what has passed or what may come. Let it remind you how strong you are. That you have fight in every breath you take. How you must live in the moment, make every second count.'

Tears stung the backs of her eyes like tiny daggers. 'Dante…' *I'm scared.*

'No fear, Eva. No more fear. Promise me this. Whatever happens,' he said huskily, smoothing his big hand down her midriff and laying his palm on her tummy in that way that tore a yearning through her heart, 'no more fear.'

Another command. Another touch. To enrapture. Inflame. Banishing all thought. All fear. Until she could no longer resist the heady pressure making her insides twitch, the blood thrum through her body. More intense than ever before. Dante flicked his thumb over her nipple, sending another bright hot spark firing to her core. And, 'Oh, God, Dante I…'

'What, *cara mia*?'

'When you do that…'

He did it again, bit into her shoulder, soothed the bite with the velvet flat of his tongue, cupped both her breasts in his hands and oh-so-lightly squeezed the soft flesh.

Wham—her body shook and sparked with the first flicker of an orgasm—an orgasm the likes of which she'd never known. And the air whooshed from her lungs as she tried to fight it off.

'*Cristo*, Eva,' he said, before murmuring hushed Italian in her ear, making her stomach scrunch, her orgasm coil tighter. God, she wished she knew what he was saying. It was the same words every time he made love to her, she was sure. Words that spoke to her heart. 'Let go.'

Another demand, blurring her vision, her mind. Until her body took over, stomach concaving with the force of the building pressure and Eva pushed her bottom towards him, seeking, a wanton cry gushing from her throat. 'Dante, *please*.'

Trembling, she hovered at the edge of heaven—or was it hell?—and heard him swear long and low. Still like cast bronze. Then shudder as if he fought some kind of evil, an internal battle, grappling with the reins of his control.

'Eva, do not beg me, *cara*,' he said, voice harder than the rock beneath her fingers. 'No protection.'

Silence. Just the soft trickle of water in the distance, the heavy beat of her heart echoing in her ears.

Silence. As if they both waited for the other to speak. *So take me, take another risk. I want you so much.*

Silence. *Speak to me, please. Tell me what you're thinking…*

A sigh, laced with resignation, dusted over her nape. Soft skin he graced with a kiss, so ardent it was almost devout as he gently flicked his thumb over her tight nipple and slid his other hand down her stomach, murmuring, 'Let go, *cara*.' He thrust two fingers inside of her, growling in her ear, 'Let. Go.'

Wham—she splintered into a million pieces, every bone cracking with the force of the orgasm tearing through her like a tornado.

'*Dante*,' she cried. Because it went on and on, whipping the air from her lungs, swirling every thought in her mind and lifting her so high she literally feared the cataclysmic drop. And still he was relentless. Thrusting his fingers in and out as she clenched and spasmed around his hand, her body convulsing, racked with pleasure.

Falling, falling, her legs buckled and Dante's hand slipped from her breast to wrap around her waist holding her upright with iron strength.

'I won't let you fall. I swear it,' he said with such fierceness she glimpsed a hidden meaning. If she could just think past the carnal oblivion…

'Again, *tesoro*.'

'I…I can't.'

'*Sì*, you can,' he said with dark intensity as he pushed inside her, hand now flexing, curling, cupping—simultaneously teasing her buttons inside and out while his heat seared her back. 'So beautiful, Eva, so very beautiful.' And his mouth licked and bit her shoulder and his thick erection nuzzled the crease of her bottom and—

Wham—another orgasm ripped through her core, all molten heat and liquid fire, tearing her apart, burning, scorching her lungs until she felt like a living, breathing flame.

Stripped to her soul, at that moment she knew the truth. She'd been lying to herself all along.

Dante Vitale owned her. Heart, body and soul. Always had. Always would.

So when her head began to spin with black ribbons and the ground lifted to meet her, she said the only thing she could. The only thing to thwart the words leeching from her heart, words embedded since she was eighteen years old. *I love you…*

'I surrender.'

CHAPTER THIRTEEN

SHIVERING VIOLENTLY, EVA roused from delirious possession to find herself straddling Dante's lap as he sat on the floor of the cave, his long legs stretched out beneath her.

Body lax, mind weak, she buried her face in his neck and surrendered to his ministrations as he wrapped her bikini sash around her breasts and tied a knot at her nape with a soothing amorous touch.

Air. She needed air. So hot. So dizzy. But, as she filled her lungs, all she could smell, all she could taste was his signature masculine scent: bergamot with lashings of the blackest amber. Dark. So very dark.

Dante raised his knees off the ground behind her and her body slipped forward until they were slick—skin against skin—and instinctively she clung to him like a life raft as he wrapped his arms around her, rocking with a gentle persuasion. As if she was his most prized possession. Such a foolish thought, her defences kicked in to frisk her skin with apprehension and shoot sanity into her mind.

Surrendering her heart to him was one thing, didn't mean she was insane enough to imagine he returned the strength of her feelings. So she didn't want to cling to him. Or need him.

I won't let you fall. I swear it…

Space. She needed space. To think. To breathe. The lines were blurring hazier by the second.

Lifting her face from the crook of his neck, she pushed at

his chest, swivelling her shoulders to twist free of the steel cage of his arms. And if a tiny part of her wanted him to hold on—to never let her go—that tiny part was crushed when he immediately released her.

'Can you stand, *tesoro*?' he asked, his voice raspy, dry.

Oh, boy. Pricked with embarrassment at the way she'd lost it, she tore her face from his view and coerced her legs to wake with a gentle flex. 'I think so.'

Curving those big hands around her waist, he lifted her to her feet, holding her in place as she tested her weight. Then, *oh, boy*, she made the mistake of looking down and his face was right *there* and…where the hell were her bikini bottoms? 'I'm fine,' she croaked. 'Really.'

Eva took a step back and leaned against the cool wet rock as Dante pushed himself up in one graceful athletic movement and swept his hands down the backs of his thighs, sand flicking in every direction.

Only then did she notice. 'Black sand.' She gave a little huff. Of course it was. What else would Dante Vitale's caves be lined with but volcanic sand?

'Wait here,' he said, veering around a corner, disappearing from view.

Within seconds her eyes were darting around the floor for a gold scrap and, *Thank you, God*, she whipped the sodden bottoms up her legs, cringing at the gritty chafe, just in time to see Dante reappear—sports duffel in hand—both owner and bag drenched.

Despite the cold seeping into her feet, she felt her lips twitch. 'Bottom of the lake, huh?'

He gave her one of those half bad-boy smiles that threatened the already precarious state of her knees as he unscrewed the cap of a water bottle and passed it to her.

Eva relished the cool liquid pouring down her tight throat.

'I believe I promised you heaven on earth,' he said, pointing to a gap in the rock before he placed the clear rim of his bottle on his lower lip...

The sight of his smooth throat convulsing acted like another blast of heat and Eva yanked the elastic hairband from her wrist, lifted the hair stuck to her nape and piled it on top of her head in a messy knot. With a quick fix of the band, she turned back to see him staring at her. Oddly.

'What?'

Brushing the back of his hand over his wet mouth, he shook his head. 'Your hair like that...reminds me of when I first saw you.'

Eva gave him a kick of her brow. Typical man. His memory was way off.

'My hair was down that day. At the tennis courts at home. You were playing with Finn and...' Eva and her friends had been glued. Mesmerised by all that yummy darkness and athletic grace. And now she'd just told him that the memory was imprinted on her brain!

Dante crossed his arms over his wide chest, shoulders bunching, pecs bulging. 'That wasn't the first time I saw you.'

Eva blinked. He had his own memory imprint? 'It wasn't?'

'No,' he said simply, then nodded in the general direction of the sliver. 'Go ahead, *tesoro*. Ladies first.'

Gaze flicking from the gap back to him, she questioned the intelligence of asking him more. Would have if he hadn't trailed his fingers down to the small of her back, her flesh quivering under the deft stroke, and gave her a little push.

Angled sideways, she breathed in and slithered through the gap, almost collapsing with relief when she made it to a wider opening, the blinding light making her recoil with a deep squint.

Anticipation was a *thump thump* of her heart, feet tentative to eke out the suspense as she gingerly made her way to the jagged archway. Sight slowly adjusting, the first sound that whispered through her mind was one of water trickling, pooling. The second was the chirp and song of a small bird, waning with the flutter of tiny wings. And the third was the echo of leaves—not thin and crisp like an autumn rustle but saturated with dewy flesh from the heights of summer.

Coarse grainy sand gave way to the tickle of scented grass and she shielded the sun's rays with one hand…and gasped, warm air snatching at her throat. '*Oh*, Dante.'

As if God had used a giant spoon and scooped a hole from the rock, they were stood at the base, surrounded by breathtaking beauty.

Waterfalls cascading, gushing into an azure lake. Trees in lush bloom, weeping exotic fruits and trailing pink and cerise flowers in elongated spirals to kiss the lush bed beneath. A butterfly fluttered past her face with wings of orange and lilac and settled on the rich green meadow smothered in tiny white flowers.

'It…it's like *Fantasia*. I didn't think places like this even existed.' The divine beauty was another physical blow and, without knowing how or why, tears stung the backs of her eyes. She had to turn her face from his view and blink rapidly to dissolve the mist.

'Hey,' he said, curving his hand around her jaw and tempting her back to meet thick dark lashes surrounding eyes that glittered. 'Do not hide your emotions from me. If it makes you feel better, I was also overwhelmed when I discovered it for myself.'

'Have you brought…?' She stopped herself in the nick of time, suddenly afraid he'd seduced a multitude of women here.

'Only you.' He brushed down her nose with the back of his index finger, then strode over to a large tree, heavy with fruit and flora. Reaching up, he plucked a large white flower from a cluster of dark purple oval fruit.

'Is that passion fruit?' she asked whilst *Only you* rang in her ears.

'A loose translation would be tryst-fruit. Very similar in

taste and texture, but immensely potent,' he said, walking back towards her, his shorts clinging to his perfectly buff body as he twirled the flower stem between his thumb and index finger.

'Like a…an aphrodisiac?' No way was she eating that stuff. Dante was potent enough and she could barely think straight as it was.

'*Sì.*'

As he drew near, the sun glinted and shimmered off the long silky tropical petals. 'It looks like an orchid.'

'I know you do not like flowers,' he said.

'Who said I didn't like—?' She winced inwardly, remembering the tongue-lashing she gave him last week. 'Oh, well, I was angry with you. Asking your secretary to fill my boutique is totally different to…to…' Trailing off, she stared into his eyes as he slid the fine stalk down her cleavage, snug behind her sash, the tiny scratch making her breath hitch.

'To what, *cara mia*?' he murmured, his fingertips grazing across the low scooped edge of her bikini, teasing. A little higher to her bare breast. Tempting.

Her eyelashes grew heavy as he cupped her with a gentle touch. Then his head dipped to the heavy aching flesh as he peeled back the gold fabric and…*oh*, he kissed her small scar. Once. Twice. Softly. Devout.

Paradise vanished behind her eyelids and her hand trembled with the need to reach up, push him into her, hold him close. And her heart…her heart gushed, overflowed.

'Different to…you choosing,' she whispered on a fluttering breath, chest heaving, 'a flower.' As a flock of butterflies began to sweep and swerve into her stomach. *Careful, Eva, you've been here before. Nothing is what it seems.*

Yet, when he lifted his head and caught her eyes, he was going to tell her something. She could virtually see his internal struggle. *Tell me, tell me. Give me something more than vague signs. Give me words. Actual words. That I can hear. That I can believe. Give me truth. Please.*

Backing up a pace, he flexed his shoulders, his posture making it clear she was pleading for the impossible, and her stomach plunged to the grass.

'This *Fantasia*, as you call it,' he said, the educated-at-Cambridge formality back in line as he set stride towards the lake, 'is one of the reasons I bought the island. Untouched, its innocence, purity called to me on some level.' His footsteps slowed and he tilted his head until she was awarded with his uber-masculine profile. 'I, the darkest, coldest of men, some say the most ruthless on earth, own such a place.' Swivelling with the predatory grace of a sleek black panther, he shot her with a killer look. 'Amusing, don't you think?'

Eva blinked. Wondering if this was some kind of trick question. Yet, from the fierce expression on his face, her opinion mattered to him.

'No, I think it's wonderful.' It spoke of his beating heart. Although, in all fairness, she would never have expected Dante to own a place so hopeful, romantic. The flip side to his cynicism, his darkness. It was bewildering. Enchanting. 'Whoever said you are cold has never met you, Dante.' Yes, he was ruthless and controlling, but cold? No. He wasn't cold. He was white-hot heat.

'I guarantee this woman knew me very well, *cara*.'

Eva crushed her lips together. 'Oh. Your ex-wife.'

His brow nipped in a split second of confusion as if she had it wrong, but then he shrugged nonchalantly.

Curling her fingers, she dug her nails into her palm. She didn't like thinking about his marriage. It made her a little jealous. Okay, insanely jealous.

Which was just ridiculous considering she had a good idea of what Natalia's life would have been like. An arid wasteland of craving for this man's love and affection.

What had he said? *Cold.*

'Why did you marry her?'

'My father desired the match. A joining of two old Italian families. One I had resisted for a long time.' The way he looked at her right then—haunted, possessive—sent a shiver scuttling over the back of her thighs. 'In hindsight, it was doomed from the start.'

'It sounds…cold.'

'Arctic, *cara*,' he said, hard, irascible. *Cold*. Then *slam*, the shutters fell down over his face. Conversation over.

Eva tried for a swallow and tugged the orchid from her cleavage, but as she looked into the pink folds shrouding the heart she realised she wasn't willing to part with it. Just yet.

Dante and her were anything but cold, right?

Right.

Threading the flower through the knot in her hair, she took a tentative step towards him as he crouched down at the water's edge and dipped his hand into the depths as if testing the temperature.

'The people from the mainland call it Dream Falls,' he said, voice thick and edged with cynicism. 'They say if you make a wish in the waters, your dream will come true.'

'Do you believe that?'

'It does not matter what I believe. But in my experience dreams are born from hard work and determination.'

Eva's feet froze a few paces away as she closed her eyes and sighed. 'Vitale. Taking Vitale to stratospheric heights. That's why you work night and day.' It was all about Vitale. Every move he made. It was like an addiction. An obsession. Ruling his every waking thought.

'*Sì.*'

'Why? Money? Power? Don't you have enough of both?'

'I care nothing for wealth.' He fingered his damp hair until it spiked and flicked in its usual effortless sexy mess and stared across the rippling waters. 'It is a question of self-worth. Pride. You take great pride in being successful at your work, do you not?'

'Yes, of course. But…you're one of the most successful men

in the world and still you keep going. What are you trying to prove to yourself?' While Eva loved her job, she knew half of what drove her was the need to make her mother proud. 'Or does it have more to do with your father?'

The muscles in his shoulders visibly tensed, his jaw locking with an audible click. And she could feel the pain emanating from him in a pulsating wave. 'There is no pleasing such a man, *cara*. I do it for myself.'

He was either lying to himself or her. Against his better judgement, he'd even married Natalia to please him.

No thought, no hesitation, she walked to the edge and sat upon the grassy lip, allowing her legs to plunge into the clear liquid.

Dante swung down to sit beside her, his tight muscular thigh dusted with dark hair mere inches away from her soft milky skin. She waited a beat, choosing her words carefully, knowing she trod in dark, dangerous depths. 'I guess you went to live with him when your mother died.'

A small jerk of his head was her only reply and she played with the grass, tearing a few blades from the root. *Easy, Eva.*

Sprinkling the grass into the water, she watched it float, drift on the slight breeze. Thinking of a perfectly natural question. 'When will I get to meet him? After all, one day he might be a grandfather.'

Dante's head shot up, eyes, fierce and deadly, careening into hers, his skin taut where he leashed the beast within. 'Hear this, Eva. I do not want my child *anywhere* near him. Nor you. *Capisci?*'

And with that brutal howling declaration came not only a plunge of unease but also the memory of his ferocious protective streak when they spoke of their child.

I will be there for our child... I am strong and powerful enough to shield him from every storm.

Licking her dry lips, she swallowed hard. 'Was he...brutal?'

'Only with his tongue, *cara*,' he said, his voice hard enough to smash glass. 'Although, in truth, at times, I would've preferred a fist.'

Crushing her lips, she closed her eyes momentarily. No matter how hard she tried, she couldn't stop her imagination firing a tirade of nasty insults and a chill pervaded her bones.

'Do you still see him on Vitale business?'

'*Sì*. But he no longer controls my world. I control his. The power is mine. Vitale was drowning when I took over and now it is also *mine*. And always will be.'

Of course he wanted control. After a life dictated by others, who wouldn't?

The silence stretched, her patience with it, until she reached up, smoothed his jaw, coaxing with a gentle hand. When their eyes met, her lips parted on an indrawn breath.

Such frustration. Such pain. God, what kind of childhood must he have had?

Fifteen years old and he'd buried his volatile mother, only to be faced with a monster specialising in mental anguish. Thrust into a heartless world—a world he'd been denied. To live with total strangers. A continual fight for his position, for the worth and self-respect his father had denied him. Was it any wonder he was so closed off from his emotions? She fancied they were buried so deep he would explode with one rattle of the key. Often times she could feel his body vibrating with power, as if they all churned inside him, threatening to burst free.

It didn't take a genius to figure out how he controlled them all. Anger. It was his first defence.

Gently, she brushed a damp lock of hair from his sun-kissed brow. 'Ah, Dante. Finally, I see you,' she said, using the exact same words he'd said to her only yesterday.

For she knew the desperation, the need to prove her worth, to prove to the world she was more than just a daughter of famous parents. More than Diva, the party girl who had drifted astray. Hadn't she spent the last week trying to prove herself to him?

Soul aching, she said in a wild whisper, 'Listen to me. I don't know one other man who could reach the heights of your success. I hope you are very proud.' Rubbing her thumb over his soft fleshy bottom lip, her mind drifted. 'What did you say to me this morning? About the good memories of my mum and dad. You said: *keep the good memories in your heart.* So I say take all your achievements, your successes and hold them in your heart. And be proud of yourself.'

Leaning forward, she kissed the corner of his mouth. 'Don't allow him to rule your life any longer. Rise above him, Dante, far, far above him where you belong. Promise me.'

For long moments he stared into her eyes. One long loaded look, the connection so startlingly intense, the world seemed to compress around them. As if they were the only two living souls on the planet. A look that said a million things and, like the mysteries of the universe, she understood none of them.

A shadow crept over her shoulder, smothering the light. As if the sun had been usurped by thick ominous clouds and a new emotion penetrated the haze.

Fear. She could feel fear in the air. Coating her skin, cool and clammy, until she struggled to breathe. It clutched at her heart and it was all from her—she knew it *must* be. Yet there was something in his eyes, those fathomless dark eyes—a look she'd seen once before—but she couldn't place it, no matter how hard she tried. So elusive. So out of reach.

And that only served to heighten her frustration. Her fear. Because, for the second time in her life, she was about to put her heart on the line for him. Such folly, she knew. But it was this place. Bewitching. Beguiling her with hope when she knew it was bad for her soul. It was his words: *how strong you are...no more fear.* Giving her strength. When she felt weak as a newborn foal.

A tremor started in her toes, swept up her legs and, before

it reached her hand, she took it from his face. Twisted her fingers in the well of her lap. 'Don't you ever want more? More than Vitale? More than success?'

From nowhere the breeze turned volatile. Wind slammed into her back to send strands of hair blowing around her face and her eyes closed in defence. Reaching up, she swept her brow and, when she opened her eyes once more, Dante's unyielding jaw was locked tight, the muscle protesting fiercely. 'What else is there to live for, Eva?'

Do it, Eva. Say it. Say it. Be brave. Be strong.

Raising her legs from the water, she hugged her wet knees to her chest and tried for a nonchalant shrug. 'I don't know. Love?'

Out went the light in his eyes, even his bronzed skin visibly paled. 'Love is not possible for a man like me.'

Eva nodded slowly, her bones colder than they'd ever been before. *You're such a fool, Eva.*

She'd been lying to herself, thinking she could marry him and stop herself from wanting more, from craving his love. When, in truth, that was all she wanted. All she'd ever wanted. His heart.

And that made her feel selfish and shameful because gaining his love would only bring him pain if she fell sick.

Oh, God, she was a horrible, horrible person because she wanted the whispering promises of this idyllic Utopia. The fairy tale. What her mum and dad shared all those years ago. The love *this* man made her remember. She wanted it all.

Sadness crept into her chest until each breath ached and she bowed her head, resting her brow on her knees, the future suddenly a scary place.

Because, yes, she desperately wanted to be pregnant, to have *his* baby, but that would lead her to a marriage bed that would surely turn as cold as his first, as she craved for his love and affection. Leaving her vulnerable. Heart, shattered fragments of pain.

The wind picked up pace, whipping around her, smacking off her wet legs, nipping her skin. Lifting her head, she focused on the surface of the water, the ripples now deep from the hard lick of the breeze.

Crushing her lips, she rocked back and forth, the hard ground biting into her flesh. 'Why did you bring me here, Dante?' *Why did you make me fall again?*

'I knew you would appreciate such vivid beauty,' he said easily, oblivious to the storm raging inside her. 'I will gift it to you if you wish.'

Eva snapped round to face him, ignorant of the pain shooting up her neck. 'Gift it?' Like when he bought jewellery for his bed-partners as a fond farewell?

'*Sì*. As a wedding gift.'

'You seem awfully sure I'm pregnant, Dante.'

He shrugged those arrogant shoulders. 'I am.'

'You really want this baby, don't you?'

'*Sì*. Very much. I have wished for an heir for a long time. It will be a dream come true for me.'

Every muscle in her body froze—*an heir*?

Mind spinning like a bobbin wheel, she began to reel in threads. 'That's why you married Natalia, isn't it? Not only to please your father but for an heir.'

'Of course. Why else?'

Oh, boy. Here she'd been dreaming of churches and christening gowns and Dante had pounced for an heir. From the start it had been about Vitale and he'd lured her in like the Pied Piper whistling his flute. First for the sake of Hamptons and now a possible heir to the Vitale empire.

My God, she could see it now. She'd bet the first thing that popped into his mind after the anger had abated from not using protection was: *Heir. Vitale. Vitale.*

And he intended to placate her with what? Sex and an island?

'I imagine it's worth quite a bit,' she said, not entirely sure what the hell she was playing at. Only knowing she wanted him to hurt like she did.

'Several million,' he said. 'It is easy enough to arrange. I can have the marriage contracts adjusted by sunset if you so desire.'

Everything stopped.

Her breasts began to rise and fall in heavy waves, while he just sat there. Pensive. Gazing across the lake. Clearly thinking of his precious Vitale. And her throat—*God*, her throat was stinging with the prick of a thousand pins.

For a split second she considered the idea she was overreacting. Being irrational. Ditched that idea right in his damn lake!

'You had papers drawn up?' she said, her voice escalating with every word. 'Like…a business contract? *Already*?'

With eerily slow movements, he turned to face her, one dark insolent brow raised over his intense glare. '*Sì*, this morning. Is there a problem?'

Eva shuffled along the grassy lip, creating distance.

She'd told him all her secrets, all her fears and he'd made love to her, shattered her every defence until she'd opened her heart. And all she'd wanted was for him to hold her and instead he'd left her in bed. Alone. To draw up a…a *marriage contract*? 'How can anyone be so cold? Heartless.'

His beautiful, despicable head jerked as if she'd slapped him. Right now, she couldn't care less.

'Why a contract, Dante?' she said as an insidious notion slithered into her mind. 'Don't you trust me?'

'It is not a question of trust.'

'Oh, yes, it is.' Clearly, he didn't trust her. After all that had happened between them. He still didn't trust her. And, *oh, God*, that hurt. 'What exactly does this contract protect your heir against?' She thought back to his mother, his childhood—his awful volatile childhood—and her heart wept for him but what did she have to do to prove herself?

Pique, which must have been as plain as the nose on her face because his brow scrunched, eyes raking over her. 'Eva, you are looking at this the wrong way. It will protect us all. You will be financially secure—'

'But I don't want your money, Dante!' she said, hating the quiver in her voice as she scrambled to her feet, stumbling backward, water dripping down her calves. 'And I will not marry a man who does not trust me. It's all so cold. I am not one of your stores to buy or tie up in a business contract. You can't control my life.'

Worst thing was, she couldn't even hate him for trying.

The gorgeous man put more faith in business contracts, what he could actually control, than the power of emotion or even human nature. So many people had let him down in his life he trusted no one. He'd become impenetrable.

Whoosh, he was up on his feet, towering over her, all six-foot-three of male dominance and seething fury.

'Hear this, Eva,' he growled, feral waves pouring off his buff frame and his eyes… There was something terrifying about the splintering power of his gaze. 'If you are pregnant we *will* marry. You may have no choice.'

'Oh, believe me, I do have a choice. That's one thing you can't control. Baby or no baby, I will never marry you.' The words lanced her throat, for how many times had she dreamed of marrying this man? But not like this.

Clouds, thick with anger, rolled across the sky and Eva felt the first drops of rain pelt her flesh.

'We discussed the need for marriage, Eva,' he bit out.

'Well, suddenly I don't care about the reputation I've fought so long and hard for. People will just have to take me as I am. I don't care about what the papers say about me. I know the truth. What's more important is that I can live with myself. So I will stand tall and tell Finn that the fault is mine alone.'

Thunder rumbled up his heaving chest before he struck her down with a bolt of lightning. 'You *know* how important it is to me that my child has my name. You gave me your word, Eva. And you question why I do not trust?'

Pat, pat went the rain, the heavy beat punishing, trickling a path down her shoulders, her chest, dousing the flaming sparks of her ire.

'I know, I'm sorry. But…don't you see? It isn't about names. It isn't about marrying me to prevent history repeating itself. You have to trust me. I'm *not* your mother. And you're *not* your father. He was a dishonourable man. A terrible dad. But you…you have honour. Integrity. Never have I doubted for a second that you wouldn't stand by me. You would be a great Dad. You're *nothing* like him.'

Shaking his head fiercely, he threw his muscular arms wide. 'Then why break your word? Why refuse to marry?'

She covered her heart with the flat of her hand. 'Because I want love. I want to get married in a beautiful little church and speak vows from my heart and know that the man standing beside me loves me for who I am. *Not* what I can give him. I want the fairy tale and I'll never have that with you.'

Dante's arms dropped to his sides, hands clenched, a look bordering on torment tightening his features. 'One night. You got your one night, Eva,' he said thickly. 'Five years late, but you got it.'

Eva stroked up her chest, fingers curling around her throat. If she wasn't mistaken, she would say he was hurt. No. Surely not. How could she possibly have the power to hurt him?

'I'm so sorry.'

Hands trembling, she closed her fingertips round her engagement ring and slipped off the heavy band. Unable to look at the beauty, the promise. Unable to even think about the words he'd whispered to her that day. Knowing she would crack in two.

Nothing is too much for the woman of my heart, tesoro.

Feet squelching on the sodden grass, she took two steps forward…took his hand, placed her ring in his palm and stumbled back. 'As soon as I know, I'll tell you. I believe I have all three of your business numbers after all.'

All that riveting beauty schooled into impassivity before her very eyes.

'Very well,' he said, throwing her ring into the air and catching it in the same hand, his lips twisting with that cynicism it had taken her a week to erase.

She just thanked God for Mother Nature's wrath because the rain now fell in heavy lashing sheets, pouring down her face. Blending, hiding the warm tears streaming down her face.

Flick, up the yellow diamond spun once more, glinting in the air as he turned to walk away…and her heart cracked in two as she heard the soft *plop* of hope, of the fairy tale, falling, falling, falling into the dark depths of the lake.

CHAPTER FOURTEEN

Two weeks later...

DANTE WRESTLED WITH the thick knot of his cerise tie, shoved his icy finger down the tight space between neck and collar and tore the top button of his white shirt free. Staring at the solid oak, he asked himself again—why? Why couldn't he knock on her door?

Cristo, he was cold. Cold through to the pit of his stomach. Colder than the dense blanket of new-fallen snow outside her boutique, colder than the now clear liquid pooling on the floor around his Italian leather–soled feet.

And, *Dannazione*, he ached. Ached only for her.

For the first time in his life he was terrified. And, as the night drew to a close, he beat and berated himself for wandering around the city—his benighted soul oblivious to the Christmas Eve cheer—preparing mental speeches, which for the life of him he couldn't recall.

Rolling his shoulders, he inhaled slow and deep. Raised his hand and rapped on the door, once, twice, bracing his taut body for the cataclysmic impact of simply taking one look.

The sound of metal sliding across metal filtered from inside and scored his sensitized skin like talons down a chalkboard. And when the solid oak swung wide...his heart stopped. Dead.

There she was. Tousled. With that adorable sleepy look

about her. The one that made him remember and covet all at once.

Eva St George.

Twenty-seven years old and more beautiful than ever. All that gorgeous caramel hair a tumble of lavish waves framing her exquisite face. A warm dove-grey jersey dress clung to her lush curves, delineating the fine bones of her décolletage, the long sleeves framing her delicate wrists and the straight-cut hem kissing her knees. But, *Cristo*, it was the bare feet that really snagged him. Perfect little toes painted pearly-white, as if she walked on heavenly clouds. And there it was again. That hint of innocence he now *knew* to be truth.

Dante closed his eyes. Inhaled a lungful of air that was a physical pain in his tight chest…

'Hello, Dante.'

…And his pulse skyrocketed into the one hundred and sixties when her soft husky voice crashed into his psyche with the ferocity of a sledgehammer.

Only then did he focus on her flawless face. Pale, she was so pale. Grey smudges of dark days and darker nights weighty beneath her eyes.

A giant fist gripped his guts, punched his heart. '*Cristo*, Eva. Are you sick?'

Huge green eyes darted over his face, her brow nipping tight. 'I was just about to ask you the same thing.'

'I do not care about me, *cara*, are you unwell?' He stepped over the threshold, hand up to feel her brow…a crucifying claw tearing at his insides, when she shrank away from his touch.

Dante stepped back. But not before he caught her pure soft scent, arousing him, clouding his brain.

'I'm not sick, Dante,' she said on a trembling rush, 'just tired. I haven't stopped since—'

'*Sì*, of course. Congratulations, *cara*. An Arunthian Princess is quite a coup d'etat.'

She tried for a small smile. 'We met at a charity dinner.

I pushed for a chance to draw up some designs. She adored them. Most of my consultations came off too.'

'I am so proud of you, *tesoro*.'

'Thank you,' she whispered, placing her hand on the soft curve of her stomach, as if she ached. That tiny movement a bolt of lightning cracking through the brume in his mind.

It was tactless and he knew she would suspect it was the only reason he was here, but, 'Do you know if you are…?'

Crushing her lips, she gave a small shake of her head and a tumult of conflicting emotions swirled inside of him. A crushing regret that she would never carry his child. Pain that he would never see her after this night. And a sharp sense of relief that he could tell her the truth without her questioning his sincerity.

'Twenty minutes, Eva. That is all I ask.'

A soft blush heated her cheeks and it took him less than a second to know its genesis. The cave. Twenty minutes for her surrender. He knew better than to hope for it again. Or even to try. This time there would be no tempting or deal-making. Only truth.

'I would like to explain,' he said hoarsely. 'To tell you something. Then I will leave and I swear I will never bother you again.'

Sweat, cold and clammy, smothered his back as he waited for her answer, his eyes narrowing on the flutter of her hand as she massaged her temple, as if he were a headache she wished to rub away.

'Okay,' she said, standing back to allow him in. 'Twenty minutes.'

Before relief stole the purpose from his stride, Dante closed the door behind him with a soft click and followed her through to the lounge, ordering his eyes to stay above her sculpted waist before visions of lacy white panties cupping her gorgeous behind enraptured his mind, stole his sanity.

Cosy. Homely. The lounge was delicately lit by a floor

lamp casting shadowy patterns over her eclectic tastes. A tall
scented Christmas fir stood before the window, bare. Open
boxes of colourful glittering baubles, blown-glass love-hearts
and golden cherubs, littered the floor, full. The Edwardian
hearth blazed a roaring fire, the crackle and spit of wood en-
hancing the aroma of fresh pine, warming his bones.

'I have disturbed your decorating. I am sorry it is late to
call, Eva, but I have been to see Yakatani—'

'Of course you have,' she said ruefully, curling up on the
sofa in her usual snuggled fashion, the sight making his chest
clench and this time he knew the reason why. He wanted her
to snuggle into *him*. Find comfort in *him*.

Her small sigh quivered in the air. 'I didn't mean that to
sound off. I'm happy for you, Dante, really I am.'

'I did not sign for Hamptons, Eva.'

Long hazel lashes blinked up at him, her full lips parted,
working around words. 'Why not?'

This was it. The culmination of two weeks, tearing himself apart wondering how the hell he'd managed to make such
a mess of everything.

Dante eyed the sofa cushion beside her, decided it was pushing his don't-touch limits to the extreme. The chair was too
far away because she needed to see his eyes. So...

He sat on the coffee table in front of her, a clean two feet
between them, braced his elbows on his knees, clasped his
hands to stop from reaching, touching, hauling her to him and
locked on to her huge wary eyes.

'Because you were right,' he said, his throat so thick he
could hear the low rasp of his voice. 'My father denied my
very existence until my mother died and he was forced to take
me in. To say his legitimate family were coloured with hate is
an understatement, *cara*. Remember when we spoke of you
and your father burying pain?'

Brow nipped tight, eyes brimming with empathy, she gave
him a jerky nod.

'I buried mine in Vitale. For the last fifteen years I worked night and day to prove that I was worthy of being one of them. That I was not tainted by my mother's bad blood. Hamptons was the jewel in my crown.' He stopped. Took a huge gulping breath. 'But, when it came down to it, I would rather make *you* proud of me. I would rather prove my worth to *you*. For you, my beautiful, loyal, selfless Eva, are more worthy of the effort and sentiment than my father will ever be. I wanted to prove to you that you would always come before Vitale. And I will not have you feeling discomfort from telling untruths for my sake.'

Her chest hitched as if she'd been holding her breath, her words no more than a whisper. 'You...you told him?'

'The truth about us, *Sì*.'

Sucking her full lips in as if to stifle a sob, she shook her head. 'I can't believe you did that for me.'

Feet flat to the floor, he had to stiffen his muscles to stop himself reaching, taking her, never letting go. But he needed to say this. Because the pain of holding it in was killing him and he'd been lying to himself, and her, all along.

No more fear.

'I would do anything for you, Eva.'

Her heavy breasts rose and fell, but she never left his gaze. Eyes that were the key to his soul... One turn in the lock and all the tension drained from his body, the words, the truth, rushing out of him.

'I would give everything I own for one more day with you. I would sell my soul to keep you well. If you got sick I would trade my life for yours.'

One glistening tear trickled down her smooth cheek but nothing was stopping him now—

'What I cannot do is make you love me. And that, my beautiful angel, was the true reason I had those contracts drawn. I tried to tell myself it was because I did not trust you. But in truth I was afraid and I was trying to keep you by my side.

Tied to me without the bonds of love. Hoping the inevitable would not happen.'

She dashed away her tears with the back of her hand. 'What are you…? What inevitable?'

He felt a weary smile tilt his mouth. 'Anyone who looked at one of your dresses, Eva, would know you wanted the fairy tale. You were fighting it. Because of your father. The risk to your health. Deep down, I knew it would come.'

Eyes fluttering closed, she nodded slowly.

'I tried, Eva. I tried to give you that fairy tale, without even realising what I was doing. Because I desired it too. From the start I was trying to make you mine. Tempting you with what I *could* give you. An engagement ring from my heart. Making love to you with everything I am. All the while thinking: she's mine. Mine. She is finally mine. And tomorrow I will tell her she must marry me. But then…*Cristo*, Eva, as soon as I touch you I lose my mind and I realise this sounds ludicrous but in my heart you were already my wife. Is that not odd, *cara*?'

Crushing her ruby-red lips, she shook her head wildly as if she understood.

'But neither of those things excuse the dishonour of not protecting you. I felt nothing but shame. Knew then I did not deserve to ask for your hand regardless. So yes, I pounced on the hope you were pregnant. Not for an heir, Eva. I pounced at the chance to have you.'

'I…I can't believe this is truly happening,' she said, breathless, pointed her unsteady hand at his chest. 'Did you just say "from the start"?'

'*Sì*,' he admitted. 'Looking back to Edward's vault, *Cristo*, I was consumed with the need to slip my ring upon your finger. Every word I said to you that day was truth. Every touch, every flower, every kiss, all from my heart.'

Another tear trickled down her face as she began to fidget in her seat. Moved to cross her legs into a yoga pose, as if she were trying to close the gap between them.

'Tell me something,' she said in a rush, her eyes darting over his face. 'When was the first time you saw me?'

In a second he was back in the cave. He'd known she wanted to ask him but he'd been too scared to lay his heart on the line. 'The night before we were introduced in the gardens, Finn and I arrived late from a club. I couldn't sleep. So I went down to the kitchen for water and there you were. Tousled. All lush hair and sexy long legs, wearing those skimpy shorts and vest tops you prefer. Looking for something to satisfy your sweet tooth, *cara*.'

'You watched me?' she asked with a pleasurable kind of wonder and he knew it was wrong, knew it was pointless, but his heart kicked with a hopeful beat.

'Oh, I watched you, Eva,' he murmured, voice thick and raspy. 'Do you want to know what I thought?'

'Yes,' she said quickly. 'Tell me.'

'I thought…' His voice cracked. So he swallowed. Tried again. 'She is an angel. I know I am not worthy of her and I know she could never love me, but I would move heaven and earth to make her mine.'

'You did?' she whispered, a beautiful watery smile touching her lips.

'I did. But that night in the pool-house, you were grieving, it was wrong to touch you. And then you asked me for only one night. One night would never have been enough for me, Eva. One million nights would never be enough.'

Her delicate hand fluttered to cover her heart and he watched her eyes fill with fresh tears and sorrow, her head bow. So much sadness and despair—neither good things, he knew—and that tentative bud of hope withered and died inside his chest.

Dante slid forward on the hard wood, closer to the edge, closer to her. 'I am leaving but I need you to know this, Eva. The true reason I am telling you all of this.'

Snap went his control and he picked up her warm hand,

wrapped it in one of his, squeezing tight. Then he tucked his forefinger under her chin, lifting her head to lock with her eyes for the last time.

Cupping her jaw, he smoothed over her cheek with the pad of his thumb. One last time. 'I know you can never return my heart but if you *ever* need me, I am here for you. Only one phone call away. I swear you would always come first. I vow I would take care of you on the darkest of days and never let you fall. Promise me you will remember that.'

'Oh, Dante.'

'Swear it to me, Eva!'

'I…I promise,' she said, tears now falling in earnest. Tears he caught, wiped away with his thumb. Tears that broke his heart.

'*Cara*, do not cry, *per favore*. I cannot bear it. I will leave.' He had her oath. It would have to be enough.

Dante stood, still bent at the waist, and leaned forward to touch her brow with his lips. Every agonised bone in his body screamed and a strange sensation stung the backs of his eyes as he spoke against her soft skin, 'I will always love you, Eva.'

Then he pulled back, to stand, to turn, to walk away…

'No!' Eva reached up, cupped his gorgeous, if a little bewildered, face, sank her fingers into his thick yummy hair and tugged his mouth down to hers. 'Don't leave me again. I need you.'

Then she kissed him, kissed him, kissed him until he *finally* kissed her back.

True, it wasn't the most passionate kiss they'd ever shared— it was messy, dewy from her tears and there were too many emotions cluttering it up, but it was stupendously wonderful. Especially when Dante snapped out of his stupor, gripped her waist and lifted her from the sofa as he stood tall, crushing her to him, lashing the strength of his steely arms around her.

Making her feel precious. His most prized possession. *Oh*, how she'd missed him. Craved him night and day.

Desperate hands touched everywhere they could reach, wild sounds of need filled the air around them and it was love. So much love. Yet the man had no idea of the love swelling her heart. Only for him.

Dante tore his mouth free. 'Eva…*cara mia*?' he said, just as breathless as her, his wide chest heaving. 'What *exactly* does this mean?'

'Oh, Dante.' Brushing a thick lock of hair from his brow, she sank into his deep, dark, tortured gaze. 'It means I love you. I always have. It was love, obsession and lust at first glance. Within ten minutes, I'd designed my wedding gown and picked out stationery and china.'

Face contorting, he shook his head, adamant. 'No. You have not always…loved me. You asked me for one night, Eva. One night.'

'Because I thought that was all you would give me. And I wanted my first time to be with you. Only you.' She remembered then, his exact words. Now imprinted on her brain. *One million nights would never be enough.* He loved her. He truly loved her. She was still having trouble believing this wasn't some pheromone-induced hallucination and from the look of it she wasn't the only one.

'*Cristo*,' he said, rocking back on his heels. And, before she knew it, he plunged down to the coffee table.

'I can't believe you didn't see it.'

'I had no idea,' he said, lifting his head. 'I thought, for you, it was just sexual attraction, passion. I didn't think love was possible for me.'

Eva blinked. 'Says the man with a jar of tattered hearts.'

'Hearts longing for my money, Eva. You ask my ex-wife why she agreed to my father's lucrative proposal. Only to sleep with my half-brother Lazio weeks later. I found them together.'

Eva slumped back down onto the sofa opposite. 'No wonder you were so cynical about women. I wish you'd told me.'

'In the seven weeks we were married I think I saw her two, three times. I sabotaged her every effort, Eva. Without really understanding why. When I found them entwined I felt nothing but anger at myself and sheer relief. Natalia said she couldn't compete with Vitale but it isn't until now I realise she was competing with you.'

'Oh, Dante.'

'I do not blame her any more. If she feels for Lazio one hundredth of what I feel for you, I understand perfectly.'

'Why didn't you tell me how you felt all those years ago?'

Raking his hand around the back of his neck, he exhaled a long ragged breath. 'My mother used to tell me I was like my father. Cold. Dark. Unlovable. But since you and I talked I was beginning to think she was beyond sad. Demoralised. I think he did that to her. And I reminded her of him every single day.'

Eva stroked down the side of his face with the back of her fingers. 'You're not cold, Dante. You're white-hot heat. And yes, you're dark, but I love you for it. It draws me in and it turns me on.' Just talking about his dark male dominance sent ribbons of heat through her veins.

Licking her suddenly dry lips, she told him, 'I crave you. All that dark smouldering passion makes me feel alive. But you have this other side too. It's always been there. Like when you held my hand the day of my mother's funeral. It's your secret side. It's Dream Falls. It's the man who showed me not to be afraid of my body. It's the man who came in here and opened his heart, expecting nothing in return. Only wishing to be there for me. It's the man I'm proud of, the man who is more worthy than any other I know. The most lovable man in the world.'

'Eva?' he said, as if doubting, trying to believe, as he swooped down for another kiss, this one no less desperate than the last.

Down, down they went, tumbling onto the sofa, his hard weight pressing her into the plush cushions. And Eva thrust her fingers in his thick hair and held on tight as he spent all his doubt, all his fears, all his anguish by making love with sliding lips, his tongue slow and easy, stirring her insides with seductive persuasion.

'Eva...Eva...tell me again, *cara*.'

'I love you,' she said on a panting breath. 'Always.'

Closing his eyes for a beat, he delved into the inside pocket of his dark suit. Pulled out his fist. Unfurled his fingers.

'Oh, Dante,' she cried, her eyes filling, spilling over, tears trickling down her face.

'*Cristo*, Eva, these are good tears, *Si*?'

'Yes,' she said, 'yes,' dashing them away. 'But how *could* you toss it into the lake? I was furious with you.'

Contrition slashed across his high cheekbones. 'Not my finest moment, *cara*. I thought I'd lost you for ever. I went back the moment you left the island. I swear it.' He slipped her beautiful yellow diamond down her ring finger, embedding the heavy weight, and everything fell right in the world.

'So many people have let you down in your life and then I did the same. But I was so scared that day. I didn't want to need your love. The only control I had was to be the one who left. Before I sank even deeper.'

Dante caught her wrist and pulled her hand down to press flat over his heart, the accelerating beat echoing her own. 'Marry me, Eva. Let me make you mine. No contracts. No baby if you wish. Just you and me.'

Fresh tears stung the backs of her eyes. How many times had she dreamed of this moment? Just like this. With pure, unadulterated love in his eyes.

Then it struck her. What he'd said.

'Hold on. No baby if I wish? But I might be already.'

'What?' He reared back a touch. 'You said you were not.'

'No, I said I didn't know yet. I've been working up the courage to do the test. Praying I was because I wanted your baby so much and I've been so miserable without you. I was half-tempted to sign your stupid contract. The pain when you're not close…'

'Ah, Eva,' he said, nuzzling deliciously down her jaw, pressing his lips to her neck. 'I feel it too, *cara*.'

'Then I felt selfish for wanting your love when it may only bring you pain. Except…'

He sucked gently on the pulse throbbing at the base of her throat. 'It is worse without one another.'

'Yes,' she said, curling her face into him, breathing in his dark, rich scent, heat spiralling down her midriff. 'Now we can do the test together, right?'

'Later.' Lips curving in that devilish half smile that made her tummy flip, he launched to his feet and *whoosh* she was in his arms and his lips were crashing over hers once more, his tongue a velvet lash of tormenting pleasure.

Body coiling with sweet anticipation, she wrapped her legs tight around his waist, gyrating against the thick length of his ardour, revelling in the growl rumbling up his chest as he made his way through to her bedroom.

'I have work to do.' He tossed her atop the bed and tore his jacket from his shoulders.

Writhing against the pearly-pink coverlet, she watched him tear off his shirt, gingerly snap his trousers open over what she guessed was a whole load of hard, pained want. Only for her. 'You still haven't given me your answer.'

Eva smiled. Rose to her knees and inched the hem of her dress up and over her head. 'Oh, so we're talking proposals here?'

Dante kicked his trousers to the floor, his gaze enraptured, burning through her white lacy knickers, his words tight. 'We certainly are. I have developed a penchant for persuading you. Teasing, tempting.'

Eva flipped the front catch of her bra and sank back against the cushions, her legs scissoring with impatience. 'Go ahead, do your worst, Vitale.'

'Fear not, *cara*,' he growled, crawling over her, all raw predator grace. 'I intend to…'

A long while later…

Sprawled on crumpled sheets, facing one another, Dante entwined his legs with hers and corkscrewed a lock of her hair around his finger, languishing in contentment, a happiness he'd never known before. 'So which of the screaming yeses was agreeing to marry me, *cara mia*?'

'All fifty of them. Your technique is astoundingly good.'

No. It was all her. Only Eva could make him feel this insatiable. Invincible. Worthy. And watching her glorious body tense in exquisite violence when she came in the throes of ecstasy was downright addictive.

'I aim to please,' he murmured, cupping her breast in his palm, luxuriating in the way she pushed into his hand. 'Although I would like to hear it one last time before that little stick turns blue.'

'Even you can't make me come in ninety seconds, Dante.'

'Wanna bet?' he growled, cinching her waist and rolling onto his back, taking Eva with him.

A purely feminine laugh stretched her lips wide as she straddled him and tugged the covers over their heads. 'I love you,' she breathed, undulating to take him inside her.

White heat unfurled high on each of his thighs and while he could still speak he said huskily, 'I love you too, *cuore mio*. Always.'

Dante gripped the delicious curves of her behind, groaning when she wrenched her lips free and leaned towards the night stand. Still he kept hold, so she never left the tight lock of his body.

'It's midnight.' White stick in hand, she came back and whispered against his lips. 'Merry Christmas, my darling.'

Heart hammering against his ribcage, he could scarcely breathe. What he'd done to deserve such a gift as Eva, he'd never know. But as he snaked his hands up her waist to wrap his arms around her, he knew he was never letting her go.

'After three we both look,' she said. 'One, two, three…'

Dante didn't look at the stick. He didn't need to. The answer was written all over her beautiful face. And right then he swore to do everything in his power to preserve that look of unadulterated joy, nourish it for the rest of their lives. Making every precious moment count.

* * * * *

A sneaky peek at next month...

MODERN™

INTERNATIONAL AFFAIRS, SEDUCTION & PASSION GUARANTEED

My wish list for next month's titles...

In stores from 20th September 2013:

❑ The Greek's Marriage Bargain – Sharon Kendrick

❑ The Playboy of Puerto Banús – Carol Marinelli

❑ The Divorce Party – Jennifer Hayward

❑ A Hint of Scandal – Tara Pammi

In stores from 4th October 2013:

❑ An Enticing Debt to Pay – Annie West

❑ Marriage Made of Secrets – Maya Blake

❑ Never Underestimate a Caffarelli – Melanie Milburne

❑ A Precious Inheritance – Paula Roe

Available at WHSmith, Tesco, Asda, Eason, Amazon and Apple

Just can't wait?

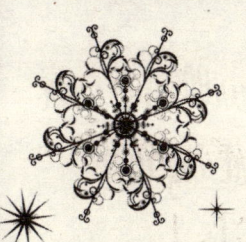

Wrap up warm this winter with Sarah Morgan...

Sleigh Bells in the Snow

Kayla Green loves business and hates Christmas.

So when Jackson O'Neil invites her to Snow Crystal Resort to discuss their business proposal... the last thing she's expecting is to stay for Christmas dinner. As the snowflakes continue to fall, will the woman who doesn't believe in the magic of Christmas finally fall under its spell...?

4th October

www.millsandboon.co.uk/sarahmorgan

1013/MB435

She's loved and lost — will she ever learn to open her heart again?

From the winner of ITV Lorraine's Racy Reads,
Anouska Knight, comes a heart-warming tale of
love, loss and confectionery.

**'The perfect summer read — warm,
sexy and addictive!'**
—Jenny Colgan

For exclusive content visit:
www.millsandboon.co.uk/anouskaknight

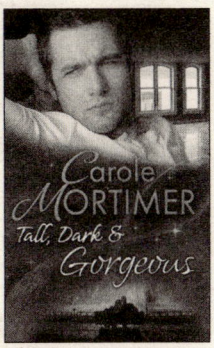

The World of Mills & Boon®

There's a Mills & Boon® series that's perfect for you. We publish ten series and, with new titles every month, you never have to wait long for your favourite to come along.

Blaze®
Scorching hot, sexy reads
4 new stories every month

By Request
Relive the romance with the best of the best
9 new stories every month

Cherish™
Romance to melt the heart every time
12 new stories every month

Desire™
Passionate and dramatic love stories
8 new stories every month